# TOWERS on the BEACH

World War II Spies and Heroes
from Ocean View, Delaware to Bremen, Germany

**J. R. Miller**

*War will tear lives apart, but the power of love
can bring them together, maybe forever.*

ARCHWAY
PUBLISHING

Certain characters in this work are historical figures, and certain events portrayed did take place. However, this is a work of fiction. All of the other characters, names, and events as well as all places, incidents, organizations, and dialogue in this novel are either the products of the author's imagination or are used fictitiously. If there are only a few historical figures or actual events in the novel, the disclaimer could name them: For example: "Edwin Stanton and Salmon Chase are historical figures..." or "The King and Queen of Burma were actually exiled by the British in 1885."

Archway Publishing books may be ordered through booksellers or by contacting:

Archway Publishing
1663 Liberty Drive
Bloomington, IN 47403
www.archwaypublishing.com
1 (888) 242-5904



ISBN: 978-1-4808-5809-1 (sc)
ISBN: 978-1-4808-5810-7 (e)

Library of Congress Control Number: 2018901245

Print information available on the last page.

Archway Publishing rev. date: 03/30/2018

# Introduction

When one drives south along the Delaware Atlantic Coast between Rehoboth and Bethany, several tall concrete towers, weathered by the ocean, can be seen sitting on the beach. Many are curious about their history. They are symbols of a nation at war and were built to safeguard the Atlantic Coast from a German sea invasion during World War II. They also symbolize how the beach communities braced for war and its transformative impact on their lives. Soldiers were stationed along the coast, and a German prisoner of war camp stood in Bear Trap, Delaware, just a few miles from Bethany Beach.

*Towers on the Beach* tells the fictional story of the impact of this time in history on the lives of families living in Germany and Delaware and how a young woman living in Ocean View, Delaware falls in love with a German saboteur.

The reader will encounter history, religion, patriotism, action, romance, love of family and the power of self-discovery.

# Prologue: Historical Perspective

History may be described as a retrospective look at the ages through the lens of one's individual personality. Individuals create war and conflict. The inhumanity of our species is displayed. Murder, violence, corruption and hate are always there. So are heroism, compassion, kindness, love and generosity.

World War II clearly demonstrated the dysfunction and collective insanity of the 20th century. It was the mightiest struggle humankind has ever seen. It killed more individuals, cost more money, damaged more property, affected more people and caused far-reaching changes in nearly every country than any other war in history. The number of people killed, wounded or missing between September 1939 and September 1945 can never be calculated, but it is estimated that more than 60 million perished. It was also the first time that one nation deployed atomic weapons of war on another country. More than 50 countries took part in the war, and the entire world felt its effects. Battlegrounds included Asia, Europe, North Africa, the Atlantic and Pacific Oceans, and the Mediterranean Sea.

On September 3, 1939, following the German invasion of Poland, the UK, France, New Zealand and Australia declared war on Germany. Canada declared war on Germany on September 10, 1939. Almost two years later, on December 11, 1941, the United States Congress declared war upon Germany hours after Germany declared war on the United States following the

Japanese attack on Pearl Harbor. The United States, for the first time, faced the possibility of attacks on both its Atlantic and Pacific shores.

A reluctant United States was at war despite its previous weak attempts at neutrality. Germany, Japan and Italy were powerful adversaries, and the US needed to mobilize quickly. Allied intelligence sources informed the War Department of Germany's intentions of a sea invasion along the vulnerable Atlantic Coast. Due to the geographic location of Washington D.C., the primary invasion area targeted by German intelligence lay roughly between New Jersey and North Carolina, but the entire Atlantic Coast was at risk, and many small coastal towns could have been targets.

How could the East Coast of the United States be protected? The War Department advised President Roosevelt that many positive military outcomes would result from the construction of concrete fire control towers along parts of the East Coast. Roosevelt studied the request and approved a plan to construct the towers in certain strategic areas along the Atlantic Coast. Eleven towers were built, three in New Jersey and eight in Delaware. They were used as artillery spotting locations and lookout posts. The towers were four- to five-story round-base concrete towers with flat observation decks.

Military was posted around the clock in each of the towers to coordinate artillery fire on enemy ships spotted off the coast. On a clear day, the military could see almost 15 miles across the Atlantic. From the uppermost decks, the spotters could scan the Atlantic for enemy vessels and direct the fire of their artillery mounted along the coast.

In 1942, the Battle in the Atlantic raged with German U-boats sinking an average of one ship per week. The *Jacob Jones* was one of those ships torpedoed off the Delaware coast, and over 130 of its crew perished.

On the morning of February 28, 1942, an undetected German submarine *U-578* submerged just a few miles off Bethany Beach, Delaware and fired its torpedoes at the unsuspecting destroyer. Several struck her port side in rapid succession. The smoke could be seen from the Delaware beaches.

The *Jones* remained afloat for about 45 minutes, allowing survivors to clear the stricken ship in life-rafts. Within an hour of the initial explosion, the *Jones* plunged bow-first into the Atlantic. As her shattered stern disappeared, her depth charges exploded, killing several survivors on a nearby life-raft.

During the period 1940 to 1945, Delaware played a critical role in keeping the homeland safe. Its many beach communities were on war footing. Many of the locals were certain that a German invasion was imminent.

Fort DuPont, Delaware City, constructed a prisoner of war camp which held German and Italian prisoners. A smaller POW camp in Bear Trap, Delaware near Bethany Beach housed mostly German POWs. Between 1941 and 1945, the camps in Delaware held over 4000 prisoners. POWs worked as dishwashers, waiters, grocers, butchers and other support roles on post. German POWs worked for civilian canneries, area farms and even for the city of Rehoboth Beach, repairing sections of the boardwalk.

From January to July 1942, some 347 civilian vessels were sunk or severely damaged by German submarine attacks off the US Atlantic Coast. The threat was real. German submarines aimed their torpedoes at tankers and freighters along the eastern coast of the United States to disrupt the delivery of oil and other supplies as well as to lower civilian morale. Sinking ships burned within sight of American civilians along the coast. The sea war in the Atlantic was now very close to coastal Delaware.

The impact of the war on the Bethany Beach area increased after the United States entered the war in December 1941. The town was blacked out at night beginning in 1942 to reduce the chance of German submarine attacks. The beach and boardwalk closed at 9:00 p.m. to make it easier for military personnel to patrol against landings by enemy agents and saboteurs. Many soldiers of the various armed forces were billeted in the town.

A large military installation stood just north of the town. German prisoners lived at Bear Trap as an Atlantic sea war occurred just two miles offshore. Hundreds of soldiers were stationed near the town, which experienced gasoline and food rationing while its young men and women were now in the military. Day-to-day life in Bethany Beach and the surrounding communities felt the mighty impact of the war.

The "Quiet Resort" was far from quiet, and all the residents in Bethany and Ocean View knew that World War II had arrived on its doorstep. Little did they know how directly some of them would be impacted by the events that would soon follow. The Nazi nightmare now darkened the world and cast a shadow on Delaware.

The horrors of war are lived at a very personal level. Some live close to its terror, others at a distance, but all feel its impact on their lives. The brutality of war touches individuals. It rearranges a person's values and their character. It pushes people to redefine themselves. Many will lead double lives—their outer and inner selves.

How could some of the families living in Ocean View, Delaware have known that their lives would be touched by a young German boy who was born in Bremen, Germany in 1920?

# The German Boy
## 1920

Kurt Wagner was born in 1920 in the coastal city of Bremen, Germany. Bremen is on the North Sea and sits on both sides of the Weser River, close to the port of Bremerhaven. Kurt was the only child of Gunter and Anna, who lived in a small redbrick single home on Leipziger Strasse. Kurt, a beautiful blond boy with large blue eyes, looked like his mother. He loved animals, especially his dog Maddie. His mother (*mutter*) was a devout Catholic and attended St. Boniface Church, which was a short walk from their home. She also played the piano for the church services and helped to prepare meals for the two priests who lived in the rectory.

Kurt's father (*vater*) had worked on the Bremen docks unloading cargo until Kurt was two years old. When World War I ended in 1918 and beginning in 1921, there was a brief call-up for soldiers to rebuild the German military.

The Treaty of Versailles imposed severe restrictions on Germany's military strength. The army was limited to 100,000 men with an additional 15,000 in the navy. The fleet was to consist of six battleships, six cruisers, and 12 destroyers. Tanks and heavy artillery were forbidden, and the air force was dissolved.

Gunter joined the German army in 1922. Because he was university educated, he quickly moved up in rank and responsibility. Since joining the German army, Kurt's father was away from home for months at a time and, due to the demands of the military, he spent little time with his son. Gunter was very strict and, on occasion, used a switch on Kurt to assure that his son was growing up in a world of rules and consequences. If rules were broken, there is punishment. Gunter demanded strict obedience. Kurt was almost three and full of energy but was afraid of his father. He loved to go on long walks with his mother. Only a short walk from their house was a beautiful park with a large lake and carousel, and Kurt always wanted to visit the park.

"Not today, little one. Your *vater* is coming home from his long trip, and we must prepare the house and surprise him with his favorite dinner."

"Will *vater* take me to the park?" he asked.

"If he has time, I am sure he will."

The front door opened, and Gunter walked down the hall and into the kitchen. Kurt ran to his arms, and Gunter gave him a little pat on the head.

"Hello, *Vater*! Will you take me to the park?"

"We will go in the morning provided *Mutter* tells me you have been a good boy," said Gunter.

"Can we take Maddie with us?"

"Yes, if you tell me she has been a good dog."

"Yes, *Vater*, Maddie is the best dog ever!"

They sat down for dinner, and Anna was excited to serve Gunter his favorite meal—a large plateful of savory fish stew. The last time all three ate together was four weeks ago. Anna insisted on a prayer, and Gunter rolled his eyes.

"Bow your head, Kurt," said Anna.

Anna said the blessing, and before she could say "amen," Kurt knocked his glass of milk to the floor. Gunter darted from the table, grabbed the switch and beat Kurt on both legs. Kurt and Anna were crying as Gunter headed out the door. Gunter was sitting on a wooden stool in the small courtyard behind the house. He was petting Maddie as Anna approached.

"How can you be so mean and cruel? He is only a little boy who wants to love you. He missed you terribly," said Anna.

"Bad behavior will not be tolerated. Kurt must learn that, and you must help with the discipline."

"Gunter, your concern should be about expressing your love for him."

"Anna, do not tell me how to raise my son. I do love him, and as he grows to manhood, he must be prepared to live in a Germany where rules must be followed and the new order obeyed. This discipline is necessary and will prepare him for the future."

Anna found Kurt crying in his room rubbing his crimson-colored legs. "I am sorry I spilled my milk, *Mutter.* I will try to be a good boy. Will *Vater* forgive me?"

As time passed, Kurt becomes very familiar with his father's hand. Anna also felt Gunter's physical abuse. Gunter seemed to be spending more time away from home, and when he returned, the relationship with his wife and son is seldom pleasant. Anna also noticed that Gunter was drinking more beer and vodka and his temper flared. He said little about his time away and told her that his military travels took him to Poland and Russia. She was curious as to why he must travel so frequently, but she was afraid to ask. She also noticed that Gunter was taking Polish language lessons every Saturday, but when she asked him the purpose of the second language, he told her it was none of her business.

Back when Kurt was one year old, Anna's parents, George and Julie Reckman, left Germany to live in Baltimore, Maryland with Julie's sister, Elizabeth, and her husband, Gerhard. Gerhard was the owner of a small German market in Baltimore, and he wanted George to work for him. George convinced Julie that life would be better in America and reminded her how much she loved and missed her sister. George had sustained an injury at work some years before and had difficulty finding employment.

The German economy was slow to recover from the Great War. Julie was apprehensive about starting over at their age in a new country, and she knew her heart would be broken because she would be leaving Anna and her grandson. She reluctantly agreed, and they arrived in Baltimore, Maryland in 1921.

Now, they live above her sister and brother-in-law in an apartment which is close to Gerhard's market, in a heavily populated German neighborhood near the Baltimore harbor called Federal Hill. Their apartment is on Cross Street.

Anna decided that it may be time to travel to America to visit her parents. It has been four long years, and even though they frequently corresponded, she missed them and they were always in her thoughts. In the fall of 1925, she wrote her parents and told them she and Kurt would like to visit as soon as the necessary travel papers were prepared. In previous correspondence with them, she discovered that her mother was having health issues and her parents knew that Anna was having marital problems. Her parents were happy that Anna has decided to visit them.

She lets Gunter know that she and Kurt may be traveling to visit her parents. To her surprise, he encourages her. "Anna, I think that would be wonderful for you to visit them. You know that I do not share my military responsibilities with you, and I have been under much pressure due to my new duties. Germany is still in a state of disorder, and the nation needs a strong military. We have just elected President Hindenburg. His friend Adolf Hitler, whom I have met, will also be one of his trusted associates within the new government. I know they will lead this country toward strength and prosperity, and they will restore respect to the German people. Within the year, I should be assigned even greater responsibility. When you and Kurt return, things between us will be different. Please promise me that you will return as soon as possible. I am not one to live a solitary life. I will deeply miss you and Kurt."

Anna explained to Kurt that they would be leaving their home and his father so that they could spend time with his grandparents in a country called the "United States of America."

Kurt asked, "Do you think Maddie will like America?" Anna tried to explain to Kurt that Maddie will not be allowed on the ship taking them to America.

"*Vater* loves Maddie, and it would be better if Maddie stayed here with him."

Kurt began to cry. "I don't want to go to America. I want to stay here with Maddie."

When Anna reminded Kurt that his grandparents have a cat named Clara, and Clara loves little boys, Kurt cried louder. "I don't love Clara. I *love* Maddie!"

Gunter had been assigned a driver and a military vehicle. On May 18, 1926, the car pulled up in front of the house on Leipziger Strasse. Kurt was petting Maddie. "Maddie, be a good dog. I love you. I'll be back soon."

Anna took Kurt by the hand, and they settled in the back seat. Gunter and the driver loaded two large suitcases into the trunk, and Anna held a large travel bag. The ride from Bremen to Bremerhaven was a quick 50 minutes in the Mercedes-built military sedan. The docks and piers were always busy, especially as summer approaches. They drove by several freighters and transport cargo ships until they find Pier 13. There sat the *SS Yorck*. It would travel light with only 230 passengers. The ocean voyage from Bremerhaven to Baltimore will take 10 days.

Kurt was excited and fascinated with the smoking stacks,

the cranes moving cargo from pier to ship, the sailors and their uniforms. His lively blue eyes darted in every direction as he took in the sights and sounds. Gunter and the driver carried the suitcases to the baggage cart and placed the luggage tags on each. Gunter said goodbye, and Anna and Kurt walked up the gangplank onto the ship. On the deck, she and Kurt turned to wave goodbye to Gunter, but he quickly walked away with his back to them. Kurt waved anyway and threw Gunter a kiss.

The wind had picked up, and the ship was rocking and swaying. Kurt was watching the crew remove the mooring lines. Anna warned Kurt not to get too close to the rail. Many passengers had gathered on the unsteady deck to watch the ship set sail. The ship vibrated as the engines began to turn over. Anna turns and recognized a family that attended her church in Bremen. Anna and Kurt walked toward Manfred and Helene Hentzel and their wide-eyed little girl, Claire.

"Anna, I am so surprised to see you! We were talking after church just a few weeks ago, and you didn't mention your travel plans."

They tell Anna that they were traveling to Philadelphia to visit Helene's brother who was a professor of German studies at the University of Pennsylvania. They will briefly visit with relatives in Baltimore and then take the train to Philadelphia.

Anna asks where in Baltimore their relatives live and learns that they reside in an area known as Fells Point, which was near the Baltimore Harbor. Anna tells them that her parents live in an area known as Federal Hill. Helene asks how long Anna will be staying in Baltimore.

"I am not sure, but perhaps a few months or so." She explained that her mother is not well and her time there will depend on her mother's health. Anna also realizes that Kurt should be attending school in the fall and that creates another issue regarding her length of stay.

"Anna, we are so concerned about the condition of this ship. This is rusty, patch-painted, and smells to high heaven. I hope the oil floating next to us is not from this ship. These 10 days cannot go fast enough. If you don't have plans, please join us for dinner tonight. It would be so good to catch up, and Claire would like to spend time with Kurt. We will send you a note concerning the time."

Their conversation was interrupted by a shipmate who announced that passengers should report to the second deck where they would be given their room assignments. Anna took Kurt by the hand, and they hurried down the stairway to the assigned area. Anna received the key to her cabin, 301 on deck three.

Anna and Kurt climbed the stairs, and she finds their room. She slowly unlocks the door. The cabin was hot and smelled of sweat and cigarettes. The communal bath is at the end of the hallway, but there was a pitcher of water and two glasses on the vanity. She also noticed a small pan under the bed. She tried to open the small, dirty window to allow some ocean breeze to enter the room, but it did not budge. Kurt began to jump on the bed. There was a knock on the door, and their luggage arrived. Anna opened Kurt's suitcase and found his little toy soldiers.

"Kurt, please get off the bed and come over here and play with your toys!"

Soon after they settle in, there was a knock on the door, and the steward handed Anna an envelope from Manfred and Helene: "See you at 6:30 for dinner."

Anna asked the steward if he would try to open the window. He stood on the bed and with his strong arms, gave the window a heavy push. The window moved a few inches, and the salt air wafts into the cabin. She handed him a few coins, and he bowed as he left the room. Anna had one hour to unpack and change her clothes. Kurt was enjoying his soldiers.

He holds up one and says, "*Mutter,* this soldier is wearing the same uniform that *Vater* wears. Do you think that one day I will wear a uniform and be a soldier like *Vater*?"

"Kurt, we don't know what the future holds. Maybe you will be a doctor or a professor at a university. Only God knows what you will be when you grow to manhood."

"*Mutter,* I think I want to be a soldier."

Anna inhales deeply and says a silent prayer, *Dear God, please no, one soldier in the family is enough!*

Anna unlocked her suitcase and found a green crepe dress to wear to dinner. Anna hopes that the Hentzels will not notice the wrinkles. She even touched her face with a bit of rouge and red lipstick. She found a fresh shirt and pants for Kurt. They left their room and walked to the small dining area next to the galley.

The Hentzels were already seated at a table close to the large window overlooking the rough, frothy ocean. They waved to Anna, and she sits next to Helene while Kurt sits next to Claire who looks away from Kurt and grabs her mother's arm.

"Kurt, you remember Claire from church, don't you?"

"Yes, *Mutter.* Hello, Claire. Would you like to see my toy soldier?"

Claire's shyness began to lessen, and she moved a bit closer to Kurt. Anna removed a pencil from her purse and found a few paper napkins.

"Here, Claire, show Kurt how well you can draw—maybe one of the seagulls sitting on the rail just outside the window."

Helene mentioned that she thought the meals onboard would be sparse and basic.

"Anna, I think we may be eating potato stew for the next nine days. I am told that tonight they are serving *Bratkartoffeln.*"

Anna says that Kurt liked the dish especially the potatoes, bacon and onions. Manfred mentioned that many of the passengers had packed boxes of food and may eat most of their meals in their cabins rather than pay the high prices for food in the galley. Helene said that they should have brought some food, but Manfred said he was not going to eat canned sardines for nine days. Helene asks about Gunter.

"Anna, we don't mean to pry, but we never see your husband even though we have attended the same church for these many years and live only a few streets away from you. Tell us about him."

Anna was surprised by the question, but other friends of hers have made the same inquiry.

"Well, as you may know, Gunter is in the German army and travels quite a bit. He is back and forth to Berlin quite frequently. He travels often and has just recently been promoted in rank. Kurt and I are very proud of him. He is not Catholic but Lutheran, so he does not attend church with us. We met in Berlin where he was attending school at the university. He grew up and went to primary school in Bremen where I did as well, but we did not know each other. We quite literally bumped into each other in the Berlin Natural History Museum. We chatted briefly and found out we lived no more than 5 kilometers from each other. He asked if he could stop by when we both returned to Bremen, and I said that I would like to see him again. I thought he was quite handsome, much taller than me, broad shoulders, sandy brown hair, and I soon found out how charming he was. We quickly fell in love and married in 1918. Kurt was born in 1920. Gunter worked at the Bremen docks unloading military cargo until 1922 when he decided to enter the army. We have so many things in common. We both love music. We enjoy the opera and are especially fond of Ursula Buckel and have seen her perform at the Bremen Opera House. We love to hike in the mountains and spend time in our garden. Kurt and I will miss him."

"We are so happy you told us about him, and we hope we can meet him when we return to Germany. Manfred is the owner of a shipping company in Bremen and frequently has business at the port and in Berlin. Manfred and I enjoy the opera as well."

Manfred asked Anna, "Have you heard about Kurt Weill's new opera, *Der Protagonist*? We just saw it at the Dresden Opera House earlier this year. Did you know that he lives in Bremen?"

The waiter interrupted with the steamy bowls along with hard crusty bread, beer, coffee and tea. Manfred was famished and enjoying his dinner when Claire pushes away her plate.

Helene asks, "Claire, why haven't you touched your dinner?"

She frowns and says, "It smells like our toilet."

Kurt looked at Claire and whispered to Anna, "Will she be switched by her *Vater*?"

Anna stared at him. "Finish your dinner, young man, or no dessert for you." Kurt quickly finished his meal.

Anna said, "I think it may be time to take Kurt to our room. *Gute Nacht.*" After saying goodnight to Helene and Manfred, she gave Claire a pat on the head. Claire waved goodbye to Kurt.

Anna and Kurt slowly walked along the promenade deck back to their room. The sea was a bit calmer, and there was a beautiful full moon casting its beam along the deck. When they return to the room, Kurt asked Anna to tell him about *Oma* and *Opa*.

Kurt was full of questions. "I hardly remember them. Will I like where they live? Will we have to visit very long? Will I like their cat? Where will we sleep?"

Anna took Kurt by the hand and told him to sit next to her on the bed. She moved the pillows behind their heads, and they both leaned back against the headboard. The moonbeam brightened the room. She held his hand. "My son, let me tell you all about your grandparents—your *Oma* and *Opa* and my *Mutter* and *Vater*. I know they seem like strangers to you. Your *Opa* was a blacksmith in Bremen and worked for the electric company. We used to tease him and say that, when the lights went out in our house, it was *Opa's* fault. He was a very hard worker. In the basement of his house, he had a workbench and carving tools, and he loved to carve circus animals of all sizes just like the elephant he gave you just before he left."

"I have it, *Mutter*! I brought it with me!" Kurt exclaims.

"Do you remember that I told you *Opa* had an accident at work and hurt his foot? That is why you remember him limping and using his cane that he made with the horse head on it. Because of his injury, the electric company would not let him work for them."

"So, what did *Opa* do?" Kurt asked.

"Sometimes he was able to find work at the markets in Bremen. Uncle Gerhard and Aunt Elizabeth decided to leave Germany and move to where we are going, the city called Baltimore. They tell me it is very similar to Bremen. Your *Oma* Julie and Aunt Elizabeth are sisters, and they missed each other, so *Oma* and *Opa* decided to leave Germany and move to Baltimore so they could all be together. Uncle Gerhard has a store in the market there, and *Opa* works with him. *Oma* says that *Opa* has made a bedroom for us next to their kitchen, so that is where we will stay. They love you very much, and they are so happy that you are coming to visit them. They say that they live near the water and *Opa* wants to take you fishing." Anna sees that Kurt is getting sleepy and strokes his head. "So, now you know all about *Oma* and *Opa*."

Anna helped Kurt put on his pajamas and pulled back the covers. In less than a minute, Kurt is sound asleep. Anna took off her dress and found her nightgown among the stuffed suitcase. She slid in next to Kurt. She thought back to her conversation with Helene and Manfred about Gunter and how they met and fell in love. How quickly those eight years of marriage have passed.

*Does Gunter really love me*? she wonders. *We were so close, and now we are so far apart. Well, maybe this absence will rekindle our love and bring us closer. I do love him so!*

She opened the drawer of the wooden cabinet next to the bed. She sees a small book with *Schone Reise!* (Good Travels!) printed on the cover across a Monet seaside painting. She paged through and sees a verse by D. H. Lawrence that captures her attention:

*To tell the truth there is something in the long, slow lift of the ship and her long, slow slide forward which makes my heart beat with joy. It is the motion of freedom. To feel her come up and slide slowly forward, with the sound of the smashing of waters, is like the magic gallop of the sky ... that long slow wavering rhythmic rise and fall of the ship, with waters snorting as it were from her nostrils, oh, God, what a joy it is to the innermost soul. One is free at last....*

Anna thinks, *Yes, this trip is a joy to my soul and perhaps a passing to a new beginning.* She turned off the dim lamp and gave Kurt a gentle kiss.

The days on the ocean pass slowly for Anna. The gale winds and rain last for three days with Anna and Kurt feeling like prisoners in their cabin. Kurt catches a cold that makes him cough and sneeze. He is not fun to sleep with. Finally, the storm passes, and Anna, Helene and the children, get together for afternoon tea in the very small lounge. Claire and Kurt were looking at a cartoon book and seemed to be enjoying each other's company. Helene asks Anna if she has noticed the changes happening in Germany since the end of the war.

"I know that Germany is slowly rebuilding from the devastating war, and that may be the reason so many Germans seem to be immigrating to the United States. My relatives in

Baltimore say that the city cannot find enough housing for all these Germans flooding into their city."

Anna nodded in agreement. "My parents have told me the same, Helene. They sometimes call their neighborhood in Baltimore 'Little Germany.' They tell me the schools teach in both German and English and that there are German speakers on the Baltimore City Council."

Helene nods. "My brother, the professor in Philadelphia, tells me that, since the war ended in 1918, over 25 million foreigners have arrived on the American shores including millions of Germans. Have you also noticed the Jewish emigration as well? My brother tells me that, since 1920, over two million Jews have left Germany to resettle in America."

"Helene, I hope my visit will be for only a few months, but I am concerned about my lack of knowledge of the English language. I know a few words and phrases but have a difficult time understanding the spoken word. My parents tell me not to worry. They have been in Baltimore only a few years, and they are taking English lessons at the church they attend."

Helene asks, "If you are staying only a few months, why worry?"

"You are correct, Helene. Why worry?" Anna passes a tray of cookies to Kurt and Claire who are getting restless.

"Anna, are you still giving piano lessons to Kurt?"

"Why, yes, it has been about two years now, and he is doing very well. I have taught him one of Bach's short preludes, and he can play it from memory. I am very proud of him and his progress at his young age. I thought that he would lose interest, but surprisingly he really enjoys it."

Helene looks at Kurt. "Kurt, your *Mutter* just told me what an accomplished pianist you are. We would like a recital when we see you back home in Bremen."

Kurt ignores the request and asks Claire if she plays the piano.

"No, but I am taking ballet lessons! Do you want to dance with me?"

"I don't dance," Kurt quickly replies and takes a bite of his cookie.

Helene asked Anna to refill her teacup. "Anna, the world is upside down and may never right itself. Germany may never recover from the effects of the Great War. America holds much promise for so many, but for my family, Germany is the motherland, the place I want to live and raise my family. I am hopeful that our political leaders won't fail us."

Anna turned her chair and moved closer to Helene. "Helene, I do not know how you feel about discussing German politics, and it is a subject I am really not familiar with, nor do I want to become familiar with it. I am a simple person, a caring wife and mother with no pretense. Ever since Gunter joined the army, he has pushed me closer to German politics and its leaders, and this troubles me. Even though I have told him how I feel, he keeps insisting that I must become more attuned to the new political reality. Hindenburg is now leading our country, and Hitler is becoming more powerful. Gunter met Hitler at a political rally for the National Socialist party, which he refers to as the Nazi party, a few years back and took a liking to him. Gunter tells me they are friends, although I have never met him. He said Hitler's ideology manifested in his speeches made him feel that Germany could begin again to regain the power it lost in World War I. From what I know from some of our church friends, Hitler is anti-religion, anti-capitalist, anti-communist and anti-Semitic. Gunter adores the man, but he scares me to death. Gunter has just received a copy of Hitler's manifesto, *Mein Kamph* (My Struggle), and it is now Gunter's bible. I am shaking all over just talking about it."

Helene touched Anna's hand and felt her trembling. "Anna, I can see how upset you are. You are such a good person. Gunter needs to understand that family and politics frequently bring unhappiness and discord, especially when each spouse has a different opinion. He must know how upsetting this is for you. He must respect your feelings. Maybe this short absence will help him understand how unhappy you are."

Anna teared up. "Thank you for your understanding, Helene, and please keep this conversation strictly between the two of us."

"Anna, please trust that I will. Now that the sun is peaking through, let's take the children for a walk around the top deck."

Their time aboard the ship settled into a routine. The seas have been rough, and a strong wind has been blowing, but Kurt seemed to be feeling better. Their last night aboard, Helene and Manfred insist on a farewell dinner together. Anna reluctantly agreed. She wore the same dinner dress, which is even more wrinkled. Manfred assigned the seating at the table with him seated between Anna and Helene. Both children were next to their mothers and well distanced from each other. Manfred ordered two bottles of wine, a red and a white. Manfred looked at Anna.

"I was surprised to find a small gift shop onboard. I am glad Helene did not find it. So, we have a few farewell surprises for our trans-Atlantic friends." He handed Anna a small colorful bag.

"Manfred, that is so kind of you." Anna opened the bag and discovered a small box of chocolate truffles. "We will share these after dinner."

Manfred pulled another box from the bag. "Kurt, since you have been such a good traveler, this is for you." He stretched across Anna and handed it to Kurt. He quickly opened it and found a small toy version of their sailing ship.

"*Danke* (thank you), *Herr* Hentzel."

"Hope you enjoy it, and when you play with it, you will be reminded of our sailing adventure. Anna, how about a glass of wine—red or white? Helene, I know you prefer the red. Let's toast: To life, love, safe travels and the fatherland."

Anna asked Manfred if he has enjoyed his time onboard.

"The 10 days passed very slowly. Claire was correct: The toilet did smell, and the bath facilities were horrible. I did meet a few passengers that I knew. I also discovered the small library. Most of the books were very dated, but someone recently added Adolf Hitler's book, *Mein Kamph*. Since I disagree with *Herr* Hitler's politics, it will not be on my reading list."

Anna seemed startled and surprised. She glanced at Helene with squinty eyes.

"Did I misspeak, Anna?" Manfred asked.

"No, not at all, but I am surprised you discovered it there."

"Why are you surprised? He seems to be in control of his party, and if it continues to gain momentum, his book will be required reading for anyone who wants to continue living in Germany."

The day for disembarkation finally arrived. The bright sun danced through the cabin window, and Anna saw the Baltimore skyline for the first time. She packed her luggage and sat it outside her door. She took Kurt down the stairs, and they waited in a long line to move off the ship.

She stroked his head and tucked in his shirt. He looked up at her with wonderment in his eyes. "Let's go find *Oma* and *Opa*, my little one!"

As she stepped upon the walkway, she wondered what the future has in store. She whispers, "*Wir schaffen das* (We can do this)!"

# The Beach Boy
# 1935

The year is now 1935, and Hugh Crosby has spent his young life in Ocean View, Delaware, just a few miles from the Atlantic Ocean. He was born in 1920. Hugh has a slender build with thick, brown hair and brown eyes. His parents are James, a carpenter, and Barbara. He has two younger siblings: Lee, a cute little girl with big, brown eyes and dark hair that her mother pulled back in soft waves, and James, Jr., who has curly, reddish-brown hair and a round face. Hugh is 15, Lee is 12, and Jimmy is 10.

They live in a two-story clapboard house on West Avenue. The house was old but accommodating, and Jim is often working on a project that Barbara would choose—replace this, change that. Barbara calls it a "turn-of-the-century house that never turned." It has a large fireplace, a wood stove in the kitchen, a pump for water, a pump house and a windmill. In-door plumbing has been a work in progress. In spite of its structural issues, it is home. Jim has refinished furniture for the bedrooms and built a handsome corner cabinet which Barbara placed in the dining room. Barbara is also proud of her grandfather clock which stands next to the front door. Its loud chiming and rhythmic ticking can be heard throughout the house. Although Barbara dutifully cares for it and winds it faithfully, it is always an hour behind, and that drives Jim crazy. Jim tells everyone the grandfather clock is the reason he is never on time.

The house sits on almost an acre of ground, large enough for Jim to plant a small garden. Thanks to the neighbors behind them, they share a barn for their two ponies, Topsy and April. The grounds also accommodate six chickens, one rooster and a large doghouse for their two dogs, Gretchen, a black and brown Dachshund, and Tasha, a tan and black German Shepherd. Gretchen seems to prefer the house to the doghouse.

The Crosby kids attend the small school near Bethany Beach for grades one to six. There are twenty-five children in the school, and Mr. Hickman is the teacher. From grade seven on, they attend the Lord Baltimore School, just a short walk up Atlantic Avenue from their home. Since Hugh is the oldest, most of the chores are assigned to him, but he frequently reassigns the chores to Lee and little Jimmy.

Hugh is usually in trouble and always the prankster who loves to tease and torment, like the day he picked up a dead squirrel on his way to school and placed it under Mr. Hickman's desk. Hugh would bring frequent letters home from Mr. Hickman advising his parents of his bad behavior. He does not like school and always finds something to distract him from his studies.

Big Jim's mother and father live nearby on Oakwood Avenue. His father, Thomas, is a stone mason and works for a small construction company. Even though Jim's father owns a 1915 Ford pickup, Thomas never pursued a driver's license. Jim, being the obedient son, became the designated driver. Most of the time, the truck is parked at Jim's house, but Jim is required to drive both his mother and father all over Sussex County. On Sunday mornings, Barbara and the three kids walk to the Bethel Methodist Church on Central Avenue. Jim drives the truck to his parents' house, and the three of them drive over to the church. Then, following the hellos and good mornings, the seven of them walk up the aisle and take their seats. After the service, Barbara and the kids walk home while Jim returns his parents to their house.

A Sunday dinner routine started a few years ago. Every Sunday, Jim's mother, Joyce, prepares a dinner that begins promptly at two in the afternoon for the family, and attendance is strongly encouraged. This meant that Jim, Barbara and the kids walk back to Thomas and Joyce's house. The kids and Barbara quickly tired of this regimented routine. Barbara wants to have Sunday dinner at her house occasionally and has asked Jim to talk to his parents about her idea.

"Barbara, you know how hard-headed they are. Why change a good thing? They buy the food. Mom works hard in the kitchen cooking it, and then we eat it. Mom says it's all about family togetherness. What's wrong with that?"

"Jim, I know your mother is always helping us. She is always baking goodies for us. She sews, mends our clothes, and takes care of us when we are sick. I love her, but we are tired of going over there every Sunday. Something has to change. The kids really hate this arrangement especially during the summer, and it has been going on much too long. We need to take a break!"

The spring flowers are in full bloom on this beautiful Sunday in May as they walk over to dinner. As they walk up the stone path of his parents' house, Jim notices their neighbor is building a large structure. Thomas walks down the front porch steps to greet them. "Dad, what's going on behind you? What are they building?"

Thomas walks Jim around back for a better view. "Miss Cecile Long Steele is building several more chicken hatcheries. The one they built a few years back only held 250 chickens now she has thousands. I talked to her yesterday, and she told me that her broiler business is really booming. She needs more room and will soon have to find a larger property. At 16 weeks, the chickens are ready to be delivered to Selbyville for processing. They weigh two to three pounds. From what I hear, she makes a good profit. Jimmy, maybe we should get into the chicken business?"

"No way, Dad. My six chicks give me one egg each per day, so I'm happy with my layers, but I am wondering if Miss Cecile might need another carpenter on the job."

Thomas places his arm on Jim's shoulder. "Jim, you've got more than enough work to keep you busy. You've got all that renovation work going on right now at the Seaside Inn up on the boardwalk, and then you've got the new building at the National Guard installation."

"You're right, Dad. Plus, it can't be much of a challenge building a chicken house."

Joyce, as she does every Sunday, rings the little silver bell that hangs on the porch, which signals that dinner is about to be served. Joyce, Barbara and Lee bring the plates of vegetables, corn bread, potatoes, ham slices and apple tarts to the table. Thomas sits at the head of the table with Jim, Jimmmy Jr., and Hugh to his right. Joyce is at the other end with Barbara and Lee to her right. They hold hands, and Joyce asks Lee to say grace. Thomas and Joyce ask the kids how they will spend their summer.

Hugh begins, "Well, I asked Dad if I could start driving Pop's truck, and he said to ask you."

Thomas is taken by surprise and stares at Hugh. "Well, let's see.... Hugh, if it's ok with Mom and Dad and you do well in your studies, I would think you could start learning how to drive next year. I did hear that Delaware may start a mandatory driver license requirement when you turn 16, but that requirement won't mean much down here at the beach."

Jim looks at Thomas. "Dad, you know Hugh had a pretty good year at school. If it's ok with you, I would like to start giving him driving lessons this summer. Hugh needs to have a summer job, and I am going to need a good helper that can drive. I think he and I will be a good team. If he works hard enough, I will give him off every Friday. That will give him some long weekends to fish, crab and swim. He tells us he has his eye on that pretty little McKenna Miller girl and wants to take her to the new Wilgus Bowling Alley they just built on the board-walk or maybe the Ringler's movie house."

Thomas looks at Barbara. "Barbara, what do you think? Is Hugh responsible enough to drive my truck, or should we wait a little longer?"

"I think that Hugh is responsible and would be a safe driver. I think we need to have another driver in the family."

Thomas looks at Hugh. "Fine with me, Hugh, but if Mom or Dad change their mind because you do something stupid, dust off your bicycle. Now, tell us about this McKenna girl."

"Well, Pop, I would like to take her out. I know you have seen her at church. She plays the piano at the nine o'clock service once a month. She has blond hair, blue eyes. We are in the same class. She lives on the Townsend farm on Woodland Avenue. Her family just moved here not too long ago from Fenwick. I talk to her at school, and she has a lot of friends. I don't know if she would go out with me, but I would like to ask her."

Barbara mentions that she knows McKenna's parents, Jeff and Lori Miller. "They are very nice. They also have a son named Tristan. You know the Townsend farm, over on Woodland Avenue, never planted last year. From what I was told, Senator Townsend had a hard time finding a good farmer to manage it after his previous tenant just decided to move out with no no-tice. Its almost 30 acres, I'm told, so they have been really busy this spring. There are mainly strawberry and beans over there this year. They did own a farm just outside of Fenwick Island, but when the depression of '29 hit, they ran into financial trouble and the bank repossessed it."

Thomas shakes his head. "Well, you know that Senator Townsend has a lot of farm knowledge but lets his superintendent, Jason LaPlante, manage all of his farm properties. The LaPlantes live on that other Townsend farm over near Bear Trap. Townsend's busy in Washington D.C. and doesn't want to get too involved in farm business. He prefers banking and legislating to farming, but now I hear he is going to get heavy into the chicken business just like Miss Cecile." Thomas turns to Lee. "Ok, Lee, it's your turn. Tell me your plans for the summer."

"No real plans, just want to go to the beach, see a movie, help Mom do some canning, and help her make me a new dress for the Fourth of July picnic. Mom and I are on the church social committee, so we will be busy. Jimmy heard that we might have fireworks this year."

Thomas looks at Jimmy, who is shy and avoids eye contact even when with the family. Some of the kids have teased him at school. "Pop, I just want to spend time with the dogs and the ponies. Maybe go swimming at the beach and catch some crabs at the Salt Pond."

Thomas looks around the table. "My goodness, you children are going to have a great summer."

Jim asks his father about the work he is doing up on the beach. Thomas says, "It's going well. Not a big job. We are building a stone breaker wall around the Life Saving Station. You know that station was built in 1907 and is in bad shape. That hurricane two years ago didn't help. Hey, kids, listen to your Pop. Here is some Delaware beach history. Did you know that before the United States Coast Guard was created in 1915 by President Woodrow Wilson, they called it the United States Life Saving Service? They paid the men just one dollar a day to risk their lives, but think of all the lives they saved. We have always had a lot of shipwrecks along the beach."

Thomas leaves the table and quickly returns, carrying a handful of coins. "I don't think I have ever showed you these. I know your father has seen them." Thomas places 12 coins on the table. "I found these when I was around 13 years old. My father and I would take our horses up to the beach near the Indian River. We would ride down the beach heading south toward Bethany. My dad called the stretch 'Treasure Beach.' One day, as we were riding, I saw something shimmering in the sunlight just below the water. I dismounted and found a coin, then another, and before I knew it, I had these. My dad told me the story of a schooner called the *Faithful Steward* that was traveling from Ireland to Philadelphia. It ran aground near the Indian River Inlet in 1785. It was carrying 400 barrels of English and Irish half-penny coins. You kids should go up there. I bet if you searched real well, you'd find some treasure. Here you go—four for each of you."

The kids are excited. Jimmy asks, "Dad, will you take us there?"

"Sure, we can all go up and take a picnic lunch and hunt for treasure. Maybe next Sunday."

Dinner is over, and everyone helps wash the dishes. Barbara is anxious to leave and glances toward Jim. She nods her head toward Thomas and Joyce. Jim understands her body language. "Mom, Dad, before we go, can I talk to you about Sunday dinner...?"

## The Senator and the Farmers 1935

Senator John G. Townsend is well known throughout Delaware, having been elected governor in 1916 and recently elected to his second term in the US Senate in 1934. He is a successful politician, farmer, banker and businessman, and one of the largest land owners in southern Delaware. He is successful because he has surrounded himself with individuals who know the business but also know how to manage the business. Every business endeavor he creates is well managed, be it his banks, strawberry farms, orchards or his chickens. He has recently hired Jason LaPlante to manage his farms. There is a small farm on Woodland Avenue in Ocean View that has been sitting, and Jason just found a new tenant farmer to manage it. Senator Townsend does not like to see his farms sit idle.

So, on this glorious Saturday morning in early summer 1935, Senator Townsend has decided to have Jason take him over to the Woodland farm to meet his new manager. The LaPlantes live on a Townsend farm near Bear Trap about three miles from Bethany Beach and a short ride to Ocean View. Jason's wife, Marna, teaches at the Lord Baltimore School. They have two boys; Connor is 16 and Cameron 14. The LaPlante farm is primarily strawberries and corn. They also have horses and chickens.

Townsend's black 1930 Cadillac Sixteen pulls into the dirt lane leading to the LaPlante house. Their dogs chase the car until it stops in front of the barn. Today, Townsend has a driver, Glen Bradshaw, a retired Marine, who drives him over from Selbyville. Jason and Marna are excited about the senator visiting. They walk out the front door and down to the car. Connor and Cameron are looking out the living room window.

Townsend is tan, tall and slender with dark hair combed straight back. He is dressed in a starched long sleeve shirt with a blue tie and tan pants with tan shoes. "Good country morning, LaPlantes. Hope all is well in Bear Trap. The fields look outstanding, Jason. How are the chickens doing? Are they all fat and happy?"

Jason points toward the chicken houses. "Your chicks are doing quite well, Senator. We just started the birds on a new diet which seems to be agreeing with them. I've been told that your veterinarian, Dr. Burton, will be stopping by next week just to be sure they are healthy."

"Miss Marna, are you enjoying your summer vacation?" Townsend asks.

"I am, Senator, and how is your family?"

"The Townsend family is doing well. They are busy preparing for our annual Selbyville Strawberry Festival, and I have friends coming up from Washington, so it will be a busy time. Good seeing you again, Miss Marna, and tell your boys I said hello."

The senator and Jason jump in the back seat, and Glen Bradshaw heads toward Woodland Avenue. The Senator hands Jason a stack of papers. "Jason, take a look at this. I asked my financial advisor in Wilmington to do a business analysis of the poultry industry in Delaware, with emphasis on my farms in lower Delaware. Most of the acreage, as you know, is in strawberries, peaches, corn, soy and potatoes, but this chicken business is exploding. If you agree with the numbers in the report, I think I will gradually begin to dedicate more of my farms to poultry. I think that chicken will be the economic driver not just here but in all of Delaware. Does Miller know anything about the chicken business? I know you are pleased with his performance so far, and leaving the farm fallow last year really hurt."

Jason looks at the senator. "How much time do I have to crunch some numbers?"

"You will be coming to the Strawberry Festival at the end of the month. How about then?"

Jason lays the report on the seat. "Senator, I don't think Jeff Miller knows much about chickens, but he is a quick study. If you decide to start dedicating more assets to poultry, he and I will make it happen."

The senator has this big broad smile. "Jason, that's just what I wanted to hear."

Bradshaw makes a sharp left turn and bounces up the rutted lane to the big white farmhouse. Jeff and Lori Miller are waiting on the porch swing. Tristan is pushing McKenna in the tire swing which hangs from the apple tree. Bradshaw parks next to the front steps. Jeff, Lori, Tristan and McKenna quickly gather around the car. Townsend opens the car door with an outstretched hand.

"Senator, good morning, I'm Jeff Miller, and this is my wife, Lori. My two kids, Tristan and McKenna."

The family shakes the senator's hand. The senator looks at the house and the outbuildings before asking if everything is to their liking.

Jeff points to the fields behind the house. "Senator, Jason and I worked out a planting schedule, and I've planted mainly beans, strawberries, peas and corn. We've got chickens here, four horses, six pigs and four goats. We are milking the goats mainly for our family. All is well. The house and barn are in good condition, and we are happy here. I will need some additional summer help when we start picking the strawberries. The kids are happy in their school."

Lori asks, "Senator, would you like to come in the house for some iced tea and blueberry muffins?"

"No, thank you. I have a very busy schedule today, so I best be going. I just wanted to meet you folks and thank you for making the farm productive. I'm sorry I didn't get to visit sooner. If there are any issues or concerns, let Jason know, and I will take care of it. Please be sure to come to my Strawberry Festival. The LaPlantes will be there, and it would be good to see you again."

The entourage gets back in the car. Townsend asks Bradshaw to stop by the Stickler farm adjacent to his on Woodland. "I want to say hello to the Sticklers. I heard Emma has been sick, so while I am in the neighborhood, I thought I would stop by."

Miss Emma, as she is called, was born in Germany and left to come to New York with her family before World War I. She met her husband Wilmer, who was an electrician in the Merchant Marine in New York. They eventually moved to the farm his parents owned in Ocean View. Wilmer's parents were also from Germany. They have passed on, and Wilmer and Emma are running the farm. Townsend always had his eye on it and would like to purchase it if the opportunity ever presents itself.

The Cadillac pulls up the lane as Wilmer is walking back toward the house. He is tall, thin, and wears a straw hat. He is carrying a basket full of large blue crabs. Wilmer is surprised to see uninvited company, but he quickly recognizes the senator as he rolls the window down. "Hi, Senator, surprised to see you in this neck of the woods."

The senator steps out of the car. Wilmer drops the basket of crabs, removes his hat, and shakes the senator's hand. "How is Emma doing? I heard she has been feeling poorly."

"Thanks for asking. She was sick most of the winter, but now she is much better. All of that vitamin D in the sunshine is what she needed."

Townsend looks around. "Is all going well here?" he asks.

"No complaints from me, just wish corn prices were higher this year."

"I agree with you, Wilmer. I am hearing the bushel price may be a bit higher come harvest time. Didn't want to bother you. Please tell Emma I said hello and was asking about her. Enjoy those crabs."

# The German Boy in Baltimore
# May, 1926

Anna and Kurt disembark the ship on this warm Saturday morning in Baltimore with a gentle breeze blowing across the water and seagulls circling above. They slowly make their way to the customs window to have their travel papers cleared. There is a long queue, and Kurt is agitated and restless. The Hentzels are at least 20 persons ahead of them. Anna finally arrives at the window and shows the clerk her papers. The clerk speaks German, so Anna feels a bit at ease. The documents are reviewed, and all are in order. A large *USA* stamp is placed in the upper right-hand corner of her papers, and she is told to enjoy her time in Baltimore.

She enters a sparsely furnished reception area. There, sitting under a large window, are her parents. Anna takes Kurt by the hand, and they both hurry over to greet them. "*Mutter und Vater, wir sind hier* (Mother and Father, we are here)." George and Julie rush toward them, and they kiss and hug and cry. Kurt is scared and begins to whimper.

Julie kneels down and hugs Kurt. "*Unser kleiner junge* (Our little boy). *Wir lieben dich* (We love you)."

"Kurt, this is your *Oma* and *Opa*."

Kurt wipes his tears and says, "Hello, my name is Kurt. I have a dog named Maddie."

George shakes his hand. "Hello, Kurt. I am George, your grandfather, and I have a cat named Clara." George asks Anna if she has the luggage tickets. Anna digs through her purse and finds them. "Anna, you and *Mutter* stay here with Kurt, and I will retrieve your luggage."

George limps down the long, dimly lit hall, banging his cane on the stone floor. He enters a large area stacked with piles of disorganized suitcases, boxes, crates and cartons. It takes some time, but he finally finds Anna's two large suitcases. He places the suitcases on a luggage trolley and heads back. Kurt runs toward George and helps him push the cart.

Julie mentions that they are using Gerhard's car. She explains that the four of them—George, Julie, Elizabeth, and Gerhard—share one vehicle, a 1921 Ford Huckster. Julie explains that Gerhard and George need the Huckster to pick up supplies for the market. They load the suitcases and squeeze into the small back seat. As George pulls away, Kurt reaches into his pocket and pulls out the carved elephant. "*Opa*, look! Here is the elephant you made me. Do you remember?"

George turns around to see the elephant. "I sure do, Kurt, and when we get to your new home, I have another surprise for you."

George parks in front of the row home they share on Cross Street, two blocks from Gerhard's market. Elizabeth and Gerhard have been watching from the window. They see George park, and they hurriedly walk toward the truck as Anna and Kurt step onto the sidewalk. Anna embraces her aunt and gives her uncle a kiss. Kurt is shy and hiding behind George.

"Where is little Kurt?" Elizabeth asks.

"Here he is." Anna grabs his arm and pulls him toward them. Gerhard and Elizabeth hug Kurt.

"Kurt, this is your new home. Welcome to Baltimore."

Julie is excited to show Anna and Kurt their apartment and their bedroom. They enter the front door and walk up the steps as George and Gerhard carry the suitcases. The living room is small but comfortable, and next to the kitchen is the bedroom that George and Julie have dressed up with paint, new curtains, and toy trucks, animals, and books for Kurt. There is a spacious closet and two large windows that look out onto the street. In the distance, Anna can see the Baltimore harbor.

"Thank you, *Mutter.* I love the room. Kurt, what do you think?"

Kurt is eyeing his new things as Clara the cat wonders into the room and brushes against Kurt's leg. "Are you Clara?" he asks as he picks up the cat and strokes its head. "I think Clara likes me."

Elizabeth has asked everyone to come to dinner in her apartment. Fresh flowers are in the center of the table. Anna spies a piano sitting in the living room. The meal is long and the conversation lively. Anna is bringing them up to date about the happenings in Germany and telling them about the ten-day voyage.

George hands Kurt something wrapped in a napkin. George clears his throat and says, "Kurt, this is for you."

Kurt grabs the napkin and quickly unwraps it to find a large carved Indian head with a war bonnet of colored feathers. "*Opa,* I love it! Thank you. What is the Indian's name?"

George responds, "I call him Chief Crazy Horse, but you should pick a new name for him. I have a book for you with Indian pictures that I think you will like to look at. If *Mutter* says it's alright, I will show it to you before you go to bed."

Elizabeth reaches for Anna's hand. "We are so happy that you and Kurt are here. We have truly missed you these many years. Have you decided how long you will be with us?"

Anna glances at her mother and father. "I really can't say. I know *Mutter* has been sick, and I would like to see her get back on her feet. I don't want to be a burden on anyone. I want to help out any way I can. Uncle Gerhard, I would love to work at the market if you need some extra help."

Gerhard sips his tea. "Anna, summer is really a busy time at the market so perhaps we could use you there, but time will tell. We will see what your schedule looks like."

Anna looks around the table. "I would really like to study English while I am here, Kurt as well. That is one thing I feel strongly about."

Julie leaves the table and brings back a large textbook. She hands it to Anna. "Here is the book we have been using to study English at Holy Cross Church. We try to speak English as much as possible, but, as you know, there are many Germans in Baltimore, so you will hear German spoken at the market and in church. The church has a wonderful instructor who gives English lessons on Friday and Sunday evenings. They have finished for the summer but will begin again in September. I will be happy to share the textbook with you, and we can review the German–English dictionary."

Anna leafs through the book and looks at Julie. "*Mutter*, that would be fantastic. I am so excited!"

Julie looks at Anna and Kurt. "Anna, we'll start your first lesson now. I am no longer your '*Mutter*.' You must call me 'Mother,' and Kurt, I am not your '*Oma*,' but you must call me 'Grandmother.' By the way, Anna, we will be going to 10:00 a.m. mass tomorrow morning at Holy Cross Church. We will leave here at 9:30."

Anna stands to take dishes off the table. "That will be fine, Mother. Kurt and I will be ready."

Anna and Kurt settle into their new surroundings. One evening shortly after their arrival, Anna writes to Gunter:

*Dearest Gunter,*

*Just wanted to let you know that we arrived safely in Baltimore. Kurt is doing well and is getting to know his family here. Our room is very nice. George and Julie send you their love, as do Elizabeth and Gerhard. Hope you are doing well and staying safe. Please write to us and let Maddie know that Kurt misses her. Our love to you,*

*Anna*

George and Julie spend their free time showing Anna and Kurt the neighborhood. They go for walks down to the harbor, and Kurt loves to see the many ships docked there. Anna takes him to Federal Hill Park where there are flags, old Civil War cannons and a spectacular view of Baltimore. Anna thinks that Kurt is becoming less homesick. George and Julie adore him, and George has taken him fishing to their favorite spot on a small tributary of the Patapsco River.

As the weeks pass, Anna notices that her mother is having dizzy spells and very bad headaches. George tells Anna how worried he is about her. He explains that she has been seeing a neighborhood doctor who has provided her with medication. George has a worried look as he adds, "She takes three pills a day, but they don't seem to be helping her."

One morning as Julie is taking one of her pills, Anna asks how she is feeling. "I have been taking these pills for the last few months, and I think they are helping, but I still sometimes feel faint. I still have the horrible headaches. The doctor thinks it is something called 'atrial fibrillation,' which could lead to thrombosis. I worry that I may fall and break some bones. I am getting old, Anna."

About a month after their arrival in Baltimore, George, Julie, Anna and Kurt are having dinner. Anna looks at her parents.

"Kurt and I have been talking. With your approval, I would like to enroll Kurt in first grade at the Holy Cross School."

Her parents are surprised. Julie has a wide smile. "Your father and I just said how wonderful it would be if Anna and Kurt would extend their stay. Having you with us has been an answer to our prayers. You know, Anna, we would love for you to stay as long as you want."

Anna's eyes brighten, and she exclaims, "Wonderful! It is decided: We will be staying at least until Christmas. I will be in touch with the German embassy. I know our papers state a six-month stay, but I am sure I can receive an extension."

Kurt is clapping his hands and looks at George. "Grandfather, you promised to take me crabbing. When can we go?"

Before he can answer, Anna asks, "Father, would it be possible for me to begin working with you and Uncle Gerhard at the market?"

"I think we could use you on Fridays and Saturdays," George responds, looking at Anna, "but I will discuss it first with Gerhard."

"Mother, if I work a few hours at the market, will you be able to look after Kurt?"

"I would love that! He and I will have fun times together, won't we, Kurt?"

The daily routine of living in Baltimore for Anna and Kurt begins to take root. Anna is working at the market and loves the interaction with the customers. Most speak German, but Anna is picking up some English words quickly. Gerhard has named his business the "Little German Country Market." He is one vendor among others who occupy the Cross Street Market. Gerhard carries various German meats and bakery items. The posted list that hangs behind the counter contains: bratwurst, liverwurst, schnitzel, sauerbraten, wieners, sauerkraut, potato salad, soft pretzels, deviled eggs, rye bread, pumpernickel, sourdough, and bakery items such as apple cake, tarts, strudel, muffins and Black Forest cake. He also carries various fruits, vegetables, and the ever-popular pickled onions. Aunt Elizabeth helps bake the cakes, muffins and tarts, and Anna's mother makes fresh potato salad and deviled eggs every day.

Sunday is the day that George likes to spend time with Kurt. One Sunday after church, George takes Kurt on the street car to the Baltimore Zoo. Kurt has carried with him several of the small wooden animals that George has carved for him. He is moving from cage to cage to compare the real animals to his wooden friends. "Grandfather, the animals you made for me look just like the real ones. You are such a good carver! Do they let you pet the animals?" George looks around and spots an attendant.

"Excuse me, but is there anywhere within the zoo that may allow children to pet the animals?"

"Yes, please follow me." The worker takes them to a small building encircled with a wire mesh fence. There are rabbits running around, a small goat, a miniature pony and two lambs. The worker says they are very tame and the children may touch them, but very gently.

Kurt moves toward a small brown rabbit and picks it up. "Grandfather, Clara needs a friend. Do you think we can take the rabbit home?"

George asks the worker if they have animals for sale.

"Yes, we do sell some small animals, and we always have a few rabbits."

As they ride the street car back home, Kurt holds the baby rabbit on his lap and asks George, "Do you think Mother will like my new rabbit? I think I will call him Cotton."

George strokes the rabbit. "I hope so Kurt, and I hope the rabbit is a boy."

In early August, Anna takes Kurt to register him for first

grade at Holy Cross School. Sister Kathleen, the principal, is seated at a small desk outside her office. Kurt is frightened by her black habit and the coarse white rope strung around her waist. She has a wide smile and converses with Anna in German. She tells them that they may call her "Sister Kathy." She reviews the instructional material and indicates that Kurt will be in a class that speaks only German. She tells Anna that Kurt will have English instruction every day. He must bring his lunch and wear the school's uniform, which will be a brown shirt, brown tie and brown pants. Brown shoes and socks are also required. She is also told that the tuition is 10 dollars, provided they use their Sunday support envelopes and are registered parishioners.

Anna asks if she may show Kurt his classroom. Sister Kathy tells them to follow her. She walks down the long hall to room 106. "This is it, Mrs. Wagner. School begins at 8:30 on the Tuesday after the Labor Day holiday."

Anna asks Sister Kathy if she knows where she can enroll in the English language class instruction. Sister Kathy walks them back to the office and opens the desk drawer. She pulls out a piece of paper labeled "English Language Registration" and asks Anna to sign her name and list her address. She says the classes are Friday evening from 6:30 to 8:30 and again on Sunday. She hands her an envelope. "The charge is three dollars, and you can bring the money to the first class."

Anna says goodbye and walks Kurt around the school to acquaint him with the location. Anna's apartment is only a few blocks from the school. As they walk back, Kurt asks Anna how he will get to school. "Kurt, don't worry. I will take you in the morning, and I will be waiting for you when school is over."

Kurt looks up into Anna's eyes. "Mother, do you think I will like school here with Sister Kathy? I will need to hurry home every day to feed Cotton."

At dinner that evening, Anna tells her parents that she

has registered Kurt at the Holy Cross Elementary School and she also registered for her English class. "I did not understand what Sister Kathy meant when she said that school begins the day after Labor Day. What is a labor day? Must everyone work on that day?"

George laughs and explains that it is a national holiday in the United States and is in honor of working men and women and the contributions they have made to the strength, prosperity and well-being of the country. It is always the first Monday in the month of September, and it is considered the unofficial end of summer. George looks at Anna. "In Germany, we celebrate a similar holiday on May first, our *Tag der Arbeit.*"

Anna nods her head. "Thank you, Father. Now I understand."

After dinner, Anna has made arrangements with Aunt Elizabeth to use her piano to give Kurt some lessons and for him to practice. Everyone gathers around the piano. They have heard Kurt play before. They are proud of him as he plays "Amazing Grace" and "Ode to Joy." Anna has explained to Kurt that "Ode to Joy" is really taken from Beethoven's ninth symphony in D minor. Anna is now teaching him Bach's Prelude in C minor. Kurt has been practicing six or seven hours a week. He loves music and loves playing the piano.

Following Kurt's brief concert, they head back upstairs to their apartment. After Kurt has had his bath and is in his bed, Anna kisses him goodnight. Now is Anna's time for her English lesson with her mother. Julie has been using the *Baltimore Evening Sun* newspaper to help Anna learn written English in the journalistic prose. They sit next to each other on the sofa under the lamp. Julie has Anna read the stories and write down the words she does not know.

Next week is the end of August, and George and Julie want to introduce Anna and Kurt to the Chesapeake Bay blue crab.

When they are all together for Sunday dinner, George tells them that he wants to have steamed crabs on Labor Day.

Anna looks at George. "Father, tell me more about these blue crabs everyone is talking about. How does one eat such an ugly thing?"

Kurt looks at Anna. "Mother, they are not ugly. They look like big spiders. Sometimes we see them when Grandfather takes me fishing. They will grab our fishing hook, and I pull them in. With their big claws, they can give you a bad bite."

George tells Kurt that he still wants to take him crabbing and looks at Anna. "We will eat the crabs next Monday on Labor Day. Uncle Gerhard will pick them up at the market. They will be alive when he brings them to the house. That's when the fun begins. I will show you exactly how to steam them, and I promise that you and Kurt will enjoy eating them."

Labor Day arrives, and in the early afternoon, George sets up a long table in the small yard behind their row house. George asks Anna to take a stack of old newspapers and spread them on the table, "just like a tablecloth." Gerhard arrives with a bushel basket full of beautiful blue crabs kicking, clawing and moving in the basket. Kurt is excited as he sees their claws snapping. Gerhard takes them into the kitchen. Elizabeth knows the recipe well and places a large pot on the stove. George takes the wooden tongs and begins to take the crabs from the basket and place them in the pot. Elizabeth quickly adds white vinegar, two bottles of beer, and a few cups of water.

As George is about to place a crab in the pot, it falls to the floor and chases Anna into a corner. She yells, "It's going to bite me!" and jumps up on a chair.

George is laughing as he runs to the crab and picks it up with the tongs before throwing it into the pot. Elizabeth quickly places the top on the steamer pot. After about 15 minutes, the crabs are silent inside the pot, and Elizabeth removes the top and generously sprinkles seasoning and salt over the crustaceans. Elizabeth tells Anna the cooking time is about 20 to 30 minutes.

Anna looks at George. "Father, are we really going to eat these nasty things? They are not blue anymore; they are red."

"Anna, you will be so surprised that something this ugly can be such a delicious delicacy. Let me find my wooden crab hammers that I just made." George dumps the basket of red hot crabs on the table. Anna's eyes are wide in amazement as she pushes her chair away from the table.

"Father, we will beat them with a hammer and eat them with our hands—not a fork?"

The Baltimore weather begins to transition from summer to fall. Kurt loves school and his teacher, Sister Regina, and has made several new friends. Occasionally after school, the children stop by to help him feed his rabbit who now has a large wired cage sitting under the back porch steps. George has also hung a swing from the apple tree.

Even though she knows in her heart that she has made the right decision, Anna is now having second thoughts about extending her stay. She knows Gunter will be furious when he finds out. She is sure he has been expecting a letter from her advising him of their return by the end of the year. Anna's hand is shaking as she writes:

*Dearest Gunter,*

*I hope this letter finds you safe and in good health. I am sure that the fall colors are soon to arrive in Bremen, and we look forward to seeing them here in Baltimore. Several things have happened that will require a longer stay. Mother continues to have health issues, and I must spend more time with her. I know I should have asked for your permission, but I took it upon myself to enroll Kurt in school. Instead of attending first grade in*

*Bremen, he will attend here. It is a Catholic school close to the house. He is in a German-speaking class, but he is also taking English lessons. We are well and keeping very busy. Please let us know where your travels have taken you and what news can you share with us. Thank you for your understanding of the situation here.*

*All of our love,*
*Anna and Kurt*

It is the day before Thanksgiving, and Elizabeth knocks on the upstairs apartment door. "Anna, this letter was delivered today, and it is for you. It looks important." She hands it to Anna and heads back downstairs.

It is a large envelope from the German Embassy. Anna quickly opens it. It contains passport extension documents with a cover letter that indicates that their passports have been extended until the end of 1927. There is a requirement that she notify the embassy in July 1927 regarding her status. It also states that there will be no further extensions. She is shocked that an extension for a year was granted.

Julie comes into the room and sees Anna reading the documents. "Did I just hear Elizabeth at the door?"

"Yes, Mother, this was just delivered. I have been advised that our passports have been extended. Not just for six months but for one year. I am so surprised."

Julie sits next to Anna. "I guess this is good news. Are you happy? Do you intend to stay that long? You know your father and I would love to keep you here as long as possible."

"I'm not sure, Mother. You know that we are happy here. Kurt is happy at school, and we love being with you and Father. I am concerned about being away from Gunter for such a long time. Kurt and I do miss him, but we have been here for six months and have received only one short letter from him."

Fall turns to winter, and a little snow arrives in early December. Anna has been playing the organ at church, and she is practicing with the choir for the Christmas concert. George has decided to erect a Christmas garden in the living room of their apartment. He wants to surprise Kurt.

One afternoon, Anna is working at the market, and George has offered to walk Kurt home from school. On their walk home, George asks Kurt if he is excited about the coming of Sankt Nikolaus and explains that, in America, he is called Santa Claus. "Kurt, would you like to have a Christmas garden at the apartment?"

Kurt's big blue eyes look up at him. "What would our garden look like, Grandfather?"

"Well, there would be a wooden platform in the living room, and on it we would a have small set of trains. Remember when we were taking our walk a few weeks ago, you saw that store that had those small electric trains in the window? Also, we must have a small village with houses and stores and miniature people. I have been making these for you. When we get home, I will show them to you. Also, when we buy our Christmas tree, we will place it on the platform. The trains will circle around it, and you will be the train engineer and run the trains anytime you want. Would you like that?"

"Oh, yes! Can we do it soon, Grandfather? That will be so much fun!"

"Yes, Kurt, we can start this Sunday." Kurt grabs George's pant leg and gives it a big hug.

Three days before Christmas, a large box is delivered to the house. It is addressed to Anna and Kurt Wagner. Kurt sees the box sitting on the kitchen table. "Grandmother, who is it from? Can we open it?"

"Not yet, Kurt. We must wait for your mother to return from the market. It is from your father."

A little later that evening, Anna arrives home and notices the large box. "What have we here, Kurt?"

"Grandmother says it is from Father. Can we open it now, please?"

Julie hands Anna a pair of scissors, and they quickly remove the paper packaging. There are several small and large boxes and a sealed envelope. Kurt quickly grabs one of the boxes and finds a small miniature chess set. He has a puzzled look because he does not know how to play chess. He hands the box to Anna. Next, he opens a box of black and red checkers and places it on the table. The next box contains dark chocolate bonbons in gold foil. The other box contains four miniature soldiers and a small tin military vehicle. This makes Kurt the most excited, but Anna frowns and rolls her eyes. There is one last small box that has *Anna* written on it. Anna opens it and is surprised to find a beautiful three-point halo necklace with three small diamonds.

She looks at Kurt, still in amazement. "I think your father has lost his mind! I can't believe he sent me this. It is beautiful."

"Father wanted you to have a Christmas present. He loves you!"

On the bottom of the box is a large Christmas card with a beautiful winter scene with children playing in the snow next to a large horse-drawn wagon. On the bottom of the card, Gunter has written: *Love you both so very much. Gunter*

Later that evening after Kurt has closed his eyes, Anna opens the sealed envelope that was in the box.

*Dear Anna,*

*Please accept my apologies for not writing more frequently during our extended separation. I have been in Bremen for only three weeks since you and Kurt departed. My superiors have me spending most of my time in Moscow and a few quick trips to Warsaw. Perhaps you have read in the news about Germany's recent treaty completed with the Soviet Union. There are many technical details that need to be negotiated with the Soviets, and I am working closely with our legation staff on several major issues.*

*Please tell Kurt that I had to find Maddie a new home but only until I return. Our neighbors on Leipziger Strasse, Norbert and Janice Petrovic, have been caring for her. I did stop by to see her on my last trip back in late October, and she is doing well and seems happy. I know the Christmas presents are meager, but you know that I am not an interested shopper. Thankfully, that was a task that you enjoyed more than I did.*

*I am sorry to hear about your mother, and I hope she improves. I understand your decision about placing Kurt in school. I was also informed that your visa has been extended, so you and Kurt are still officially German.*

*I am writing this from Moscow and will be here until the end of January. We have just had an epic blizzard, and the city is completely shut down. Hope Baltimore is sunny and warm.*

*Love to all,*

*Gunter*

As Anna reflects on the tenor of Gunter's letter, her eyes are moist, and a tear trickles down her cheek. She closes her eyes and thinks, *I do love him. Perhaps I have misjudged him, and he does truly love us. I will not tell Kurt about Maddie. That will break his heart.*

As Christmas approaches, excitement is building. The family gathers to discuss how they will spend Christmas day. Gerhard and Elizabeth will host dinner in their apartment. They will all walk to church and attend the 10:00 a.m. mass. Anna reminds everyone that she needs to meet the choir 45 minutes before mass begins. Julie wants to show Kurt the live manger scene in front of church and the *Krippenspiel* (Nativity play).

George wants to set up the *Weihnachtsbaum* (Christmas tree) and garden on Christmas Eve so Kurt will wake up to the lights on the tree and the train. George asks Anna, "Do you need one of my socks so Kurt can hang his stocking?"

"Father, I forgot all about the stocking! Thank you for reminding me."

Christmas Eve arrives, and everyone is gathered around the piano. Anna begins to play, and everyone sings along to "*Stille Nacht, Heilige Nacht* (Silent Night, Holy Night)" and then "*Oh Tannenbaum.*" It is then Kurt's turn. He plays "*Herbei,o ihr Glaubigen* (O Come All Ye Faithful)" and "*Kling Glockchen* (Jingle Bells)." After more music and song, Elizabeth and Julie place cookies, candy and cider on the table. They light candles throughout the house. The house is aglow and radiates the warmth of family. Anna walks over to her mother and gives her a long embrace. She looks at the faces gathered about the table and savors this precious moment.

"Aunt Elizabeth, Uncle Gerhard, Mother, Father, thank you for making our time here with you so special and loving. Thank you for taking care of us and especially thank you for embracing Kurt with your love and kindness. I love you, and *Fröhliche Weihnachten* (Merry Christmas)!"

Christmas is a fleeting memory as everyone returns to the work, school routine. Anna notices that her mother is having more headaches and dizziness and is spending more time in bed. George takes her to the doctor. When they return, Anna is waiting.

"Tell me what the doctor said. I am so worried about you!"

Julie sits on the sofa, exhausted. George helps remove her coat. He looks at Anna with troubled eyes. "Well, he gave her more pills to take. She is running a fever, and her blood pressure is up. He thinks it may be flu-related, so he wants her to rest and drink fluids."

That evening at bedtime, Anna notices that her father is bringing sheets, a blanket and a pillow to the sofa. Anna has a puzzled look.

"I think your mother needs a more restful sleep. I know my snoring bothers her. I will be fine here." Over the next few days, Julie seems to be getting worse, and her fever has reached 102 degrees. Anna thinks that she needs to be admitted to the hospital.

"Perhaps you are correct, Anna. I will call her doctor in the morning."

January, 25, 1927 will always be remembered. As the sun begins to rise, Anna hears George sobbing, "Julie, don't leave me." He yells, "Anna, please come! Your mother is gone. My Jesus, don't let this be happening!"

Anna and Kurt come into the room. George is kneeling next to the bed holding Julie's hand. Julie's eyes are open but staring at the ceiling. Anna checks her pulse, but there is none. Through her tears and cries, she tells Kurt to run downstairs and get Aunt Elizabeth and Uncle Gerhard.

Elizabeth runs up the steps and cries out, "No! Please no, don't take her from us!" She kneels next to George and places her head on Julie's shoulder. Anna gently kisses her mother on her cold forehead. She reaches down and closes Julie's eyes.

Sobbing, Kurt climbs up on the bed and places his head on Julie's chest. "Grandmother, please come back. I love you!"

The funeral mass is three days later. The church is crowded on this very cold and dreary morning. The priest, Father Kirsch, knows the family well. Following his homily, he asks Anna to come forward, and he meets her at the head of the casket. "Anna has asked if she may read a poem in tribute to her mother."

Anna places one hand on the casket and unfolds a sheet of paper. In a halting voice, she begins reading in English:

*We little knew that morning that God was going to call your name.*
*In life, we loved you dearly; in death, we do the same.*
*It broke our hearts to lose you; you did not go alone,*
*For part of us went with you, the day God called you home.*
*You left us beautiful memories; your love is still our guide,*
*And though we cannot see you, you are always at our side.*

"Mother, my love for you is eternal. You are the woman I always wanted to be. Please ask Jesus if he will let you be the guardian angel that will always watch over our family."

# Summer in Ocean View, Delaware 1935

This Sunday in June is bright and warm in Selbyville, Delaware, and the town is buzzing with excitement. Today is the annual Strawberry Festival held on US Senator John Townsend's estate. The home is Tudor-styled with gable dormers, steeply pitched rooflines and a long front porch. There are beautiful gardens and ponds with Japanese koi fish. There are dogwoods, wisteria, azaleas, tulips, hydrangeas and wild flowers.

Many of Delaware's public servants are here, including several members of the US Senate and House of Representatives and many Delaware politicos including Governor Buck. Senator Townsend's children will be there, and they still mourn and miss their mother who was killed a few years ago in an automobile accident when the senator was governor. It was even rumored that Mrs. Roosevelt may be in attendance. The Roosevelts and Townsends have a close relationship in Washington, and the President refers to him as his "go-to" man in the Senate. Many refer to Senator Townsend as the "Strawberry King" of Selbyville. Also in attendance will be many of those currently or previously employed by the senator in his various business activities, among them the LaPlante and Miller families who manage his farms in Ocean View and near Bear Trap. The guest list also includes political supporters from across the state, including the Sticklers and the Crosbys from Ocean View.

The senator loves to entertain and wants everyone to eat, drink and enjoy Delaware hospitality. The menu today will include traditional south county Delaware home cooking with most of the food coming from a Townsend farm. Today, they will serve a lunch of fried chicken, rock fish, country salads, green beans, potato salad and a variety of desserts including fresh peaches and, of course, strawberries. Many of the adults and children will be given baskets and will fill them with fresh-picked strawberries to take home. There will be guitar and violin music, and Miss McKenna Miller has been asked to solo at the piano.

The senator mingles through the crowd, greeting his many guests. He stops to talk to Jason and Marna LaPlante and their two boys, Connor and Cameron. Then he then walks over to Jeff and Lori Miller, who are seated next to their two children, Tristan and McKenna. Both families are together at one large picnic table. Jason hands the senator an envelope and tells him that it is his assessment of the proposal regarding the expansion of the senator's poultry business.

"Thank you, Jason. I will take a look at it and get back to you." The senator looks at McKenna. "Miss McKenna, you look so pretty in your blue sundress. I understand you will be playing the piano for us this afternoon. What songs will we be hearing?"

"Thank you, Senator. Yes, I am excited to play three songs that I hope everyone will enjoy. I wrote them down for you." She hands the note to him.

"I know everyone is excited to hear you play. Let me walk you over to the stage so we can begin."

Jeff and Lori are beaming as she comes on stage. Hugh and Lee Crosby, who are seated with their family, move closer to the stage. Hugh looks at Lee. "Did you know that McKenna was going to be the entertainment today?"

Lee turns toward the stage. "No, I have not seen her since school let out. I thought she only played church music. Hugh, has she ever talked to you about the piano music she can play?"

Hugh looks toward the stage in amazement. "No, we only talk about school stuff and sometimes about how her brother picks on her."

The senator pulls out the piano bench and helps McKenna into her seat. She sits behind the piano facing the audience. The senator moves toward the front of the stage and in his loud bravado begins the introductions.

He introduces the guitar and violin players, two brothers from Bethany Beach, and says, "But, first, it is my pleasure to introduce to those that may not know her, Miss McKenna Miller. She attends Lord Baltimore School in Ocean View. Her parents are here. Jeff and Lori, please stand up so they can see you. McKenna is an accomplished pianist, and I have been told she has been playing the piano since she was six years old. She tells me she has three piano renditions to entertain you with, 'Stardust,' 'Georgia on My Mind,' and 'I Get a Kick Out of You'. Following McKenna, please grab your partner and dance to the music of the Dawson Brothers." McKenna begins, and her hands move gracefully across the keys. Several people in the audience know the verses, so they begin to sing along. Quickly, all three songs are finished, and there is applause from the audience. The Dawson Brothers break out in country music, and some of the guests begin to dance.

Marna moves over next to Lori and Jeff. "Wow, your daughter was fantastic! She is quite the celebrity today. She didn't seem the least bit nervous."

Lori looks at the stage. "She loves to perform, and her dream is to someday go to New York and play with one of the big dance bands, like Benny Goodman or Duke Ellington. She really likes jazzy blues music."

McKenna makes her way back to the table. As soon as she is seated, Tristan, Connor and Cameron ask permission to go play baseball with some of the other kids. People are coming by and complimenting McKenna. Hugh and Lee Crosby sheepishly approach the table. McKenna spots them. "Hi, Hugh! Hi, Lee! I saw you earlier with your family but didn't get a chance to say hello."

Hugh, although a bit timid, speaks up, "Just wanted to let you know how much we liked your music. You really play well." McKenna stands and walks toward them.

"Thank you so much. Let's walk over to the ice cream stand. I need to cool off a little."

Lee winks at Hugh. "You two go. Mom wants me to see what Jimmy is up to."

Hugh is on top of the world as he and McKenna walk over to the patio behind the house which has several large tables full of all types of yummy desserts. They both ask for strawberry ice cream. They walk over to a bench beneath a large oak. Hugh asks McKenna how she likes living in Ocean View.

"It's great. We have been here almost a year now. We like the house and the farm. I love our animals, especially the dogs and the horses. Tristan and I like the school."

Hugh drips some ice cream on his pants and hopes McKenna didn't notice. He looks at McKenna. "You know that we are practically neighbors. I live less than a mile from your farm. Maybe I could stop by one weekend, and you could show me around? Dad is teaching me how to drive my grandfather's truck, so maybe we could ride up to the beach or something?"

"That sounds like fun, Hugh. Maybe next Sunday after church?"

Hugh's face is aglow. "I'll check it out with my parents. More ice cream?"

Jeff Miller and Jason LaPlante are in the beer line. Jason points to his cup. "A few years back when we still had prohibition, everybody would sneak into the barn for the beer. Townsend always pretended it wasn't there."

Behind them is Jim Crosby. Jim taps Jeff on the shoulder. "Hi, are you Jeff Miller? Your daughter is an exceptional pianist. I know everyone really enjoyed her music. My son Hugh is in McKenna's class, and we attend your church. I know you are new to this area and are managing the Townsend farm on Woodland Avenue."

Jeff asks Jim if he knows Jason.

"No, I don't believe I have had the pleasure."

They shake hands and order their beers. Jim leaves to walk back to his table. "You gentlemen take care. Hope to see you soon." Jeff and Jason smile and wave and walk away with their beverages.

Jeff asks Jason about the report he gave to Townsend concerning the financial analysis of Townsend's growing poultry business. Jason shakes his head. "From what I read, Townsend would be a fool not to expand his poultry business. Since he controls most of the production sources, like corn, transportation, land and the other things the farms can supply, he has a monopoly. I think most of his farms will be chicken farms in the next couple of years, and he will be the chicken king and not the strawberry king. I think you and I need to be quick studies on the poultry industry!"

The next Sunday, Hugh sees McKenna after church and asks if it would be ok to stop by later on. She checks with her mom. "Mom says that will be fine. How about one o'clock?"

Hugh lets his parents know about his visit to the Miller farm. He walks over to Woodland Avenue and slowly meanders up the driveway. McKenna sees him approaching and walks down to meet him. Hugh is surprised by a quick hug.

She points toward the horses who are standing near the picket fence. "Hugh, have you ridden much? My dad says we can saddle them up if you want to ride them."

Hugh's face is full of excitement. "I have two ponies that we sometimes ride. Lee and Jimmy, more than me. That would be fun."

McKenna begins to saddle the horses as Hugh hands her the tack. McKenna is sweating as she fastens the last cinch. "Hugh, these Western saddles are heavy! These two are Quarter Horses, and they are fun to ride. We have two Arabians that my dad likes to ride, but they have bad tempers. This one is Sadie, and yours is named Toby."

Hugh looks at McKenna as they ride along the fence. "Where to?"

McKenna gives Sadie a kick. "Follow me. There is a trail that will take us over to the river." Hugh is bouncing along, holding the saddle horn, and McKenna quickly realizes that Hugh may need some riding lessons. They reach the river, dismount and walk the horses over to a sandy clearing. They tie the horses to an old scrub pine. "Hugh, let's take off our boots and get our feet wet."

They wade out a short distance, and the water is still cold and tingly. McKenna splashes Hugh. "So, Hugh, tell me what you have been doing since we got out of school."

Hugh splashes back. "Well, mainly I have been helping my dad. He is a carpenter, and we have been finishing up a job at the Seaside Inn. Next week, we start work at the National Guard camp north of town."

McKenna trips and falls into the water. Hugh is laughing hysterically as he runs to help her up. "Now I am soaked! It will be a wet ride, but I guess we should head back."

Hugh and McKenna spend a lot of time together during the summer of 1935. They swim in the ocean, go bowling on the Bethany boardwalk, see movies at the Ringler Movie Theatre, have picnics at church and on the beach, and ride the horses. McKenna frequently spends time at Hugh's house and often is invited for Sunday dinner. Even though their friends describe their relationship as "going steady," they really are "just friends" who enjoy each other's company. As a result of the friendship of their children, the Millers and the Crosbys are also becoming close friends. Tristan and Hugh develop a friendship and like to fish and crab together. Summer quickly passes, and school begins. Hugh continues to struggle with his studies, and McKenna and Tristan offer to help him with his math and English.

The Sunday dinner schedule has changed for Tom and Joyce. They host dinner at their house once a month, and on the last Sunday of the month they go to Jim and Barbara's house. On this fall Sunday, all are gathered at Jim and Barbara's. Thomas always wants to engage the grandkids in conversation. Lee mentions that she and Jimmy are going to be in a Thanksgiving play at school. She is a Pilgrim, and Jimmy is an Indian.

Hugh puts down his fork and says, "Well, I am not totally sure about this, but I think this is going to be my last year in school. I hate school, always have. I'm tired of failing grades and teachers that give you a hard time. I want to continue to work with Dad. We are a great team, and I really like that kind of work. I did real well working for you this summer, didn't I, Dad?"

Jim gives Hugh a frowning stare. "We did work well together, Hugh, and I loved working with you. What surprises me is that you would make this big announcement now. Don't you think this is something that you should have discussed with Mom and me? You have always had your ups and downs in school, and I know Mom and I were disappointed with your first report card, but you usually improve as the school year moves on."

Hugh is trying to control his temper. “Dad, you didn’t finish high school, and you are my role model. So, what’s wrong with me following in your footsteps?”

Jim is hanging onto his anger. “Are you trying to be sarcastic or funny? Let’s end this discussion now, but we *will* continue it later!” Barbara is uncomfortable and embarrassed. Thomas and Joyce are poking at their meal with their heads down.

Lee looks at Jim and Barbara. “May Jimmy and I be excused? We need to feed the ponies.”

# Return to Germany
# 1927

Back in Baltimore, so much has changed, and it amazes Anna that life as she knew it just a few short weeks ago is now totally different. George is grieving, and depression has set in. He is staying in his room and comes out only to eat. He is not communicating with Anna or Kurt. Anna sees him sitting on his bed, staring out the window and clutching Julie's pillow while holding a small framed photo of their wedding day. He and Julie had known each other since they were in upper school in Bremen. He attended Julie's $16^{th}$ birthday party. They married at age 20, and Anna was their only child. They were inseparable. While in Germany, Julie was a seamstress and occasionally made custom slip covers for family and customers. George would help her on larger jobs, cutting the material, fixing the sewing machine and hand-sewing when asked. They loved music and would sing German folk songs every evening when they washed the dishes. Anna knows that there is a deep hole in her father's heart.

Even Kurt can see the change. He asks Anna, "Will Grandfather ever feel better? Every day, we would have fun together. Now he seldom talks to me."

"Kurt, Grandfather needs some time to himself. He loves us, but he is thinking about how much he loved your grandmother. He misses her, and he is sad."

Gerhard and Elizabeth try to console him. Elizabeth finally gets George to take long walks with her. She calls it their "walk and talk." Gerhard asks George to come back to the market. Slowly, George's attitude improves, but Anna notices a change in his appearance. His eyes appear hollow; the lids are dark and heavy. His grooming is shabby, and his beard is heavy. Anna forces the issue about his appearance. "Father, let me have a load of your wash, and tomorrow I will take you to the barber shop for a fresh haircut and shave." There is no response from George, so the following day, she stands in his bedroom and spies a pile of dirty clothes in his closet.

"Ok, Father, all of this into the wash! Let's pick out some fresh clothes for you to wear to the barbers."

So, George has fresh clothes and a new haircut and shave. That afternoon, he surprises Kurt by setting up the chess set he received from Gunter. Kurt and Anna arrive home from school, and Kurt finds George sitting at the table arranging the chess figures. With enormous eyes, Kurt exclaims, "Grandfather, today at school, Sister Regina asked us to close our eyes and pray for someone. I prayed for you and asked God to make you feel better. Are you going to teach me how to play chess?"

George rubs Kurt's head. "I am, Kurt, and we will also play checkers if you want."

George continues to slowly improve. Every Sunday, he stops by the little corner florist shop and picks up two red roses. He takes the street car to the cemetery to visit Julie's grave. He says a prayer and leaves her the roses. "I will always love you, Julie."

Spring begins to arrive with warmer temperatures and fresh spring flowers budding. This seems to have a positive impact on the entire family. George is back at work with Gerhard, and

Anna continues her English lessons. She has decided to return to Germany after Kurt completes first grade. She wrote to Gunter soon after Julie's death, and now writes to let him know that she and Kurt will book passage in July.

One evening after Kurt is asleep, Anna asks George to sit next to her on the sofa. "Father, I have decided to return to Germany. We will book passage on the Italian liner *SS St. Anthony Padua* leaving from Philadelphia on July 10$^{th}$ and arriving back in Bremerhaven on July 20$^{th}$."

George does not appear surprised. "Anna, Mother and I knew that you and Kurt could not stay here forever, and your wonderful visit would eventually have to come to an end. I am so thankful that you were with us when Mother passed on. I will miss you, but I understand that this is what you must do."

Anna holds his hand and looks into his troubled eyes. "Father, would you think about returning to Germany with us? We would love for you to live with us."

"Anna, I am unhappy without your mother, and now with you and Kurt returning to Germany, I am so upset I don't know what I should do. Let me think about it and discuss it with Elizabeth and Gerhard. I love you and Kurt with all my heart and soul."

George takes his time to make a decision. He is now an American citizen, and returning to Germany would create immigration and other issues. He has also heard about some of the political changes there. Although he would never share this with Anna, Gunter's rise in the German army concerns him. Several weeks have passed, and one evening, Anna asks him if he has made a decision about living with her in Germany.

"Anna, it was so kind and sweet to ask me to live with you. I have spent many a sleepless night thinking about it. I think I have made the decision to stay here. Returning to Germany creates too many issues for me. At my age, it is not easy just to pick up and move. This is my home now. I will dearly miss you and Kurt, but I must stay here and be near your mother. Gerhard and Elizabeth will look after me."

Anna gently kisses him on his cheek. "I understand, Father. I know the trip is a long one, but please promise to visit us. Mother was the letter writer, but now that will be your responsibility. You must write often as I will to you."

In late April, Anna receives a note from Sister Regina.

*Mrs. Wagner, we are planning our May Procession and school recital. With your permission, we would like Kurt to play the piano at the school assembly. Let me know if you approve. Of course, parents and family are invited to attend. Following your approval, I will send the sheet music home for the selection, which is "Bring Flowers of the Rarest" (Mary Walsh, 1871). Thank you, Sister Regina*

Of course Anna approves, and Kurt begins to practice. On the afternoon of the procession and assembly, Anna and George enter the school hall and find seats close to the stage. There is a May altar with beautiful, fragrant spring flowers. The children process through the hall following the eighth grade May Queen, who wears a flowing white gown and carries a bouquet of flowers. The children gather on stage, and Kurt is seated at the piano. With the direction of Sister Regina, they begin to sing to Kurt's accompaniment. Following the song, Kurt leaves the piano and joins the choir. Anna is holding George's hand. She is so proud of all that Kurt has accomplished this school year. She reflects on her time in Baltimore. Kurt has loved his time here. First grade at Holy Cross School was the right decision. He is speaking excellent English, and Anna has been pleased with her progress with her lessons. She will miss her Baltimore family. She wonders what life holds next as she ponders her return to Germany.

Kurt has mixed feelings about his return to Germany. He

has made many friends at his school. He enjoys being close to the water and spending time with his grandfather. He misses his father, but he does remember his strict discipline and finding his mother crying in her room following many of her heated arguments with Gunter. He hopes that, when he returns, things will be better for both of them. George has offered to take care of his pet rabbit, and it seems that Clara has been most affectionate of late. As he pets her, he looks forward to seeing Maddie when he returns home.

The time has come to leave Baltimore. Anna is packed, and a taxi waits at the curb to take them to the train station. She is told that it takes about two hours to travel to Philadelphia and then another quick taxi ride to the ship terminal. There is a big family hug, and everyone is crying, especially George and Kurt.

"I love you, my little pal, and I will greatly miss you. Be a good boy and take care of your mother."

Kurt gives him a long hug. "Grandfather, please come and visit us."

George hands Kurt a little box. "Kurt, open this when you get to the train station."

Anna and Kurt arrive at the station and buy their tickets. They find a spot on a long wooden bench. Kurt opens the box. "Look, Mother! Grandfather carved for me a wooden rabbit, and his name is on the bottom: *Cotton.*"

# Ocean View, Delaware
# 1938

The last two years of high school have been a struggle for Hugh. Jim and Barbara pleaded with him to complete his high school education and contacted Marna to ask if she would tutor him in his math and English classes. At the end of the school day, Hugh stops by Marna's classroom, usually two days a week. Marna's son, Connor, has become a good friend of Hugh's. They play baseball together and hang out on the weekends. Hugh is still McKenna's "best friend," and Connor is dating Hayden, a friend of McKenna's. Hugh and McKenna went to the senior prom together, and they still like to ride horses on the beach, go to the movies and just enjoy each other's company. Hugh is driving, and Jim has purchased a beat-up 1930 Ford Model A pickup which they both have been working on. When the stars align, Hugh is allowed to drive the truck on Saturday nights.

One Saturday evening, after a movie at Bethany Beach, Hugh drives McKenna back to her house. They hold hands, and Hugh asks McKenna if they can sit on the porch swing. Hugh is still holding her hand when Lori turns on the porch light and opens the front door.

"McKenna, I thought I heard voices out here. Hi, Hugh. You should have told me you were home."

"Hi, Mrs. Miller. I won't stay long." Lori closes the door and turns off the light.

Hugh holds her hand tighter. "There is something I want to talk to you about."

"What is it, Hugh? Is there something wrong?"

"Not really, but it does affect our relationship. I am just trying to decide where my life is going. I know we have talked about my big question mark before. Do I want to be a carpenter the rest of my life like my dad? I like working with him, but not for a lifetime. You seem to know what you want to do. You like your new job at the post office, and you are playing the piano at the Seaside Inn on the weekends. I know someday you will be famous and maybe move to New York or Philadelphia and play with one of those big dance bands we hear on the radio. I am thinking about joining the Coast Guard. Dad and I have been doing some work at the old Life Saving Station, and one of the men who is working with us has been telling me all about the opportunities I would have in that branch of the military. His son joined up a few years ago and is stationed in Florida. My mom and dad think it is a good idea. Dad even talked to Senator Townsend about it. What do you think?"

McKenna is totally surprised and wonders why he has not mentioned his plans sooner. "Hugh, this news about joining the Coast Guard breaks my heart. I am sad to hear this. I know it is your life, but I thought you knew me well enough to have talked to me about this before now. You always keep your secrets from me. You seem to have your mind made up. What do you want me to say? If you join, I probably will never see you again. I guess you are telling me that our relationship is over!"

She lets go of his hand. Hugh places his arm around her shoulders. "Well, I just want to pause our relationship, not end it. Who knows what life has in store for us? Maybe you will fall in love with my uniform, and someday we will get married."

McKenna gives him a quick kiss on the cheek and heads into the house. "Maybe you are right. Follow your heart. Goodnight, Hugh."

The door slams, and Hugh slowly walks back to his truck. He forgot to tell her about Connor joining him.

The next day, Hugh picks up Connor at the LaPlante farm. Connor emerges from the barn with two fishing rods, a large tackle box and a can of worms.

Connor's brother, Cameron, is feeding the animals and walks out of the barn. "Hi, Hugh! How is the truck running? Maybe next time I can go fishing with you guys?"

"Hi, Cam. You look busy. Yeah, maybe next time."

Connor throws the gear in the back seat. "Let's head over to the Salt Pond." They park the car and head through the pines down to the water. It is sunny and warm, and the fish are not biting. Hugh is baiting his hook. "Connor, did you talk to your parents about our plan?"

Connor is surprised with a quick nibble and jerks on his rod. "I did, and they liked the idea of me joining the Coast Guard. I guess I will never be a professional baseball player, and farming the rest of my life is not for me. I did tell them that you were thinking about it, too. They said they were going to talk to your parents. Dad and Mom said that I am not a kid anymore and they would respect my decision. They feel that I need to be more responsible, and the military might be what I need to do right now."

In early September 1938, Hugh and Connor say goodbye to family and friends. They have enlisted in the US Coast Guard and are off to start boot camp in New London, Connecticut. Jim and Jason take their sons to the Selbyville train station. Jim embraces Hugh and shakes hands with Connor. "You boys don't know how proud we are of you. Promise to write home as much as you can. The next time we see you, in eight weeks, you will be finished your boot camp and all decked out in your new uniforms."

Hugh wipes a tear from his eye. "Dad, I promise to make you proud. I will miss you. Please tell Mom I love her very much and give Lee and Jimmy a hug from me. Dad, would you please see that McKenna gets this?" Hugh hands Jim a small white envelope.

Jason hugs Connor and places a twenty-dollar bill in his hand. "Hope this is enough until your first paycheck."

"Thanks, Dad. Can't wait to see you in a few weeks."

On the Sunday following Hugh's departure, Jim, Barbara, Lee and Jimmy attend the service at the Bethel Church where McKenna is playing the piano and conducting the choir. After the service, they wait for her at the back of church.

"Hi, Mr. and Mrs. Crosby. Hi, Lee. Hi, Jimmy. So good to see you. Have you heard from Hugh?"

Jim steps forward and hands McKenna the envelope from Hugh. "No, we haven't heard a word since we took him to the train. I am sure they are very busy and getting adjusted to military life and the Coast Guard discipline. Here is a letter he wanted me to give you the next time we saw you."

"Oh, that was so sweet of him. When you get his mailing address, please let me know. I do want to write him."

They say goodbye, and McKenna walks back into the empty church, sits in the last pew and opens the envelope.

*Dear McKenna,*

*I miss you already, and I am so sorry I upset you. I should have talked to you about my plans long before our last night together. I regret that, and I know you were surprised to find out that Connor was enlisting as well. You know my reputation for*

*doing stupid things. I hope you find it in your heart to forgive me. My parents may be coming to visit when I finish boot camp in about eight weeks from now. Maybe you would be able to travel with them. I know they would not mind. They care so much for you. I have the small cross you gave me a while ago and carry it in my wallet. It is my way of keeping you close to me. I will miss our times together, your laughter and support. You were always there for me. I hope that you will think of me often and write me when you can. I hope that someday we can pick up again where we left off. Stay safe and be a good girl. Your "best friend,"*
*Hugh*

She places the letter back in the envelope and gently places it into her purse. Her eyes tear up as she looks at the sanctuary, says a silent prayer and asks herself, *Where are our lives going?*

# Coast Guard Recruits 1938

The first week at boot camp has been a whirlwind for Seaman Recruit Connor LaPlante and Seaman Recruit Hugh Crosby. Both have new haircuts, all kinds of shots and vaccinations, uniforms, and the signing of all types of documents. This processing lasts for three days. During this time, the new recruits are led by temporary company commanders. These temporary company commanders are tasked with teaching the new recruits a basic overview of the Coast Guard and how to march while preparing them to enter into their designated company. On the fourth day, Connor and Hugh are introduced to their permanent company commanders, Petty Officer 2nd Class Pappas and Petty Officer 2nd Class Nicholson. There are about 50 recruits in their company. These commanders will remain with them for the duration of their boot camp. Day four begins the routine for the next few weeks: Reveille is at 5:30 a.m., then they take muster, shave, brush teeth, make racks, and get to "chow."

The morning starts off with a one-mile run. Then follows a regimen of various physical activities including push-ups, crunches, rope climbing, swimming and marching. They are also learning leadership skills and team building. They attend classes that walk them through Coast Guard operations with special emphasis on the Coast Guard's Creed, which they must memorize. Hugh reads the Creed, written by Vice Admiral Hamlet, to Connor:

*I am proud to be a United States Coast Guardsman.*

*I revere that long line of expert seamen who, by their devotion to duty and sacrifice of self, have made it possible for me to be a member of a service honored and respected, in peace and in war, throughout the world.*

*I never, by word or deed, will bring reproach upon the fair name of my service, nor permit others to do so unchallenged.*

*I will cheerfully and willingly obey all lawful orders.*

*I will always be on time to relieve, and shall endeavor to do more, rather than less, than my share.*

*I will always be at my station, alert and attending to my duties.*

*I shall, so far as I am able, bring to my seniors solutions, not problems.*

*I shall live joyously, but always with due regard for the rights and privileges of others.*

*I shall endeavor to be a model citizen in the community in which I live.*

*I shall sell life dearly to an enemy of my country, but give it freely to rescue those in peril.*

*With God's help, I shall endeavor to be one of His noblest Works...*

A UNITED STATES COAST GUARDSMAN.

*Semper Paratus* (Always Ready, the Coast Guard Motto)

They are a bit overwhelmed but like the classes on seamanship, search and rescue, instrumentation, defense readiness, beach patrol, firefighting and marksmanship. The abandon ship drills are exhausting. They also participate in a survival float class. The suit they put on includes a life vest. It is made for waters 60 degrees and lower. It covers their whole body except for the hands, feet and face. They learn two positions that will help keep them afloat and help retain their body heat. Connor thinks it looks like a big sponge with a hood. Hugh says, "I wish McKenna could see me now."

One evening in the mess hall, Hugh is seated across from Connor. "Connor, I can really tell something is going on inside of me. For the first time in my life, I feel that I am growing physically, mentally and spiritually."

Connor shakes his head. "I know what you are trying to say. I feel that now I am part of something bigger than myself. I know it is a new attitude. It is a sense of pride within myself. I like the way I feel. I know the next few weeks will not be easy, but we will make it. We are a team. I can't wait to join the fleet and serve my country."

Back in Ocean View, McKenna has been thinking about Hugh and Connor over the last few weeks, and she really misses them. Fall is returning to the beach. Harvest time is mostly finished. Lori and McKenna have been canning much of the produce. The crops did well this year, and Senator Townsend was pleased that the farm made a small profit. He sent a congratulatory note to Jeff thanking him for his hard work and promised more help next year.

McKenna is in her bedroom with a small lamp sitting on her dresser next to her chair, a pad of writing paper on her lap. The window is open, and the cool coastal air moves the curtains. Hugh has been gone about three weeks. She has a waste can full of letters started, but she could not express how she really feels about him. Does she just like him as a friend, or does she feel a special emotional connection to him? She couldn't describe their relationship as romantic. They seldom held hands, rarely embraced, and she thinks Hugh was too shy or afraid to kiss her. How difficult it is for an 18-year-old girl to define her deepest inner feelings. She is determined that tonight she will get the letter finished, no matter how brief.

*Dear Hugh,*

*Thank you for your letter, and I am sorry I didn't write sooner. I know you have been busy, and I have talked to your parents, who have told me all about your new life so far away from me. You really did upset me when you hit me with your big decision that so surprised me. I am slowly accepting the fact that my life and future will never be what I was dreaming, and I thought you shared the same dream as me. I miss you so, and many nights I have cried myself to sleep thinking of you and holding your picture. I still feel that God has a plan for us and that someday we will be together. Your parents have asked me to join them when they travel to see you graduate from boot camp. The anticipation of seeing you is building up in me like a kid on the night before Christmas. I can't wait to see you, and I know you will be so handsome in your uniform. Keeping you close to my heart and counting down the days.*

*McKenna*

November 1938. McKenna, along with the Crosby and LaPlante families, travel to the Coast Guard Training Center to celebrate the graduation of Hugh and Connor. They have received a briefing letter explaining the day's schedule and advising them that they cannot see the boys until the graduation ceremony is completed. The Commander has invited all the families to breakfast beginning at 8:30 a.m. Following breakfast, there is a briefing in the auditorium for all families and visitors, which provides an overview of the recruit training. They are told that the graduation is a formal military ceremony beginning at

11:00 and lasting for approximately 45 minutes. During breakfast, they hear words to describe Hugh's and Connor's new status. "Shipmates" and "Coastie" are used as descriptions of honor and respect, titles earned because of what will be demanded of them as they serve and protect their fellow citizens and their duty of sacrifice to help and assist others. As McKenna and the boys' families hear the accolades, they begin to understand the Coast Guard mission and appreciate the rigorous training. They understand, for the first time, that these are not the same boys that left Selbyville, Delaware just eight week ago.

The LaPlante and Crosby families enter the auditorium and take their assigned seats. McKenna sits next to Jimmy at the end of the row. Columns of recruits, dressed from head to toe in their sharp service dress blues, file in and take their seats. Hugh and Connor are separated by their company. The patriotic music with flags waving and Coastguardsmen marching stirs McKenna. There are many speeches, and then the highest-ranking commanding officer comes to the stage and addresses the recruits and the families.

"Greetings to our Coastguardsmen, their families and friends, and distinguished guests. It is with great pleasure that I welcome you to the Coast Guard family! I share your proud feelings today as you gaze upon these men of the US Coast Guard. Just eight weeks ago, you said farewell, and now a new person stands before you. They have completed basic training and graduate as proud members of the US Coast Guard, basically trained, physically fit, and smartly disciplined, ready to execute Coast Guard missions worldwide. This graduation ceremony is an occasion that you will remember for a very long time.

We have pushed you mentally, tested you physically, and now you are a proud member of the United States Coast guard Team. At times, you doubted your capability and ability, but you succeeded and overcame the challenge. You worked hard, and everyone here is proud of your accomplishments. You will now embark on a new adventure. You may travel the world, sail the Seven Seas, fly to the greatest heights. No matter where you go or what you do, the Coast Guard team is with you. You will not walk alone.

The world as we know it today is a dangerous place. Sadly, the winds of war are blowing again around the world. As you listen to the radio and read the newspaper, you see that the seeds of another possible world conflict are being sown primarily by German aggression. Hitler is making moves against Czechoslovakia, and President Roosevelt has said we will for the foreseeable future remain neutral. Many of us in this room can remember the fighting of the last world conflict, and God help us that we will not be party to another world conflagration. Be assured that, if or when our President calls, we will be ready to serve and defend. Remember we are *Semper Paratus*."

"As we conclude our ceremony, your newly minted Coast Guardsman is free to depart on five days of well-deserved leave before reporting to their new duty station. Thank you, be safe, and may God Bless America!"

Following the graduation ceremony, the families find each other in front of the auditorium, and there are family hugs and kisses. McKenna waits her turn, and Hugh rushes over to her. They embrace, and McKenna is crying. Hugh's uniform is transformational. He looks so handsome. He steps back and looks at her from head to toe. "McKenna, you look beautiful!"

Her greenish gray dress does make her stand out from many of the other young women in the crowd. Her blond hair is longer than the last time they were together, and a touch of summer sun still lingers on her face.

Connor comes over to them and gives McKenna a big hug and kiss. He steps back and salutes her. "Welcome aboard, McKenna! Doesn't Hugh look good? We both lost 10 pounds."

McKenna's eyes are big and bright. "I can't believe how great you both look."

Everyone wants to know where their new duty stations will be. Jason asks Connor, "Well, son, by the time we get you home to Delaware, you will be leaving again. Where will you be stationed?"

Connor pulls out his papers. "I am not going to be too far away from home. I'll be at the Coast Guard Station in Cape Charles, Virginia."

McKenna is staring at Hugh. "Well, Hugh, where will you be heading?" she asks.

"I'm heading north to the Coast Guard Manhattan Beach Training Station in Brooklyn, New York."

McKenna mumbles, almost to herself, "Does the Selbyville train go there?"

# Bremen, Germany
# 1927-1937

July 1927. Gunter is waiting for Anna and Kurt in the vast Bremerhaven passenger terminal. He sees them making their way to the baggage claim area. He is wearing his gray-green military uniform. Gunter runs toward them, and Kurt runs to his arms. Anna trails behind. With Kurt in one arm, Gunter hugs and kisses Anna. Gunter can't believe how much Kurt has grown in the 12 months they have been apart.

"Kurt, I really have missed you! Guess who will be waiting for you when you get home?"

Kurt looks at him wide-eyed. "I hope Maddie is there. Do you think she remembers me?"

Gunter takes his hand. "Yes, I am sure she remembers you. She will be so happy to see you!"

Gunter loads the luggage in the car and makes his way to their house in Bremen. The summer weather in Bremen is warm but not hot, and it has been a rainy month. As they pull up to the house, the flower boxes in the front windows are colorful with red geraniums.

"Gunter, how lovely the house looks! I am so glad to be home." Kurt opens the front door, and Maddie runs to greet him. Kurt runs outside and into the yard, and Maddie is at his heels, jumping with delight.

The house is just the way Anna had left it. At times, it feels that she hasn't been away. Anna is anxious to talk to Gunter about their time apart. The evening of her return, they all enjoy dinner together. Later that evening, she kisses Kurt goodnight and comes into the kitchen. Gunter has large maps spread out over the kitchen table. She comes up behind him and places her arms around his waist and holds him close.

"Tell me, Gunter: Did you miss me?"

He slowly turns toward her and gives her a long, loving kiss. "Anna, I did miss you, and I am so happy you and Kurt are here and we are a family again. I have so much to tell you, and we have some important decisions to make. I am now a captain in the army, and as I mentioned in my letter, I have been traveling most of the time you have been gone."

She looks at him with a sad smile. "Gunter, tell me what you are doing. Why must you travel so much?"

"Anna, the military continues to add personnel, and my responsibility is to keep the troops supplied with the armaments and vehicles they need to meet their expanding requirements. We need to build warehouses near our military bases and procure goods and services. It is a demanding task, and that is why I have been traveling. Many of our suppliers are outside of Germany. I must travel to Italy next week and will be there for two weeks. I am negotiating a large contract for a new weapon called the Breda machine gun. So, now you have an example of what I am doing."

Anna holds his arm. With a puzzled look, she asks, "Why does Germany need all these weapons that you are purchasing?"

"Anna, how can you forget how our country was crawling on its hands and knees after World War I? We are vulnerable. The Soviet Union is at our doorstep with all its Marxist ideology and Communist propaganda. The British are no better, and we can never trust the French. This is a dangerous world we live in, and we must be prepared to defend the homeland. You must promise me that any information I share about the military will be kept very confidential. Do you promise?"

"Yes, of course I promise, but I am so worried about you. How can we have a normal family life if you are never home?"

Gunter walks over to the cabinet and finds the bottle of vodka. He pours a large drink and motions Anna to sit next to him. "Something else we need to discuss. When I am not traveling, most of my work is in Berlin. I think it would help if we took an apartment there. Maybe we can find someone to rent the Bremen house. The Petrovics who took care of Maddie might know of someone who would rent it. That way, we would see each other more often. We need to decide quickly because Kurt must register for school."

Anna rests her head in her hands and begins to cry. "Gunter, I was not expecting to have to deal with all of this on my first night home."

"Don't cry, my love. It will all work out. Come, I have a surprise for you." She follows him into the dining room. In the corner sits a large wooden cabinet. He lifts the lid, and Anna looks at a phonograph and below it a radio receiver. He takes out a large disc and lays it on the turntable. A soft Mozart piano sonata begins to play.

"Thank you, Gunter! I love it, and now we can listen to the opera any time we want. Kurt will enjoy it as well."

August 10, 1927. Anna, Kurt, Maddie and Gunter move into their third-floor apartment in Berlin. It is modest but has two bedrooms. There are three floors in the building with two apartments on each floor. From the kitchen window, Gunter can see his office in the elegant Chancellery building on Wilhelmstrasse about four blocks away. Nearby is the elementary school that

Kurt will attend. It is called the *Weimar Grundschule*, and Kurt will begin second grade. Despite Gunter's protests, Anna has insisted that Kurt continue to take English as a second language, and she was happy to hear that the Weimar school has an excellent English language program for grades one through six. Many of the diplomats who live in Berlin near their embassies also have their children enrolled at the Weimar school. Many of the French, Polish and Spanish children who speak German also study English there.

Berlin is a beautiful city with many cathedrals, museums, parks and gardens. It is the capital of Germany and has a population in 1927 of almost three million people. Anna is having a difficult time adjusting to her new life in such a large city. A big issue for her is the fact that she had to leave her piano in Bremen. Gunter has refused to move it because he said it will crowd their small apartment. The piano controversy has been going on for several weeks, and Gunter finally gives in. With the help of several of his soldier friends, they make the trip to Bremen. The truck pulls behind their apartment building, and they struggle to move it from the truck and up the rear fire escape. Despite some minor scratches, the piano finally rests in a space outside their bedroom. Anna and Kurt are very happy that it is now in their new home, and Kurt is first to play it. Anna has also found a new church, St. Hedwig's Cathedral. It is an easy walk from the apartment, and Kurt loves the large pipe organ and the beautiful stained glass windows and the looming bell tower. Anna has also joined their choir.

Many of the tenants who reside in the building have stopped by to wish them welcome. They have met the family who lives next to them on their floor. David and Sandra Brack are a young military couple. David is in the German navy and has an office in the same building where Gunter works. They have a daughter, Amie, and a son, Jason, who both attend the Weimer school.

Below them live Ernest and Glennis Baldersohn, an elderly couple with grown children. Anna is fond of them, and they remind her of her grandparents. They have taken a liking to Kurt, and Ernest takes him and Maddie on walks to the nearby Berlin Botanical Garden where Ernest was employed. Kurt loves to walk among the garden beds and parkland, and he enjoys the carousel. Ernest educates Kurt about the many species of plants and takes him through the large greenhouse that displays tropical plants, birds and butterflies.

On a warm Friday evening, Ernest invites the Wagners to join Glennis and him for an outdoor concert at the Gardens. The concert will feature local and international musicians and is located in a picturesque and sheltered garden between the main greenhouses. They decide to take the tram over from the apartment to the Gardens. On their way home, as the tram approaches the Berlin Concert Hall, it begins to slow and then comes to a sudden stop. They see the now-familiar red-and-black swastika flags hanging from the front windows of the building. There are several hundred people waiting in line and spilling into the street. Police are attempting to move the crowd so the tram and other traffic can pass.

Anna looks at Gunter. "Can you see what is going on? Is it a traffic accident?"

Gunter stands to get a better view. "No accident. I think it is another rally of the Nazi Party, and Adolf Hitler is making a speech tonight."

Ernest looks at Gunter and asks, "Tell me about this Hitler fellow, Gunter. Do you like him?"

Gunter glances at Anna and then looks at Ernest. "I do like him, and I think he is what Germany needs at this moment in our history. He deeply cares about Germany, although his opinions about certain social issues are very controversial. Many of the military have joined the Nazi Party, me included. If you have not read his book, *Mein Kampf,* I would highly recommend it."

Kurt stares at Gunter. "Father, can you get their flag for me? I like the design and colors." Anna looks at Glennis and rolls her eyes with an annoyed look on her face.

Time in Berlin moves quickly. Kurt seems to enjoy his new school and has made many friends. Sometimes he walks to school with Amie, who lives next door. Anna has been volunteering at the school and on occasion is a substitute teacher. Gunter continues his travels. Anna has been keeping in touch with her father in Baltimore and tells him about their new life in Berlin. She has encouraged him to visit with them, perhaps this coming summer.

Kurt has a new interest, pigeons. Raising pigeons has been a hobby of Ernest's since his boyhood. Behind the apartment at the back of the courtyard, there is a large overhang where he has constructed a pigeon house for his six racing birds. Most days, after school, Kurt and Ernest will tend to the pigeons—feeding them, placing straw in the nest, grooming them. These are homing pigeons called Tumblers, and Ernest has explained to Kurt how they can travel long distances and were used way back in history to deliver important messages to soldiers in battle. He is told that the German army still uses them. One of his pigeons has flown over 500 miles in one day. Ernest has raced two of the birds in a competition, and he shows Kurt the award medals they have won. Kurt is reading many books about racing pigeons and hopes to buy a pair that he can raise and race.

One morning in late spring, a short, rotund man in a police uniform knocks on Ernest's door. "*Herr* Baldersohn, I am Officer Schmidt. Your neighbors are complaining about your filthy pigeons. They are attracting rats and mice, and you must remove them within the next 10 days." Ernest tries to explain how he keeps the coop clean and removes the bedding and keeps the food covered, but the police officer will not budge.

"Did you not hear me, *Herr* Baldersohn? The birds must go, no excuses!"

When Kurt arrives home from school, he sees a note on his door: *Kurt, come see me. Ernest.*

Kurt knocks on the door, and Glennis greets him with sad eyes. "Hello, Kurt. I know Ernest wants to talk to you. He is in the courtyard with the pigeons." Kurt runs down the stairs and sees Ernest standing next to the coop.

"Bad news, Kurt. I have been told that the pigeons cannot stay here. I must quickly find them a new home."

Kurt stands on the step ladder and looks at the birds, who are resting comfortably. "But, why must they leave? They are quiet and don't make a mess."

Ernest unlocks the small hinged door to the cage and takes out one of the birds and hands it to Kurt. "I wish I could put them in my bedroom."

Ernest strokes the bird. "I wish you could, Kurt, but that would not work. Your mother and father would not approve. I'll start searching for a new home for them. Ask your parents if they know of a place where we can move them."

Ten days later, Officer Schmidt returns and finds Ernest in the courtyard feeding the birds. "*Herr* Baldersohn, I gave you 10 days to remove the birds, but I see they are still here. You have exactly 12 hours to remove them. Do you understand?"

Ernest does not look up but continues to fill the trays with bird seed. "I hear you, but it has been difficult to find them a new home. Please be reasonable. Can I have five more days?"

The officer steps closer, red-faced, and yells in his ear. "I said 12 hours, no more!"

He turns and slams the courtyard gate. Early the next morning, Ernest heads to the courtyard to check on the pigeons. He is staggered by what he finds, and he holds his chest. He feels faint. His heart is racing as he runs to the cage. All six birds lay motionless, their necks contorted. Someone has killed his pigeons, and he is grief stricken. He can't believe that someone would do this. It is like losing a family member. He has had these birds for almost five years, and each has a name. Three boys and three girls—Dirk, Jorg, Max, Elsa, Petra, Sophie. Ernest knows who did this. It is obvious where the suspicion lies. Officer Schmidt will pay.

Anna is heading down the stairs and sees Ernest sitting on the steps, holding his head. It is apparent that he is very upset. "Good morning, Ernest. Are you alright?"

Ernest stands and faces Anna. "Someone has killed my pigeons, and I think I know who. I know Kurt will be very upset when he finds out. Anna, would you please let him know? I can't bear to see his face when he is told."

The next day, Ernest is taking down the coop and stacking the lumber when Officer Schmidt walks into the courtyard. He walks over to Ernest. "I see, *Herr* Baldersohn, that you found a new home for your pigeons."

Ernest tries to suppress his anger. "You know very well what happened to my birds! You, sir, killed them."

Ernest rushes the officer and pushes him to the ground. Schmidt strikes his head on the blue stone patio. The officer staggers to his feet and wrestles Ernest to the ground. He tells Ernest he is under arrest for striking a police officer and places him in handcuffs.

David Brack is leaving the apartment to walk to work when he sees Ernest being escorted down the street with his hands cuffed behind his back. David approaches the officer. "Officer, I know this man. He is my neighbor. Tell me what is going on."

The officer walks faster and looks at David. "Sir, this is none of your business, but in deference to your naval uniform, I will inform you that he is under arrest for assaulting an officer and making a false accusation." David can see that the officer is holding a bloody handkerchief to his head. "I am taking him to the police station. His future disposition is not in my hands."

Ernest yells over his shoulder, "David, please tell Glennis what is happening!"

David hurries back to the second-floor apartment, and Glennis opens the door. "Good morning, Glennis. May I come in?" He walks her to the sofa and sits next to her. "Ernest has been arrested. I don't know the details. He was being taken to the station a few blocks from here by a police officer. With your permission, I will see what is going on. Maybe I can help him."

Glennis is terribly upset and shaking. "Please, David, by all means. I can't imagine why he is being arrested. Maybe it has something to do with his dead pigeons."

David enters the police station and talks to the officer at the desk. He asks if he may speak with *Herr* Baldersohn. After waiting for some time, he is escorted back to the holding cell. Ernest moves toward David and grabs the bars. "Ernest, I have spoken with Glennis, and I told her I would help you. Tell me what happened this morning."

Ernest tells him all about the murdered pigeons and his uncontrollable anger. "I am at fault, David. I should not have pushed him, but I know the swine killed my birds."

"Ernest, my military office has many contacts within the Berlin police. Let me see what I can do to get you released as soon as possible."

Ernest touches David on the hand. "Thank you for helping me. I will be forever grateful. Your kindness touches my heart."

A few hours later, the jailer walks up to where Ernest is sitting and unlocks the cell. "Here is a box with your keys, wallet and valuables. Sign here, and you are free to go."

That evening, Ernest has contacted the other tenants in the

building and asked them to join him in the courtyard at 7:00 p.m. Most of the tenants are there, and they are wondering why Ernest wants to meet with them. Ernest speaks to the group and explains exactly what happened.

"Thank you for your understanding, and I am sorry if I have embarrassed any of you by my actions. I was at fault, and my anger overtook my emotions. I am especially grateful to David for his intercession today."

Two days later, there is a knock on Ernest's door. A large man with a fat face introduces himself. "*Herr* Baldersohn, I am *Herr* Dieter. I know all about your arrest and release. It was the Nazi party that interceded on your behalf, and it was the party that secured your release. Lieutenant Brack is a loyal party member, but we took over where he left off. I understand you and your wife are not members of the Nazi party. I have here a membership form. I would strongly suggest that you consider joining and forwarding the signed form to the address listed, along with your generous monetary donation. Look upon it as an insurance policy. *Heil* Hitler!"

October 24, 1929. Gunter has finished dinner and picks up the evening newspaper, *Berliner Tageblatt.* On the front page, he reads the lead story about "Black Thursday" in the United States. Earlier in the day, most of the radio news was all about the Wall Street crash and the financial meltdown in New York City, which was also spreading throughout the United States. Millionaires became paupers overnight. Bankers and stock traders were jumping from the windows of the skyscrapers. Share prices on the New York Stock Exchange fell rapidly. Share prices plummeted as owners tried to minimize their losses. There are dire warnings about the future economic and social effects that may spread to other countries. Gunter shows the paper to Anna.

"Gunter, what does it all mean? Will those problems come to Germany? Will we not have enough food? Will they close our schools? I am so worried. I remember an economics teacher of mine once said, 'When the USA catches a cold, the rest of the world gets pneumonia.' The German economy is not strong. What will we do?"

Anna was correct. Due to the Great Depression in the United States, Germany and the rest of Europe quickly begins to suffer from its economic effects. As a result of World War I, Germany was required to borrow heavily from the United States to prop up its economy. All loans from the United States to Germany cease in 1929. Many American financiers begin to "call in" their outstanding German loans. This has a disastrous effect on the German economy which is not resilient enough to withstand significant withdrawals of capital. German banks struggle, and consumers lose confidence in their financial institutions. German industrialists who had prospered in the 1920s now find little demand for their products.

Anna quickly notices the changes in Berlin. One evening in early 1930, Anna has prepared dinner, and she tells Gunter and Kurt about the long line she encountered in the market and how the shelves of many items such as coffee and sugar were empty. "No meat tonight, Gunter, just some potatoes and carrots." She also saw a long line at their bank and a large crowd pushing and shoving as they waited their turn to enter.

"People want to withdraw as much as they can, but the bank will not allow it. Glennis told me that Ernest has much gold deposited there, but they will not let him remove it. Many of the students at Kurt's school have a parent that is unemployed. Gunter, I am really concerned. Will we have to beg on the sidewalk?"

Gunter pushes back from the table and looks sternly at Anna. "Please remember that I am an officer in the German military. Soldiers do not starve nor beg for food. Our family will have enough to eat. I will be sure we are taken care of. Please, Anna, do not worry, and don't upset Kurt with your talk."

In early April, Ernest is heading down the stairs and sees Anna in the hallway. "Anna, I have some good news. The Botanical Gardens are allowing employees and retirees to plant a small vegetable garden in the meadow behind the garage next to the greenhouse. I am going over today to help prepare the soil for planting. I will plant enough for your family as well. By May, we should have more than enough produce for the table."

Anna is surprised. "Thank you, Ernest, for thinking of us and for your kindness."

"You are welcome, and also please tell Kurt that they will let me have a small pigeon coop for a few birds. I will stop by and talk to him about the pigeons when he gets home from school."

Anna is having a difficult time adjusting to the military feel of the city. Hitler restores much of the population's hope with vague promises of employment, prosperity, profit and the restoration of German glory. Hitler is a powerful and spellbinding speaker and attracts a wide following of Germans desperate for change. He promises the disenchanted a better life and a new and glorious Germany. Swastikas fly everywhere along with thousands of Third Reich banners. They are even hanging from her apartment house.

Anna is very concerned about the direction that the political winds are blowing in Germany, but she is more concerned about her father. She writes him once a month, but he has not responded. Finally, she receives a letter from him postmarked from Baltimore in April 1931:

*My dearest Anna,*

*I am sorry that I have not been a faithful writer. My prayer is that the economic situation in Germany is improving. Unfortunately, the depression in the USA continues, and*

*Baltimore is greatly impacted. There are many unemployed. Your uncle Gerhard has encountered hard times at the market. Many of the vendors there have closed and shuttered their stalls. We have lost many old customers, and many of those that shop are using rationing coupons issued by the government. As summer approaches, we have agreed that, due to the downturn, I will take some time off from the market. I know that I am a burden on him and Elizabeth. I will be joining a group of 30 from the church who will be spending the next few months on a large farm about 30 miles north of Baltimore in a place called Aberdeen. The wages will be meager, but we are told we will be well fed. We will sleep in tents or in a converted barn. Please do not worry as I am in good health and the country air will be good for me. Hope that better times are ahead. Please tell Gunter and Kurt that I send my greetings.*

*Love and miss you,*
*Vater*

Gunter has kept his promise during the long and painful depression. Despite widespread starvation throughout Germany, the German army has plenty to eat. Gunter continues to bring boxes of canned food home and shares it with the Baldersohns. Gunter has made them swear that they will not mention his continued supply of various household items including flour, cooking oil, soups, razor blades, detergent and various and sundry items. David Brack, the German naval officer and Gunter's neighbor, is apparently doing the same thing. One Sunday morning, Gunter notices that a military vehicle has pulled into the street next to the apartment. Gunter walks down and finds David unloading several nondescript boxes and placing them on the sidewalk. "Good morning, David. Do you need some help with these Christmas presents?"

"No thanks, Gunter, I can manage. I know Christmas is

coming a bit early for us, but we must take advantage of the situation we are faced with. Are you still able to obtain enough Christmas presents for your family?"

Gunter notices that the boxes look heavy. "Yes, my family has enough presents, and we will have a good Christmas. *Heil* Hitler!"

Kurt continues his schooling and has made friends there, many of whom are also children of German military officers. His best friend is Grant Mueller, whose father is also in the German army. Gunter knows his father, Major Raymond Mueller, and has traveled with him. The Wagner and Mueller families have spent time together. Raymond's wife Kathi and their daughter Kate are members of Anna's church and sing in the choir. Raymond and Gunter are also members of the Nazi party, and both personally know Hitler, mainly from party meetings and other political gatherings.

Gunter and Raymond take Kurt and Grant to a large rally in the Berlin *Sportpalast*. Crimson swastika flags flutter from every lamp post and window. Hitler is there, and the rally is all about the Hitler Youth organization. Hitler believes that youth support is vital to the future of the Third Reich, and his goal is to produce a generation of loyal supporters of his Nazi views. He wants German children to revere him. Hitler explains that this will be an essential paramilitary organization for male youth throughout all of Germany. He likens it to the Boy Scout movement in America. Several young boys are there, smartly dressed in brown shirts and black short pants and proudly displaying the Nazi insignia on their arm. Kurt and Grant like the uniforms but are a bit apprehensive about joining. Their fathers feel that this type of organization will mold their character and help the boys understand the Nazi views on racial purity. They know that Hitler Youth will be mandated training if the boys want to join the German military. The fathers push their sons to join.

Kurt graduates from upper school in 1937. To satisfy his father's wishes, he applies for entry into the German Institute of Military Studies. Admission is controlled by the German high command. This is a very elite school, and Gunter will do everything within his power to make sure his son is accepted. In July 1937, Kurt receives a letter stating that he has been accepted to apply for admission and to complete a battery of tests. In September, he arrives at the sprawling campus of Friedrich-Wilhelms Universitat in Berlin, which houses the Institute of Military Studies.

By the beginning of 1933, the Nazi regime was firmly in control of all academic and administrative functions at the university, as with most German universities. On May 10, 1933, some 20,000 books written by those opposed to the Third Reich were burned in the main square of the university. During the same period, over 200 Jewish professors and employees were required to leave the university, and numerous doctorates were withdrawn from Jewish professors.

Kurt knows about this history of the university and accepts it as part of Germany's transformation. He is anxious to be accepted and anxious to please his father. As his admission process begins, he knows he must compete with 200 other candidates aged 16 to 19. Only 100 will be accepted. If accepted, he will take part in a two-year program of intense academic and military study. If he graduates, he will receive a commission into the German military.

On his first day, he must be on the field by 6:00 a.m. The instructor assembles them in rows of 20, arranged from the shortest to the tallest. At six feet tall, Kurt is in the last row with the tallest boys. Everyone is handed their uniform, a red shirt with swastikas on both sleeves, blue trousers, red socks and black military high-top boots. He is housed in a cold, damp dormitory in a room with three other candidates. Electricity is spotty, and the showers spray cold water. Nazi banners hang from the ceiling. Kurt reads the slogans taped to the walls: *All cowards please stand here* and *Death is honor.*

He will endure rigorous mental and physical punishment over the next 12 weeks, but he is ready. Each day is demanding. His instructors yell, scream, demean and physically abuse him. Physical fitness is a top priority. They do push-ups until the muscles in their arms lock up. They climb walls, rappel from ropes, and crawl through small tubes and other obstacles. After the first five weeks, 80 boys have dropped out.

He knows that, in week 12, he must run over five miles within 90 minutes with 35 pounds of gear on his back, so every evening Kurt and his roommates place 35 pounds of river rock in a sack and run with it around the quarter-mile track until they drop from exhaustion. He is totally tired of marching and the Sunday morning parades.

As he readies himself for bed one evening, totally exhausted, he continues to kneel at the foot of his bed, blesses himself, and prays silently the evening prayers Anna taught him when he was a child. He has been faithful to his prayers even though he knows that his roommates are staring at him. He knows how important the prayers are, and he asks the Lord to provide him with the strength and stamina he needs to complete this demanding course. He climbs into bed and thinks of his mother, and his time in Baltimore, which seems so long ago. He questions the path his father has set him on. Are his father's values misguided? Must it be country before moral principles? Will patriotism and religion be compatible, or will one win out over the other? He admires Hitler for unifying the country, but his Jewish policy sickens him. He asks himself, *What does "anti-Semitic" really mean?*

His 12 weeks at the institute are finished. He has survived and feels confident that he will be selected for admission to the

Military Institute. Gunter and Anna have been worried about his time there and are surprised that he looks so good in spite of the physical punishment. Three weeks after completing the entrance course, Anna hands him the letter he has been waiting for. He quickly opens it. His eyes read only the first line: *Congratulations, you have been selected for admission to the German Institute of Military Studies.*

He reads it aloud to Anna. She tries to read his face and is not sure if she sees happiness or sadness, but she knows Gunter will be extremely pleased. She also realizes that Kurt is no longer her son. He now belongs to Germany and to Hitler. She walks toward the window and wipes a tear from her eye. Kurt hears her gently sobbing and walks over to his mother and places his hand on her shoulder.

"Mother, why are you crying?"

# The Stickler Farm, Ocean View Delaware 1938

November 1938. Back on Woodland Avenue on a Sunday afternoon, Emma Stickler has just taken two apple pies from the oven. She takes one of the pies and slowly walks down the lane and over to the Miller farm. Emma has mostly gray hair combed straight back. She never wears make-up and is pudgy with fat arms. Her voice sounds hoarse and gravelly. She always wears eyeglasses that hang from a gold chain around her neck. As she slowly approaches the porch, she sees McKenna sitting on the swing reading a book.

"Hi, Miss Emma. Something smells delicious!"

"Hello, dear, I have not seen you nor your family in months. We have more apples than we know what to do with, so I wanted to bring a pie over for you and your family. Are you still working at the post office?"

"I just started a new job last week. I am a teller at Senator Townsend's bank, Baltimore Trust."

"Good for you, McKenna! That sounds like a nice position. I would think that the post office job was boring. Tell your parents that I said hello."

"Oh, by the way, Miss Emma, did you hear that my friends Hugh Crosby and Connor LaPlante joined the US Coast Guard and just completed their basic training? Connor is now stationed in Virginia, and Hugh is in New York."

"No, I did not know that. Honestly, I don't know those boys that well. I did meet their parents. I hope they will be safe. The world is on fire again. I don't know if you follow the news on the radio or read the paper, but I think Germany will have to protect itself from its many enemies like Poland, Austria and the Soviet Union. There is also the Jewish issue. Wilmer and I call our dear president 'Franklin D. Roosenstein.' He has some Jewish blood. Rather than becoming German's ally, he wants to remain neutral. I am convinced that the Jews started the depression in '29, and now they want to take over Germany. I am so happy that Adolf Hitler has a plan for them. I still have family in Germany, and my brother Heinrich is in the German military. They were so happy when Hitler became chancellor, and he has doubled the size of the German army. Germany needs to stand tall and not be pushed around anymore."

McKenna stares at her gravely and doesn't know how to reply. She knew that Emma was from Germany and had a German accent, but she had no idea how Emma felt about world politics until now. Emma's tone and intensity are frightening.

"Well, thank you for the pie. Have a good evening." McKenna walks into the house, and Lori emerges from behind the front door.

"McKenna, I was not eavesdropping, but I was wondering who you were talking to. I moved close to the open door and could hear everything she was telling you. That woman frightens me!"

The Sticklers have friends in New York City who share their feelings about a strong German nation as well as the issues concerning the Jewish resettlement. Emma travels to New

York a few times each year. Over dinner with friends one evening, she is made aware of an organization called the Friends of New Germany, also known as the German American Bund (Alliance). She likes what she hears and wants to join the movement. She is introduced to its leader, Fritz Kuhn. Kuhn was a former Bavarian infantry officer in World War I and a chemical engineer from Munich. In 1934, he was granted American citizenship. Kuhn has been called the "American Fuehrer" by the press. Emma discovers that the Bund has several thousand members throughout the United States and that Kuhn's organization has created training camps to educate new members. He mentions that several of these camps are secret and provides as an example the one just started at the Deutschhorst Country Club in Pennsylvania, just outside of Philadelphia. Kuhn is always looking for new members and says that there are thousands of Germans who immigrated to the United States for various reasons. He tells her about a new recruit who faced imprisonment in Germany for murder and extortion and made his way to the US through Mexico. Now he is one of the Bund's top officials.

Emma is fascinated by Kuhn, and he captures her imagination and vision. She would like to learn about his political views and wants her husband to meet him. She talks to Wilmer about the Bund and pushes him to spend a weekend at the camp in Pennsylvania. Fall and winter are usually slow times on the farm, so he agrees to attend the last weekend in November 1938. It is a three-hour drive from Ocean View, but all goes well. He is staying at a small hotel in Sellersville, and Kuhn has made arrangements to transport the attendees over to the camp. Wilmer finds it amusing that a country club is the location of a Bund training camp.

On Saturday morning, Wilmer sits down to breakfast with a dozen others, mostly men although there are two women. Most are from New York, New Jersey and Pennsylvania. Following breakfast, they move into a conference room. On one side of the room is the flag of the United States, and on the other side is the Nazi flag with the swastika. Kuhn introduces himself and two other men he calls his "assistants." Kuhn is heavy set and balding with large ears and penetrating eyes. He provides a broad overview of the organization and its ties to Hitler and the German Nazi movement. Kuhn mentions that he and a few other Bund members traveled to Berlin to attend the 1936 Summer Olympics. During the trip, he visited the Reich Chancellery, where his picture was taken with Hitler. He proudly passes the picture to those in the room. Kuhn wants the Bund to become a powerful political force in the United States that will someday rival the Democrats and the Republicans. He talks about a huge rally and parade that is scheduled for October 30, 1939. He describes the uniforms that many will wear when they march in the parade, the marching bands, the floats, and he says it will be larger than New York's Thanksgiving Day parade.

Over the course of the two days, Wilmer sees how persuasive Kuhn's rhetoric is. Kuhn mocks the weak administration of President Roosevelt. He attacks Jewish groups, both in the United States and Germany, he hates Stalin and derides communism, but at the same time he says that the Bund is not anti-American. At the end of the two days as the attendees are leaving, Wilmer shakes Kuhn's hand and mentions that his wife Emma would like to attend the next "camp," perhaps if one is scheduled in New York. Wilmer also mentions to him that Emma has a brother who lives in Berlin and is a member of the Nazi party. Kuhn grabs a pencil from his coat pocket and writes down this information and thanks Wilmer for mentioning that to him. He hands Wilmer a piece of paper on which he has written his home telephone number. "Wilmer, call me at this number when you get back home. Call me on a Sunday evening after 7:00 p.m. I have something to discuss with you."

January 1939. Emma receives a letter from Fritz Kuhn inviting her to attend a Bund conference in New York City in early March. She takes the train from Philadelphia and arrives in the late afternoon. She takes a taxi to the Commodore Hotel, which is where the meeting will take place. The following morning at 9:00 a.m., she makes her way to the conference room on the eighth floor. As she enters, she finds the room displayed much like the one Wilmer had described when he attended the meeting in Sellersville with crimson banners, swastikas and the American flag. She also notices several men dressed in brown uniforms, black boots and soft field hats.

There are about 30 in attendance, mostly men. Emma sits next to three other women. Kuhn moves to the front of the room, which is arranged classroom style, 10 to a table. Four uniformed men are seated behind him. Kuhn greets the attendees and provides an update of Bund activities. He stresses the Nazi ideology that all Germans are united by blood and all Germans living in the United States need to be awakened to their racial duties in support of Hitler. He states that 25% of the US population can trace their ancestry back to Germany. He points out that the state of Wisconsin, noted for its beer and bratwurst, has a 45% German population, mostly first-generation German American. Kuhn emphasizes that the Bund is not part of the Nazi party, but they are organized according to the Nazi leadership principle which demands absolute obedience to superiors. He displays an organization chart which shows the Bund's regional districts within the United States. He also talks about the recent creation of a youth program and states that he is looking for individuals who will host youth camps this coming summer.

He points to the men seated behind him. "How do you like our uniforms?" There is awkward applause from the audience.

At the close of the conference, Emma lets Kuhn know that she wants to host a Bund summer camp at her farm in Ocean View, Delaware. Kuhn shows excited interest.

"Emma, that would be a fantastic experience for our boys. The camps usually run from Saturday to Saturday, and I would like to have about 10 to 12 boys there. They would stay in tents, and I would have four or five adults there to supervise. There ages will be from 12 to 16. July would be a good month if that works for you. Think about it before you give me a firm commitment."

Emma shakes his hand. "No need to think about it. How about the second week in July?"

"Let's plan on it, and thank you. By the way, when Wilmer was at the meeting in Sellersville, I asked him to call me. I did not hear from him, and I know he must be busy. During the course of our conversations, he mentioned that he was an electrician in the Merchant Marine. I realize that farming now takes up most of his time. I have an important time-sensitive project that I would like to discuss with him."

"I am sorry that he didn't call you. I will talk to him when I get home. He *will* be in touch with you!"

Emma arrives back home and tells Wilmer all about her Bund conference and the upcoming summer camp in July. She scolds him for not calling Kuhn about his "important" project.

"Emma, I have no idea what he wants me to do, but I will call him."

Wilmer calls Kuhn on the next Sunday, just after 7:00 in the evening, as directed.

Kuhn picks up on the first ring. "Thanks for calling me, Wilmer. I am working on a very important project directly for the German counter-intelligence office in Berlin. Would it be possible to meet you in Philadelphia within the next two weeks? I don't want to talk over the phone and would prefer to see you in person."

"Yes, I can meet with you. How about next Friday?"

"Thank you, my friend. I will have one of my couriers deliver a letter which will let you know the location of our meeting and provide additional information. Can you reserve the dates of September 21 to September 25 (1939) for a trip to New York? I will pay all of your travel expenses and give you a nice check for your efforts. See you next Friday."

# Manhattan Beach Training Station 1939

January 1939. Seaman Apprentice Hugh Crosby arrives by bus at the Manhattan Beach Training Station in Brooklyn, New York. He has been assigned to train as a boatswain. He has memorized the job description: *Boatswain mates are masters of seamanship. They are capable of performing almost any task in connection with deck maintenance, small boat operations, navigation, and supervising all personnel assigned to a ship's deck force. They have a general knowledge of ropes and cables, including different uses, stresses, strains and proper stowing. Boatswain mates must operate hoists, cranes and winches to load cargo or set gangplanks, and stand watch for security, navigation or communications.*

Hugh will be training here for the next 14 weeks. His dream job is to one day pilot a Coast Guard cutter and do search and rescue. He is not sure if being the captain of his small row boat in Ocean View counts as "previous experience," but he knows that he loves the ocean and loves being on the water. He is assigned to Company J along with 40 others. His quarters contains

30 double stacked bunks, rifle racks, six commodes, three sinks, one towel, five shower heads and plenty of cold water.

Every day is a new adventure. He has practiced for the last three days how to abandon a ship without a lifeboat. He spends several days jumping 20 feet into a large tank with fire burning on top. The challenge is to swim out of the flames without catching your hair on fire. He learns semaphore and practices along the beach with red, white and blue flags. He is sick of tying and untying knots. This week, they are driving for four hours by military bus to Sea Girt, New Jersey for gunnery training. They practice on targets being towed by Navy aircraft. This has been the most fun so far. He also likes rifle and pistol practice. In week four, he makes time to write home and to get a letter off to McKenna.

*Dear McKenna,*

*Hope everything is good in Ocean View and you are settling into your teller job at the bank. I know winter at the beach can be dreary. It has been cold and wet here, but I am getting used to it. I am fine and training hard. I really like boatswain training and will tell you all about it when I see you. In the next few weeks, I will be eligible for leave. New York City is a quick ride from the Coast Guard Station. Maybe we could meet somewhere and tour the sights like the Empire State building, go to Macy's or visit Central Park. I know it would be a long trip for you, and I guess your mom and dad would want to come along. Maybe I am just daydreaming. I really do miss you. My return address is on the back of this letter. Please write me and let me know how you are and what your plans may be. Hugs and kisses,*

*Your best friend,*
*Hugh*

McKenna is so excited to hear from Hugh. She brings the letter to dinner. After the meal, she picks it up and says, "I got this letter from Hugh. He likes his new assignment, and he is really training hard. He says he is very close to New York City and would like us to come visit him when he can take leave time."

Lori looks at Jeff. "I know it will never happen, but wouldn't it be fun if we all took a long weekend trip to New York City, maybe over the Easter holiday?"

Jeff glances at Tristan and looks at Lori. "You know, we do have a farm here with animals! Things are very busy with the planting. Why don't you and McKenna go? That would be a great experience for her, and she always talks about playing in one of the clubs there."

McKenna's blue eyes brighten up. "Mom, do you think we could?"

That evening, McKenna quickly gets a letter off to Hugh:

*Dear Hugh,*

*So good to hear from you and hope all is going well. I mentioned to my parents your idea of visiting you in New York City. Dad and my brother would not be able to come. You know how busy the farm work keeps them, but Mom and I would like to meet you when you have your leave. Maybe your mother would like to come with us. Send me the dates you have in mind. It will be so exciting to see New York and to spend time with you. Mom said she won't get in our way, and she is good company. We will take the train up from Wilmington and meet you at Grand Central Station. Would they allow you to spend two nights? I am jumping up and down just thinking about it. Please write soon and let me know. Hugs and kisses back to you,*

*McKenna*

In mid-March, Hugh gets two days of leave and travels into New York City to meet McKenna and Lori at Grand Central Station. Hugh is disappointed that his mother cannot make the trip, but he is excited to join McKenna and her mother for a couple of days. This will be everyone's first trip to New York City. Hugh waits for the arrival of their train and can't believe the size of the station and the crowd. He orders a soda and grabs a newspaper. Before he can take the first sip, McKenna sees him and comes running over to him with Lori trailing behind pulling two small suitcases. "I saw your uniform before I saw you, Hugh. I think you have lost more weight." She throws her arms around his neck and gives him a hard kiss. Lori is next with a kiss on his cheek.

Hugh grabs the suitcases. "So great to see both of you! How was your trip?"

They make their way through the station and out to the taxi lane. They quickly jump in the waiting cab. The driver asks, "Where to, folks?"

Lori searches for a folded piece of paper in her purse. "The Hotel Chesterfield at 130 West 49th Street, please."

Hugh is sitting near the rear door with McKenna next to him. Lori is straining her neck to see the passing skyscrapers. McKenna grabs his hand. "I forgot to tell you where we would be staying. Your room is directly next to ours on the ninth floor."

They check in, and Lori insists on paying for Hugh's room, but Hugh hands her 40 dollars. Lori places the money in his uniform pocket. "Take this, Hugh. The rate was just 19 dollars a night, and the clerk said military receive a discount. Also, our breakfast is included."

They quickly drop the suitcases in their rooms and head back down on the bumpy elevator to the lobby. Since it is still early, they decide to head over to the Empire State Building. The taxi drops them off on Fifth Avenue at 33rd. All three look up at the same time and are awestruck. They enter the building, and on the wall is a plaque that highlights facts about the building. Hugh reads aloud, "It is 102 stories and was completed in 1931. Its name is derived from the nickname for New York, the Empire State. It is one of the world's tallest buildings, standing at a total of 1,454 feet. There are 1,860 steps from the lobby at street level to the 102nd floor. Lightning strikes the building about 100 times a year."

There is a long line waiting for the elevators. They crowd in and arrive at the observation deck on the 102nd floor, and McKenna is nervous. She never has liked heights. Hugh coaxes her and holds her arm. Lori is already at the railing, wondering at the panorama view of all of New York. They can see the entire city, most of the skyscrapers and Central Park. It is more than breathtaking. On this bright, sunny day, they can see for miles, and Hugh thinks he can see the Atlantic Ocean.

They return to the hotel and ask the bellhop where would be a good place to eat dinner. He mentions the Manhattan Grill just a block down the street. At 7:00, they meet in the lobby. To their surprise, the restaurant is not crowded, and they are quickly seated. They enjoy their meal, and Hugh is full of stories about his training and the friends he has made since his arrival. McKenna tells Hugh that recently she has been playing piano on Sunday afternoons in the lobby of the Sandbar Hotel on the Rehoboth Beach boardwalk. She also mentions that some friends at the Sandbar told her about a club here in New York, not far from their hotel on 52nd Street, that has jazz music. It is called the Club Downbeat. She looks at Lori. "Do you think the three of us could go there after dinner?"

Lori stares at Hugh. "What do you think, Hugh? Should we walk over? I'm not really into jazz, but McKenna has been playing a lot of it lately."

Hugh's eyes are excited. "Sounds like fun! Let's do it." Hugh tells McKenna that he found out from his Coast Guard friends that the legal age to consume alcohol in New York is 18.

Lori hears the conversation and says, "That is why you two need a chaperone!"

They arrive and have to wait in the lobby until a table is available. Lori spots the small sign next to the door surrounded in twinkle lights. There is a five-dollar cover charge per person. Lori points out the sign to Hugh and McKenna. "Not too bad for New York City on a Friday night."

There is also a larger sign announcing a special guest appearance: *Hoagy Carmichael tonight at 10:00.* McKenna loves Hoagy, and she is bouncing off the walls. She has played many of his songs and knows most of his lyrics by heart. She especially loves "Heart and Soul" and "Georgia on My Mind." They take their seats at a table, and the jazz band is not far away on a small stage next to the bar. There are four musicians: piano, drummer, guitar and trumpet. As the evening moves on, the place is packed. McKenna orders a glass of white wine, Hugh a beer and Lori a gin and tonic. Lori almost shouts at Hugh and McKenna, "You two are only allowed one drink! I can have two or more." Hugh and McKenna are laughing and enjoying each other.

At exactly 10:00, the lights dim, and the master of ceremonies walks on stage. "Ladies and gentlemen, it is my pleasure to introduce to you Mr. Hoagy Carmichael. Besides composing popular hits, he has also recently appeared in the movie *Topper* in which he serenaded Cary Grant and Constance Bennett with his hit song "Old Man Moon." We are so pleased that he has stopped by tonight. Here he is—Hoagy Carmichael!" The audience applauds and whistles. He is wearing a gray suit with a white shirt and blue tie. He is tall with dark brown hair.

Lori whispers in McKenna's ear, "My god, he is so handsome!" McKenna shakes her head in agreement. For the next 30 minutes, he plays all of his most popular songs including

McKenna's favorites. He stands, waves at the crowd, and walks off stage. He passes by their table and slightly brushes against Lori. McKenna asks Hugh if he thinks Hoagy would give her his autograph. Hugh raises his arms. "Give it a try. All he can say is no."

She runs to the back of the room and sees Hoagy talking to several men in tuxedos. As he turns, McKenna asks, "Mr. Carmichael, may I have your autograph? I am a huge fan of yours. I play the piano and know most of your music."

Hoagy is a bit startled, but this happens all the time. He takes her notebook and pencil. In a bold hand, he writes his autograph across two pages. He is taller than McKenna, so he bends down and gives her a kiss on the cheek and says, "Young lady, I am looking for fresh new talent for a new radio show I will be doing. If you would be interested in auditioning, contact my agent. Here is his business card."

McKenna is in a state of shock as she takes the card. "Thank you so much, Mr. Carmichael!"

He touches her arm. "Please call me Hoagy."

McKenna rushes back to the table. "Look! I got his autograph, and he said he is looking for new talent for a radio show he is going to be doing. He said to call his agent if I wanted to audition!"

Lori gives Hugh a nervous look. "McKenna, settle down. He probably says that to every pretty girl that asks for his autograph."

Hugh's brief leave in New York is a distant memory. He had hoped that he and McKenna could have some time alone to talk about where their relationship is going, but that did not happen. Every time they had a moment alone, Lori surfaced for this or that. Maybe McKenna will try out for the radio show and come back to New York. He can't believe she idolizes someone that he has never heard of with a crazy name like "Hoagy." She did seem to want to tell him something. He saw an anxious look on her face. Maybe she will write something.

Every Friday morning before breakfast, all the Coasties assemble for a briefing by the commanding officer, David Ebert. Usually it is about mission, new equipment, training or critical concerns. On this morning in early April 1939, Commander Ebert is somber and formal. His talk is about Hitler and German aggression:

"Good morning, all Coast Guard stations have received a notification and updated information from the State Department with a sign-off by President Roosevelt concerning troubling news about the current situation in Eastern Europe. Last August, as we have heard, Adolph Hitler mobilized the German army. In November of last year, it was reported that over 7,500 Jewish shops were destroyed and over 400 synagogues were torched and sacked throughout Germany. Just a few weeks ago, on March 15, Germany invaded Czechoslovakia. Our intelligence sources confirm the existence of concentration camps operated by the German military. It is apparent that Europe is close to all-out war. We are on high alert, and we stand at the ready to respond to possible threats against the United States and our sovereign territories. Port security and beach patrol will be our main emphasis until we receive further orders. Stay vigilant, train hard. Leave will still be granted, but this could change quickly based on unforeseen developments. Thank you for your attention. *Semper Paratus*. Dismissed."

# German Institute of Military Studies 1937

December 1937. Anna has still not accepted the fact that she is losing her son, her only child. She has seen over the years how Gunter has deeply influenced Kurt's life and the path it is taking him. Deep within her, she feels that Christmas 1937 will be their last Christmas together. Kurt insisted on erecting his Christmas garden which he has done every Christmas since his return from Baltimore. It became a Wagner tradition, and his grandfather, years ago, shipped him the electric trains that he played with under the Christmas tree back in 1926. The Baldersohns are invited over for Christmas Eve. Ernest is not in good health, but they are happy to celebrate the holiday with Gunter, Anna and Kurt. Still, they are sad that Kurt is leaving home. Ernest has a present for Kurt. He hands him a small box in red wrapping.

"Here, Kurt, this is from Glennis and me. We will miss you. When you look at this, please think of us."

Kurt opens the box, and inside is a small silver compass. Kurt shows it to Anna and Gunter. Glennis looks at Anna and then Kurt. "Kurt, with this, you will always be headed in the right direction toward conviction and courage. It symbolizes your moral compass. It will keep you on the best path in your life ahead. Think of this as your moral reference point. You will have to make difficult decisions, and for each decision you make, there is a consequence."

Kurt nods his head in agreement. He thanks them and gives both a warm embrace. "I will be coming home for brief visits, so you will be seeing me from time to time. I will write to you when I can. You both have been like grandparents to me, and I will always carry the good times we have had in my heart."

It is cold and snowy in Berlin when Kurt must say goodbye to his mother. Kurt is in his military uniform. Anna thinks back to the toy soldiers he played with when he was a little boy and remembers his question: *Mother, do you think one day I will be a soldier like Father?*

He pulls her close and holds her in his arms. He kisses her gently and whispers, "Mother, I love you and will miss you."

Anna can't hold back her tears. "Kurt, I will always be here for you. Stay safe, and be true to yourself." She hands him a rosary that her mother had given to her when she made her First Communion. "Always keep this with you."

Gunter has the car waiting at the curb. Kurt blows his Mother a kiss as she stands on the porch waiving to him. He thinks, *I know I am breaking her heart!*

Gunter continues to advance in rank and status. He has been promoted from captain to major. He is well liked among the German military hierarchy and has caught the eye of three of Hitler's top deputies, Heinrich Himmler, Admiral Wilheim Canaris and General Reinhard Heydrich. Following his quick goodbye to Kurt, he is driven to the Berlin Military airport for a flight to Munich and then on to Vienna, Austria. Later in the day, he will meet with Himmler, Canaris and Heydrich. Gunter has not met Himmler or Canaris but has had several encounters with Heydrich, whom Hitler has called "the man with the iron heart."

His plane lands, and a soldier is waiting to drive him to the Austrian Parliament Building. Gunter has been here before and is always impressed with its Greek revival architecture. He grabs his bag, exits the car, and stops to take in the beauty of the Pallas Athena fountain. Athena is the Greek goddess of wisdom and war, and her statue looms large in the fountain. Although contradictory, the wisdom and war theme seems to fit Germany at this moment. He enters the building and sees Heydrich standing next to the Greek statue of Hermes. Gunter seems to remember that Hermes is the god who leads the souls of the dead into the afterlife. He thinks of the irony between the two. Heydrich spots Gunter and walks toward him with outstretched arms. "Let's hurry. *Herr* Himmler does not tolerate lateness."

They make their way through the maze of hallways, offices and conference chambers. They stumble upon room A10. Himmler has assembled a group of army intelligence officers around a large conference table. Gunter knows most of them. Several were involved in constructing and operating the first "detention and resettlement camp" in Dachau in 1933. Himmler is clearly in charge and introduces everyone. He advises them that General Heydrich has been chosen to head the Gestapo Intelligence Office (the SD).

"Our mission is to secure the safety of the Fuehrer and the German nation through various methods including surveillance, covert activities, sabotage, incarceration and other appropriate means. We will accelerate the construction of additional internment camps as we acquire additional territory. To that end, today I am naming Admiral Canaris as Commander Heydrich's chief deputy, and he will head Abwehr. His operational department will play a critical role as we execute the

Fuhrer's plan for new territorial expansion. Major Wagner will be Commander Heydrich's chief operational officer. Although still top secret, I have been authorized to communicate to you that Austria will be annexed as part of the German Reich on the 12$^{th}$ of March (1938). Most of this building will be occupied by German military. It should be a peaceful takeover, but one never knows until it happens. This is only the beginning. Also, Admiral Canaris will take over full control of the operation to inventory all Jewish property within the Reich. This will include all personal and business property. Those that do not comply will be confined. These inventories will be used to compile a registry of Jewish wealth and will be the basis for our Jewish taxation."

# Return to Bremen 1938

Anna has decided that she would like to move back to Bremen by the end of the year. Berlin has changed, and now that the Nazis have taken control, she worries about her safety. She has witnessed drunken SS soldiers in their black uniforms beat street vendors for no apparent reason, and a prominent businessman who was a member of her choir has suddenly disappeared.

The house in Bremen had been rented. The last tenants moved out several months ago, and the house now sits vacant. Gunter would prefer that she stay in Berlin. He understands that, with him spending more time traveling and Kurt away at the Military Institute, she is very lonely. Bremen is more inviting, and she has stayed in touch with many of her friends there.

Anna is in her apartment sitting at the kitchen table. She hears someone knocking and finds Glennis standing there with her arms wrapped around a large, engraved silver bowl. "Glennis, please come in, and I will make some tea. Where did you get such a lovely piece? Is that just plating or real silver?"

Glennis comes into the kitchen and places the bowl on the table. "Anna, I hope that we are alone." Anna nods yes. "This is a very strange story. You know our neighbors on the first floor, the Steiners? Well, Edna just came up this morning and knocked on my door with a large box full of beautiful silver bowls, platters, spoons, and other items. You will have to come over and look at it. I know what she gave me is very valuable. The Steiners have been here over a year now, but I don't know them that well. They seem very nice. I did not know that her husband, Elmer, was Jewish. She showed me a document that was slipped under her door. It looked official and requires them to submit a listing of all their personal belongings and its estimated value. It threatens imprisonment if they don't comply. Edna said she is going to give all her valuables away rather than submit a list to the Nazi government. She was very upset and crying. I felt so sorry for her. She said that they will be moving and that they don't feel safe in this building with two Nazi soldiers living above them."

Anna pours hot water into two tea cups and hands one to Glennis along with a teabag. "Glennis, I don't think Edna has anything to be worried about. Gunter mentioned to me a new program that requires this, but he said it was only needed for tax purposes on those that are not of pure Aryan blood. She certainly should not feel threatened living here. If anything, she should be happy that David and Gunter are her neighbors! Remember, Jews lost their citizenship in 1935, so *Frau* Steiner should be very careful!"

Gunter has been working in Berlin for the last several weeks. In early August, he comes home, and Anna can see that he is very agitated. He has started smoking and always lights a cigarette and pours a glass of whiskey before dinner. Anna puts the food on the table, and they sit down. Gunter has hardly spoken since he walked in, and he only nibbles at his food. Anna touches his hand. "Gunter, tell me what is on your mind?" she asks.

He looks at her with troubled eyes. "I am worried about Kurt. On the 12$^{th}$ of August (1938), the German army will be mobilized by order of the Fuhrer."

Anna rolls her shoulders. “What does that mean?”

“It means that Kurt will no longer be able to attend the Military Institute and all the cadets there will enter the German military. He will be a soldier and not a cadet. I know most of the war planning is secret, but I can tell you that Germany will soon be party to a new global conflict. We are mobilizing and expanding our military, and this is just the beginning.”

Anna can’t believe what she is hearing. “Gunter, this cannot be! You share the blame for this. You are placing our son in danger. He always adored his soldier father and wanted to follow in your footsteps. You encouraged him every step of the way. Will you guarantee his safety? Of course not! I guess you are proud of the fact that your son will be shot at. Well, I can’t bear to see him go off to war. My heart was broken months ago when he kissed me goodbye and now this. It is all your fault! How can you live with yourself?”

Gunter jumps up, knocking over his chair. “Anna, how can you place such guilt on me? I am going to see Kurt, and I am not sure when I will return.” He quickly gathers some belongings and slams the door.

Anna has not seen Gunter since his abrupt departure several weeks ago. She has been spending time with Glennis and has helped her take care of Ernest, who has been bedridden for several weeks. She also had a surprise visit with Manfred and Helene Hentzel. Anna has corresponded with Helene over the years and saw them about five years ago. One evening, Helene called to say that they were in Berlin and they should get together for dinner. They met at a restaurant a few blocks from Anna’s apartment. They were excited to catch up on where their lives have been taking them. Their daughter, Claire, has been living in Philadelphia since she graduated from upper school and is attending the University of Pennsylvania, where Helene’s brother is still a professor. Anna is surprised to find out that

Manfred and Helene want to leave Germany and are hopeful that their visa will be approved so they can move to the United States. Her brother has contacts within the United States government, and he is helping to obtain the necessary documents.

Anna tells them about Kurt, but does not mention Gunter. Helene probes, "So, how is Gunter?"

Anna drops her eyes. "Oh, he is fine. Still in the military and still traveling. He is gone most of the time. I will be moving back to our house in Bremen. I will miss seeing you. Can you believe it has been 12 years since we traveled together to Baltimore?"

The dinner with the Hentzels is a distant memory. It is late September, and she receives a letter from Kurt.

*Dearest Mother,*

*I cannot find the words to tell you how much I miss you. I can't believe how my life has changed so quickly. I know Father has told you that I am now officially in the German army. When we received word that our training at the Institute would be interrupted due to the call up, I was ordered to proceed directly to Munich for additional training. Because of Father's connections, I am now assigned to the German high-command service for espionage, counterintelligence and will be training here until the first of December. I will have two weeks off until I receive my final orders. I will be back in Berlin for a brief time. My thought was to help you relocate to Bremen and you would be settled in before Christmas. I know that you and Father had a disagreement, and I received a letter from him telling me that he has been spending most of his time in Austria. I am not sure if he has been in touch with you. Please know that the German military has been my choice, and I want to serve my country and protect it. I love you and cannot wait to see you.*

*Your loving son,*

*Kurt*

Anna will never forget November 9, 1938. She spends the day packing boxes for the upcoming move to Bremen. That evening, she attends choir practice at St. Hedwig's Cathedral and is walking back to her apartment. On her way back, she can smell smoke and can see flames coming from the synagogue several blocks away. She sees gangs of boys in brown shirts running down the street. One is pushing a wagon full of bricks. When they come to certain stores, a brick is thrown through the glass. Smoke and flames are also coming from many of the buildings. They enter one shop and drag out a man who tries to break free. Anna recognizes him. It is Elmer Steiner, her neighbor. They beat him with clubs and kick him. A crowd of men and some women encircle the melee and cheer the boys on. The poor man lies motionless with blood pouring from his eyes and mouth. Anna can't believe what she is witnessing. Anna screams, "My God, someone help him!" She attempts to move toward him, but the boys push her back and will not let her through. Anna hurries along as the night is turning into a full-scale riot. She hears screams and sirens.

As she approaches her apartment, Glennis is standing on the front porch. The smoke is heavy in the air. "Anna, are you alright? Tell me what is going on?" Anna tells her what she has just witnessed. They decide to go inside and knock on Edna Steiner's door. Anna tells her about Elmer.

"No, no, not my Elmer! I must go find him!"

She runs down the steps and toward his shop. Glennis tells Anna she heard on the radio this morning that a young Jewish man mortally wounded *Herr* von Rath, a German diplomat, as he was coming out of the German embassy in Paris. Could this riot be the result of his assassination? Germany is on fire this night, and the Jews are in the crosshairs.

Three weeks before Christmas is not a good time to say goodbye. Anna is crying as she leaves Glennis and Ernest's apartment. They have talked most of the morning, and she will miss them. She loves them, and they are both getting up in years. Anna has watched over them for these 11 years that she has lived in Berlin and will worry about them. She knows she can find them a suitable apartment in Bremen, but Glennis has lived in Berlin all her life, and moving is out of the question. Also, Ernest has been very sick, and Glennis does not want to move him.

Kurt arrives, and he has secured a military truck to help with the move. His two new friends, Alex and Eric, are in the German Military Intelligence Corps and are assigned to the same unit as Kurt. They have offered to help him with Anna's move. She has given much of her furniture away, and she still has some things stored in the basement of the Bremen home. Kurt stops in to say goodbye to the Baldersohns.

Ernest sits up in bed and stares at Kurt. "Kurt, you are a handsome soldier in your uniform. I can't believe how quickly you grew up. It seems like yesterday we were feeding our pigeons and you were riding the carousel at the Gardens."

Kurt walks toward Ernest and leans over the bed to give him a kiss on his forehead. "*Herr* Ernest, I will always remember the times we spent together and all the new things you taught me. I will miss you and Glennis, and I know Mother does not want to leave you here."

Ernest looks at Kurt with his weak eyes and holds his hand. "Kurt, stay safe and stay close to your mother. She needs your love and support. Remember to always carry your compass, and don't forget that the shortest distance between two points is a straight line."

Kurt smiles. "I'll remember that and all of the other advice you have given me over the years." Kurt gives Glennis a hug and kiss. She is crying as Kurt waves goodbye.

Everything is packed in the truck. It is about a four-hour

drive from Berlin to Bremen. The only thing left in the apartment is the piano. "Mother, what about your piano?"

"I gave it to Sandra Brack. I no longer wanted it. It only reminds me of you when you were a little boy. Like so many things, it makes me sad when I look at it. We had so many good times when you were a small child. Now it's just old furniture that needs to be discarded."

Alex and Eric shake hands with Kurt and say goodbye to Anna.

"Thank you both for helping. See both of you next week as we settle into our new assignment."

Kurt and Anna pull up to the house in Bremen. "Mother, I always loved this house, and Bremen has grown more beautiful over the years."

Anna nods in agreement and looks at Kurt. "I wish we could have stayed here, but your father insisted that we move to Berlin. I am sure you have been in touch with him. I have not heard from him since he left when he got mad at me and ran out of the apartment in August. You would think he would be concerned about me. I thought he would say goodbye."

Kurt avoids her comment. "Let's get this truck emptied before it begins to snow. Are the Petrovics still able to help us unload?"

"Yes, Norbert said he would keep an eye out for your truck. Do you remember that he and his wife, Janice, kept Maddie when we were away in Baltimore?"

Norbert arrives, and the truck is quickly unloaded. Anna went to grade school with Norbert and his wife, and they have kept in touch and visited while Anna was living in Berlin. "Norbert, please stay, and I will fix some hot tea to warm us up."

"No thank you, Anna. I must get back. Janice has been sick with the flu. So glad you are back in Bremen. I am sure we will see you in church. How is Gunter?"

Anna stands at the stove with her back to him. "Oh, he is fine and has been traveling out of the country. Thank you for helping, and please say hello to Janice." She turns and gives Norbert a quick hug.

Kurt finds a flashlight and has made his way to the damp, dark cellar. He shovels some coal into the furnace as it rumbles and shakes. He then places logs in the fireplace in the living room and lights the kindling. Quickly, the fire begins to crackle and spit, and the red embers are aglow. The house slowly begins to warm, and Kurt and Anna sit at the kitchen table sipping their tea. She looks at Kurt and touches his face.

"Kurt, I miss you terribly. You are still my little boy. I know you are almost 19, but you will always be my little boy. I worry about you so! Can we have a frank and serious conversation?"

Kurt places his cup on the table and sits straight up and stares into her eyes.

"I don't see a future for your father and me. I would prefer never to see him again. The Nazis have demonized him, and they will do the same to you. I know he is involved in the Jewish concentration camps, and I can never forgive him for his actions. I know he would say that he must follow the orders of the Fuehrer. How can he and you be loyal to someone who is forcing the military to commit genocide? Hitler has created a godless society absent all our traditions that held our country together. He closes our churches, kills nuns and priests. He sends the Jews to the concentration camps and burns their synagogues. Just last July, our beloved pastor was arrested by the Gestapo, and no one knows where he may be. Nazi mobs break into our Catholic schools and remove the crucifixes. Your father would not let me hang a crucifix in our apartment. At mass, a Hitler Youth and a Nazi soldier stand on either side of the altar. All we see now are flags, uniforms, parades, fighting in the street and burning our books. The government controls the telephone, the radio, the newspaper. Everything we nurtured and loved is gone. Kurt, how can you be loyal to an army that is morally corrupt? The work you do and the orders you follow are abhorrent. How can you embrace and condone such criminality? We are at the doorstep of another world war. Can't you see that? You did not experience the first one; I did!" Anna has held her composure, but now she cannot continue and begins to sob.

Kurt hands his mother his handkerchief. "Mother, first, please know how much I love you. As I have told you, the military was my choice. We were a weak nation until the Fuehrer came to power. Do you want to live under Soviet rule with the Communists running Germany? Stalin is much worse than Hitler. You and millions of other Germans need a strong military who will protect our country. I don't want my children and your grandchildren to fight a third world war. Three great wars in the same century is unfathomable. I will stand and fight for our country. This is just an unfortunate interlude. In a few years, this will all be over. I pray that you and Father can then have a normal relationship. As far as I know, Father is still in Austria but will be returning to Berlin early next year. He has written me, and he asks about you. I know he loves you and wants to see you if you would only let him."

"Kurt, I am not sure I still love him. He is not the man I married. There is no way I can ever accept Nazi dogma. Love, hope and truth are casualties of this reign of terror. Why can't you accept that? Please don't worry about me. I will be fine here. Bremen is home, and I will reconnect with our neighbors and my friends at church. I may even rejoin the choir. Before you leave, I have an old sewing machine down in the basement. Would you mind bringing it up? I want to start making you some warm clothes. So, tell me: Where will you be traveling?"

"I will leave here in the morning and head back to Berlin to return the truck. Then I will meet Eric and Alex at the train station for a quick ride back to Munich. I will continue my training at the Military Intelligence unit there. I may not be back to see you until next July, but I promise to write."

Anna grabs the teapot and pours Kurt another cup. She raises her cup and says, "*Frohe Weihnachten* (Merry Christmas), my son. May the Lord watch over and protect you." She walks over to a large paper bag sitting next to the stove and brings him a brightly wrapped box. "*Ich werde dich immer lieben* (I will always love you)!" Kurt opens it. It is the small wooden rabbit that his grandfather carved for him in 1927.

# The Senator Meets with President Roosevelt 1939

September 1939. It is still hot and steamy in Washington D.C., and Senator Townsend is working late in his office when he receives an unexpected telephone call from President Roosevelt's Senate liaison, Michael Rogosky.

"Hello, Senator, Mike Rogosky here. Hope all is well. The President would like to meet with you as soon as possible. It is about a national security issue. Might you be able to make some time this coming Saturday morning at 9:00 a.m.? The President would like to meet on the Presidential Yacht *Potomac* rather than the White House. Hope to see you then."

Townsend was going home to Delaware for the weekend, but of course a meeting with the President is top priority, so he will change his plans. Townsend wonders what the President has on his mind. Europe is exploding, and US coastal security has to be a hot topic that needs more attention. Even though Townsend is a Republican, he and Roosevelt have a close relationship and a mutual respect. Their disagreements have been few.

Townsend arrives at the Washington Naval Yard, and the guard sees that he is on the Congressional list provided by the

President's staff. The guard salutes him, and he is quickly met by Mike Rogosky, who walks him along the pier toward the *USS Potomac*. This is Townsend's first visit to the Presidential Yacht.

The *Potomac* is a beautiful ship, all steel, 165 feet in length with a cruising speed of 13 knots. Rogosky tells him that Roosevelt prefers the *Potomac* to the *USS Sequoia* used by his predecessor, Herbert Hoover. Roosevelt has been a paraplegic since 1921 when he was stricken with polio at age 39. One of his greatest fears is to be caught in a fire and not be able to escape. Roosevelt had a hand-operated elevator installed by the Coast Guard inside a false stack on the ship, and the President—who has developed an extremely strong upper body—can use ropes and pulleys to move the elevator up and down between the salon and upper boat deck. During the sultry summer days in Washington D.C., he enjoys cruising on the *USS Potomac* rather than staying in the White House. The *USS Potomac* gives the nation's 32$^{nd}$ President much-needed respite from the cares of governing. He prefers holding informal strategy sessions with close advisors and Congressional leaders in the privacy and seclusion of the yacht. He loves the sea and spending time on this beautiful ship.

Townsend asks Rogosky what's on the President's mind. "I think it's all about coastal security."

Off the ship's salon, the President has a small office. Townsend walks in and sees that he is seated in his wheelchair smoking a cigarette. There is a large, thick binder that he has been reading which he quickly closes as Townsend moves closer to shake his hand. The President looks tan and well rested as he removes his glasses and sets them on the desk.

"John, so good to see you and hope your family is well. Did you have a good summer? How are things in Delaware?"

Townsend settles into a plush leather armchair and slides it forward so that he is directly in front of Roosevelt. "Things are fine, Mr. President. Delaware is in good shape, but the folks there, just like everyone else around the country, now have their eyes on Germany and the war in Europe. As you know, I have been appointed as one of the senators assigned to the Special Committee on Un-American Activities. We are investigating Nazi influence in the US and taking a close look at the Bund and their activities."

The President opens his binder. "John, that ties into why I asked you to see me today. Let's label our conversation 'top secret' so we don't have to make denials later on. Secretary of State Hull just gave me an update on the war, and it looks like we may be drawn in, but our intelligence cannot determine a timeline. We knew that, as soon as Germany invaded Poland, Britain and France would declare war on that maniac Hitler. The Nazis are exterminating the Jews, Christianity is being threatened, Mussolini has all but imprisoned the Pope, and all hell is breaking out all over Europe. I want us to stay out of it for as long as possible, so I will be pushing Congress to have the United States remain neutral. That's why I made the speech to the country on September 3rd. What I want is to remain neutral and remain safe.

"What I am also concerned about is sabotage here in the US, especially on the East Coast. We know that there are saboteurs amongst us. There has been domestic terrorism going on. I can't be too specific, but J. Edgar Hoover briefed me on Friday and gave me a list of ongoing FBI investigations. Here is a sampling: Bombs have been planted in military plants producing weapons, trucks carrying munitions bound for Europe have mysteriously disappeared, a two-star Army general, responsible for weapons procurement, was found dead in a public restroom here in Washington with his throat cut, and a dynamite bomb was planted at the Glen L. Martin plant outside of Baltimore that manufacturers sea planes. Thank God it was found and diffused before it could detonate. We know the Germans now have more submarines than any other country, and they could or maybe already have landed saboteurs on our shores. John, I want to appoint you to a secret committee, just five members of Congress that will work with Hoover and Army, Navy, and Coast Guard personnel to begin to set up a security blanket along the entire East Coast.

"I was reminded by Hoover that it is only 125 miles from Rehoboth Beach, Delaware to the steps of the White House. If a German hijacked a car, he could be sitting at my front door in four hours or less. While there is a lot of coast from Maine to Key West, I want to quickly beef up coastal security along New Jersey, Delaware, Maryland and Virginia. I want to build fire control towers on the beach with patrol dogs, horses, jeeps and the Coast Guard. Since Delaware is your baby, that's where I want to start and place the emphasis."

Townsend has been quiet, listening to the President express his strong feelings. "Mr. President, I share your concern. There is also a strong possibility that a sea invasion on either our Atlantic or Pacific coast could occur. I will be honored to serve in any capacity you would like. I totally agree with you regarding East Coast security. The sooner we begin to agree on a strategy and implement the plan, the better. I assure you that there will be timely and accurate information provided to you regarding our progress. Delaware will be the model for others to follow."

The President moves his wheelchair from behind the desk and positions it next to Townsend's chair. His eyes are glittering as he motions toward the water outside the window and toward the capital in the distance. "John, that capital belongs to the nation, and we will keep it out of harm's way. I know I can count on you."

The following weekend, Townsend is back home in Delaware. He has asked Jason LaPlante and Jeff Miller to join him for lunch. The three are seated at a large table on a screened-in porch just off the kitchen. They are enjoying fried chicken as they bring the senator up to date on farm issues.

Jason pushes back in his chair. "Senator, Jeff will be harvesting the rest of the sweet corn next week, and then we have the last of the tomatoes scheduled to be picked the week after. We both have expanded our chicken population, and the profit margins on that segment are increasing."

Townsend nods in agreement and has a pleasing smile. "Gentlemen, you both have done an outstanding job, and I am very pleased with the way you both are managing the farms. Today, I want to talk about another issue, a national security issue that will have a big impact on you and the farms. As you know, we have a war going across the Atlantic, and how we keep the East Coast safe and free from saboteurs and spies is something I'm working on in Washington. The war over there will require us to reconfigure our business plan for the farms. I can't share with you all the details due to secrecy, but be assured that the plans we will begin implementing have been vetted by top military brass and have the approval from the highest levels of the government. The Delaware beaches will be the starting point for a high-profile security strategy all along the East Coast from Maine to Florida. Since my farms are so close to the beach, in the near future, we will begin to accept horses and dogs that will be used by the Coast Guard for beach patrol. The mounted training for the horses will not be done here. That job will be done at the Elkins Park Training Station in Pennsylvania and the training center in Hilton Head, South Carolina. They will also train patrol dogs there. Your job will be to manage the construction of kennel space at both farms for a minimum of 20 dogs. We will need to build two new barns, one on each farm with stalls for about 20 horses, 10 on each farm. Also, think about how much fencing we will have to install. You two are the experts, so can you work on a project plan and cost it all out."

Jason and Jeff are trying to envision and internalize what they are hearing. Jeff takes a sip of his iced tea. "Senator, this is a huge change of direction. There are a lot of moving pieces that need to come together. It's going to take some time to get all this work done. Sounds like we will have an equal number of horses and dogs on each of our farms. We will have to transfer corn crop to alfalfa for grazing the horses. We need some direction from the military folks and a timeline so we can meet the deadlines they may have. Once the dogs and horses arrive, we may need help to care for them."

The senator hardly touches his food and swats at a fly that just landed on his plate. "Boys, I know this sounds like a lot of work, but I know you can make it happen. This is all about patriotism and keeping our country safe. I will set up a meeting with the Army and the Coast Guard to brief you on more of the specifics within the next 30 days. Remember: Keep what I have shared with you today to yourselves. Be careful what you say to your families. I am sure the press will get tipped off at some point, so if you get any calls asking questions, refer them to my Washington office."

In Ocean View in October of 1939, the season is shifting, and fall is changing the tempo and rhythm with crisp mornings and shorter days. The "shoulder season" usually means a slower pace. This fall, the LaPlante and Miller farms demand longer work days and more farm help.

Emma and Wilmer notice that the Miller farm next to them is swarming with trucks delivering lumber and building supplies. Emma's curiosity gets the best of her as she spies Lori walking down the drive to her mailbox. Lori has been trying to avoid her neighbors ever since that day Emma frightened

McKenna with her Hitler conversation, but this day there is no place to hide.

"Good morning, Lori. Would you mind if I dropped off some freshly baked strawberry tarts? It has been a busy summer, and we have missed seeing you and your family."

"Hello, Miss Emma. Hope all is well. That would be fine. Do stop in." Lori rushes back to the house and tidies up just before Emma knocks on the door.

"These are still warm. Hope you like them." Lori thanks her and places them on the table next to the window. "Tell me, Lori.... Wilmer and I have been curious about all the trucks and building supplies that we see being delivered. Looks like more chickens are coming?"

"No, Miss Emma, nothing to do with chickens. Jeff tells me that Senator Townsend wants to build a new barn for some horses that he wants to board here and a kennel for some dogs he will breed for hunting. I think he wants to keep some thoroughbreds here for racing at some of the nearby tracks."

"Dogs and horses? I never thought we would have a kennel next door to us. I hope it is far enough away from our house so that we don't hear that constant barking. I am surprised Townsend didn't drop by to tell us what his plans are. Maybe it's his way of pushing us to sell our farm to him. I will have to get in touch with him."

Lori motions toward the kitchen chair. "Please have a seat, Miss Emma. Since you seem so curious about what is going on here, I have some questions for you. I should have talked to you about this before now. Our family noticed that you had a crowd over at your place in July. We first thought that you were having a family reunion. Then we noticed tents going up and young boys marching around in uniforms. We noticed some flags hung on your barn. We thought it resembled the Nazi swastika. We also saw some of the boys throwing stones at our horses. Quite honestly, we were frightened, especially after your conversation with McKenna about Adolf Hitler, and now there is a war going on in Europe. What was all that activity about? Many of the neighbors think you and Wilmer are Nazi sympathizers, and it frightens them."

"Lori, I am sorry that we upset you. I should have told you about the summer camp we were sponsoring. Wilmer and I belong to a group called the German American Alliance. It operates all across the United States and is headquartered in New York. It has received some negative press because of its association with Hitler. I can assure you the organization is non-political, and you should not have been frightened. There were 12 boys, and they camped, crabbed, fished and went swimming. It was just a small group of boys having summer fun. The leaders stress discipline and character building. Most of them were from Pennsylvania and New Jersey. I am sorry if they were bothering your horses. Lori, Wilmer and I are Germans first, and we have great loyalty to our homeland. All Germans are united by blood. We may live in Berlin or Ocean View, but our blood is the same no matter where we live. We will try not to bother you in the future. Please tell your husband that we said hello." Emma quickly leaves and hurries down the driveway.

That evening at the dinner table, Lori tells the family of her conversation with Emma. "Jeff, I think you should tell Senator Townsend what is going on next to us. The German American Alliance she is talking about is also known as the Bund. She says they are non-political, but they love Hitler. I was listening to the news the other night on the radio, and they were talking about how the Germans are taking over Jewish property and arresting Jews for no reason. I am glad we are not Jewish. If we were, Emma and Wilmer would be trying to take over our farm!"

Jeff nods in agreement. "Don't worry. Senator Townsend is on top of things, and he is part of a plan to provide more security to coastal towns, starting here in Delaware. Emma is not breaking any laws by flying a swastika on her barn and hosting a summer camp for a group of boys. That is what free speech is all about. Tristan, tell Mom what you were discussing with me earlier today."

Tristan looks surprised. "Well, we know there is a war going on in Europe, and soon we will be brought into it, no matter what Roosevelt says. Connor and Hugh are now in the Coast Guard, and I am thinking about enlisting in the Navy. Mom, I know your dad was in the Navy, and he has told me so much about his experiences. It is a way to see the world. If we are brought into the war, they don't usually draft into the Navy. I'd rather be on a ship somewhere than in a foxhole in Germany."

McKenna listens with grave eyes. "Tristan, it will not make any difference what branch of the military you will be in. If we go to war, you will be in danger—and forget the part about you seeing the world. You need to decide if you want to dodge bullets or torpedoes."

# Aboard the Coast Guard Cutter *William Taft* 1939

The last few months have been very busy for Hugh and everyone stationed at Manhattan Beach. Hugh has completed boatswain training and is now a boatswain mate. He proudly wears two crossed anchors on his uniform. He has been assigned to the Coast Guard Cutter *William Taft*, and they are doing port security all along New York City's waterfront and into the Atlantic. He is learning navigation and will be training to pilot the cutter.

All the military in the United States is on heightened security since Britain and France declared war on Nazi Germany on September 3, 1939. Although still technically assigned to Manhattan Beach, Hugh has been spending most of his time on the cutter. He is in his bunk, totally wiped out, after a busy day on the water involving a series of maneuvers alongside cargo ships delivering coal to New York City.

His bunkmate, Roger Trotta, settles in above him. "Hugh, did you hear the news about the sinking of the British passenger ship, *Athenia*? Here is a copy of the dispatch we just received."

*On September 1, 1939, the* Athenia*, commanded by Captain*

*James Cook, left Glasgow for Montreal via Liverpool. She carried 1,103 passengers including about 500 Jewish refugees, 469 Canadians, 311 US citizens and 72 UK subjects, and 315 crew. Despite clear indications that war would break out any day, she departed Liverpool at 13:00 hrs on 2 September without recall, and on the evening of the 3rd was 60 nautical miles (110 km) south of Rockall and 200 nautical miles (370 km) northwest of Inishtrahull, Ireland, when she was sighted by a German submarine which tracked the* Athenia *for three hours until eventually, at 19:40, when both vessels were between Rockall and Tory Island, two torpedoes were fired. The first exploded on* Athenia's *port side in her engine room, and she began to settle by the stern. 128 civilian passengers and crew were killed with the sinking condemned as a war crime. The dead included 28 US citizens.*

"My God, Roger, those Nazis didn't waste any time sinking a passenger ship. They must have known it was carrying Jewish refugees. With Americans among the dead, Roosevelt can't just sit back and do nothing!"

Roger takes the dispatch from Hugh, folds it and places it under his pillow. "Hugh, Captain Barr wants to see us at 0600 sharp tomorrow morning."

At 0530 hours, Hugh and Roger make their way to the small room outside of the captain's quarters. It is standing room only with a mix of officers and enlisted men. Everyone grabs a coffee cup. As the captain enters, everyone stands and salutes. "At ease. Does everyone have a copy of the dispatch concerning the sinking of the *SS Athenia*?" It is the same dispatch that Roger showed to Hugh last night.

"As you know, President Roosevelt has issued the Neutrality Act. He has just extended the Pan-American Security Zone to include Canada and Iceland. Effective immediately, we will begin providing escorts within this region. The Germans have torpedoed their first unarmed passenger ship with loss of life.

The dispatch indicates a death toll of 128, but I have been told that the death toll is much greater. Our mission, effective immediately, will be to provide escort to ships and convoys entering or exiting New York Harbor and other Atlantic ports as required. We may be sailing as far as Montreal, Quebec, Halifax and Iceland. We will be in port at the New York Navy Yard to have some retrofit work done. We will be there about seven days. They will install depth charge tracks, and they will be adding a 5-inch 51 caliber gun. New duty assignments will be made and posted this afternoon. Gentlemen, things are heating up, and I know I can count on each of you. Dismissed."

Hugh finds out that they will be arriving at the Navy Yard within the next two days. Some of the crew will be given leave while in dry-dock, but not Hugh. After evening chow, Hugh writes letters to his parents and to McKenna. The letter to his parents is all about his new deployment and how excited he is to be part of the Coast Guard team that is providing coastal security. His letter to McKenna is difficult to compose. He has received only one short letter from her since their meeting in New York. It was all about her audition for the Hoagy radio show and how disappointed she was that she was not selected. He knows his new duties will keep him away from her, and he is not sure when he will see her again. In his heart, he knows that it would not be right to expect that she not date other men. That big question about where the future will take them will not be quickly answered.

*September 12, 1939*

*Dear McKenna,*

*I hope that you are well and things are quiet in Ocean View. I'm sorry that you were not selected by that Hoagy guy for his radio show. Obviously, they don't know exceptional talent when they see it. Maybe it was for the best.*

*I am now assigned to the Coast Guard Cutter* William Taft. *Even though the US is not at war, our new duty assignment really places us on a war footing. My hope is that the German U-boats stay far away from our shores, but if they come, we will be ready. I don't mean to frighten you, but that is the reality of the life I now have.*

*I have not seen you in so long, and it feels like years. When I close my eyes, I can see your beautiful face. I have so many great memories of our time together. I know I never liked high school, but I loved the time we spent together after school and on weekends. Remember our summer horseback rides down to the river and the long walks on the beach? Those great memories will forever be locked away in my heart.*

*To ask you to save a place for me in your heart is being selfish. You are young and beautiful, and I know a lot of boys at the beach would love to ask you out. Probably already have. When they do, please accept. I really don't want you to wait for me because you may be waiting a very long time. We really don't know if God has a plan for us, and it may be quite a while before we find out. Enjoy your life, and we will keep in touch as best friends should. Hugs and kisses!*

*Your best friend,*
*Hugh*

On Sunday, September 24, 1939, the cutter *William Taft* is on escort duty. They are tasked to escort the British ocean liner *King James* out of New York Harbor and into the Atlantic on her way to Liverpool, England. Since hostilities began between England and Germany on September 3, many British nationals living in Canada and the US are rushing to return to England to stay close to family. The liner is carrying 903 passengers, including Canadians, US citizens, UK subjects, and crew. She leaves at 2:00 p.m. and slowly makes her way southeast away from New York Harbor and into the Atlantic moving at approximately 18 knots.

Hugh is assisting with navigation duties on the bridge. The day is clear and crisp with a hint of chill in the air with calm seas. He always salutes as he passes the Statue of Liberty. The out and back of this escort should take about eight hours. The *William Taft* is about a half mile ahead of the liner. At approximately 6:35 p.m., Hugh hears a loud explosion. He runs out onto the deck and hangs over the rail as he sees the *King James* engulfed in flames. Hugh can see a gaping hole on the port side with flames climbing up the side of the ship. Hugh's heart is pounding as he runs back to his duty station just as Captain Barr is sounding the emergency siren. All the Coast Guard crewmembers are now on high alert as the cutter circles back toward the ocean liner. As they approach, the liner is listing and taking on water. The crew of the liner is making ready the lifeboats. Already, there are people in the water.

Captain Barr has radioed all ships in proximity to assist in saving passengers. As the cutter moves closer, more flames and smaller explosions can be heard as the liner convulses. The *William Taft* lowers its lifeboats and begins to bring aboard survivors, some burned, others badly injured, and many have drowned. Hugh can't believe what he is witnessing. There are woman and children in life jackets screaming for help. There are deck chairs floating among the debris with people clinging to them as they would an inflated inner tube. Grimy dark oil floats on the surface. Clothes, suitcases, boxes and wooden crates float and bump against those in the water. The cutter quickly reaches its limit and cannot take on any more survivors. Two freighters, one from Bermuda and the other from Cuba, quickly arrive and begin to assist in saving lives. Medical staff aboard the cutter are working on those severely injured, and a triage process is taking place. Hugh is now helping medical staff attend to those lying on deck. Crewmembers are bringing their mattresses from their bunks and placing them on the deck. Slowly, the wounded are placed side by side, and those crewmembers who have medical training are attending to them. Many are horribly burned. The dead are moved inside and covered in blankets. Hugh passes a little girl, maybe 10 or 12 years old, who has lost most of her arm and has blood seeping from her eyes. He says a silent prayer as the medical team attends to her. The captain announces for all crew to return to their normal duty stations so the cutter can return to New York at top speed. They have radioed ahead, and medical help will be awaiting their arrival. This will be a day that Hugh will never forget as long as he lives.

Night slips into day after their arrival at New York Harbor. Late in the afternoon, Hugh and Roger are sitting on their bunks sipping coffee. "Roger, I heard Captain Barr tell some of the officers that it will be some time before a final death toll is counted. The *King James* went under at 8:15 p.m."

Roger takes a sip of coffee and stares ahead with blurry eyes. "I'm thinking that we had about 150 wounded on our decks, and someone counted 53 dead. Who would ever believe that on our first escort mission something like this would happen? Captain Barr knows it was not a German U-Boat attack and thinks someone planted a bomb or several bombs on the liner. I heard the FBI have been called and will lead the investigation. Even though this happened in international waters, it might prompt Roosevelt to move away from his neutrality position. Hugh, I am sure German saboteurs or sympathizers did this. This is an act of German aggression."

On Sunday, October 1, 1939, Lori and Jeff Miller have invited the Crosby and LaPlante families to their farmhouse on Woodland Avenue for dinner. All three families now have sons in the military. Connor LaPlante is in the Coast Guard and stationed at Cape Charles, Virginia. Jason and Marna's younger son Cameron is attending college at the University of Delaware and living in Newark. He was a straight-A student in high school and was awarded an academic scholarship. He has told Jason and Marna that he wants to be a veterinarian. Lori and Jeff's son, Tristan, recently enlisted in the Navy and will soon be leaving for basic training. All the parents gather in the kitchen. The topic of conversation is Hugh Crosby and the explosion onboard the British ocean liner *King James*. McKenna doesn't want to listen and takes Lee and Jimmy outside.

Jeff hands Jim and Jason a beer. "Jim, tell us about Hugh. We were so worried when we heard the bulletin come across the radio last Sunday about the sinking of the *King James*. As soon as McKenna heard that the Coast Guard cutter that Hugh is on was part of the rescue, she totally lost it, and we could not console her. Lori and I are worried about her. She spends most of her time after work in her room. She so misses Hugh and is worried about him. She now tells us she wants to quit her job and go to college and wants to teach. She may need a change in scenery."

Jim looks at Barbara. "Barb, tell them about your phone conversation with Hugh."

Barbara pulls out a chair and sits down at the kitchen table. "We were so upset when we heard about the explosion. He had told us in a letter a few weeks prior that his cutter was going to be escorting ships out into the Atlantic, and he mentioned that last Sunday would be their first mission escorting a British ocean liner. We heard a bulletin on the radio late Sunday evening that there had been an explosion aboard the *King James*. I think McKenna heard the same news. She called our house when she heard that the cutter *William Taft* was involved. All of us had a good cry. Hugh wasn't able to call us until late Monday afternoon. He didn't share with us many of the details but said he was fine and not to worry about him. They had dead and injured onboard, and he felt really bad for all those poor, innocent people who just wanted to return home to their families in England. Hugh is convinced it was sabotage. He said that investigators believe someone planted several bombs in the ship's engine room."

McKenna, Lee and Jimmy are behind the house looking at the construction work for the new barn and kennel. McKenna's two horses, Sadie and Toby, are grazing nearby. Lee looks out at the horses. "McKenna, which horse did Hugh ride?"

"Hugh always rode Toby, and I rode Sadie. Sadie is the one with the white mark on her face."

Jimmy tries to reach over the fence to touch Sadie. "McKenna, do you miss Hugh?"

McKenna begins to cry, and Jimmy is startled and moves closer to her. "Don't cry! Hugh is ok, and I'm sorry I asked you such a stupid question. Maybe we should go back in the house?"

"You and Lee go. Let me stay here a little while." She remembers her last letter from Hugh and what he wrote: *Remember our summer horseback rides down to the river and the long walks on the beach? Those great memories will forever be locked away in my heart.* Tears come back as she slowly walks into the house and sits down at the piano. Lee timidly walks over to McKenna.

"McKenna, will you be able to teach me how to play? You play so well. I feel like you are my big sister."

"Here, Lee, sit next to me. Here is your first song." McKenna shows Lee the keys to strike for "God Bless America."

"There you are," McKenna encourages as Lee plays. "Great job! Lee, I would love to give you lessons, but in January I will be leaving for college."

Lee looks surprised. "Where will you be going?"

"I'm going to the Maryland State Teachers College in Salisbury. It is not that far away, and Dad said I can come home most weekends if I want. I decided that working as a teller is not for me. I really want to be an elementary school teacher, and Salisbury has an excellent teacher education program."

After dinner, everyone is sitting around the table. Marna mentions that Connor has applied for flight school. "Connor wrote us two weeks ago and said his commanding officer posted a notice that the Coast Guard was looking for applicants for aviation training. He is keeping his fingers crossed. He was always fascinated with airplanes ever since he was a small boy and saw the planes towing the banners down Bethany Beach. He should know within the next 90 days whether he has been accepted."

Jeff asks Jason how Cameron likes the University of Delaware. "He is adjusting, and I think he is homesick. He told me he is applying for Army ROTC and would start next semester. Looks like both my boys will be in the military. Jeff, when does Tristan leave for basic training?"

"He surprised us with his decision to enlist. I think Connor and Hugh had a big influence on him. He will be heading to the recruit training center in Great Lakes, Chicago. We thought he would go to Bainbridge in Port Deposit, Maryland for basic training, but since he wants to train on submarines, they are sending him to Illinois. He will be leaving next month."

Jim Crosby gives a curious look to Jeff and Jason. "So, tell me more about the dogs and horses. I just saw the article in the *Coastal News* about the President's coastal security initiative and that Delaware will pilot the plan with towers and security patrols with dogs and horses. Looks like Senator Townsend is in the thick of it. My dad found out that his company just bid on a contract to build several towers along the Delaware beaches. The contract will be awarded by the War Department in Washington. They will build eight towers in Delaware on the beach. Dad showed me the drawings. The towers will be four- to five-story round-base concrete towers with flat observation decks. They will be used as artillery spotting locations and for observation of ship traffic in the Atlantic. When they are completed, the Coast Guard will man them and patrol the beach with the dogs and horses. Now I know where the dogs and horses will stay. You guys will really be busy. Looks like we are heading to war, and the talk around town is concern that there may be an invasion along our Atlantic coast by the Germans. The *King James* explosion only reinforces the idea that it may happen, so it makes sense to be ready."

Jason suggests they move outside to look at the barn, stalls and kennels that are under construction. The three of them walk over to the barn. "Jim, Jeff will have 10 horses here, and I will have 10 at my farm. They haven't told us how many dogs will be coming, but they are building kennels for 10 at each farm. Jeff and I have meetings scheduled with the Coast Guard early next year to finalize the details. Looks like 1940 is going to be a year to remember. I pray to God to protect our boys and our country."

# German Intelligence Service 1939

January 1939. Kurt arrives in Munich for training at the German Military Intelligence Service of the Abwehr. He has studied the basics of espionage, counterintelligence and sabotage. He has been learning how to decode British radio transmissions and how to assemble wireless transmitters. In early April, he is ordered back to Berlin. He is appointed special assistant to Admiral Wilhelm Canaris, who now heads all German military intelligence and reports directly to Hitler. Kurt is working with another soldier in a small office. They are investigating those Jews who have not paid special tax assessments on their property. He is also tracking Polish spies working in Germany and Austria. He is surprised to accidently uncover some very sensitive information about Canaris.

Kurt is busy pulling files when his phone rings. "Kurt, this is your father. How do you like your new job?"

Kurt is unsettled and catches his breath. "Father, I can't believe it's you. Where are you?"

"I am one building away from you. Are you free for lunch? Let's meet at the restaurant *Schlossgarten.* Do you know where that is? Two blocks east and on the corner. If you get lost, use the compass that Ernest and Glennis gave you. Only joking! See you there in an hour. Is that acceptable?"

It has been almost a year since Kurt has seen his father. The restaurant was once a beer hall, and it is very crowded. He sees Gunter at a table next to a large window and waves. He works his way through the narrow aisles. Gunter stamps out his cigarette and puts down his newspaper. He comes around the table and gives Kurt a warm embrace. "Kurt, you look so good. I see you now wear the new Gestapo uniform and they have issued you the Walther PPK pistol like the one I carry. I have been keeping my eye on you. Berlin is a much better place to work. Your duties will be more challenging. How do you like Canaris? You know you can be honest with me."

"Father, I like him. I had a long discussion with him when I arrived in his office, and of course your name came up. He has warm feelings for you. He is very straightforward and does not sugar-coat his words. Apparently, he was a naval hero during the Great War, and Hitler must like him. He wants me on this special project to identify those criminals who owe the Reich thousands in back taxes, primarily those Jews that refuse to pay and attempt to hide their wealth. I just started, so I think it will be interesting. We are also identifying Polish spies who may be in Germany. He also likes the fact that I can speak English and says I am one of the few he knows who speaks it without a German accent. He mentioned that soon he wants to utilize my language skills but was not specific. I have missed you. Were you in Austria all of the time you have been away?"

"First, let me tell you how happy I am that you are in this intelligence unit and not part of our ground troops. If you were, you would be on your way to Prague. I knew for some time that we would invade Czechoslovakia on March 15, so I made some phone calls and found out that Admiral Canaris was adding staff. So, here you are. I have been in Austria since we took over the government there (March 1938). Vienna is not a bad assignment. I am still reporting to Heydrich, who is a real jackass. He yells, screams and beats his fist on his desk. I take it but ignore it. He knows I am good at what I do and will always get the job done. I will be here in Berlin for two more weeks. How is your mother doing? I heard you helped her move back to Bremen. I know she appreciated you doing that. I still love her, though she probably doesn't think so. The Nazi military does not bode well for a strong marriage. I am in too deep now and can't turn back. The three of us are victims of turbulent times. It will not get better. Hitler wants a global war, and only God knows our destiny. Tell me: What does she say about me?"

"I guess you would say that she has mixed emotions. I know she doesn't say much to me about her true feelings about you. She knows that I love and respect you and would never hurt you, and that makes her cautious. I feel like the pawn on the chess board pushed and pulled in so many directions. She did open up a little. She said she was not sure she still loves you and you were not now the man she married. She is totally anti-Hitler and said that she could never give allegiance to Nazi principles. I do worry about her. She is mostly alone except for a few neighbors. Maybe she needs a dog or a cat to keep her company. I don't know what would be best for her."

"Kurt, I do worry about her. I am still in love with her. She is a traditionalist and strong in her Catholic faith. That will not help to bring us close. She never cared or worried much about world affairs. She was focused only on our family and her parents. When I decided to enter the military, my life completely changed, and she could never accept that. I admire her for being the perfect mother. I just wish she was more understanding. It really breaks my heart that the times we live in have hurt our marriage and the way she feels about me. I want to see her before I go back to Vienna."

July in Bremen is warm and wet. Kurt has one week of leave and will spend two nights with his mother. When he arrives, he finds her sitting at the large oak kitchen table with family pictures sorted in various piles. He places his hands on her shoulders and bends over to kiss her. "Looks like you are busy arranging the family album. I've been wanting to ask you about Grandfather. The last time you heard from him, he told you that Aunt Elizabeth had died and Uncle Gerhard was trying to sell the market in Baltimore."

Anna motions toward the chair. "Please sit and help me place some of these old photographs in this album. I just received a letter from him last week. He seems to be well and still helps out at the market. I thought it would have sold by now. He is very active at his church. Can you believe it has been 12 years since we saw him? I always thought he would come here to visit or perhaps even move here. Grandfather will be 70 years old this August 17th. I worry about him. There is no one to look after him in Baltimore except Uncle Gerhard, and he is 73. Father says Uncle Gerhard is a bit feeble, can't climb the steps and very forgetful."

Kurt hands Anna a photograph of him sitting at the piano in the house in Baltimore. Kurt stares at the photo. "I remember Grandmother took this. Let's pray that things change here soon and maybe we could travel back to Baltimore."

"You are not a realist. It will be a very long time before things change here. I would love to see him one more time before he passes, but I don't see that happening."

"Did you know that I had lunch with Father? He has been spending his time in Vienna but came back to Berlin for a few weeks. Mother, did he come to see you?"

"Yes, he did stop by. He did tell me about your lunch. We had a long conversation. He told me he still loves me, which I don't believe. I was honest with him. I told him I do not love him. We cried. He held me close and said he hoped that I would change my mind. I said that the Nazi military has destroyed our marriage and I couldn't see any hope for a return to the life we had and the love we once shared. I also told him that I would never forgive him because he took you from me." Anna starts to cry. "He did bring me a present." She walks into the living room and returns holding a little black kitten.

"I have named her Adelina. She does keep me company, and I talk to her constantly."

The visit with his mother was much too brief, and Kurt hates to see her living alone. Sadness grips him when he remembers her standing in the doorway waving goodbye to him, wiping tears from her eyes. It seems that his parents will never be together, and he believes what she said about not loving his father. Their lives are heading in different directions. It would be irrational for him to think that the three of them will ever come together again as the family they were.

Kurt is back to work in the office of Admiral Canaris. Germany is at war. On September 1, 1939, Germany invades Poland. Two days later, Britain and France declare war on Germany. Questions remain about the neutrality of the United States and the Soviet Union. Kurt's office is chaotic, and he is working 16-hour days. He has been busy decoding intercepted transmissions between the United States and Britain.

On September 12, Canaris travels to visit Hitler at his underground compound on the outskirts of Berlin. This is not a trip he wants to make. He is compelled after hearing reports of massacres in Poland and hearing eyewitness accounts from several high-ranking military he has been in touch with. He wants to personally register his objections to the atrocities and his protest with the Fuehrer himself.

As he arrives at Hitler's headquarters, he is stopped by

General Wilhelm Keitel. He is Hitler's door keeper, and no one can enter unless they receive Keitel's personal approval.

Canaris looks at Keitel with wide, grave eyes. "I demand to speak to him. I have information that mass executions are being planned in Poland, and that members of the Polish nobility and the Roman Catholic bishops and priests have been singled out for extermination. Please let the Fuehrer know that I am here. He is expecting me."

Keitel will not move and straightens his stance. "My dear admiral, if you want to remain in the German military, leave now, and we will pretend this did not happen. I will provide an excuse for your absence. Hitler is well aware of the plans you want to bring to his attention. I would not characterize them as 'atrocities.' They may be referred to as 'strategic military action plans.' They have been approved by the Fuehrer, and they will be carried out. I suggest you leave now. At some time in the future, you will thank me."

Canaris decides to leave and follow the advice of Keitel. Shocked by these incidents, he begins to secretly work more actively, at increasing risk to himself, to overthrow Hitler's régime. He knows this maniac must be stopped.

Late Friday afternoon on September 22, Major Josef Huber hurries into the office and hands Kurt an envelope. "Please see that Admiral Canaris receives this immediately. It is urgent and time-sensitive. *Heil* Hitler!"

"The admiral is in a meeting. I will see that he gets this as soon as he returns."

Thirty minutes later, Canaris returns, and Kurt rushes into his office and hands him the envelope. "Admiral, this was hand-delivered by Major Huber, and he indicated that it was extremely urgent."

The admiral opens the envelope as Kurt stands in front of his desk. Canaris reads it. His eyes are wide and darting from line to line. "Kurt, this is the same message you decoded just an hour ago. It's from our man in New York. Take a look."

Kurt takes the paper from Canaris and carefully reads each line:

*Attention: Admiral Wilhelm Canaris—Regarding* King James. *New York to Liverpool. Three steaks are in the oven. Well done as ordered. Timer set for 18:35 hours on 24 September.*

Canaris returns the paper to Kurt. "Take this to Himmler's office. I will call the Fuehrer to let him know the details and will tell him that Himmler has the transmission. This will make our leader very happy!"

On Monday at four in the morning, Corporal Ansel Justus enters the dormitory room that Kurt shares with 12 other soldiers assigned to the intelligence unit. He leans over and shakes Kurt's shoulder. "Admiral Canaris wants to see you, now!"

Kurt jumps out of bed and quickly dresses. Within 20 minutes, he is in Canaris' office. Six members of his immediate staff are gathered around the radio, including his deputy, General Hans Oster. Kurt stands next to Ansel in the corner of the office but close enough to hear the BBC news concerning the explosion aboard the *King James* and its sinking at 8:15 p.m. last evening approximately six miles off New York Harbor. The room is buzzing, and a few of the staff applaud.

Canaris calls the Fuehrer. After a bit of a wait, Hitler gets on the line. "*Was der dringlichkeit ist* (What is the urgency)?"

"*Mein Fuehrer*, thanks to your saboteurs in New York City, the *King James* exploded and went under Sunday evening. There are few survivors."

"Excellent work, Admiral. Thank your staff for me, and transmit my congratulations to our men in New York."

On November 8, 1939, Kurt has been asked by Admiral

Canaris to travel with him along with General Oster and four others of his staff to attend a speech Hitler is giving in Munich. The flight is a brief 35 minutes. During the flight, Kurt sits behind Canaris and Oster. Corporal Ansel Justus sits next to Kurt. Canaris has a bit of a hearing problem and speaks with a loud, booming voice. Kurt overhears Canaris say to Oster that Hitler will be surprised how his speech ends. Kurt and Ansel give curious looks to each other.

Hitler has asked several of his top commanders and other high-ranking Nazi officials to join him to celebrate the $16^{th}$ anniversary of his infamous 1923 coup attempt that resulted in his arrest. This is a commemorative speech that the Fuehrer gives every year. This is an annual ritual for Hitler and one he thoroughly enjoys. On this day, he will be addressing a large group of his old guard party members and supporters along with other political functionaries as well as soldiers who have been loyal to his fascist party since the early days of its inception. Hitler takes the stage. Canaris has directed his group to stand at the back of the hall. They are approximately 80 meters (240 feet) from the podium.

Hitler cuts his speech short, and it lasts only 45 minutes. He stresses that Germany had to defend itself and had no choice but to invade Poland. Hitler wants the conflict to be brief. He states, "Germany only wants lasting peace." The speech is over, and the crowd cheers and sings the German national anthem. Hitler leaves the stage and begins to slowly walk toward the exit. He is surrounded by his security team.

Canaris whispers to Oster, "The speech was supposed to last one hour. We had better get the hell out of here." Kurt and Ansel follow as Canaris rushes out of the building. Hitler and his entourage move toward their waiting cars. As he enters the rear of his sedan, there is a bellowing explosion from inside the hall that shakes his car. Smoke and fire engulf the rear of the building. Hitler is safe, but many are killed and wounded, including civilian and military personnel.

Canaris and his group immediately head to the Munich airport for the flight back to Berlin. The Fuehrer's plane lands at 10:20 p.m. Canaris' plane arrives 10 minutes later. Hitler wants all his immediate staff including his military high command at a meeting in the Chancellery at 8:00 a.m.

Canaris, Oster, Reinhard Heydrich and Heinrich Himmler are told to bring a preliminary report with them so that the Fuehrer has the most current briefing on the assassination attempt. There are 12 military commanders assembled around a large conference table as Hitler enters the room. The Fuehrer is completely nonplussed, somewhat confused, and very angry. He is red-faced with bulging eyes. Had his speech yesterday been just a bit longer, today the Fuehrer would be described in the past tense. Soon, he will know all the facts, and retribution will begin.

Canaris stands and hands out their report. Hitler doesn't look at the paper. He looks at Canaris with glazed eyes and a fixed stare.

"*Mein Fuehrer,* I must preface my comments by stating that this is a very preliminary assessment concerning yesterday's explosion. I can confirm that seven were killed and 63 were wounded. A dynamite bomb with a timer mechanism was hidden in a wooden pillar behind the speaker's platform. I am told that the perpetrator is one George Elser, a Munich carpenter who is a known communist. He is in custody and has admitted his guilt. His questioning continues, and I will provide additional details as they are confirmed to me. I can assure you that your security detail will be increased in number with better-trained soldiers."

The next day, the Nazi party official paper, the *Voelkischer Beobachter,* squarely places the assassination attempt on British secret agents. Hitler even implicates British Prime Minister Neville Chamberlain. Now at war with Britain, he stirs up hatred for the British and whips the German people into a war frenzy.

Canaris, Oster and a few top generals know the assassination attempt was not at the direction of the British. It is the work of a secret German anti-Nazi/Hitler military conspiracy, and they are the major players. Canaris has named the group *Toten um zu Leben* (Kill to Live). Kurt is slowly being brought into Canaris' inner circle. Canaris is secretly creating a safe haven within Abwehr for a select group of German soldiers who share his hatred for Hitler.

# Delaware Braces for War
# 1940

June 1940. Senator Townsend has arrived at Jason LaPlante's farm in Bear Trap. It is a hazy warm Sunday afternoon with a hint of ocean breeze moving the leaves in the big walnut tree that sits in front of the old farmhouse. The senator has been campaigning most of the morning and just attended a big rally in Georgetown. He has not visited the farm since the barn, stalls and kennel were completed. Six horses and four dogs are new residents.

The senator pulls his car into the lane and parks next to the barn. Jason hurries over to greet him. "Welcome, Senator. Hope all is well! How is the campaign going?"

"Jason, good to see you. Hope the family is well. I heard that Connor is going to flight school and Cameron is at the University of Delaware. You must be so proud of those fine young men. Yes, the campaign is going well. This is my toughest race, and James Tunnell is a worthy opponent. This may be a very close election. That reminds me—before I go, I want to give you a few *Vote for Townsend* signs.

"I talked to the President just last week, and he has given Delaware an executive order which allows our state to pilot the use of dogs and horses on the beach for security purposes. He wants to expedite the tower beach construction. He assures me that all of his military brass are plugged in. The *King James* sinking has really got him worried about coastal security. I know you have been following the news, and it amazes me how Hitler has captured Europe. He has invaded Poland, Denmark, Norway, and is advancing on France and Belgium, but we have the Battle of the Atlantic going on just a few miles east of where we are standing. The folks here at the beach are really concerned. Those German U-boats are tearing us up and moving closer to our shores. Let's take a look at the horses the Army just delivered."

Jason and the senator walk over to where the new Arabian horses are grazing in the pasture. "Senator, I was surprised to learn that these horses are the property of the US Army but are assigned to the Coast Guard. Same goes for the dogs. I thought our involvement with the animals would be more labor-intensive. All we are required to do is feed them, bed them down at night and pasture them in the morning. The military comes by to exercise and groom them. I am told they will use our veterinarian, Dr. Burton, if they have any health issues. I don't think I told you that my son Cameron will be working with Dr. Burton this summer as one of his assistants. Cameron wants to become a vet, so this will be a great experience for him. Are you going to stop by the Miller farm?"

"Not today. Actually, I am heading back to Washington tonight. Sounds like you and Jeff have everything under control. Jason, I also heard that the Army wants to purchase 10 acres here in Bear Trap. They want to quickly build a detention camp and a radar station. I heard a couple different stories about who they will detain there. If I hear anything definitive, I will let you know."

That evening, there is a knock on the door. Marna looks

out the window and sees that it is Dr. Burton. "Please come in, Doctor. What brings you out on a Sunday evening?"

"Hello, Mrs. LaPlante. Please, call me Bob. I wanted to stop by to talk to Cameron about his summer schedule. Is he here?"

"I believe he is out back feeding the horses and the dogs. Let me get him."

"That's not necessary. Let me go out to the barn. I'm sure I can find him."

Dr. Burton finds Cameron filling the trough that the dogs have in each kennel with food and pouring water into their bowls. "Hi, Cameron. You look busy. How are these new dogs and horses doing?"

"Hi, Dr. Burton. You startled me! I wasn't expecting you to stop by."

"I had an emergency at a farm not far from here. A mare had a difficult delivery. So, I thought I would stop by so we could talk about your schedule. I also was hoping to check out the new dogs and horses the Army delivered. I heard you have four dogs and six horses here and the same number at the Miller farm. The dogs look fit and healthy." Dr. Burton kneels down to pet one of them. "Are they all German Shepherds?"

Cameron moves the bag of food out of his way and bends over next to the dog. "I think the one over there in the corner is a Belgian Shepherd. The others here at our farm are German Shepherds. The Belgian stands out and is all black with just a little white on her neck."

"You don't see many Belgians. They are smaller and faster than the German Shepherds and should do a good job for the Army when they start beach patrol."

Burton stands up and looks out at the pasture. "Let's take a quick look at the horses."

Cameron and Dr. Burton walk over to the barn. Cameron and Jason just finished moving them into their stalls for the evening. "Handsome Arabians and beautiful coloring. I understand they moved them here from the Elkins Park Training Station in Pennsylvania. So, they are trained and ready to go. All the military needs now is to train some riders."

They both walk back toward the house. "Cameron, I have something for you in the car."

They walk over to his car, and Dr. Burton hands Cameron a large, thick textbook.

"Here you go. It's a copy of *Black's Veterinary Dictionary.* It is well worn and over 400 pages. My parents gave me this when I started veterinary college at Penn State. You will refer to this often. It is an essential reference tool, so keep it handy."

Cameron quickly leafs through it. "Thank you, Doctor. So kind of you. What days will you want me to work? Dad said he will let me drive his car, so I can drive over to your office."

"Great! How does Thursday, Friday and Saturday sound? I may have to call you on short notice if I have an emergency that I can't handle on my own. Is that ok with you?"

"Dr. Burton, that sounds good to me! I'm anxious to help and learn as much as I can. I am excited and look forward to working with you! Thanks for this great opportunity!"

# War Touches Bremen, Germany 1940

January 1940. The German winter of 1939–1940 is the coldest in 50 years. Waterways, canals, and even the bay have frozen over. The temperature on January 5th was -15 degrees. Bremen is feeling the effects of the weather and the effects of Germany at war. Food rationing began August 27, 1939. Anna's neighbor, Norbert Petrovic, delivered baskets of vegetables from his garden in the fall. Anna was able to can tomatoes, green beans, beets and corn so she has had to wait in the two-hour queue for rationing coupons only once. Schools closed early for the Christmas holiday and stay closed due to lack of coal. The school authorities are calling it a "coal holiday," and they may stay closed until spring.

She opens her front door and watches a young mother walk past her house pushing a baby carriage with a sack of coal sitting behind her baby with another sack balanced on the mother's shoulder. Everyone in Bremen is grumbling about the food and coal shortages. Just about everyone wears coats and sweaters inside their homes all day and all night. Water pipes break all over the city.

Anna has organized a group of women at her church to

show support for the soldiers by knitting socks, gloves, blankets and scarfs. Around 10 to 12 women usually join the group after the 12:00 mass each Sunday. Yarn and double-pointed needles are in short supply, but they seem to have more than enough to fill a large box that will be taken to the German army supply depot in Bremen. She has also made up a special box for Kurt, although she is not sure where he is spending his winter. She has received only a few short letters which listed an address but no telephone number.

The church group looks after each other by pooling their rationing coupons. Since Anna is living alone, she usually has more than enough coupons, so she makes sure some of the women, especially those with children still at home, have what they need. Anna has tried to help her women's group find coal, which is also being strictly rationed. Norbert, who works for one of Bremen's largest coal distributors, has been able to provide coal to those in need through Anna's efforts.

Norbert has also offered to help her place blackout paper at her windows. Just after dinner, there is a knock on her door. Anna looks out the window and sees her neighbor shivering and stamping his feet.

"Anna, I wanted to finish the blackout paper tonight, if that is alright with you? The Nazi security patrol has inspectors who will fine you if the windows are not darkened by the end of the month."

"Yes, Norbert, I so appreciate your helpfulness. Please come in."

Anna helps and hands him the step ladder, hammer, tacks and scissors. Soon, all 10 windows are papered over.

"Thank you, Norbert. That did not take too long. Just another depressing thing for me. I so enjoyed looking out at the yard, the snow and that red cardinal that snacked on my seeds and nuts. Now darkness will be a constant companion."

"Anna, how is your coal bin? Is it full? I have a truck delivering to my house tomorrow, and I could drop off some to you if you are in need. Don't worry about the rationing coupons. I will cover the delivery."

"That would be wonderful. I am about half full, so that delivery may last the rest of the winter."

"Anna, I don't mean to frighten you, but they are broadcasting the possibility of air raids on our German cities, especially if we begin to bomb Britain. You need to be ready in case you lose electricity and water. I just placed in my cellar 10 buckets of water, a supply of candles, and some battery-powered torches. We also filled our bathtub with water. Janice has been placing cans of food down there. You need to take the same precautions."

"Norbert, do you really think we will be bombed by British aircraft? I have read in the newspaper how well our city is protected with artillery that can fire shells as far as 10 kilometers. Large concrete spotting towers are being built along the coast as well as more police and fire protection. But, I should be more prepared. I will have to purchase some buckets as you suggest."

"Anna, don't worry. On Saturday, I will bring some buckets and help you make ready. You never know what the future holds. I also heard that many families are moving out of the city. Last weekend, there was a long line of traffic moving southwest toward the countryside near Hannover and Dusseldorf. That exodus will only continue."

Anna continues to keep herself busy and pretends that her life alone is as it should be. She wonders if moving back to Bremen was a terrible mistake. She has been packing her china, carefully wrapping each piece in newspaper, and stringing twine securely around each box. After many trips up and down the cellar stairs, all are now secure under her steps. She has also wrapped some beautiful framed watercolor art depicting Giverny, France that has been displayed in her living room and moved those pieces next to the china. She misses her piano but is glad it is no longer with her—just more bad memories. She has noticed that she has lost weight and her clothes are a bit baggy.

It has been a beautiful spring in Bremen, and she stays outside as much as possible and eats most of her sparse meals on her small patio when the sun is setting and the air is warm. This evening, she has been busy with her small flower garden and enjoys the company of Adelina. Just as she is about to go back into the house, she hears the frightening sound of the air raid sirens. Is this just another drill or the real thing? She picks up Adelina and runs to the cellar. She lights her torch and glances at the calendar hanging on the basement wall next to the shelf where she has stocked her canned goods. It is May 17, 1940. She opens an old wooden folding chair and sits down with Adelina on her lap and her rosary around her neck. In the stillness, she can faintly hear repeated explosions and feel the ground beneath the cellar shake and rumble. Somewhere nearby, bombs are hitting their targets.

The next morning, Anna turns on her radio and hears that 24 RAF bombers attacked Bremen oil installations just 12 kilometers from her house and the death toll near the refineries may exceed 50. The Reich reminds the citizens of Bremen that the anti-aircraft emplacements that surround the city took down five of the planes. The broadcast fails to mention that the oil and refinery targets were totally lost and the fires continue to rage. This is the first of many air attacks on Bremen.

The day following the bombings, Kurt makes a surprise visit. At noon, he pulls up in front of the house in a black Mercedes. He opens the trunk and grabs hold of a large box. He runs up the front steps and knocks on the door. Anna swings open the door and blinks in disbelief. She throws her arms around his neck, and the box falls to the floor. The box opens, and cans of vegetables roll across the floor. Anna also sees flour, sugar and coffee.

"Kurt, I can't believe it is you and you are bringing me gifts! What are you doing here? I have missed you so! I am mad at you for not writing me. I worry about you and pray that you are safe."

"Mother, are you alright? As soon as I heard that Bremen was bombed last night, I asked Admiral Canaris if I could take some leave for a quick visit. He insisted that I use one of his assigned cars. Drive time from Berlin was almost four hours, and I have to be back for a 3:00 p.m. meeting tomorrow. I hope this box of food will help. Do you have enough to eat?"

"I have enough, and our church women look out for each other. Let me get you something to eat and drink, and then you can tell me what you have been doing all these many months."

Anna places apples, sausage and cheese on a large plate and sits it on the table in front of Kurt. She tells him all about the help she has received from her neighbor Norbert and his wife, Janice. She mentions the knitting group at her church. She walks over to the closet and brings him a box of clothes she has knitted for him.

"Mother, so kind of you." He tries on the gloves, and Anna places the scarf around his neck.

"Last night, I was so worried about you when I heard that Bremen had been targeted and the Brits were bombing the oil refineries here. I know you were frightened. I see that your electricity is still off."

"I was scared, but Adelina keeps me company. I know we have people from the neighborhood that work at the oil depot there, and I hope they are safe. Many in our church have left the city for safer places to stay until this nightmare is over. Kurt, you know how stubborn I can be. I will not be leaving here. I will be fine, so don't worry about me. Now tell me all about you.

I know most of what you do is secret. Is there anything you can share with me?"

"Mother, what I am about to tell you can never be revealed to anyone. I am glad that Father was able to secure a position for me with Admiral Canaris. The admiral must follow orders, but he is a good man who wants to remove the Fuhrer as quickly as possible. Last November, his group tried an assassination attempt but was unsuccessful. I am sure you read about it. I uncovered some documents that prove the military, with orders coming directly from Hitler, are killing Jews, the religious, the mentally ill, and Polish military in our so-called 'detainment camps.' The atrocities that I have seen and read about sicken me. I know for a fact that 6,000 Poles were shot and buried in a mass grave in the woods near Neustadt. Over 1,700 hospital patients were executed in Bromberg. This is just a small sampling. The Nazi propaganda machine continually denies these atrocities. I know they are happening, and I have pictures to prove it. This military, this government is morally corrupt, and I must do whatever I can to help Canaris.

"I always admired Father, and since I was a little boy, I wanted to follow in his footsteps. I should have listened to you. We should have returned to Baltimore years ago. I have made a horrible mistake, and I hope God forgives me. Hitler must be eliminated somehow and by whatever means available to us."

He reaches into his pocket and places the compass given to him by Ernest on the table. "Mother, I always carry this with me. Remember, Ernest called this my 'moral compass'? I am hoping it is pointing me in the right direction."

"Kurt, you are doing very dangerous work, and this is just another nail in my heart. I wish you would not have told me these things. I don't know how I will be able to live with this. Does your father know anything about this?"

"Mother, I wanted to be honest with you. I had to tell you

what is going on in my life. No, Father does not know, and this is a closely held secret among just a small number of Canaris' inner circle."

"Kurt, you are a good man, and you have a good heart. You are a victim of this war just like millions of others. The Germans are good people. It is Hitler that has betrayed us. I pray that God will protect and watch over you. You once said to me that these times of travail will quickly pass and our lives will return to normal. I had hoped and prayed that would happen. Now I know the German nation, as we knew it, will never return."

The summer settles in, and Kurt's visit is a fleeting memory. Every morning and evening, Anna is able to tune in a BBC channel on her radio. On the morning of August 29, 1940, Anna listens through the static as the announcer discusses the first major air attack by the German Luftwaffe on Liverpool, England. "Last evening, over 160 German Luftwaffe bombers attacked the city of Liverpool. The death toll is in the thousands. The port facilities were heavily damaged."

She turns to the German military broadcasting channel and hears the Third Reich military music and German marching songs. The German broadcaster proclaims the victory of the Liverpool air war. She thinks, *We only hear the good news, never the bad.* She turns off the radio, and her body shakes as she ponders her future.

# Submarine School
# 1939

Tristan Miller bounced around for a few years after his high school graduation. He spent most of his time working on the farm with his dad in Ocean View but decided to enlist in the Navy in October 1939. His decision was motivated by his friends, Connor and Hugh, and the stories they shared with him about their life of adventure in the Coast Guard. He also loved to hear his grandfather tell him all about his naval career including his time at the Naval Academy. He has always lived close to the ocean, so this love of sea must be ingrained within his DNA.

As a Naval recruit, he underwent eight weeks of basic training at the Naval Station Great Lakes, North Chicago, Illinois. He remembers the long bus ride to Chicago from Wilmington, Delaware. He will never forget his boot camp at the *Quarterdeck of the Navy.* After graduation, he still was not sure which branch of the Navy he wanted to pursue for his so-called "apprenticeship." He developed a close friendship with his group commander, Brian Russo. Commander Russo was a submariner at heart and encouraged Tristan to consider submarine school. Tristan remembers the commander telling him that submariners make more money, have more shore leave and travel to more exotic places than the sailors on destroyers or aircraft carriers. He also told him to be prepared to work in a confined space for at least 90 days and that safety is paramount on a submarine. "Tristan, everything is magnified in a 300-foot-long, 30-foot-wide, three-story capsule operating at depths down to 800 feet. Your shipmates will rely heavily upon your abilities. You will hold mutual trust in high regard. It will be all about teamwork."

Tristan liked what he heard and transferred to submarine school at New London, Connecticut for another eight weeks of training. As soon as he completed submarine school, he was assigned to the *USS Terrapin* which was just launched, fitted out and recently finished sea trials. The boat validated all its systems, components and compartments as well as submerged for the first time and conducted high-speed tests on the surface and underwater. He was excited about his new life onboard the *Terrapin* and becoming a "submariner."

Tristan likes his assignment as a torpedoman's mate and begins his training to learn how to store, load, operate and fire eight torpedoes, four from the stern tubes and four from the bow tubes. He knows that the *Terrapin* is one of the ultimate hunters of the sea. She is a fast-attack submarine designed to find and destroy enemy ships. She carries five officers and 65 enlisted sailors. The *Terrapin* was fitted out and departed from Portsmouth, New Hampshire in April of 1940 for her shakedown cruise which lasted for almost 10 weeks and took the crew to the Panama Canal. The *Terrapin's* next assignment was to the Pacific Fleet. Her home port will be San Diego, California. She docked in San Diego in October of 1940.

Tristan has written a few short letters home. When you spend your time underwater, letter delivery becomes a bit unreliable. Now that he is not at sea, he decides to write a letter home.

*October 16, 1940, onboard the* USS Terrapin

*Dear Mom, Dad and McKenna,*

*I hope this letter finds all of you in good health and you are winding down the harvest. I guess the new patrol dogs and horses are settling into their new homes. I know they have important jobs keeping the Atlantic coast safe. In a way, I am like a patrol dog, keeping the West Coast safe. What is troubling is that the East Coast of our country is preparing for an invasion from Germany and I am here on the West Coast. Does that make any sense?*

*We arrived here in San Diego last Sunday, and I am anxious to find out how long we will stay here. Scuttlebutt onboard has it that we may be heading to Pearl Harbor, Hawaii. We should have official word by the end of the month. Some of the guys think we will be there for Christmas.*

*I am fine, eating well and getting familiar with the moving parts onboard this brand-new sub. My bunk is cramped, and when they turn off the ventilators, my bedding is damp and musty, and perspiration permeates the air. But, that is a small annoyance that I will get used to. Sometimes I close my eyes and long for the cool ocean breeze back in Ocean View and think of all of you. We did have rough seas for most of our voyage here. When the forecastle hits the waves, there is this thud after thud that keeps me awake. I'm accepting the rhythm and beginning to sleep better. I am with a great team here onboard, and they are like my brothers. We are very close and have formed a tight bond. We really look out for each other.*

*I am anxious to hear how McKenna likes the Maryland State Teachers College at Salisbury and if she is still playing the piano on the weekends. Please write to me as much as you can. I have sort of lost touch with Connor and Hugh, so if you see their parents, please give them this address in San Diego. If we get reassigned quickly, I am told the Navy is good about forwarding mail.*

*I love you and miss you more than you will ever know.*

*Tristan*

Every day, Lori hurries to the mailbox, and today she finds the letter from Tristan that she has been waiting for. She runs up the dusty driveway littered with the fall leaves from the large oaks. Jeff is in the barn as she runs over to find him. "Jeff, here it is, the letter from Tristan." They both sit on a bale of straw, and Lori reads the letter aloud. She drops the letter in her lap, and her eyes are teary.

"Jeff, can you believe our son is on a submarine in San Diego, California?" Jeff places his arm around Lori. "He grew up much too fast, and now I am so proud of what he has accomplished. Our son may be in Hawaii for Christmas?"

McKenna comes home for the weekend from Salisbury. Her weekends are very busy, and she is still playing the piano at the Seaside Inn on Saturday nights. At breakfast, Lori tells McKenna how excited and happy she was to receive Tristan's letter.

"McKenna, please read his letter. He is doing well, and he may be on his way to Hawaii. You must get a letter off to him. He wants to know what you are doing. Do you miss him as much as we do?"

"Mom, I do miss him and pray every night that God keeps him safe. I will write him before I leave and give you the letter to mail. I wanted to tell you and Dad that I met three guys at school, Brian, Michael and Joey. They play in a jazz band. Brian is the bass player, Michael plays the drums and Joey the trumpet. Once a month, they go to Baltimore and play Friday and Saturday nights at the Belvedere Hotel. They are looking for someone to sing and play the piano, and I told them I might be interested. I have never been to Baltimore. I know you and Dad have. They said they would pay me 50 dollars for the two nights and pay for my hotel room. We would leave after class on Friday and return on Sunday evening. I think it would be a great experience, and they are really nice guys. They want me to start the first weekend in November. What do you think?"

Lori has a surprised look. "I have mixed feelings. I know you are a big girl now, and I trust you to make the right decisions. I know Dad will not be crazy about the idea."

"That's why I wanted to discuss it with you before I mention it to Dad. If you are ok with it, I know we can get Dad to agree."

"Is there any way we can meet these boys? Why don't you invite them over for a Sunday dinner? I do know that the Belvedere Hotel is one of the finer hotels in Baltimore. That is a long ride for you from Salisbury to Baltimore. I hope they have a reliable car. I don't want this to affect your studies. If I see your grades slip, that will be the end of it."

"Mom, you know my dream has always been to play in a jazz band, and I am getting tired of the Seaside Inn. I want to become a music teacher, so this will look good on my resume."

"Ok, ok! I will talk to your father, and then the three of us can discuss it. Maybe I will travel with you the first couple of times just to settle my mind and make sure you will be safe there."

That evening, McKenna writes a letter to her brother.

*October 29, 1940*

*Dear Tristan,*

*I hope you are doing well and staying out of trouble. I read your letter of the 16th, and we miss you so much. This will be our first Thanksgiving and Christmas that we have not been together, and that is so sad. I see, sailor boy that you may be in Hawaii for Christmas. How exciting is that? You asked about school. I love Salisbury, and I am taking basic freshman courses, like sociology, English, algebra, history and PE. All my professors are great. My dormitory is basic, and I love my roommates. My time there can't go fast enough, and I hope I can make it through. I do want to be a music teacher in elementary school.*

*I may be playing in a small jazz band in Baltimore, provided Dad gives it his blessing. Mom is ok with it. I would play on Friday and Saturday nights, once or twice a month. I think it would be a good experience for me, and I will make a little money. I will keep you posted if it happens.*

*I have not heard from Hugh or Connor. You knew about the sinking of the* King James *and that Hugh's cutter, the* William Taft, *was involved in the rescue. The event had a huge impact on him. He is still in New York, and I heard he has been to Iceland and Halifax. Connor was home for five days before he left for flight school. I heard he is now stationed in Mobile, Alabama. Did you know that Cameron is at the University of Delaware on a full scholarship? He wants to be a veterinarian, and he has been working over the summer with Dr. Burton.*

*I guess my relationship with Hugh is pretty much over ... if you want to call it a "relationship." He told me to date other guys, and I have. Oh well, who knows what our next steps will be? And that goes for you, too, Tristan. Have they let you use the periscope? That is the only part of a submarine that I know anything about.*

*Oh, by the way, the Sticklers now have a small German flag, not the Nazi one, sticking in the ground next to their mailbox. I think they are just daring someone to take it. They are so strange.*

*Be safe,*
*Love you,*
*McKenna*

# The Arrest of Dr. Erik Reinhardt 1941

July 1941. Dr. Reinhardt has the look of an academic with his distinguished face, glasses, gray-speckled goatee and thinning hair. He is totally exhausted as he steps off the crowded train at Baltimore's Pennsylvania Station. It is a warm, humid evening, and sweat gathers under his starched collar. Yesterday, he flew on a new Lufthansa Condor long-range airliner non-stop from Berlin to New York, spent the night at the Waldorf Astoria, then took the morning train to Baltimore. It was a quick cab ride to the Admiral Fell Inn near the Baltimore harbor and close enough to Johns Hopkins University. He ate an early dinner and was in bed by 9:00 that evening. He wanted to be fresh for his presentation to the symposium of aerospace engineers on the Hopkins campus. He was particularly excited to meet with American physicist Robert H. Goddard. Goddard and Reinhardt have occasionally shared scientific research on rocket propulsion and have developed a friendship. Reinhardt speaks poor English, and Goddard speaks a little German, so the conversation should be interesting.

Reinhardt has worried about this trip and was surprised that his superiors allowed him to travel to the US with the war raging in Europe and the US restricting German travel to America. Thanks to Goddard and some diplomatic pull, he is attending the first American-sponsored conference dealing with the development of rocket technology and the new field of aerospace engineering. He does not mention the fact that he is a member of the Nazi party. Hitler approved Reinhardt's trip and is hoping that he will return with some sensitive intelligence about the progress of the US rocket program.

Following the three-day conference in Baltimore, he is scheduled to travel with Goddard to Annapolis, Maryland to meet with his American counterparts at the Engineering Experimental Station housed on the Naval Academy campus. The scientists that are stationed there are working on long-range missile propulsion control systems, and Reinhardt has completed extensive research in this field. Goddard has asked Reinhardt to speak to this group about his theoretical applications regarding large-scale liquid propellants for rocket applications.

Reinhardt welcomes the break and will enjoy his time in Maryland. For the last three years, he has been working very long days at the Peenemunde Army Research Center. Peenemunde is a German municipality on the Baltic Sea. Hitler has personally visited the facility and met with the German scientists working there. He has ordered them to develop what is secretly referred to as the "V-2 project." Hitler's aggressive goal is to develop a long-range rocket that can deliver a new, never-before-deployed warhead to England within the next 18 months. Most of the research has been completed, and test rockets have been fired from the rocket launch facility at Peenemunde.

Dr. Reinhardt is passionate about his science, but not about the Nazi application. He has a deep hatred of Hitler, and he was forced to join the Nazi party in order to keep his doctorate in physics that he earned from the University of Hamburg. He knows that Hitler needs him and his team of scientists, so he is the critical linchpin to make the V-2 a success and perhaps help win the war. Following the meeting in Annapolis, he will travel back to Baltimore, spend the weekend at the Admiral Fell Inn, and then take the train to New York to catch the next scheduled flight back to Berlin.

When Dr. Reinhardt arrived in New York and cleared the passport check, the FBI's New York office was notified. Due to his scientific credentials, he was immediately placed on a person-of-interest watch list. New York FBI notified the Baltimore field office, and as soon as Dr. Reinhardt stepped off the train at Pennsylvania Station, he was under surveillance.

In Washington, the dossier of Dr. Erik Reinhardt quickly reached the eyes of J. Edgar Hoover, who immediately informed the President. On Wednesday morning, while Reinhardt is on the Hopkins campus, Hoover sits in front of President Roosevelt. "Well, J. Edgar, we have got a top Nazi scientist sitting in Baltimore. Our spy network in Berlin tells us that he is Hitler's lead scientist on the V-2 project. I can't believe they let him travel here, and we can't let him return to Germany. You know that, if the V-2 succeeds, it will just about wipe out all of the UK and perhaps most of Europe. Hell, the Luftwaffe has already bombed most of London and just destroyed the House of Commons last month."

Hoover nods in agreement. "Mr. President, he has been under our surveillance as soon as he stepped off the train in Baltimore. He is also scheduled to attend a meeting in Annapolis. I would suggest that he should miss that meeting. Perhaps he will experience an unexpected traffic accident or a sudden appendectomy."

The President glares at Hoover. "J. Edgar, take him into custody this evening, and keep me informed on his future travels."

Dr. Reinhardt is pleased with his presentation and feels

good following his meeting with Dr. Goddard. There was much scientific data exchanged, and he was surprised how much his American counterparts knew about his V-2 project. He has invited some colleagues to join him for dinner at a popular German restaurant in Baltimore called Haussners. They will join him at 7:00 at the hotel bar.

As he walks down the stairs at the Admiral Fell Inn to the lobby, he is joined by two men in dark suits. They immediately grab him by his arms, and the taller one says in textbook German, "Dr. Reinhardt, please follow us this way."

They walk him through the lobby, out the front door, to a waiting car. They place him in the back seat with one of them on each side. As the car speeds through the streets of Baltimore, he knows he is not in a good situation. The man on his right pulls an identification badge from his breast pocket. As he shows him the badge, he says, "Dr. Reinhardt, we are with the United States Federal Bureau of Investigation. We have received orders to take you into custody. We are taking you to our office for questioning and detainment."

The next morning, Roosevelt is handed a brown envelope clearly stamped, *TOP SECRET.* He quickly opens it. *GERMAN ALIEN E.R. IS IN CUSTODY AND IS NOW DETAINED AT FORT MEADE, MARYLAND.* It was signed *J. Edgar Hoover* and dated July 17, 1941.

It has been 10 weeks since Dr. Reinhardt was taken into custody. He has been "detained" at Fort Meade, Maryland. He has been kept in a small, stuffy, windowless cell. He has met with a US Army lawyer who has advised him that he will have a hearing before a Justice Department Hearing Board.

On October 18, he appears for his hearing before three military judges collectively known as the Alien Enemy Hearing Board. The hearing is brief, lasting for only 20 minutes. Reinhardt's military lawyer reads a statement of facts concerning why he was in the United States. It is noted that he is not in the US as an official German diplomat but was attending an academic conference. He also points out that Germany and the US are not at war, and he specifically mentions the Neutrality Act. It is also noted and read into the transcript that Dr. Goddard has protested Reinhardt's detainment to President Roosevelt.

One of the judges addresses Dr. Reinhardt. "Sir, are you aware that just yesterday the destroyer *USS Kearny* was torpedoed and damaged by one of your country's U-boats near Iceland, killing 11 of our sailors? Has your country no regard for the neutrality of the United States? It is the opinion of this board that you are to be detained indefinitely. You are a danger to the peace and safety of this nation."

# Fire, Brimstone and Death 1940

December 1940. Anna and a few of her friends from church have decided to volunteer at the St. Joseph Krankenhaus, a hospital in Bremen. The city has an apocalyptic feel. Although thousands have fled the city, the hospital is beyond capacity, and beds have been placed in the cafeteria, halls and lobby area. Since August, the RAF bombing raids have been more frequent, and the civilian casualty numbers continue to climb. Anna is over the initial shock she felt when the air raids began, but each day brings more devastation and misery. When she quickly walks to the hospital, the streets and sidewalks are filled with small craters, burned-out houses and dead animals.

Anna volunteers usually three days a week. She primarily helps in the kitchen and feeds patients. Her neighbor, Norbert Petrovic, is one of the most recent patients. He was working on his parents' house when the air raid sirens screamed. After the all-clear was sounded, he saw that the library across from their house was on fire. He was helping with the bucket brigade and assisting the firemen when a gust of wind carried heated timbers toward them. His shirt caught fire, and he was severely burned. The doctors have told him it will be a long recovery. Children, mothers and the elderly fill the beds. Anna thinks, *How much can we endure?*

The city struggles to provide basic services. Electricity and water service are spotty at best, and many homes are not heated. The cold winter has settled in. As Christmas approaches, she decides to cut a small white pine she had planted during the summer. She places it in a large bucket and drags it into the house. She is determined to have a Christmas tree and hopes that Kurt will pay her a surprise visit. When the oven is working, she bakes a few dozen cookies with the remaining flour that Kurt brought her last summer. She has saved one bottle of wine, Kurt's favorite, the Riesling from the Baden region. She muses, "When he comes, we will have our cookies, drink our wine, and sing Christmas carols. Maybe we can attend midnight mass together at St. Boniface. It will be a perfect celebration, just like in years past."

Christmas arrives without a visit from Kurt. A few days before the holiday, she receives a Christmas card from Kurt with a brief note:

*Mother, I hope you are well. I am on assignment in Paris. I should be back in Berlin in late February and hope to visit then. Father is here as well. He is on the general's staff for our occupation forces here in France. He sends his love.*

*You are always in my thoughts and prayers. You know how much I love you!*

Fröhliche Weihnachten *(Merry Christmas)*

*Kurt*

Anna spends New Year's Day, January 1, 1941, at the hospital. She brings Norbert a brightly wrapped box with a large red ribbon.

"Thank you, Anna! What a surprise!"

Norbert's hands and arms are heavily bandaged. Anna takes the box. "Let me open it. Here are some cookies for you! *Frohliche Weihnachten*! Norbert, have you enough to eat? You need to gain some weight. Let me get you something from the kitchen."

"No thank you, Anna, I'm not hungry. They provide enough food, and I really don't have an appetite. I know that I am lucky to be alive. I just want to get out of here and go home to my family."

Anna looks at him with concerned eyes. "Healing takes time, and you must be patient. I am so sorry that this happened to you. You are such a good person. When will God stop inflicting this punishment on us?"

"Anna, as we both know, Adolf Hitler is responsible for the wrath brought upon us. His inhumanity is what causes our suffering. There is this evil in the souls of so many Germans." Norbert shakes his head. "Have you heard from Kurt? Did you see him during the holidays?"

"No, I was hoping that he would visit. I received a Christmas card from him. He said he was in Paris. They say that Paris is relatively safe. I did hear that there is a resistance movement and some German soldiers have been killed. General de Gaulle wants his country back. Norbert, you take care. I better get back to the kitchen."

Norbert looks at her and slowly raises his head off the pillow. "Anna, before you go, I want you to consider moving in with Janice and me until the situation in Bremen improves. It is too dangerous for you to continue to stay alone at your house. We have a spare bedroom since the boys were drafted into the Army. Janice thinks she can help you move some things, and maybe within the next few days you can start living with us. Don't worry about Adelina; you know we love cats."

"Norbert, that is so kind of you. I may take you up on the offer. Let me talk to Janice in the next day or so. I don't want to be a bother."

Anna is tired after a long day of cooking and feeding those in need. She leaves the hospital and quickly walks the mile back to her house. It is dark, cold, and the wind is howling. There were 12 houses on her street; now only seven are still standing. The previous bombings have taken their toll. Her house has some minor damage with a few shattered windows, missing bricks, fallen rainspouts and hanging shutters.

She enters her empty house and places some kindling sticks in the fireplace and lights a fire. She adds some oak logs, and quickly the room begins to warm. She has been sleeping on the sofa to be near the fireplace. Anna sits on the sofa and covers herself with her knitted blankets. Adelina joins her and snuggles on her lap. As the fire crackles, she closes her eyes. Sleep is what she longs for.

Her brief nap is over as she hears the booming wail of the air raid sirens. She covers her ears to silence the air war happening directly above her. The house shakes, and the dishes rattle. She jumps up, grabs Adelina, and heads to the cellar. Another few hours of sitting with her cat in the darkness. She wonders why the British bombers are targeting Bremen. *Haven't we suffered enough?* She knows that Hamburg was bombed in November, then recalls that the Luftwaffe had been bombing London and most of England since last August. It is all about retaliation. She thinks, *Why can't the world live in peace?* She can hear the shrilling sound of the anti-aircraft guns. Exploding bombs are not too far away.

Three hours later, the all-clear is sounded, and she slowly walks up the cellar stairs with Adelina under her arm. The fire has died, and she can see her breath. She lights her many candles and makes another fire. Anna notices that her glass angel that sat on the top of her Christmas tree has fallen and broken its wing. The wounded angel stares up at her. She steps over it and walks out the front door. She stands on her steps. The air is heavy with smoke, and she can see the nearby flames. Just three blocks away, a house is burning, and down the street, a car is on fire. She softly speaks aloud to herself, "Happy New Year!"

As she awakes on January 3$^{rd}$, there is snow on the ground and the house is very cold. She is quickly running out of firewood, and the coal bin is nearly empty. She shares the same plight as many of her friends at the hospital and at St. Boniface. She thinks, *We are strong. We will survive. Tomorrow, I will see Janice, and maybe by the weekend, I will be rooming at her house. It is so kind of them to think of my welfare. They are good people!"*

She decides not to go to the hospital. The snow is gathering on the sidewalks. She takes some stationery from her closet and begins to compose a letter to Kurt.

*My dearest Kurt,*

*I miss you, and it was a very lonely Christmas without you. Thank you for your Christmas card. I never know where you will be. I sent you a card to your address in Berlin. I always wanted to travel to Paris, but your father had other priorities. I hope the destruction of war does not transform the beauty of Paris. The bombing of Bremen continues, and I have been lucky so far. Many of the neighbors, whom you know, have lost their homes. I have some minor house damage, and Norbert has offered to help with the repairs when the situation here improves. I don't think I told you that he was badly burned on his chest, hands and arms just before Christmas. He was helping to extinguish the fire at the library across from his parents' house. He will recover, but it will take some time. He and Janice have asked me to move in with them, and I have accepted. Within the next week, I will be living at their house.*

*This war has destroyed not just houses and property but the beautiful life we had in a country that we loved. Happiness is an emotion we no longer know. Our lives will never be the same. I am worried sick thinking about the peril you are facing.*

*I miss my little boy and can't wait to see you. You are young, and I hope you live a long and happy life. I want to be a grandmother to your children. May each of your special moments live on to be cherished memories. I know your grandmother is your guardian angel, and she will be sure that the Lord watches over and protects you.*

Ich liebe dich mein Sohn *(Love you, my son)*

Anna will take the letter to the hospital and place it in the mail room. *Lord knows when Kurt will receive it.* Until then, she places it in an envelope and slides it under a vase in the kitchen.

She makes some soup with the vegetables she canned in late summer and even found an onion. Just as the winter sun begins to set, she hears the scream of the air raid sirens. She knows the drill. Turn off the stove, pick up the cat, walk to the cellar. This will be the third night of bombing.

She sits on her folding chair at the front of the cellar. Adelina is in her lap as she begins to pray her rosary. This night sounds different. Aircraft are flying overhead, and she can hear the high-pitched sound of their engines. The thump of bombs shakes the cellar floor. A tremendous concussion followed by a loud bang shatters her eardrums. A whistling sound echoes in her head. For the first time, she can smell smoke.

"My God, the house is on fire!" She is choking and can now see red glowing timbers at the back of the cellar. She runs to the top of the stairs and can feel heat on the door. She knows she is trapped as she moves down the stairs to the corner next to the coal bin. "Please, Jesus, don't let me die down here!"

She hears a loud crash and sees that the back of the house

has collapsed. Flames are now intense as she picks burning splinters of wood from her hair and dress. She can feel the concrete wall getting hotter. Her legs give way, and she falls to the floor with her rosary still in her hand. "Pray for us sinners, now and at the hour of our death...."

# Towers on the Beach 1942

January 1942. It is a cold and clear morning as Jason and Jeff pull up in Jason's truck to the Warren Restaurant on the boardwalk in Bethany Beach. Jason had received a call from former Senator John Townsend to join him for breakfast on this Saturday. The restaurant is warm and inviting and almost empty. Townsend is already seated near the window overlooking the frothy Atlantic.

Townsend motions for them to sit down. Jason and Jeff shake Townsend's hand, and Jeff asks, "Can we still call you 'Senator'?"

"Jeff, those days are behind me now. I can't believe it has been over a year since I left office. Since we are friends and business associates, 'John' will do."

The waitress comes to the table and takes their order. Townsend always orders blueberry pancakes and black coffee. Jeff and Jason order the egg and meat special. Townsend stares out at the ocean. "In politics, you never know if you will be celebrating or lamenting. It was a very close race. I fell only a few thousand votes short. You know, 12 years is a long time to serve in the US Senate. It was a great experience that I will never forget."

Townsend sips his coffee and places the morning paper on the table. "It's crazy, but it seems that I have seen less of you two since leaving office. I know you had a busy summer with the growing chicken business and the patrol dogs and horses. Now the world is really burning. Pearl Harbor was a surprise, and now we have a European war and a Pacific war going on—and don't forget the battle just a few miles offshore, right here on the Atlantic coast. Jeff, how is Tristan? I think the last we talked, his submarine was in Hawaii."

"You are correct, John. He was in Hawaii from December to March of last year; then he sailed to Australia. When the attack on Pearl Harbor occurred three weeks ago, he was in Moreton Bay, Australia for some engine overhaul work. They are now on their way to Guadalcanal. We heard that they sunk their first Japanese warship, the *Kimsu Maru*, on January 4th. He is in the thick of it. Lori and I pray to God every day for his safe keeping."

Townsend picks up the paper from the table. "I can't believe our War Department didn't have some advanced warning about the Pearl Harbor attack. Let me read to you this article in the *New York Times*: 'Reports from Hawaii indicated that Honolulu had no warning of the attack. Japanese bombers, with the red circle of the Rising Sun of Japan on their wings, suddenly appeared, escorted by fighters. Flying high, they suddenly dive-bombed, attacking Pearl Harbor, the great Navy base, the Army's Hickam Field and Ford Island. For the first time in its history, the United States finds itself at war against powers in both the Atlantic and the Pacific.'

"I just can't believe we were taken totally by surprise with no warning. Over 2,500 Americans were killed within a few hours. Our military intelligence really dropped the ball! We had to know they were planning something. Jason, what is the latest on Connor? I think you told me he was going to flight school?"

"He did go to flight school, and now he is a Naval pilot, not a Coast Guard pilot. As you know, last November, the entire Coast Guard shifted from the control of the Treasury Department to the Department of the Navy. He is flying the new P51 Mustangs and is stationed in Daytona Beach, Florida for the time being. I am sure he won't be there long now that the Pacific war has started."

"Ok, I am current with Tristan and Connor. How are McKenna and Cameron doing?"

Jason looks at Jeff. "Well, Cameron is in his last year at the University of Delaware, and now he wants to go to veterinary school at Penn State. He is also in ROTC and may have to defer vet school if there is another call up."

Jeff wipes his mouth with his napkin and takes a sip of his coffee. "McKenna is still at Salisbury and has one more year to go before she gets her teaching degree. She still plays piano and has been playing at a hotel in Baltimore on the weekends."

"You and your wives have done an outstanding job raising your children, and I know you are very proud of them. Sorry to call you out on a Saturday morning. I was wondering if you wouldn't mind riding along with me so you could show me the patrol dogs and horses at work. We are going to meet Captain Mackley at the National Guard camp and follow him up to the two new towers on the beach just below Dewey. I think he said there are dogs and horses patrolling there around the clock. They tell me those towers are used to coordinate artillery fire on enemy ships spotted off the coast."

Jason pushes back his chair. "We're good to go, Senator—I mean John. You know how winters are on the farm. Jeff and I are anxious to see the towers as well. You mentioned the war at our doorstep. Marna's cousin, Jennifer, lives on Fenwick Island. She telephoned our house just two days ago and said that around 3:00 in the morning, they were awakened by a huge explosion and it felt like an earthquake hit her house. Her bed shook; glasses fell from the shelves. She ran to her window, and just offshore she could see a great reddish fireball and a towering column of black smoke. She thinks a German sub torpedoed one of our oil ships heading north to New Jersey. I know we have the blackout along the coast, but things could really get bad if they start firing shells at us. We are very vulnerable."

Townsend heads out the door. "It is very scary, and I think I heard something about that explosion on the radio. Let's jump in my car, and I will drive up."

They pull into the National Guard camp and find Captain Mackley. He leads the way in his brown jeep. They cross the Indian River Inlet and soon arrive at the first concrete tower which sits about 100 yards from the water. As they walk toward the tower, two armed Coastguardsmen walk toward them, each with a patrol dog on its leash. The dogs seem to recognize Jeff, and after a good sniff, Jeff bends to pet them. Jeff notices that the dogs are wearing small canvas boots.

He looks at Captain Mackley. "Where did you find their little boots?"

"The sun, sand and oyster shells are hard on their paws, and they walk at least five miles a day, so the vet that looks after them—I think his name is Dr. Burton—designed these, and they are made by the Bata Shoe Company in Maryland."

The Coastguardsmen salute Captain Mackley.

"At ease. How is it going here?"

"All is well, Captain. We are working our 12-hour patrol and will be replaced at noon. It was quiet last night, but a few nights ago, we could see the explosion near Fenwick. Reconnaissance aircraft circled for a few hours looking for the German sub, but she got away."

"Yes, I know. We had a detailed briefing about that. The German subs are moving closer, so you must remain vigilant. I'm going to take our guests to the top observation area so they can check out the view. Follow me, gentlemen."

They climb the suspension ladders to the top observation area. The wind and cold hit them in the face. It is a clear day, and with the binoculars provided by the Captain, they have a spectacular view of the coast. While they are watching, two Naval aircraft fly low overhead, and they can almost touch their wings.

Townsend looks around. "Wow, I guess they are chasing those German U-boats!"

Jeff asks the Captain, "Are these towers prefabricated and just stacked here?"

The Captain holds onto his hat as the wind howls. "No, these are built by using a sliding tube-shaped form. A ring of reinforced concrete was poured. When that solidified, the form was slid up and more concrete was poured. The whole tower was formed this way except for the top, which required a form of its own. The whole process took only three days. The towers here have different heights, and some of them have only two viewing slits, while others have four. They can withstand strong hurricanes and nor'easters! We are here around the clock to look for German ships, submarines and saboteurs. On a clear day, like today, we can see out 15 to 20 miles. From the upper level, the spotters can direct the fire of the guns mounted along the coast. We will take readings on the offshore targets. Those readings will be radioed back to a gunnery room at Fort Miles near Cape Henlopen. The triangulation calculations are turned into coordinates. Their big 12" and 16" barreled guns are positioned along the coast, hidden in sand dunes and camouflaged in salt grass, and will be fired in the direction that coordinates with the incoming enemy ships. I see some of the mounted horse patrols approaching, so let's head down. I understand these horses are the ones you are keeping on your farms."

They slowly make their way down the ladder, and as they open the metal door, the two Coastguardsmen dismount and salute the Captain. The Captain returns the salute and motions toward Jeff and Jason.

"These two gentlemen are keeping your horses on their farms, not far from here."

The riders bring the horses closer. Jeff pets the Arabian on the nose. "I think this is the one we call Cassie. She is so gentle and has beautiful eyes. She is the only one with the chestnut color and a touch of white on her front knees."

The Coastguardsmen shake hands with Jeff and Jason. "Thanks for taking good care of them. Good to meet you!" They remount and head down the beach toward the Indian River Inlet.

Jason notices the rifle scabbard attached to their saddles. "Jeff, they look different with the saddle, saddle bags and the rifle scabbards. They almost look like the ones in our Fourth of July parade."

Townsend watches the horses head down the beach. "This is no parade, gentlemen. We are at war! We better run. Captain Mackley, thanks for taking time out of your busy day to show us the towers. We going to take a quick ride over to Bear Trap where they are building the prisoner of war camp. I heard that the first group of prisoners will be arriving around the beginning of March."

Townsend heads back down to Bethany so Jason can pick up his truck. He and Jeff follow Townsend on the short ride down Atlantic Avenue, through Ocean View, and then southwest to Bear Trap. Townsend pulls up to the Army guard patrolling the entrance, and Jason and Jeff can see that he is showing the guard his license and a folded piece of paper, which the guard opens and reads. The guard then salutes to Townsend and lets him pass. Jason follows, and the guard waves him in. The road is unpaved, and there are several Quonset-style buildings that line the narrow road. They pull up to one of the buildings, and a uniformed officer comes out and bends over to look at Townsend behind the wheel of his black Cadillac. Townsend gets out and shakes the officer's hand. He motions to Jeff and Jason to park next to him, and they walk over to Townsend.

"Gentlemen, this is Lieutenant Johnson. He is in command here. He will give us a quick tour and briefing."

The lieutenant shakes their hands and points at the building they are standing next to. "This is a rush project due to the President's order to round up German, Italian and now Japanese aliens here in the US. We have 10 of these Quonset huts in place and 10 more to follow. Each will hold 20 prisoners. There is also a mess hall and a latrine and shower building. The buildings here have sides made of corrugated steel sheets. The two ends were covered with plywood, which have doors and windows. The interior is insulated and has pressed wood lining and a wood floor. They are heated and will have bunk beds. We sit on about 10 acres here in Bear Trap. I guess you noticed the 10-foot-high fencing with razor wire on top. I am told that many of the German prisoners coming here are now housed at Fort Meade in Maryland."

They spend time walking around the property and thank the lieutenant for the quick tour. As Townsend, Jason and Jeff head back to their vehicles, Jeff looks at them. "Can you believe we have lookout towers on the beach and prisoners of war in Bear Trap? Delaware *is* at war!"

# Prisoner of War, Bear Trap, Delaware 1942

March 1942. Dr. Erik Reinhardt has been in detention at Fort Meade, Maryland since October of 1941. At the time of his arrest, he was advised that he was not a prisoner of war but a "detainee." That classification changed when Japan attacked Pearl Harbor, Hawaii on December 7, 1941 and Germany and Italy declared war on the United States on December 11, 1941. He has been issued a new uniform. He wears a denim shirt and pants, but now a larger "PW" is emblazoned on the shirt. He has noticed a slow trickle of other German prisoners beginning in January of 1942.

One new prisoner is Werner Kohler, and he is in a cell next to Reinhardt. Kohler and Reinhardt spend a lot of time together and share stories about life in Germany. Kohler lived in Hamburg during the time that Reinhardt was a student at the University of Hamburg. He also sailed his small sailboat out of Peenemunde, where his grandparents lived. Reinhardt shares with him stories about his time in Peenemunde working on rocket research projects. They both share a deep hatred for Adolph Hitler.

Kohler tells Reinhardt all about his problems with the German police and how he left Germany and fled to the United States in 1936 to avoid being arrested for robbery. He eventually settled in Annapolis, Maryland and worked as a cook in several restaurants on the Annapolis harbor. He was able to save enough money to purchase a sailboat and kept it at the dock near the US Naval Academy. He soon left his small apartment and lived on his boat. Kohler had an expired visa and knew it was only a matter of time before he would be deported. When the war began with Germany, he decided that he would sail to Bermuda and start over there. He was stopped by the Coast Guard only a few miles out into the Atlantic. They seized his sailboat and sent him to Fort Meade. They charged him with sabotage and spying for the Third Reich.

After the war with Germany began, Fort Meade was assigned a top-secret activity by the War Department. The Enemy Prisoner of War Bureau was created and housed at Fort Meade. One of the responsibilities of the new bureau was to serve as the central depository for all letters and packages addressed to German, Italian and Japanese prisoners detained within the United States. Once they were screened and recorded, they were forwarded to wherever the prisoner was detained. This created a clerical nightmare for the understaffed bureau, and they decided to use prisoners to work in the mail room. Since Reinhardt and Kohler were going crazy from boredom, they both volunteered for the work.

One evening at supper, Kohler tells Reinhardt that, when he can feel that an envelope may contain money, he has been secretly opening the envelopes and taking the money. He says that he has coins and bills in various currencies hidden in his cell. He tells Reinhardt that he uses the US currency to bribe one of the guards to mail letters to his relatives who live in Bermuda from the secure post office at Fort Meade.

In March 1942, Reinhardt and Kohler receive word that they are being transferred to another POW camp somewhere in Delaware. Reinhardt sees Kohler on the loading dock unloading bags of mail from an Army truck. He walks up to Kohler and whispers, "We will be packing our bags tonight. Looks like no more money will be heading to Bermuda."

Kohler shakes his head and replies, "Don't worry about that. I'll find a way. My bags will be a bit heavier than yours, if you know what I mean!"

They find out that they are being transferred to a camp near Bethany Beach, Delaware that one of the guards called a bear trap. Reinhardt and Kohler understand a little English and are puzzled. They ask the guard, "Why are we being transferred to a bear trap?" They are among the first 20 prisoners to arrive at the POW camp in Bear Trap, Delaware.

# Safe Haven for the Saboteur
# 1942

Wilmer is feeding his chickens late in the afternoon when a military jeep pulls into his driveway. Lieutenant Johnson sees him and walks over to the chicken house. "Excuse me, sir, I'm looking for a Wilmer or Emma Stickler."

"I am Wilmer Stickler, and who are you?"

"I'm Lieutenant Johnson. I was told that you and your wife may be able to help the United States Army. Perhaps you have heard that a prisoner of war camp is located a few miles from here in Bear Trap. We have just received about 20 German prisoners, and we are looking for German translators. Do you think you and your wife would be interested in working for us a few hours a week until we receive a German-speaking US soldier?"

"My wife Emma is not here at the moment. Let me speak to her about it, and we will get back to you. Can you leave me your telephone number? Also, can you tell me who gave you our name and address?"

The lieutenant takes a pencil out of his uniform pocket and writes his number on a piece of paper.

"That would be great. I am not sure how frequently we

would need your services, but we would give you a few hours' notice and send a driver over to pick you up. I think the pay would be one dollar per hour, but don't quote me on that. Oh, it was former Senator Townsend that told us you may be interested and said you were the only persons he knew in this area that spoke German."

The lieutenant gets back in his jeep and heads down the gravel drive to Woodland Avenue. Wilmer goes back to feeding the chickens, and soon Emma is dropped off by Lori Miller. She waves goodbye to Lori and sees Wilmer behind the house.

"That was so nice of Mrs. Miller to take you to the doctor. We just had a visitor, a soldier from the Bear Trap POW camp. They need German translators, and Townsend gave them our name and told them we may be interested. I still can't believe they are building a prisoner of war camp in Bear Trap."

"Wilmer, what did you tell him?"

"I told him I would talk to you, make a decision, and call him. He gave me his telephone number."

"This may be a good way to help our German brothers. I think we should contact Fritz Kuhn in New York. He just sent us that letter a few weeks ago which said German intelligence told him the location of several POW camps being built here in the US, and Bear Trap was one of them. That shows you how well placed our German spies are within the United States government. Wilmer, call him back and tell them we are interested. It is our patriotic duty to help the US Army."

On a quiet Sunday evening in early May 1942, the phone rings at the Stickler farm. Emma quickly grabs the receiver. "Emma, this is Arnold Bauer. I work for Fritz Kuhn. Hope you and Wilmer are well and helping the US Army with our fellow German prisoners at Bear Trap. Just wanted to let you know that, sometime this week, a Bund member will be stopping by your farm for a quick visit. His name is Jacob Baden, and he will be driving a dark blue Buick Roadmaster convertible. He will be delivering an important message. Take care, and *Heil* Hitler!" Before Emma can speak a word, the conversation ends. She finds Wilmer in the kitchen and tells him about the strange call from someone who works for Fritz Kuhn.

"I met both Arnold and Jacob when I was in New York working on the *King James* project. They were working directly with the German Intelligence office in Berlin concerning the planning of the *King James* bombing. It must be something big coming up for them to send Jacob to see us."

A week later and again on a Sunday evening, Emma's phone rings. "Hello, is this Emma? This is Jacob Baden. Would it be possible to stop by your farm tomorrow afternoon?"

Emma looks at Wilmer with big eyes. "Yes, that is fine. We will be expecting you."

The bright sun begins to throw long shadows from the trees lining the front yard. Emma and Wilmer are eating lunch on the porch when the large Buick convertible makes it way up the stony driveway. Jacob Baden slams the car door and quickly makes his way up the steps carrying a large black suitcase and a file folder. Emma and Wilmer stand to greet him.

"Hello, Emma. Wilmer, so good to see you again. Would you mind if we went inside to discuss an urgent matter?"

They walk through the front door, and Emma leads them back to the kitchen. Jacob places the suitcase on the kitchen table and pulls out a chair. Emma and Wilmer sit next to him.

Baden looks concerned. "I understand you have been to the POW camp at Bear Trap. I just drove past it on my way here. Looks like a lot of construction going on and Army guards in great numbers. I also understand that you have talked with Dr. Erik Reinhardt."

Emma nods. "Yes, Wilmer and I have been going to the camp generally twice a week. We are the only interpreters they use. If someone is sick, we may get an emergency call. Both of us have talked to Dr. Reinhardt. He told us about his work on the German rocket program and his imprisonment at Fort Meade. The American Army officers there have told us they want to begin to send some of the prisoners to various farms in the Bethany and Ocean View area to help with the harvest. We will be one of the first farms to receive them."

Emma has placed an ice tea in front of Jacob. "Thank you, Emma. Reinhardt is what my visit is about. We have orders coming directly from the Fuehrer. They have dispatched a German Intelligence Officer named Kurt Wagner to land in Bethany from submarine U-202 sometime between June 12 and June 15. We will know the exact date by the beginning of June. He will stay with you as he works to free Reinhardt and return him to Germany. If there is some way you can convince the Army to have Reinhardt work on your farm, the abduction of the good doctor will be very easy. If that is not possible, then Wagner will have his job cut out for him. We want to avoid bloodshed, but it may be necessary if things get complicated."

Wilmer sits straight in his chair. "Emma and I love Germany and want to help in any way. What we don't want is bloodshed. For now, we are citizens of the United States and don't want to be arrested and hung as traitors. Emma and I know we must flee the country quickly as soon as this work is completed."

"I understand how you feel, and I am sorry to worry you. I can assure you that the plans to free Reinhardt have been crafted with your safety in mind. I also want to talk about an escape plan for the two of you."

Baden opens the suitcase and lifts out a wireless transmitter and an antenna. "Kurt will need this upon his arrival. He will be communicating with his superiors in Berlin. Do you have a good hiding place for it? Also, we need a high perch for the antenna."

Emma has a frightened look. Wilmer is wide-eyed. "I have

a place for this in the barn. The antenna can be placed in a spot above the hayloft. Tell me more about the saboteur that will be staying with us."

Baden sits and takes another sip of his drink. "The cover story is that *Herr* Wagner is your twenty-two-year-old nephew visiting for the summer from Baltimore. While he is here, his American codename will be Paul Lukas. He will have a driver's license and other identification bearing that name. From what we have been told about *Herr* Wagner, he is the son of a highly placed officer in the German army. His mother has been recently killed in an RAF air raid on his home city of Bremen. He speaks excellent American English with no German accent. His grandfather does live in Baltimore. He and his mother spent time there when he was a young boy. Some may ask why he has not been drafted. If that comes up, the cover is that he has a medical deferment due to an asthma condition. He will have documents to prove his draft status if he is challenged by authorities. When I have better information on the exact time of his landing, I will let you know."

Baden looks for a map inside the file folder and spreads it out on the table. "He will come ashore here near the Inlet and then walk south. He has been told that Wilmer will be waiting for him in your black pickup truck at this location. You must be there at 5:00 a.m. and wait no more than three hours. If he doesn't appear, you will leave. He has been told to make his way to your farm on his own."

Wilmer looks at the spot Baden is pointing. "That is a very busy area—Atlantic Avenue and Garfield Parkway. It will be busy with military personnel and those coming to the beach for vacation. Also, what about the spotting towers and the military patrols along the beach? We have patrol dogs and Army horses on the farm next to us. The soldiers are there every day picking up the animals."

"Wilmer, Wagner is highly trained and is aware of all of the potential threats. If he is captured, he will take his cyanide pill, and none of this ever happened. Here is your briefing information that contains all the details we discussed. When he first approaches your truck, his identification will be confirmed when he asks you the question, 'Are the fish biting today?' If you are aware that there may be an unforeseen critical development at that moment that would prevent you from taking him in your truck to the farm, reply, 'Not today, they will be biting tomorrow.' If all is as planned and you have no immediate concerns, you reply, 'Today is a good day to catch some fish.' Once in your truck, he is yours until Reinhardt is secured and they rendezvous with the submarine."

Baden lays a brown envelope on the table. "Here is a down payment on this important mission. *Heil* Hitler!"

# The Making of a Spy
# 1942

April 1942. Kurt has been reassigned from Paris to the newly created Abwehr sabotage school in the wooded German countryside a few kilometers from the city of Brandenburg, Germany. Admiral Canaris is there to speak to Kurt and 19 other soldiers as they arrive. Hitler has ordered Canaris to plan and implement an aggressive sabotage operation against certain targets within the United States. Several spies have been active in the US for several years, but Hitler's new plan is much more aggressive. Canaris has assembled the group in a large conference room. He strides to the front of the room.

"As you know, the Reich is now at war with the United States. The Fuehrer wants Roosevelt to know that his country is vulnerable, and America will be our target despite its distance. Our spies have had some success within the United States. We have exploded bombs in military weapon plants, we have assassinated some high-ranking military officials, and our operatives have sunk the *King James* passenger liner. Here at Brandenburg, you will hone your skills in the fine art of sabotage. Your major objective is to create panic and terror in the United States. You will also perfect your English language skills. At the conclusion of your training here, several of you will be selected to enter coastal towns along the Atlantic coast of the United States. Military industrial targets have been selected. They include major hydroelectric plants, bridges, canals, and the water supply system of several major cities including Washington D.C. and New York City. When your training here is completed, you will be experts in explosives. You will be in teams of four with a few exceptions. You have been selected because you represent the very best of the German Military Intelligence Corps. I am confident of your success. *Heil* Hitler!"

After a very long day, Kurt climbs into his bed. He is still grieving the death of his mother and thinks about her constantly. He sleeps only three or four hours a night because his mother is always on his mind. He takes personal responsibility for her death. He remembers the short telephone call from his father, absent any emotion: *Kurt, your mother was killed during the bombing of Bremen a few nights ago. A bomb exploded near our house, and the burning debris ignited our roof. She was in the cellar and did not survive. I loved your mother, and you can't imagine how difficult it is to have to break the news to you. I would have preferred to be standing next to you so we could grieve together. Sadly, that is not possible. Be strong, and I hope to see you soon.*

His mother's death only heightened his hatred for Hitler and the Nazi movement, but, for now, he continues to serve the wishes of the Fuehrer.

The next morning, a soldier stands next to his bed. "Admiral Canaris wants to see you within the hour." Kurt makes his way to the command headquarters and finds Canaris standing in the hall.

"Good morning, Kurt. Follow me to my office. I must brief you on a very urgent matter."

Kurt slides into a chair across the table from Admiral Canaris, who grabs a thick manila folder from his briefcase and leafs through the pages.

"Kurt, I have a very high-priority issue for you to handle, and it comes directly from the Fuehrer."

Canaris describes in great detail the prisoner of war, Dr. Erik Reinhardt, and his place of imprisonment just outside Bethany Beach, Delaware. He gives Kurt several photographs taken of Dr. Reinhardt. Canaris stresses that the Fuehrer demands a successful return of Reinhardt, who is responsible for all German rocket research.

"Kurt, the Fuehrer thinks that Dr. Reinhardt has much to do about who will win this war. That may be true, but not because of the rocket program. It's because he is a member of my resistance group."

Canaris slides a large map across the table to Kurt. "Kurt, this map is important to you. You will note that there are several locations circled. You must memorize every road, bridge, intersection. You will board submarine U-202 on May 28th at our naval base in Lorient, France. After you go ashore, you will have only a few short weeks to secure Dr. Reinhardt. George Dasch and his team will travel with you on U-202. The Dasch team will land on the south shore of Long Island, New York near East Hampton. You, just you, will land on the south shore of Delaware where the Indian River meets the Atlantic." Canaris points to the location on the map.

"You will note on the map the location of spotting towers that the Americans have placed along the Atlantic beaches. They are manned by their Coast Guard along with mounted horse patrols and guard dogs. You will land at night and make your way south as designated on the map, to the town of Bethany Beach. Don't hesitate to use your pistol and knife if you encounter any guards or dogs. Those American spotters loyal to the Reich that watch that beach area advise that this section of beach has very little patrol activity at that time of the night. Let's hope you have rain and fog that evening. You will meet a Bund member at the intersection of Atlantic Avenue and Garfield Parkway." Canaris taps the location. "He will be driving a black pickup truck and will be wearing a tan shirt and a straw hat. His name is Wilmer Stickler. He will be there at 5:00 a.m. and will wait no longer than three hours. If, for whatever reason, you are delayed, you must make your way to Woodland Avenue." Again, Canaris traces with his finger the route down Atlantic Avenue to Woodland Avenue. "You will be staying at the farm of Emma and Wilmer Stickler, which is on the west side of the Woodland road. They will have a small German flag next to their mailbox. The Bear Trap detention camp is approximately five kilometers from their farm. Kurt, remember, U-202 will be waiting offshore near Ocean City, Maryland to secure you and Reinhardt. You will be in touch with German Intelligence by wireless transmitter, and they will provide you with more details concerning the rendezvous with our submarine."

Canaris lays a bundle of US currency on the table and separates it into three piles, each containing 1,000 dollars. "Do you think you can spread these American dollars out over your time ashore? Also, here is another 2,000 dollars, which you will give the Bund husband and wife team where you will be staying. You will assume a new identity. Your codename will be Paul Lukas. The cover story is that you are the nephew of the Sticklers who is visiting them from Baltimore, Maryland. I believe you told us that you lived there for a time when you were a young boy. You have an asthma condition and have a medical deferment from the US military. Here is your Maryland driver's license. The Sticklers have been vetted, and you can trust them. Wilmer was instrumental in the sinking of the *King James* passenger liner. He and his wife both like the Reich's money. The Sticklers have a small farm, mainly fruit, vegetables and livestock. They both have a clearance to move in and out of the camp where Reinhardt is detained. They are working as German translators for the US Army. It is our understanding that they have seen and talked to Dr. Reinhardt. They will be instrumental to the success of your mission.

"Head back to your room. Tomorrow, you will fly to Lorient, France along with the Dasch team. There, you will be briefed on more specifics and logistics. Remember, Kurt, this is not a soccer game. It is all about living and dying. In our line of work, there can only be winners. Losing means self-destruction. Stay safe. I know you will be successful. When you return to Germany, I will have another major mission for you."

Canaris shakes Kurt's hand. Kurt stands and salutes before grabbing the map, the money and the file folder. He quickly heads back to his barrack.

The following morning, he is transported along with his fellow saboteurs to the airfield, and three hours later, they land in Lorient, France, a seaport in Brittany. His group is bussed to the dock, and he sees U-202 for the first time. This will be his first submarine experience. He looks around the harbor, and it appears that the entire German fleet is docked there. He sees destroyers, submarines, barges, tankers, long boats and cutters, all ready for war.

That afternoon, he joins George Dasch and his team in a small room tucked inside a large warehouse on the pier across from U-202. Everyone stands as Major Raymond Mueller enters the room and sits at the head of the table. Mueller is medium height with brown hair, glasses and a strong build. Kurt thinks, *I know him*. Mueller reports to Canaris and has assembled the Dasch team. He was briefed only a few hours ago about Kurt's mission. Dasch, Kurt and the others stand and salute Mueller.

Kurt is surprised to see Mueller. This is the same officer that his father was friends with when Kurt was attending school in Berlin. He also remembers his son Grant, who was his schoolmate and one of his best friends. Kurt walks forward and reintroduces himself.

"Kurt, so good to see you. It has been a few years. When I saw your name listed, I thought it might be you. I heard you were assigned to Canaris. How is your father? I lost track of him."

Kurt updates the major about his father and mentions his mother's death.

"Kurt, you know this is a critical mission for you. You must be successful. I know the captain of the sub you will be on, so let me know if there is anything I can assist with. Also, please tell your father that I wish him well."

Kurt has heard about Dasch. He served in the German army during World War I and then spent time in America. He returned to Germany in 1939 when war broke out. Besides Dasch, there are three other members of his landing team: Ernest Burger, Heinrich Heinck and Richard Quirin. Dasch's team has been given an aggressive mission. They will plant a bomb in the Niagara Falls hydroelectric plant. They will also bomb an aluminum manufacturing plant in Philadelphia and then bomb the locks on the Ohio River between Louisville, Kentucky and Pittsburgh, Pennsylvania. Their mission also requires them to plant bombs in Jewish-owned department stores in New York and Philadelphia and in railroad stations on the East Coast.

Mueller orders them "to speak only American English beginning now! You will act like Americans. Smoke cigarettes and cigars, swear and use slang. Know who their most famous actors and actresses are and their most current and famous movies. Read their newspapers and magazines. Remember that the people you meet hate Germans and Germany. They are our enemy. Don't ever forget that!"

Kurt's singular mission is to free Dr. Erik Reinhardt, a POW at the Bear Trap internment camp in Bethany Beach, Delaware and return him safely to Germany. Mueller provides an overview of the outcome expected from both Dasch and Kurt. Mueller reminds the Dasch team that, if anything happens to Kurt, they may pull a member of the Dasch team to complete Kurt's assignment. Mueller states that Dr. Reinhardt is the high-priority target, and a failed mission will have consequences.

"The Fuhrer will be watching and wants daily updates on how the mission is progressing." He reminds all the men that they are about to embark on a very dangerous mission. "If they discover that you are spies, your death will be by hanging in an American prison or suicide with your cyanide pill."

The Dasch team is supplied with small, waterproof wooden crates. Three contain dynamite, and some pieces are disguised as lumps of coal. The last box contains fuses, timing devices, wire, incendiary pen and pencil sets, and sulfuric acid. Mueller tells them that this is their "starter kit" and other explosive supplies will be provided by saboteur operatives already in the United States. Following the meeting with Mueller, they grab their bags and equipment and are led to the submarine.

As Kurt enters the submarine, he takes one last look at the radiant, cloudless blue sky and the spring green trees behind the harbor. He takes a deep breath and descends the ladder while bouncing his duffle bag down the metal steps. He and his group are led to the torpedo room, which has a string of small bunks tucked away into a dimly lit corner. He quickly notices how cramped the spaces are. He is told by the sailor directing him that the rule onboard is "bend, duck and dodge." He is also told that the crewmembers sleep in shifts and share bunks. During the voyage, when he is not working on the details of his mission, he will help out in the mess preparing meals.

U-202 leaves Lorient harbor on May 28th. The 3,000-mile trip across the Atlantic will take about 15 days to reach Long

Island and two more to reach the outer banks of Delaware. Life onboard is boring, windowless and timeless. U-202 travels underwater during the day and on the surface at night. Kurt plays cards, checkers and chess with Dasch and members of his team. Stacks of newspapers and magazines are sitting on the floor next to their bunks. Kurt sees copies of the *Baltimore Sun Newspaper* sitting on top of the pile.

Dasch regales the others with stories of his job as a waiter in New York City and his many girlfriends. Ernest Burger tells his cohorts that he was actually a member of the Milwaukee National Guard and became an American citizen. Kurt sees that the group is anxious to tell their life stories, but Kurt really does not have an interesting story to share. To the others, he seems too young, shy and withdrawn and a poor choice to take on such an important mission upon the direct orders of the Fuhrer.

Burger looks at Kurt. "Kurt, what about you? Any interesting stories to share?"

Kurt stares at the group. "Not really. I've been in school and the military most of my life. Never had a girlfriend. My exciting life just started when we left France."

Kurt is also tired of peeling potatoes and washing dishes, and he tries to sleep as much as possible. He needs to be well rested when he goes ashore. He spends time cleaning his pistol and sharpening his knife. He carries a picture of his mother and the compass from Glennis and Ernest along with his rosary. Tomorrow, the landing will take place for the Dasch team and then two more days before Kurt goes ashore.

On Friday evening, June 12, U-202 comes within sight of the Amagansett, New York coastline. Amagansett is about 115 miles east of New York City on Long Island. She surfaces and is now just a few kilometers offshore. Dasch and his team climb the steps and through the hatch and make their way to an inflatable raft manned by two German sailors. The sailors wear life jackets over their tight rubber body suits. There is heavy fog, strong surf and poor visibility. The two sailors paddle their way toward the shore while Dasch uses his flashlight to check his compass reading, shouting directions as they head to the beach. Upon Dasch's signal, they stumble out of the raft and are in waist-deep water. They are handed their crates and wade onto the beach. They quickly open one of the crates and change from their German uniforms to civilian clothes. They dig a large hole in the sand and bury their uniforms and place the crate on top, pushing the sand back until everything is covered. The sailors on the raft quickly paddle back to U-202. The submarine makes its way to deeper water, submerges, and heads south toward the Delaware coast.

Kurt is called to meet with the sub's captain. "Come in, Kurt." Captain Gretner leans over a chart lying on a small wooden desk. He looks at Kurt and points to a spot on the chart. "This is where we are now. We are moving slowly at 3 knots and are passing Cape May, New Jersey." Gretner points to the Indian River Bay inlet and says, "You know there are military towers on the beach in Delaware, and here is where they are located," as he runs his finger down the chart. "As you know, you will go ashore here and make your way to the town of Bethany Beach. The weather is windy with some light rain falling. Your landing craft will be the one we used for the Dasch team. I know your mission will be successful and we will be waiting for you and Dr. Reinhardt. Keep in touch with the Intelligence Office in Berlin and let them know if there is a change in plans. *Heil* Hitler!"

About five hours after Kurt's meeting with the captain, he is in his bunk and studying the Bethany Beach, Delaware street map. Suddenly, the entire sub is rocked, and there is a deafening sound of a screeching siren. The submarine shakes from what feels like a destructive hydraulic shock.

The sailor next to him jumps out of his bunk. Kurt asks him

what is happening. He yells over his shoulder, "Depth charge!" Loose objects are flying, and the lights dim.

Kurt moves down the narrow corridor toward the control room and wonders if the sub has been hit. He hears one sailor yell, "American naval destroyer sees us on sonar and is dropping depth charges. They missed us, and the captain has taken evasive action. We will power down and sit on the bottom until the destroyer moves away from us. Let's hope the worst is over!" Silence engulfs the submarine, a silence that will last for several hours.

Kurt makes his way back to his bunk. Hours later, he finally hears the engines turning and the submarine slowly moving just above the ocean floor. He wonders if this delay will impact his rendezvous with Wilmer Stickler.

At 2:30 a.m. on Sunday, June 14, 1942, he has his answer. Kurt is told that he will be leaving the submarine in 30 minutes. He feels the sub slowly rising to the surface. His heart is jumping as he packs his heavy canvas duffel bag. He places his Walther pistol in a waterproof holster and his knife in its sheath. He has khaki pants, shirts, socks, underwear, a leather belt, identity papers, maps and his compass. He also has the American dollars given to him by Admiral Canaris. His cyanide pill is carefully placed in a tiny metal box. He will wear civilian clothes so he will not have to change when he hits the beach, even though he knows he will be drenched from the pounding surf. He prays that he will avoid the military beach patrols and dogs.

Kurt meets the landing team, and they slowly make their way to the stairs that will take them to the hatch that opens onto the deck of the submarine. The two sailors slide the rubber raft across the deck and secure it to the side of the sub. Kurt is sweating as he takes a deep breath and looks up at the canopy of white stars twinkling through the misty night. There is no moon, and a light rain is gusting from east to west off the choppy Atlantic.

The waves are small but growing as he hands his duffel bag to the sailor in the raft. A salty spray hits his face. Kurt is wearing a full-length Army rain slicker. His pistol and knife are attached to his belt, and his compass hangs from a chain around his neck. He has memorized the landing coordinates. Slowly they pull away from the submarine. He keeps his duffel bag between his legs and keeps his hands tightly wrapped around the rope that runs along the sides of the raft. He briefly turns on his flashlight and checks the coordinates on the map against the ones on the compass: 38 degrees north/75 degrees west. He yells a slight directional change to the sailors. The raft is taking on some water as the waves gain in intensity. Suddenly, the sailors stop rowing and point toward the shore. Kurt can barely see lights that appear to be coming from a moving vehicle, probably a Coast Guard beach patrol truck, as it makes it way south along the coast. They are the only lights they see.

Kurt can tell that they are close to landing. He hears the screeching gulls and the sound of the waves pounding the beach. The raft hits the beach and is carried backward by the breaking waves. Both sailors jump out into waist-deep water and move the raft on to the shore. Kurt throws his bag to one sailor, and the other helps Kurt jump out and onto the sandy beach. They quickly pull the raft back into the waves, jump in, and row hard against the incoming surf. Quickly, they disappear into the darkness.

Kurt walks away from the surf. He takes off his rain slicker and places it in the duffel bag. He removes his pistol and knife and places them in the pocket sewn to the side of the duffel bag. He finds his wallet, which has his Maryland driver's license and 30 dollars. He places it deep in his pants pocket. He lifts the bag and places his arms through the straps as he struggles through the sand. To the east, he sees the first glimmer of the orange sun peeking above the misty horizon. He looks south and, in the distance, sees vehicle lights moving north along the beach. At the top of the sand dune, he can see a small house sitting next to a road. The house is dark, and he moves closer. There is a small screened in porch on the back of the house sitting on stilts which lift it a few feet above the sand. He squirms under the steps and pushes his bag as far back as possible.

He can no longer see the lights, but he can hear the engine and the sounds of men talking. They continue moving north, heading toward the Indian River Inlet. Their sounds slowly disappear into the darkness. Kurt pulls out his map and flashlight. He estimates that he is approximately five kilometers from the meeting location with the American Bund member. If all goes well, he should be there in less than one hour and would be there just before sun rise. He quickly climbs out from under the porch and carries his bag. He finds the road and walks south toward Bethany.

As he is walking along the road, a car slows, and red emergency flashers begin to blink. A military jeep stops, and an American soldier holding a cigarette motions him to move toward the car. The soldier shines his flashlight into Kurt's fearful blue eyes.

"Are you a soldier?" he asks.

"No, just spent the night hitchhiking to the beach from Baltimore. Wanted to enjoy some vacation time with my relatives in Ocean View. Is there a problem?"

"Okay. Just checking. With that military duffel bag, we thought you might be a soldier whose car broke down and needed a ride. Didn't mean to scare you."

"Oh, this is my grandfather's duffel from World War I. Holds a lot of stuff."

The jeep speeds away, and Kurt is shaking. He thinks, *I hope that was a convincing performance.* He hurries along the roadway toward the town of Bethany. He finds Atlantic Avenue and discovers a boardwalk with benches overlooking the sand dunes and the Atlantic. The orange sun is rising, and the misty haze is lifting. He sees a few of the houses turning on their lights and finds the boardwalk empty. He places his bag next to him and stares out at the glimmering ocean. He thinks, *I can't believe I'm here on the shores of America!*

It is after 5:00 a.m., so he hopes that his ride will be waiting for him. He continues walking and comes to the intersection of Atlantic Avenue and Garfield Parkway. There on the corner, he spots a black pickup truck with someone dozing behind the wheel with his head back on the seat, mouth open. Paul Lukas sees that the man is wearing a tan shirt and a straw hat. He taps on the hood of the truck, and Wilmer opens his eyes and cautiously looks around. Paul walks up to the open window. "Good morning. Are the fish biting today?"

Wilmer clears his throat and replies, "Today is a good day to catch some fish." Paul walks around the truck, places his bag in the truck's bed, opens the door, and sits next to Wilmer. Wilmer looks around and slowly pulls away, heading west. Along the way, the traffic is sparse, mostly Army jeeps and khaki-colored trucks.

"So, you are Paul Lukas, and how was your ride from Baltimore?"

"Yes, that is my name for the next few weeks. The ride from Baltimore took 15 days and was very scary, especially when some military police stopped me a few miles up the road. Also saw some military patrols on the beach, but I was in a good hiding place."

Wilmer glances over. "Paul, this is just the beginning of what may be a very scary few weeks."

# Paul Arrives in Ocean View 1942

Emma Stickler is looking out the front window as she sees Wilmer's truck making its way up the driveway. She has been so nervous and upset knowing that the German saboteur would be arriving this morning and that her life was about to change. She sees the pickup door open, and Paul follows Wilmer toward the front door. She is somewhat relieved knowing the rendezvous went well and is taken aback with Paul's appearance. He is tall with short, honey-blond hair combed straight back. She can't see his eyes, but he is lean and trim as he carries his duffel bag over his shoulder. He is wearing a short-sleeved blue denim shirt and tan pants. The door swings open, and Emma is standing in front of him. She thinks, *Yes, his eyes are robin egg blue, and he looks like a movie star. He is an incredibly handsome man!*

Wilmer looks at Emma and points at Kurt. "Meet our nephew from Baltimore, Paul Lukas."

Paul drops his bag on the floor and shakes hands with Emma. "So good to meet you, and thank you for allowing me to stay at your home."

Emma thinks, *So the show is about to begin,* and responds in German, "*Bitte* (You are welcome)."

Paul responds, "Excuse me, Aunt Emma. We'll speak only English while I'm here, ok?"

Emma is impressed with his American English and his deep baritone voice. "Come in, Paul. I just took some corn muffins out of the oven. I know you must be starving. I must get used to you calling me 'aunt.' Tell me: Do you like your eggs scrambled or fried?"

The three gather at the kitchen table, and Paul tells them about the submarine experience and the depth charge scare. He glances from Wilmer to Emma. "So, tell me what you know about Dr. Reinhardt."

Emma pours Paul another cup of coffee. "Well, we have met him. He is mostly bald with a grayish goatee, and he wears glasses. He has been sick and has lost weight. The Army has him isolated from the other prisoners. He eats with the others, and I think that is the only time he comingles with them. When they question him, they want me in the room. He speaks poor English, and sometimes he doesn't understand the questions. He was arrested in July of last year (1941). He was detained at Fort Meade in Maryland, and then he was transferred here. There are currently 20 prisoners at Bear Trap. They tell me many more will follow over the summer. He is a German scientist, so they are very interested in the secrets he could tell them. One day last week, they questioned him for six hours. He told me he has had no contact with his family in Germany, and they will not let him write letters to them."

"Wilmer and I are on good terms with Lieutenant Johnson, who is the acting warden, if you want to call him that. I take him cakes and cookies, and he likes us. He told me that they will start moving prisoners very soon to various farms around

Ocean View to help with the harvest. I am hoping to convince him to let Dr. Reinhardt work at our farm."

Paul looks at Emma. "When will you return to Bear Trap?"

"We never know for sure. Usually we get a call on Monday, and they tell us what days they may need us."

"My capture of Dr. Reinhardt depends on many variables, and I have a deadline. I rendezvous with the submarine in about 30 days or less. That timeline may be adjusted, but I have limited flexibility. If he becomes a field hand on your farm, my work becomes much easier. If they will not allow him to leave the camp, my work is much more complicated. Do you see my point? Wilmer, can you show me the farm? Also, did you receive a transmitter and antenna?"

"Yes, it is in the barn, well hidden. Let's take a walk, and I will show it to you."

They walk out the back door and move toward the barn. Wilmer points to the strawberries and potatoes fields. "Paul, as of today, this is a working farm, but that is about to change. I have a few men that work for me during harvest time. They should get the berries picked within the next few weeks, same for the potatoes. I think Emma and I have a good chance of persuading the Army to allow Dr. Reinhardt and a few other German prisoners to come over to help us. If that doesn't happen, then we will take Reinhardt whatever information he needs from you to plot his escape. One reason I think they will consider sending him here is that the farm next door to us—you can see their house from here—has horses and dogs that the military uses to patrol the beaches. The Army is over there every day with guards and trucks moving the animals to the beach area. The farm next door is managed by Jeff and Lori Miller. They have two kids. Their son is in the Navy on the West Coast, and there is their daughter, McKenna, walking up the driveway." Wilmer points in McKenna's direction.

Paul sees a beautiful blond girl with shorts and a white blouse walking along the fence line toward her house.

"Paul, Emma talked to them and told them your cover story that you are our nephew and will be spending a few weeks here at our farm. They said they would like to meet you, and that is probably a good idea to meet the neighbors. We have to appear that everything is normal."

Paul keeps staring toward McKenna. "I will meet them, but I will be keeping to myself and hope they don't get too nosy. Show me where you hid the transmitter."

For several hours, Paul and Wilmer work to set up the transmitter and the placement of the antenna in the highest place in the barn, about 10 feet above the hayloft tucked away behind some rough-hewn beams. The transmitter is hidden away in a stall behind the barn door. The hardest part of the work was running the wire from the antenna to the transmitter, and Paul was concerned that they might not have enough cable to make the connection. Finally, he flips the switch, and the transmitter buzzes as the lights begin to blink. He clicks in the code and talks into the microphone.

Berlin is six hours ahead of Ocean View time. Paul knows the Berlin Intelligence Office is manned around the clock and is communicating with officers throughout the world. He makes contact and lets them know he has arrived at the Delaware location and all is well. He ends his conversation with, "Will make contact with Reinhardt this week."

Paul and Wilmer make their way back to the house, and Wilmer tells Emma all about the transmitter in their barn. Paul finds his folder inside his duffel bag and sits at the kitchen table and begins to take notes.

"Wilmer, when the Bund member dropped off the transmitter, did he mention a contact in Ocean City, Maryland? Someone who operates a charter fishing business? I see on the map the location of the Ocean City Inlet and easy access to the Atlantic. It appears to be a quick ride from here to the Inlet. Maybe about 18 miles?"

"Jacob Baden was the name of the person who delivered the transmitter. He did mention a Delmont Richter, who has a fishing boat near the Ocean City Inlet. Here, I wrote down his name and was given this telephone number by Jacob. He said you would be most interested in contacting Captain Richter."

"I must anticipate variables and unforeseen twists and turns to successfully free Reinhardt and get him back to Germany. The best option is to free him when he is here working on your farm, get him to Richter in Ocean City and then to the submarine rendezvous five miles off the Inlet. Other options include cutting through the fence into the Bear Trap camp, finding Reinhardt, taking him out of the camp, and driving him to Ocean City. This is risky and may include some bloodshed. Another option would be for Reinhardt to fake an illness, hope the Army would take him to a medical center, grab him from his sick bed, and get him to Ocean City. If the boat in Ocean City falls apart, I will have to get him to New York and place him on an ocean liner heading to Portugal or Spain. Using your truck will be necessary. Let's hope you can convince the Army to bring him over here to pick some strawberries. It has been a long day for me. I think I will say goodnight."

Emma shows Paul to his bedroom. She returns to the kitchen and looks at Wilmer. "Can you believe what we just heard, and did he say this may include some bloodshed? My God, what did we get ourselves into?"

Wilmer gives her a sharp frown. "Baden said the same thing about possible bloodshed, and don't say *we*. You are the one that got us involved with your Bund friends!"

Emma glares back. "That may be true, but it was your choice to help them plant the bomb on the *King James*!"

# Roosevelt's United Flag Day Prayer 1942

June 1942. Jeff, Lori and McKenna are eating their Sunday dinner. It has been a busy day on the farm. All three attended church, and McKenna played the piano and conducted the choir. She is home on summer break from college. Jeff hands McKenna a dish full of mashed potatoes. "McKenna, the church music and the choir were exceptional. I loved when you played 'God Bless America' and everyone stood and held hands. It was heartwarming to see the American flags with today being Flag Day. So many of our young people attending the service in their uniforms. Wish Tristan could have been there. At 7:00 tonight, I want to listen to Roosevelt addressing the country on this very patriotic day."

"Thank you, Dad. I agree that it was inspirational. I'd like to listen to the President with you. I love to hear him speak with that New York aristocratic voice of his. I do admire the fact that he has had to cope with his paralysis while dealing with a nation at war. I am glad I placed those small American flags along our driveway. Can you believe that the Sticklers still have their German flag sitting next to their mailbox? How un-American!

I saw Wilmer today walking a young man around his barn. I wonder if that is the nephew Emma said was going to spend the summer at their farm?"

Lori glances toward the Stickler farm. "Must be. She told me she was expecting him around the middle of June. I told her that we would like to meet him and thought we could have them over for dinner. Maybe next Sunday?"

Jeff frowns. "They are so strange, especially Emma! That's fine. I would like to meet the young man."

At 7:00 that evening, Jeff, Lori and McKenna sit on the living room sofa next to the radio. Jeff tunes in the station just as Roosevelt begins to deliver his address to the nation:

*"God of the free, we pledge our hearts and lives today to the cause of all free mankind.*

*"Grant us victory over the tyrants who would enslave all free men and nations. Grant us faith and understanding to cherish all those who fight for freedom as if they were our brothers. Grant us brotherhood in hope and union, not only for the space of this bitter war, but for the days to come which shall and must unite all the children of earth.*

*"Our earth is but a small star in the great universe. Yet of it, we can make, if we choose, a planet unvexed by war, untroubled by hunger or fear, undivided by senseless distinctions of race, color, or theory. Grant us that courage and foreseeing to begin this task today that our children and our children's children may be proud of the name of man.*

*"The spirit of man has awakened, and the soul of man has gone forth. Grant us the wisdom and the vision to comprehend the greatness of man's spirit that suffers and endures so hugely for a goal beyond his own brief span. Grant us honor for our dead who died in the faith, honor for our living who work and strive for the faith, redemption and security for all captive lands and*

*peoples. Grant us patience with the deluded and pity for the betrayed. And grant us the skill and the valor that shall cleanse the world of oppression and the old base doctrine that the strong must eat the weak because they are strong.*

*"Yet most of all grant us brotherhood, not only for this day but for all our years—a brotherhood not of words but of acts and deeds. We are all of us children of earth—grant us that simple knowledge. If our brothers are oppressed, then we are oppressed. If they hunger, we hunger. If their freedom is taken away, our freedom is not secure. Grant us a common faith that man shall know bread and peace—that he shall know justice and righteousness, freedom and security, an equal opportunity and an equal chance to do his best, not only in our own lands, but throughout the world. And in that faith let us march, toward the clean world our hands can make. Amen."*

Jeff, Lori and McKenna have tears in their eyes. They are thinking of Tristan, Connor, and Hugh, and other men and women this war has touched—even the young man who has just arrived next door, though they do not know it.

# German Farm Help
# 1942

June, 1942. At 7:30 a.m. the Sticklers' phone rings, and Emma rushes to answer it. "Emma, this is Lieutenant Johnson. Would you be able to come to Bear Trap this morning around 10:00 a.m.? If you can make it, I will send a car over to pick you up."

"Yes, I can come this morning. How long will you need me?"

"Maybe just an hour or so. We don't need Wilmer, just you."

Paul and Wilmer are sipping coffee as Emma walks over to the table. "That was Lieutenant Johnson. They need me for a few hours this morning at Bear Trap and will send over a car to pick me up. They don't need you, Wilmer, just me."

Paul has a curious look. "Did he give you any idea why he needs you?"

"No, not a clue."

Wilmer looks at Paul. "Paul, we can saddle the horses, and I'll show you around the farm."

The Army jeep pulls into the Stickler driveway, and a corporal comes to the front door and escorts Emma down the porch steps and into the jeep. It is a quick ride as she enters the compound and waves to the armed guard at the main gate. They pull up in front of the headquarters Quonset, and Lieutenant Johnson comes out to meet Emma.

"Thank you, Emma, for coming on such short notice. I have an important announcement to make to the prisoners and wanted you to translate my talk to them so there is no confusion about what is being said. I will assemble them now out in the recreation area, so please give me a few minutes."

The guards gather the prisoners, and they stand shoulder to shoulder in their khaki trousers, blue shirts and fatigue caps. The letters "PW" are emblazoned on the backs of their shirts.

Lieutenant Johnson stands on a small wooden platform, and Emma stands next to him. After each sentence, Emma translates Lieutenant Johnson's message into German. Johnson takes a quick drink out of his canteen and begins, "This is an important announcement concerning your confinement here. For those of you who have been imprisoned for more than two months, I have received permission from my superiors to allow you to leave the camp on certain days and work on various farms within a close distance to this camp. We have a list of farms, and you will be rotated to them on a weekly basis. You will work mainly Monday to Thursday. The farmers are willing to provide food and drink to you while you are working there. You will arrive there at 7:00 in the morning, and we will pick you up at 5:00 in the evening. There will be four workers assigned to each farm, and you will work under the supervision of one of our armed guards. You will work as a team and will be used primarily to pick produce at the direction of the farmer who owns the property. There may also be some other farm chores you will be asked to do, such as carpentry or painting. When you leave here in the morning, you will be searched and your pockets emptied. Same for when you return at the end of the day. Any interaction with the farmer and his family or his workers will be through the guard assigned to you. If there are any infractions, you will be taken off the farm work and placed in isolation here. You will begin farm work next Monday. We will provide you with work clothes and boots. Are there any questions?"

The prisoners look at each other, and there are no questions, just some quiet murmurs.

Lieutenant Johnson dismisses them, and they are returned to their quarters. He thanks Emma. "Emma, you and Wilmer will receive four prisoners next Monday. Jeff Miller will also receive four prisoners. My corporal will confirm with the Millers when he takes you back. All the farmers in the area who are participating have signed an agreement form. I am hearing good feedback, and the farmers seem happy to receive free labor at this time of the harvest season.

Emma removes her glasses. "Thank you, Lieutenant. We are anxious to receive them. I know Wilmer hopes they will be good workers and praying that we will not encounter any problems. I can sign the form now if you would like?" Emma stares at Lieutenant Johnson, considering for a moment. "I think it would be a good idea if the farmers had the names of the prisoners who will be working for them. Is that possible?"

"We already thought of that, Emma. Each week you will receive four new prisoners. I have a calendar schedule taped to the bulletin board over there. It shows the farmer's name and who will be working there each week for the next month. Here, let me show you."

Emma follows him over to the bulletin board and looks at the calendar for the remaining weeks in June and all of July. She sees that Dr. Reinhardt will be at her farm the week of July 5.

Back on Woodland Avenue, Paul and Wilmer walk out to the barn, and Wilmer halters two horses and throws saddles on them. Paul swings his leg into the stirrup, grabs the saddle horn, and mounts his horse. He slowly walks the horse out of the barn, and Wilmer is just behind him.

"Wilmer, where are we headed?"

"We will walk the fence line, and then there is a trail that leads to the river. Just follow me. When was the last time you rode a horse?"

Paul looks comfortable in the saddle. "I guess it was a year ago. It was part of our training, and I rode three times a week for three months. Mainly mountain trails. We also shot our rifles while we were mounted and in gallop. I love horses."

As they are riding, Paul can see McKenna in the garden behind her house working with a pitchfork. Her blond hair is tumbled, and she is wearing a short-sleeved flowered shirt, jeans and sandals. Her skin is beginning to tan. She stops, looks toward them, and waves. Wilmer waves back, and Paul stares ahead. McKenna wipes her hands on her jeans and gets back to work.

Paul can see that the Stickler farm is heavily planted and the land is flat. There are chickens, pigs, and apple and cherry trees. A warm breeze slowly turns the windmill next to the barn. Paul inhales deeply and can taste the ocean air. He thinks, *Is there a war going on?*

That evening at dinner, Emma tells Paul and Wilmer about her meeting with the prisoners. "Lieutenant Johnson actually let me look at the schedule and said we will receive a copy of it so we will know the names of those that will be working here. Prisoners will be here Monday to Thursday beginning next Monday. They arrive between 7:00 and 7:30. The Millers will have four prisoners as well. Dr. Reinhardt will be here at our farm the week of July 5. I saw him in the crowd, and he gave me a quick wave."

Paul walks over to the calendar sitting next to the stove. "Ok, so he is scheduled to be here July 6, 7, 8 and 9. I hope they don't start making changes to this schedule. If it holds, I'm thinking the good doctor will be on his way to Germany on July 9 if all goes well. Wilmer, since my week is pretty much open, can we take a quick trip to Ocean City to visit my taxi ride to the submarine?"

Wilmer smiles. "Sure, Paul, let's head down there early tomorrow morning, assuming he can meet with you."

"Let me call Captain Richter and see what his schedule looks like for tomorrow morning."

Wilmer and Paul drive toward Ocean City, along the Coastal Highway. Captain Richter had a chartered fishing party on his boat in the morning, so there was a schedule change to the afternoon. "Paul, where we are heading was not on the map in 1932, just 10 years ago. In August of 1933, a major hurricane battered Ocean City. It changed the geography of the area we are going. It created a new 40-foot-wide, eight-foot-deep inlet at the south end of the town. It separated the southern end of the town from an area known as Assateague Island. It is now a direct route into the Atlantic, and commercial fishing is now a big business here. Bethany got beat up a little but not as bad as Ocean City. Just wanted to share a little bit of beach history with you in case a question comes up."

"That is interesting. We don't have hurricanes in Germany. Although the Fuhrer has created more damage, death, and destruction than 10,000 hurricanes ever will. Wilmer, if this plan works out and I get Reinhardt back to Germany, what are your plans after I leave? You know the authorities will be all over you, and they will quickly find out the truth. There is a good chance you and Emma will be arrested and imprisoned. Have you two thought about that?"

"Paul, we have, and we knew as soon as you arrived that our lives would be changed forever. When Jacob Baden was here, we talked about that. We have a plan that begins the day you leave."

Wilmer works his way through the small streets in Ocean City and finds the marina where Captain Richter keeps his boat. He parks the truck. "Paul, I'll stay here while you talk to Richter."

Paul walks along the pier and sees a fishing boat with the name Richter gave him, the *Dawn Riser.* He sees a short, stocky man wearing a white baseball cap with the word *CAPTAIN* emblazoned on the front. Richter is smoking a cigar as he stands near the wheelhouse.

"Good afternoon, Captain. I'm Paul Lukas. I talked to you yesterday about a charter fishing trip."

"Oh, yes, I remember the conversation. Come aboard."

Paul jumps from the pier to the boat, and the captain takes him inside the cabin. "How do you like my boat? It is only two years old, 40-foot with a trusty diesel engine. Took a group out this morning, and they went fishing for blues and marlin. They had a good time and caught some big ones."

Paul looks around the boat to see if anyone else is onboard. "Captain, I think you know why I am here, and it is not about catching fish. I believe Jacob Baden explained that I would need your assistance to take me to a rendezvous with a German U-boat. The date I am looking at is July 9. I am told the submarine will be at the five-mile marker. I will give you exact compass coordinates when we arrive, which will be early. I can't give you our exact time. So, you will be on standby for that day."

"I have done other work for the Bund, and they know I am loyal and can keep sensitive information to myself. No one will know about this except you and me. You can count on me being here and ready on July 9. If that date needs to be changed, let me know as quickly as you can. Will it just be you?"

"No, it will be me and one other person. Here is your down payment." Paul hands Richter a small brown envelope. Richter opens it and counts out 500 dollars.

He looks at Paul with sunken eyes and takes a long puff of his cigar. "See you on the $9^{th}$."

That evening after dinner, Paul and Wilmer walk out to the barn, and Paul activates the transmitter. Soon, he has a connection, and he grabs the microphone. "Rendezvous date with U-202 is changed to noon on July 9." German Intelligence confirms, and Paul quickly disconnects.

# Time with McKenna
## 1942

The following Sunday, Emma, Wilmer and Paul walk next door to have dinner with the Millers. Lori sees them walking up the drive and meets them at the door. "So good to see you, and glad you could join us for dinner. This must be your nephew?"

Paul steps forward with an extended arm. "So nice to meet you, Mrs. Miller. My name is Paul, Paul Lukas."

Lori is staring at Paul and thinks, *What a handsome young man!* Jeff and McKenna come into the room. Jeff shakes Paul's hand. "Hi, Paul. I'm Jeff. Welcome to the beach!"

McKenna steps forward, and there is a brief hesitation as Paul's eyes meet McKenna's. There is an intense gaze between them. "Hi, Paul. I'm McKenna. I saw you and Wilmer a few times, once when you were riding."

"Yes, I remember. You were working hard in the garden using that pitchfork. Good to meet you!"

They gather around the large wooden table just off the kitchen. Lori has made crab cakes, and there are large red summer tomatoes and white corn.

Lori passes the corn to Paul. "Paul, do you like crab meat?"

"I do, Mrs. Miller. I started eating steamed crabs when I was a young boy in Baltimore, and my grandfather always had them on Labor Day. My mom and dad have passed on, and I live with my relatives in Baltimore. Aunt Emma told me that you have a son in the Navy."

"Yes, his name is Tristan, and he is stationed on a submarine in the Pacific." Paul doesn't respond, although he has had some submarine experience that he could tell them about.

Paul looks at McKenna. She is wearing a sleeveless yellow sun dress, small shell earrings and lightly tinted pink lipstick. "I understand you are attending college?"

McKenna takes a sip of iced tea. She gazes into Paul's blue eyes. "Yes, I have one year to go, and hopefully I will graduate next May. I will be looking for a teaching job somewhere nearby."

Jeff looks at Paul. "So, Paul, what line of work are you in back in Baltimore?"

"Well, I have been bouncing around a little bit from job to job. I did work for my uncle at a market in Baltimore and part-time in a restaurant, mainly as a waiter and bartender. Still searching for a permanent job that pays well."

Jeff has a suspicious look. "How did you avoid the draft?"

Paul stares at Jeff. "I have a medical deferment due to my asthma condition."

Wilmer jumps into the conversation. "Jeff, looks like we will be receiving some free labor courtesy of the US Army. Couldn't come at a better time. I have more than enough work for them to do."

"I agree, Wilmer. Same with me. I would like them to repair some fencing and string some fence wire. Lieutenant Johnson said that would be fine. What concerns me, though, is having a military police officer standing guard with a rifle. I hope nothing serious develops while they are here."

"Jeff, you know that Emma and I have been over to Bear Trap. The Army asked us to be translators. We met a few of the prisoners. They seem passive, and I think they are looking forward to some fresh air and some new surroundings. I think things will be fine."

McKenna is sitting next to Paul and gently touches his hand. "So, Paul, you have never visited Bethany? How did you get here?"

"I was here years ago when I was very small. I do remember playing in the ocean and catching sand crabs. My parents didn't own a car, so we always stayed close to home. For this trip, I could have taken the bus, but I decided to hitchhike. Rides were easy to catch, and the people that picked me up were very nice."

McKenna looks surprised. "Sounds like an exciting ride! I think with a war going on people are trying to be more helpful. Maybe tomorrow evening, I could take you into town, and you could check out downtown Bethany."

"Thanks, McKenna. I would like that. Mr. and Mrs. Miller, is that ok with you?"

Lori glances around the table. "Fine with me. You two are adults, so you don't need our permission." Jeff nods in agreement. The Sticklers are quiet.

Lori looks at McKenna. "McKenna, why don't you play us something on the piano while I make some coffee?"

Everyone walks into the living room while McKenna sits at the piano. She looks around the room. "Any requests?" No one speaks up, so she plays a new song by Duke Ellington, "Don't Get Around Much Anymore." Everyone applauds.

Paul walks over to the piano and slides onto the bench next to McKenna. "McKenna, mind if I play something?"

McKenna slides over to give Paul room. "What a great surprise! No, not at all. We would love to hear you play."

Paul plays the Bach prelude that his mother taught him

when he was a boy. He also plays "Clair de Lune" by Claude Debussy.

McKenna and the others applaud, and McKenna exclaims, "Wow! Where did you learn to play classical music like that?"

Paul has a shy look. "I've always loved the piano. My mother played, and she was intent on giving me lessons. I don't play as much as I did. Glad you liked it!"

After everyone leaves, Jeff and Lori are doing the dishes. "I wonder about Paul. He seems like a nice young man. Lori, I know you have always told me I have a suspicious nature. I'm thinking that some things about him and his relationship to the Sticklers seem disconnected."

"Jeff, he is so nice. Why try to find fault with him? It seems that McKenna likes him."

"That's part of my concern. First of all, to me, he has a slight accent, and it's not a Baltimore accent. Did you notice it? Also, why haven't the Sticklers ever mentioned a family in Baltimore, and why hasn't he visited them more frequently over the years? Is he Emma's sister's son, or is he on Wilmer's side of the family? I don't know. Certain things about him just don't add up. Also, did you notice how quiet Emma was?"

"Oh, Jeff, stop your worrying. He is only here for a few weeks; then he will be gone. I think it was nice of McKenna to offer to show him around Bethany. No, I didn't notice an accent, and I am glad Emma was quiet!"

On Monday evening, June 22, Paul walks over to the Miller farm, and McKenna is waiting on the front porch. "Hi, Paul, hope you had a good day. My dad said it was ok to use his pickup truck to drive to the beach. There is a 9:00 blackout, so we have only a few hours."

Paul stares at this beautiful young woman. She has her blond hair brushed straight back from her forehead, and her ponytail is held in place with a pink rubber band. She is wearing a pale blue cotton print dress.

There is a lot of summer traffic on Atlantic Avenue, and McKenna tries to find a close parking space near the boardwalk. The wind is calm off the ocean, and the beach is spotted with blankets and umbrellas. A good crowd wants to soak up the remaining sunshine. Who would realize that there is a war going on?

McKenna grabs Paul's arm. "Let's walk down and get our feet wet." Paul nods in agreement, and they find a bench and take off their shoes. Paul rolls up his pants to his knees. McKenna notices how white Paul's legs are. "Paul, your legs and arms need some sun. You are as white as a ghost."

"I know! When you are bartending for 10 hours a day, it's hard to get a suntan."

The waves break on their ankles, and McKenna's dress is wet. McKenna notices that Paul's pants are wet. "I should have brought a bath towel and a bucket so we could collect some shells."

Paul stoops down and picks up a small star-shaped shell and hands it to McKenna. She admires it and hands it back to him. "Can you put it in your pocket for safe keeping?" She thinks, *My first present from Paul.*

They walk down the beach carrying their shoes, and Paul notices the shops and restaurants just off the boardwalk. "McKenna, I'm thirsty. Is there somewhere we can get something to drink?"

"I'm thirsty, too. There is a little snack bar not too far up the boardwalk. I love their root beer."

Paul's face is blood red. He had been afraid this might happen—a word, phrase, or comment he is not familiar with. Is root beer the same as the German beer he is familiar with? "Did you say 'root beer'?"

McKenna looks at Paul with a puzzled look. "Yes, root beer. *R-O-O-T* beer. Don't you have root beer in Baltimore?"

"Oh, root beer. Of course we do. I have it behind the bar in bottles. We don't sell much of it, but I know what it is. I don't like it. Does the place we are going sell real beer?"

"'Fraid not. I said it was a snack bar, not a real bar."

They walk up to the snack bar, and McKenna orders a large root beer with plenty of ice. "Paul, what would you like?"

He see a *COKE* sign and points to it. "I'll have one of those—plenty of ice, please!"

McKenna sips on her beverage and stares out at the ocean. "I love the ocean, and I try to come here as much as possible. Sometimes I will ride my bike up to the boardwalk and just sit in the sand and lose myself in the tranquility. To me, it is almost a religious experience."

Paul stares into McKenna's blue eyes. "I would love to live near the ocean. Maybe someday."

"Maybe someday you will. Do you have a steady girlfriend back in Baltimore?"

"No, I don't have a steady girlfriend. I have dated a few girls. Never got interested in any of them. When you are locked into one place, it is hard to meet people."

"You should have a ton of girls chasing you, especially with a war going on and so many young men in the service."

"That hasn't happened to me yet. I'll keep looking for the right one."

"Look at that beautiful sunset! We better get going. Sorry you didn't get your real beer. What are you doing next Sunday? We could go horseback riding if you want. There is a great trail behind the farm that leads down to the river. Also, think about joining our family for our Fourth of July celebration." McKenna wonders why Paul didn't ask her if she has a boyfriend.

Paul gently touches her hand. "Sounds like fun. I will let you know."

McKenna takes a slow drive down Atlantic Avenue to her farm. Paul says goodnight and then walks back to talk to Emma and Wilmer. The night air has a salty taste. He can hear the shrill voices of the cicadas and frogs.

Emma is sitting next to the radio, listening to her favorite opera channel. "Paul, tell me about your evening while I get you something to drink."

"Emma, you listening to the opera reminds me of my grandparents and my mother. They loved the opera. McKenna is fun to be with, and I enjoyed her company. Is Wilmer around?" Just then, Wilmer walks in the back door.

Paul gestures toward the kitchen table. "Can the three of us talk?" They sit at the table, and Emma pours hot tea.

"I wanted to discuss the next steps so we are all on the same page. Obviously, we have a bit of a slowdown since Reinhardt is not scheduled to work here until July 6, and I have made arrangements with the Ocean City captain to take me to the submarine on July 9. Reinhardt has no idea that I will be taking him back to Germany, which is probably a good thing at this point. Assuming we are on our way back to Germany, let's talk about your plans."

Wilmer points at Emma. "I told you, Paul, that Emma and I have a plan. After you have secured Reinhardt that morning, Emma and I will take you to the fishing boat in Ocean City. You will board and be on your way. The day you leave is the day we leave. We will lock our door and never return. Emma and I will be going to the bank tomorrow and secure a large loan. Most farmers here at the beach have a credit line with a bank, so it will not be unusual to ask for a large amount of cash. I have been liquidating assets over the last few months and have a sizable amount of cash hidden around the house. From Ocean City, we will drive to Norfolk and board a Spanish freighter which will take us to Brazil. We hear there are many Germans living there that have been displaced by the war. All of our travel plans and necessary documents have been made by Fritz Kuhn and Jacob Baden. Emma and I realized that, as soon as we agreed to have you stay here, we would be guilty of treason. We are looking forward to a new life. Perhaps after the war is over, we will resettle in Germany. Only time will tell, but we should be fine, so don't worry about us. By the way, you owe us some money."

Paul has a surprised look. "I can't believe you will just walk away from this farm."

Wilmer looks at Emma, who is holding back her emotions. "There is nothing to keep us here. We have no children and no family nearby. Our loyalty is to Germany, not this country. In time, the bank will auction off the farm, and I'm guessing a former US Senator will step up and purchase it. All will be well."

Paul goes to his room and comes back to the kitchen with an envelope. He hands it to Wilmer. "Here is your final payment."

As the days roll by, Paul keeps himself busy helping Wilmer and Emma. Every day, he uses the wireless and checks in with his counterparts in Berlin. They pack up two large suitcases and hide them in the barn. He helps Wilmer load some cattle and pigs into the truck for a trip to the slaughterhouse in Selbyville. Wilmer told Jeff Miller he is getting out of the chicken business, so they have been herding his flock over to the Miller farm. McKenna reminds him that they have a date on Sunday.

A few evenings, he drives Wilmer's truck over to Bear Trap. He sketches the layout of the camp and its buildings. As he slows the truck, he sees one watch tower and one sentry at the main gate. There are soldiers patrolling the fence line along with their dogs. He notices that a section of the barbed wire fence runs through a stretch of large pines with some branches overhanging the fence in a secluded spot behind a large storage shed.

In his mind, he maps out his backup plan if Reinhardt does not appear at the Sticklers' on July 9. He makes a mental note to ask Emma if she knows in which building they keep Reinhardt.

It is a beautiful, cloudless Sunday as Paul walks over to meet McKenna. She is in the barn saddling her horse, Sadie. Paul stands by the barn door and watches. She is wearing riding jeans tucked into her brown boots with her short-sleeved yellow cotton top. She has her hair pulled back into that ponytail he saw the other day. He thinks almost aloud, *She is a beautiful woman!* He quietly walks toward her, gently touches her shoulder, and whispers, "Good afternoon."

She is startled as she steps back and almost stumbles into his arms. "Oh, hi, Paul. You scared me! Here, hold onto Sadie's reins while I saddle Toby."

Paul is dressed in jeans, work boots, and one of Wilmer's short-sleeved shirts, untucked. "No, I can saddle him. I can't let you do all of the work! Where is his tack?"

Soon, they both mount, and McKenna leads the way out of the barn and through the bean and tomato fields. She looks at Paul and notices his arms, face, and neck are burned a brownish red. Studying him, she thinks, *The hot summer Bethany sun works fast.* He seems comfortable in the saddle, which surprises her. "Paul, did you take riding lessons somewhere? There are not too many farms left in Baltimore."

He wants to say, "*Yes, at the German Intelligence School outside of Brandenburg, Germany,*" but he responds, "More farms than you may think. When I was younger, our family would spend summers on a small farm just north of Baltimore in a place called Aberdeen. We would mainly pick produce for the farmer, but he had some horses, and he let me ride them around the farm. I remember he had a pony and would hitch her to a pony cart and give the kids rides. We enjoyed our time there."

He remembers what his instructors told him at Brandenburg:

*A spy must be a gifted liar. It is all about deceit and betrayal.* Kurt is not comfortable with this new person, Paul.

Paul notices a basket strapped to the back of her saddle. "What's in the basket?"

McKenna checks to make sure it is secured. "Just some fried chicken in case we get hungry and some soda pop to wash it down."

"Sounds good. I didn't know you could cook. No root beer?"

McKenna laughs. "Mom made the chicken, and we are out of root beer."

As McKenna rides along the path to the river, she thinks about the times she rode with Hugh along the same path.

They eventually come to a shady spot next to the sandy bank. "Paul, this is a good spot to stop. Are you hungry?"

They dismount and secure the horses, and Paul helps McKenna take the basket off of Sadie. McKenna spreads a small red blanket on the sand."

Paul is eating his chicken leg and notices McKenna staring at him. "Is something wrong?"

"Oh no, I'm sorry! Just watching you eat." She wants to say, *I love your eyes!*

"I didn't tell you that I have been playing piano in Baltimore on the weekends, usually once a month with some guys from my college. Have you ever been to the Belvedere Hotel? We play in the Owl Bar. It's been fun, and I get to see what Baltimore looks like. Do you like living there?"

Paul knows nothing about the Belvedere Hotel, so he evades that question and hopes McKenna doesn't notice. "I do like Baltimore. I live in an area called Federal Hill. It's near the Cross Street Market. Do you know where that is?"

"No, I have not seen that part of the city. I've met some students from Johns Hopkins University who like to visit the bar and listen to our jazz music. We did drive over to their campus.

Maybe the next time I come to Baltimore, you could show me around? How long will you be staying here with the Sticklers?"

"Not that long. I need to get back to my job before they decide to fire me. Wilmer said he will drive me back."

"Remember what I said about coming over to our place to celebrate the Fourth. We have steamed crabs but no fireworks again this year because of the blackout. When will this damn war be over? Emma and Wilmer are invited. We usually have a large crowd."

"Thank you for the invitation. It sounds like fun."

The sun is very hot despite being in the shade, and the flies are beginning to bite. McKenna packs up the basket and moves the blanket closer to the water to catch more of the sea breeze. "Paul, let's sit here awhile and get a little sun before we go back. I'm starting to compose and write music, and I wanted to show you what I am working on. I have a copy book in the basket."

Paul is hesitant and doesn't trust his emotions. "Maybe not a good idea, McKenna. I'm really sunburned already. The horses are getting restless and need some water. Maybe I can look at your music a little later. Let's just head back."

"Wow, you really surprise me. I thought you were enjoying our time together, but I understand. Maybe you are right. Do I frighten you?"

"McKenna, I do enjoy being with you and our time together. No, I'm not afraid of you! It's myself that I am afraid of."

McKenna shakes her head and has a quizzical look.

Paul looks at her as she mounts her horse and thinks, *If you only knew.*

McKenna gives Sadie a kick and looks over her shoulder. "Race you back to the barn!"

Paul unsaddles his horse and says goodbye.

McKenna yells, "See you on the Fourth!" She takes her time and brushes both horses. She thinks about their time together.

*I really like him. He is handsome, kind, and seems sincere. I feel a strange, indescribable attraction when I am around him. He is shy and a little standoffish. He seems to keep his emotions locked up inside of him. Oh, well, maybe a brief little summer crush that isn't going anywhere.*

# The Fourth of July in Ocean View 1942

McKenna always looks forward to the Fourth of July. She gets up early and helps Jeff and Lori prepare for the day. She has 24 small American flags the she stands along the driveway. She finds their large American flag and hangs it across the front porch. Several wooden tables are set up on the back patio between the house and the barn. At noon, neighbors and friends begin to arrive. Jeff has invited the Dawson Brothers to come and entertain with their country music. The afternoon wears on, and McKenna spends time catching up with friends and the LaPlante and Crosby families.

Marna and Jason tell her all about Connor and Cameron. "Connor is now stationed in San Diego and flying out of the naval base there. He thinks eventually he will be transferred somewhere in the Pacific. Cameron has been accepted into the veterinary school at Penn State. He wanted to come today, but he is working with Dr. Burton. With all of the dogs and horses the military has here, they have been working 12-hour days."

The Crosbys are sitting at the same table. McKenna chats with Lee and Jimmy and asks about Hugh. Barbara responds and tells McKenna that he is fine and is now second in command of a Coast Guard cutter stationed in Iceland. "He seems to like what he is doing and always tells me not to worry about him. Doesn't he know that we read the newspapers? There are thousands of American troops now stationed there, and then there is always the risk of the German U-boats. I know he is in danger. I can never forget the sinking of the *King James*."

"Miss Barbara, the next time you write, please tell him that I asked about him and that he is always in my prayers." McKenna leans over and gives Barbara a kiss on the cheek.

The day is passing quickly, and McKenna is on edge. She keeps looking toward the Stickler farm and wonders why Paul, Emma and Wilmer have not stopped over. Lori can tell that McKenna is very nervous and upset. She asks McKenna to help her bring out more food. When McKenna hands her a tray of lunch meat, Lori asks, "Wonder where Paul and the Sticklers are?"

McKenna gives Lori a quick, snappy answer, "Who knows? I invited them, and Paul said they were coming. Maybe I will walk over and check on them."

As the afternoon fades into evening, a few of the guests are beginning to say goodbye. McKenna can wait no longer. She walks over and knocks on the Sticklers' front door. No one answers. She walks down the steps and around the house and can see Paul standing in the back of the barn. As she walks closer, she can see a strange black suitcase sitting on a bale of hay as Paul measures out rope. She sees a pistol lying behind the suitcase.

As she walks in, Paul quickly closes the suitcase and throws the rope on top of it.

"Paul, I'm disappointed that you did not come over to our party. What's going on?"

"Oh, hi, McKenna. Sorry I didn't stop over. Both Emma and Wilmer are sick. They think it was something they ate. I felt uncomfortable coming over alone since I really didn't know anyone."

She walks over and stands directly in front of him. "Paul, I was looking forward to spending time with you today. You know me and my mom and dad! That's no excuse!"

She is staring into his wide blue eyes, and she knows at that moment she wants to kiss him. She pulls him close, and he places his hands on her shoulders. Her heart is pounding. *Is he feeling what I'm feeling?* He gently lifts her chin and kisses her. His lips are warm and soft. She could scream with excitement. He places his hand on the back of her neck and pulls her closer to him. He kisses her again with more intensity, and she suddenly pulls away. He steps back and sees that her eyes are moist.

She looks at him with tenderness in her eyes. "I better get back to the party."

Paul touches her arm. "Let me walk you over."

"No, I'll be fine. Get back to whatever you were doing. Be careful with that pistol. My dad keeps his under his bed. You never know when the Germans will land." She slowly walks back to her house. Her mind is racing. She thinks, *This is crazy! What just happened?*

# The POWs Arrive
# 1942

On a cloudless, hot Monday morning (July 6), a US Army cargo truck with a closed cab and canvas covering known to the military as a "Deuce and a Half" pulls up the Stickler driveway and parks behind the house and next to the barn. The driver gets out and walks behind the truck. A soldier, Corporal Bromwell, is sitting with his rifle next to Dr. Reinhardt and seven other prisoners. One other guard sits in the back of the truck, pointing his rifle at the floor. The driver drops the tailgate of the truck. Reinhardt along with three other POWs and Corporal Bromwell jump down. The other four POWs along with their guard are heading to the Miller farm.

As the truck pulls away, Emma, Wilmer and Paul walk out of the barn and stand in front of the corporal and the four prisoners. Emma shakes Corporal Bromwell's hand, then steps forward and says in German, "*Guten morgen* (good morning) and *willkommen* (welcome)." Since she has met Dr. Reinhardt, she says to him, "*Hoffe, dass sie sich besser fühlen* (Hope you are feeling better)."

He stands erect in his work clothes and responds slowly in English, "Much better, Miss Emma, thank you."

Corporal Bromwell ask Wilmer what tasks the men will be doing today. Wilmer points to the paint buckets sitting next to a large pine tree.

"I would like them to paint my split rail fence that runs along the road. I think that will take most of today."

Corporal Bromwell looks at Wilmer and points his rifle at the POWs and says, "Let's get it done!"

Wilmer gives the men instructions in German, and they grab the paint buckets and brushes and march single file down the driveway with their guard behind them.

Paul whispers to Emma, "Boy, that was easy!" as they watch them head toward the fence.

As the week moves on, the POWs paint, cut firewood, pick beans and strawberries, and do other odd jobs. Paul has some limited conversation with Reinhardt and tries to keep Corporal Bromwell happy with sandwiches and buckets of iced tea. He notices that the guard has a hard time staying awake, especially after lunch.

On Wednesday afternoon, Reinhardt is picking tomatoes as Paul walks over to him holding a basket. Bromwell is dozing under an apple tree a good 50 yards from Reinhardt. Paul walks toward Reinhardt and hands him the basket. In German, Paul, in a very quiet voice, says, "*Herr* Doctor, I know this will surprise you. I am a German spy. The Fuehrer has asked me to bring you home to Germany. Tomorrow morning you, only you, are on your way. Tell no one. Emma and Wilmer know our escape plan. No one else. Please believe me. This will happen!"

Reinhardt wipes his sweaty face on his shirt and looks up at Paul with a confused stare. He says in German, "You must be kidding!"

Paul quietly says, "No, this time tomorrow, you will be on a German submarine. Trust me, and when the time comes, do exactly as you are told."

Reinhardt gets back to work. Later that afternoon, the truck returns, and the four POWs are taken back to Bear Trap.

On Thursday, July 9, at exactly 7:15 in the morning, the Army truck pulls into the Stickler driveway and parks in its usual spot. Corporal Bromwell and the four POWs jump out, and the truck slowly moves on. The corporal asks Wilmer for the daily work assignment.

Wilmer approaches the corporal and points toward the barn. "Let's go into the barn so I can show you what I would like done?"

Reinhardt leads the way as the other three POWs follow. Corporal Bromwell walks behind them with his rifle slung over his shoulder. Wilmer walks them to the back of the barn and into one of the stalls, where Paul is waiting.

Bromwell sees Paul. "Hey, Paul, what's going on today? You are looking good this morning!"

Paul pulls his pistol from his back pocket and yells at the guard, "Drop your rifle. NOW!" Bromwell is wide-eyed as he shakes in fear. Wilmer blocks the entrance to the stall and picks up the rifle.

Paul points the pistol at the corporal. He grabs Reinhardt by his shirt sleeve and moves him next to Wilmer. Paul says in German, "Everyone on the floor with your hands behind your back." He repeats the same command to the corporal in English.

Bromwell exclaims, "What the hell is going on?"

As they lie next to each other, Wilmer quickly binds their hands tightly with the rope lying on the floor of the stall as Paul stands over them. There are two wooden support poles behind the stall toward the back of the barn. Paul and Wilmer get the men on their feet and push them toward the poles. The men are securely tied, two to a pole. Wilmer ties handkerchiefs tightly around their mouths. Paul pushes Reinhardt out of the barn and toward Wilmer's truck. Emma rushes out of the house.

The bed of the truck is packed with two suitcases and Paul's duffel bag. Paul explains to Reinhardt that he will lie in the bed of the truck, which they are covering with a canvas tarp. Wilmer will drive with Emma and Paul next to him. Reinhardt does as he is told. Paul finishes strapping the tarp to the bed. "Dr. Reinhardt, I apologize for the tight space. It is a short ride to where we are going."

The truck pulls out of the driveway and heads up Woodland Avenue. Emma takes one last look at her house, the barn, and the fields. "Wilmer, I can't believe we are doing this!" She then looks at Paul. "Are you happy? Everything seems to have gone as planned. I hope they stay tied to those poles for a long time."

Paul stares ahead. "Me, too—at least until this afternoon when the truck returns to pick them up. Can you imagine the surprise that awaits Lieutenant Johnson when he discovers Dr. Reinhardt is no longer his prisoner? The best plans are the least complicated. Let's find a good spot to pull over when we are just outside of Ocean City so I can check on Reinhardt. I want him to change into some of Wilmer's clothes. Wouldn't look good if he is walking down the pier wearing his POW uniform. Oh, by the way, you can now call me Kurt."

It is an easy ride from Ocean View to Ocean City, and Wilmer is taking it slow. A speeding ticket would not be helpful at this point. He makes his way to the piers close to the Inlet. Kurt knows that this will be his last conversation with Emma and Wilmer.

"I know our time together has been brief, and I realize that you have placed your lives in my hands. This world war brings out the best and worst in people, and how you see this war depends on your inner self and your view of the world. It amazes me that someone like Adolf Hitler has brought us together 3,000 miles from Germany. I can never thank you enough for your assistance. I pray that your life ahead will be just as you planned it. Be safe!"

Emma is teary-eyed as she touches Kurt's arm. "You be safe. Your world will be much more dangerous than ours. *Sicher reist zu dir* (Safe travels to you)!"

Wilmer finds the pier where Captain Richter keeps his boat. Reinhardt is now squeezed into the small space behind the truck's front seat as Kurt quickly explains to him what happens next. Wilmer pulls into a small parking lot next to the docks. Kurt jumps out, and Reinhardt is behind him. Kurt lifts the tailgate and grabs his duffel bag. He touches the pocket just to be sure his pistol is there. They quickly walk down the pier toward Richter and the *Dawn Riser.*

Emma looks at Wilmer. "There goes a German spy and a German scientist and the end of our life here as we knew it. Funny, Paul—I mean Kurt—didn't look back. Did you say it is a three-hour ride to Norfolk?" She watches them board Richter's boat as Wilmer pulls the truck back onto the road and over the bridge that takes them south to Norfolk, Virginia.

Captain Richter pulls away from the pier and guides the *Dawn Riser* through the narrow inlet and into the Atlantic. It is overcast with some fog which will burn off quickly. Kurt has given Richter the compass coordinates: *Latitude north 37 degrees 44 minutes, Longitude west 74 degrees and 37 minutes* where the submarine should surface. Richter looks at his navigational chart. "We should be there in about two hours. Enjoy the ride!"

Kurt and Reinhardt sit on a bench next to the cabin. Reinhardt rubs his hands through his hair and shakes his head. "I can't believe what just happened. This morning, I was in a prisoner of war camp in Bear Trap, Delaware, and now I am on my way to Germany. I thought I would be sitting in that camp until the end of the war."

"You are vital to Germany winning this war, and the Fuehrer wants you back at Peenemunde so you can help develop the bomb and rockets that will destroy half of this planet. Admiral Canaris has other plans for you. I am pleased with the way your escape played out. Thanks to the Bund network, they made my assignment very easy. I was afraid that this would be much more difficult and there would be bloodshed. I am also glad that Emma and Wilmer were part of our team. Their help was vital. They have given up their lives in America for the German cause."

Reinhardt takes a deep breath. "I must tell you that I have mixed feelings about my return to Germany. I do miss my family. Bear Trap and Fort Meade are no comparison to our slaughter houses at Dachau and Buchenwald. In a way, Bear Trap was almost like being on holiday. The war wasn't raging. I felt safe in a strange sort of way. I had enough food and plenty of fruit and fresh air from the ocean breeze. They told us we were going to repair the boardwalk north of Bethany in a beach town they called Rehoboth. In a way, I was looking forward to that assignment. We knew that, if we did what we were told, they wouldn't bother us. Kurt, may I tell you something? I trust that you will keep it to yourself. I despise Hitler and how he has destroyed our German nation! I swear to you that I will do everything in my power to destroy him! I am anxious to begin working with Canaris."

Kurt stares into Reinhardt's eyes. "Dr. Reinhardt, all of our conversations will be kept in confidence. I assure you that you can trust me." Kurt knows what Reinhardt is trying to express. "My time here was very brief compared to your confinement, but I know what you mean about feeling safe. I know the people here are our enemy and they and their allies are bombing and killing German soldiers and civilians. Their bombs have killed my mother! The few Americans I met were kind, friendly, and displayed a moral character. That does not exist in my world. Perhaps someday I may return to Ocean View as a tourist."

They both laugh, and Reinhardt says, "Maybe I will join you!"

Emma and Wilmer make their way to Norfolk, Virginia. Military convoys pass them loaded with military cargo bound for the US freighters and the naval fleet docked there. Their escape plan has been given to them by Jacob Baden along with false passports and new identities. As soon as they arrive in Norfolk, they will board the Spanish freighter *Alfonso* taking mostly farm equipment to Brazil, but also a few passengers.

Wilmer had not expected to see a gated entry with an armed naval officer checking identification at the dock. He has to show his new driver's license. They are asked to stand next to the truck while it is searched. Emma is tense and shaking as the guard waves them in. Wilmer slowly passes cargo ships until he comes to the berth where the *Alfonso* is sitting. Emma opens the truck door and stands by the curb as Wilmer unloads their luggage.

"Emma, I will park this in the location Baden gave us. I will place the keys inside the engine, and Baden will retrieve it at his convenience. Stay here until I return."

Emma is slowly baking in the hot July sun. Twenty minutes later, she sees Wilmer quickly walking back toward her. She glares at him. "What took you so long?"

"I'm sorry! I thought I was being followed by two men. I think I lost them. Let's get moving."

Wilmer drags the two suitcases, and Emma carries a large handbag. They slowly walk down the pier toward the *Alfonso*, which is scheduled to sail around 4:00 this afternoon. They see the boarding area and move toward a large metal shed where the customs officials will check their documents. As they enter the shed, two men walk through the door and toward them.

Wilmer thinks, *Why are they wearing suits and ties?* He then realizes these are the men that were following him.

Both men, tall and very muscular, walk up to them. One points toward a larger building behind the boarding shed. "Please follow me."

Wilmer's fear is apparent, and he can hardly speak. "What about our luggage?"

"Just drop it here. It will be in good hands!"

Wilmer and Emma are led to a small office with a noisy fan blowing stale hot air. They are seated on two metal folding chairs. The older man asks to see their passports. "So, you are the Beckmans, and you are traveling to Brazil to visit a sick relative. Is that correct?" Emma's shaking is apparent, and she is sweating as she nods her head.

Wilmer takes a deep breath. "Yes, that is correct. Is something wrong?"

"Mr. and Mrs. Beckman, we are agents with the Federal Bureau of Investigation. We have received information that you may be a couple involved in a plot to free a German prisoner of war and conspiring with a German saboteur. You fit their description, and the truck you were driving is registered to a Wilmer Stickler residing in Ocean View, Delaware. Is there some mix-up here? Are you sure you are not the Sticklers?"

Emma grips her chair and looks at Wilmer. She has the wide-open eyes of fear and screams, "Wilmer, for God's sake, tell them the truth!"

After several hours of interrogation, the agent stands up and says sternly, "Both of you are under arrest for treason and conspiracy against the United States. Please follow me." Emma faints and falls off her chair as Wilmer tries to catch her.

# Kurt's Homecoming 1942

The *Dawn Riser* is slowly churning through the waves. Captain Richter thinks, *It's a beautiful day to do this kind of work. Clear blue skies and not much wind, and these guys are waiting for a submarine! This is crazy!* It's not quite noon when Richter is five miles out in the Atlantic and at the compass location given to him by Kurt. He takes his enormous cigar out of his mouth and yells above the engine noise to Kurt, "We are at the location you gave me. I will circle until we see something."

Kurt gets his binoculars from his bag and moves to the front of the boat. Richter also has his binoculars scanning the horizon. It has been almost one hour since they arrived at the rendezvous site, and Kurt is beginning to worry. Suddenly, the Captain sees the sub surfacing on the starboard side. "I see it, and it's moving toward us. I'll kill the engine, and they can come up next to us."

Slowly, the sub moves closer, and Kurt can almost touch it. Two German sailors lift the hatch and move along the deck of the sub toward the *Dawn Riser.* They tell Richter to throw them his docking rope. The *Dawn Riser* is secured to the sub, and just that fast, Kurt and Dr. Reinhardt are aboard U-202. Kurt is still dragging his duffel bag and hands it off to one of the sailors. When they are safely aboard, the sailors throw the rope back to Richter. Kurt, Reinhardt, and the two sailors enter the hatch and make their way into the sub. They are taken to the same bunk area Kurt occupied on the trip over from France. He looks at Reinhardt. "Welcome to your new home for the next three weeks. It's not spacious, and you will not feel the ocean breeze. You will have a lot of time to reflect on what waits ahead."

Kurt can feel the sub slowly descending, and it soon levels out. He and Reinhardt are sitting in their bunks when the sub shakes and they can hear in the distance a faint explosion. Kurt thinks it could be another depth charge attack, but there were no American Naval ships in sight. Reinhardt looks around and asks one of the sailors standing nearby, "What was that? Are we under attack?"

The sailor smiles. "That was one of our torpedoes hitting the boat you just left. Direct orders from our captain. I guess we needed some target practice."

Kurt thinks, *My God, Richter's dead!*

The long ride back to the harbor in Lorient, France is a monotonous routine mixed with an occasional torpedo attack on unsuspecting Allied vessels as the Atlantic sea war continues. U-202 is on the surface at night and underwater during the day. Several days of high seas make for an uncomfortable ride, and Kurt notices that the sub is not riding as smooth as it did on the way over. Even some of the hardened crew are seasick, as is Dr. Reinhardt. The footing is treacherous with falls, stumbles, and split heads.

Kurt has a hard time sleeping, and when he is just lying in his bunk, his mind is on McKenna. He thinks of his brief time with her and how good she made him feel. He thinks of the twists and turns his life has taken and wonders what she will think when she discovers what has happened at the Stickler farm. He thinks, *I am glad that I left when I did. I think I was falling in love with her! Soon, she will know the truth about me! I'll always remember our kiss!*

Kurt and Dr. Reinhardt are summoned to the small cabin of Captain Gretner. Kurt introduces Reinhardt to the captain, and they shake hands. "Welcome back to Germany! The Fuehrer has sent greetings and well wishes to you. Kurt, he and Admiral Canaris also congratulate you for your successful mission."

Kurt asks Gretner if he has any information about the Dasch team who landed in New York. "Their mission seems to have been compromised. I was told that Dasch and his team have been arrested. Both of you must now relax as best you can and decompress. I know you will be extremely busy when you are back on German soil."

# Understanding the Question Marks 1942

Late Thursday evening, July 9, at the Miller farm on Woodland Avenue, everyone is trying to understand and process the events of the day. They can't believe what has taken place in such a beautiful, tranquil part of Delaware. A crowd begins to assemble on Jeff and Lori's front yard as word of the abduction of a German POW by a German saboteur spreads throughout the community. Jason and Marna LaPlante have arrived along with former Senator Townsend. The Crosby family is also there along with local law enforcement and Army and Coast Guard military personnel. The Ocean City police chief is there concerning the explosion and sinking of a fishing boat. John Townsend has been gathering information since late afternoon when he received a call from Lieutenant Johnson at the Bear Trap POW camp. Two FBI agents have arrived as well. They have searched the Sticklers' farmhouse and barn.

Townsend asks Lori and Jeff if he, along with the other officials, may use their house to sort through the facts and establish a timeline. Townsend asks the group to give them some time to get the details in order before he will provide an update as soon as possible based on the information they have collected.

About 20 people are gathered on the front porch and in the front yard. Jeff is being asked all kinds of questions from his curious neighbors. Jeff stands at the top of the steps and asks the crowd to gather around.

McKenna moves close to her father. She still can't believe what she is hearing.

"I know everyone is anxious to know what happened today, so let me tell you what I can."

Jeff reminds the crowd that Bear Trap POWs were working at several farms in the Ocean View area. He also mentions that the Sticklers were being used by the Army at Bear Trap as German translators.

"From what we've been told, it appears that our neighbors, Emma and Wilmer Stickler, became involved with a group of German sympathizers who had connections with Adolf Hitler and other German military intelligence officials. A few weeks ago, June 14 from what we can tell, a German submarine landed a German saboteur on the beach near the Indian River Inlet just north of Bethany. He eventually made his way to their farm, and they introduced him as their nephew who was, we were told, visiting from Baltimore. All along, it was the plan of this German agent to secure the release of a German scientist from the Bear Trap POW camp and return him to Germany. We were totally fooled and had no idea a German spy was living next to us. They had a wireless transmitter hidden in the barn so they could establish a radio link to Berlin. We even invited him to dinner at our house, and our daughter showed him around Bethany. This morning, the spy overpowered several of the prisoners who were supposed to be working on the Stickler farm along with their guard—and Wilmer helped him. They were tied up in Wilmer's barn soon after they arrived this morning. When the

Army truck came around 4:00 this afternoon to pick them up, they realized what had happened. Emma, Wilmer, the spy and the German scientist all left in Wilmer's truck. They hightailed it out of here about 7:30 this morning. That's about all I know at this point."

Jason LaPlante is standing next to Jeff. "Does anyone know where the Sticklers or this spy could be hiding? Could they still be in the Bethany area? I can't believe that Emma and Wilmer were involved in something this sinister and unpatriotic. They have committed treason against our country. They just decided to walk away from their farm to help old Adolf! That is incredible!"

As the sun is setting, Townsend and Lieutenant Johnson along with the other officials come out of the house and see that a large crowd has gathered. Jeff tells Townsend that he has told them what he could. Townsend says, "The Army and the FBI are taking the lead on this, so Lieutenant Johnson will fill in some of the question marks that may help explain what Jeff told you."

Lieutenant Johnson steps forward and takes a deep breath. He restates much of the information Jeff shared. "I heard a question about where the Sticklers may be. The FBI just gave us an update on them. This morning, they left here and drove the spy and the scientist to Ocean City. They left their passengers on the dock near the Ocean City Inlet to board a fishing boat belonging to a Captain Richter. Having dropped them off, they drove to Norfolk, Virginia and attempted to board a freighter that was taking farm equipment to Brazil. They both were arrested as they were about to board and are now being held by the FBI in Norfolk. I am told that J. Edgar Hoover and the President have been briefed. We have to assume that the spy and the scientist had a successful rendezvous with a submarine just a few miles off of Ocean City. We are also told that Captain Richter and his boat, the *Dawn Riser*, cannot be located. There are unconfirmed reports that there was an explosion seen in the general area where we think his boat would have been. The Coast Guard is searching the area."

The crowd slowly trickles away. Near midnight, Jeff, Lori and McKenna sit together at the long kitchen table. Jeff stares out the window. "What an unbelievable day it has been. I can't wait to let Tristan know all the details."

Lori walks over to the stove and brings the coffee pot over to the table. "Thank God no one was killed or injured. McKenna said she saw the pistol that Paul had in the barn, and we had soldiers here with rifles. It could have been a massacre! Paul was a very good actor. Can you believe our daughter was alone with him!"

McKenna is still very upset and emotional. "The funny thing is, I really liked Paul. He seemed genuine. When I was with him, he was kind, gentle, and a really sweet guy. He loved music. I think this is the first time in my life that someone has truly deceived me. I thought I was a pretty good judge of someone's character. I would never have guessed in a million years that he was a German spy."

Jeff is animated as he stands up and walks toward Lori. "Well, I don't want to say, 'I told you so,' but I told you so. I knew he had some kind of accent, but no one would believe me. I really didn't buy the asthma medical deferment story. McKenna, you are so lucky that he didn't hurt you or take you as a hostage. Can you believe that Roosevelt and J. Edgar Hoover now know about a small farm on Woodland Avenue in Ocean View, Delaware! There is something else I don't understand. We have towers on the beach with guards, horses and patrol dogs, and somehow a German sub can land a spy on our beach. I guess it's all about timing! All of this is just unbelievable!"

# Arrival in Lorient, France 1942

August 3, 1942. U-202 slowly lumbers into the Lorient harbor and moves into its concrete housing pen. Major Raymond Mueller is waiting for them as Kurt and Dr. Reinhardt disembark. Kurt introduces Reinhardt to Mueller as he shakes his hand. "Hope the ride back to France went well. Follow me to my office, and I will give you both an update."

Kurt is back in the same warehouse building where he previously met Mueller prior to boarding U-202. Mueller hands both Kurt and Reinhardt a stack of papers in tan folders. He looks at Reinhardt. "Doctor, your family has been notified regarding your return to Germany, and we have made arrangements for them to meet you in Berlin tomorrow afternoon. The Fuehrer will meet with you there, and then I am told that you will then return to Peenemunde. Kurt, you will travel with him to Berlin and then meet with Admiral Canaris. You need to leave Lorient quickly. Just three days ago, the Allies bombed the harbor here for the first time. We are now moving much of the fleet away from here with the exception of our submarines."

Kurt and Reinhardt are led to a bunker which houses German officials, a short walk from the harbor. They enter a small, windowless room with two beds, a sofa, a bath, and a nightstand with a phone. The overhead light barely brightens the room. Kurt throws his duffel bag and papers on the bed and flops into the chair. Reinhardt sits next to him. He notices that some civilian clothes have been hung in the closet. Kurt sees that a new uniform is placed in his.

Reinhardt takes a deep breath and looks at Kurt. "Can I be truthful with you? When you spend three weeks in a submarine with someone, you really get to know them. I know that you are still grieving about the loss of your mother, and please know that you have my sincere condolences. What a beautiful person she must have been. I think you know how I feel about Hitler, and I know that you share the same feelings. Perhaps my confession to you will cost me my life, but I do think I can trust you. So, can we be candid and open about where this war will take us?"

Kurt straightens up and sits erect. "Dr. Reinhardt, first let me tell you that I have great respect for you. I know that you and I are in similar positions due to the tragic circumstances this war has visited upon us. I can't reveal certain specifics, but I can tell you that there is a group of conspirators within the military who have and will continue to make the effort to assassinate the Fuehrer. You might remember the attempt in November of 1939 when a bomb exploded during his speech in Munich. We were so close, but he left the hall and was in his car just as the bomb detonated. For the good of Germany and for world peace, I do want him dead, and I will do whatever is necessary to make that happen."

"Kurt, you are brave to be willing to lay down your life to eliminate this monster. Can you believe I will meet with him tomorrow? Maybe I should strap a bomb to my stomach?"

Kurt smiles. "I think Canaris has other plans that may be more appropriate, so maybe we don't need you to do that."

"Kurt, please tell Admiral Canaris that I am anxious to be part of his anti-Hitler movement. I know he will be able to contact me."

August 13, 1942. Canaris is back at his office in Berlin, having just visited the German consulate in Madrid, Spain. Kurt arrives for his meeting and is told that Canaris will be with him shortly and to take a seat. On the other side of the room, a young German in an army uniform is sitting and playing with his watch. Kurt recognizes him from his time at the sabotage school in Brandenburg. Werner von Horne was a few beds down from Kurt's. He remembers him from the bomb making and self-defense instruction. Kurt sits down next to him, and Werner has a surprised look as he extends his hand.

"Kurt Wagner, good to see you again! Are you meeting with Canaris as well? What have you been doing since we last saw each other?"

"I am. I just had a quick mission to free a POW from a camp in the US."

"Hope that was successful. Were you on the same submarine as George Dasch? I heard that his mission failed and he and his team were arrested in New York. Are you aware of that? The Fuehrer has been saying that he will soon have his storm troopers in America. So, I guess you were testing the waters?"

"Yes, I just heard about that when I returned. I was very lucky. My mission was successful. What have you been doing?"

"I just returned from Spain. I was with Admiral Canaris on a quick trip to Madrid. Top secret, but I know he will tell you all about it."

The desk clerk comes over to them. "The admiral will see you now."

They enter the large office, and Canaris is seated at his conference table. They salute him, and he points them toward two chairs next to him. He stands and walks over and secures the lock on his door. "Please consider our conversation top secret. If you don't know, Germany is in a critical state. Despite what the Fuehrer has stated, we are losing the war on the Russian front, and I fear an Allied invasion will soon begin. Kurt, Werner and I just returned from Spain. My goal while there was to contact our defectors who are now working with the French, Italian, and German resistance in England. They will provide assistance, and we must move quickly to eliminate Hitler and overthrow this Nazi government. This *coup d'état* must be successful. I know you will be in grave danger. I also know that you share my hatred for the Fuehrer. The number of my co-conspirators is growing, and I think we have reached a critical mass. I have handpicked a very select group of trusted members of our military intelligence team. There are 10 more men from the Intelligence School, and all 12 of you will meet tomorrow to begin planning and designate assignments. The codename for the group is the Apostles. Werner, you will be in charge of the group. Your codename is Peter. Kurt, you will back up Werner, and you will be called Andrew."

Werner and Kurt smile, and Werner makes the sign of the cross. Werner notices that Canaris has a small grin. "Admiral, if we are the Apostles, then your codename will be Jesus."

"Please, let's not take His name in vain. My codename will be the Shepherd." Canaris blesses himself. "I pray every day that He guides me along the right path and forgives the sins that I have committed in service to the Reich. Our success will depend on divine intervention! Kurt, glad you are back on German soil. My gratitude for your successful mission and the return of Dr. Reinhardt. As you know, he is on our team. I knew you would be successful. Also, a new promotion for you to lieutenant."

The next day, at 2:00 in the afternoon in Canaris' conference room, all 12 German intelligence officers are gathered around the conference room table. When the Shepherd walks in, they stand. Instead of the Nazi salute, they see that Canaris places his hand over his heart.

"Our group will not profess the *Heil* Hitler salute. Hand over heart will signify our select group. Please be seated. As you are aware, this group has been handpicked by me for one of the most important missions in German history. I know each of you are committed to this effort. The Fuehrer and his cohorts must be removed. We must seek a peace treaty with the Allies. While each of you are equals, for military purposes, I have asked Lieutenant Werner von Horne to be the team leader and Lieutenant Kurt Wagner will be second in command. We must show the world that not all Germans are butchers and barbarians. I have many co-conspirators, but my closest ally is my deputy, General Hans Oster. I have given him a list, so he has your names. The codename of this group will be the Apostles. My codename is the Shepherd. Most of you have met Oster, and he will be meeting with us as soon as he returns from Casablanca. You should also be aware that Himmler is on our side. We are about to commit high treason for the sake of our country. If we are successful, thousands of lives will be saved. We must show the world that there are Germans that do have a moral conscience and barbarism will not be tolerated. Our efforts to kill him will be at a high cost. Arrest and execution are real possibilities, but we must try. The future of our Fatherland demands it. The British, the US, and even Pope Pius XII will be supporting us. All the pieces are coming together, and I am confident that we will be successful."

Canaris sees the grave look on the faces of these young men. "If any of you have the slightest reservation concerning the mission of this group, please excuse yourself now. I will respect your decision, and I will find an appropriate reassignment." There are glances around the table, but no one leaves.

Canaris looks at each one. "As you know, the Fuehrer spends

most of his time now at the *Wolfsschanze* (the Wolf's Lair, located near Rastenburg, East Prussia). On occasion, he will venture out, and that is when we will have our best opportunity for assassination. I have been asked by Himmler to assign four of you to a security detail at the Wolf's Lair. The following Apostles will be stationed there within the next five days: Andrew (Kurt), James, John, and Phillip. Himmler indicated that the four of you will be assigned as drivers and security detail for the Fuehrer. Peter (Werner), you will work with me and the other Apostles here in Berlin concerning strategy, planning and special projects. Andrew (Kurt), we will be in touch with you concerning next steps. This team will be successful. My thanks, and you are free to leave."

As Kurt is walking toward the door, he hears Canaris, "Kurt, may I see you in my office?"

Kurt follows Canaris down the hall and into his office. "Kurt, have a seat." Canaris pulls up his chair next to Kurt. He has a grave look as he places his hand on Kurt's arm.

"Kurt, I have bad news. It saddens me to tell you that your father was killed two days ago in an artillery barrage outside of Stalingrad. They tell me he was leading his troops toward a cluster of houses when the shell landed within 20 meters of where he was. He was buried in a mass grave nearby. I will try to get more details for you and will pass them along. He was a good man and the perfect soldier. As you know, he was also a very close friend of mine. He will be missed, and you have my sincere condolences."

Kurt sits motionless, and his face is ashen, but no tears. "My God, I knew he was in danger. For some reason, I always thought he would return unharmed. I envisioned a time when peace returned and we would enjoy each other's company. First Mother, and now Father. I hold Hitler responsible for both of their deaths. If you are looking for an assassin, I am first in line!"

Five days later, Kurt is now stationed at the Wolf's Lair in Rastenburg, East Prussia. The location is top secret. It is built in a vast forest and encompasses 12.5 square miles. Kurt is surprised to learn that over 2,000 soldiers and civilians live and work there, mostly in underground bunkers. The stone buildings are heavily camouflaged with bushes, grass and artificial trees planted on the flat roofs. From the air, it is unnoticeable and looks like a vast woodland.

Kurt and his three associates are greeted by Major Raymond Hintenach, codename Judas. Most of the military personnel at the Wolf's Lair are members of the SS under Himmler's command. Hintenach is a member of the SS and reports directly to Himmler and has been one of Hitler's bodyguards. He is also one of the conspirators working with Canaris, Himmler and Oster.

Hintenach shows them to their assigned barracks. Hintenach is large in stature and wears wire rim glasses which fit snugly over his ears. "Tomorrow at 7:00 a.m., I will take you to the bunker where the Fuehrer has his breakfast. You will be introduced, and you will escort him on his morning walk with his German Shepherd, Blondi. You speak only when spoken to. You do *not* touch, pet or talk to his dog. You will follow him but from a distance of approximately 20 feet. I will accompany you for the first day. Tomorrow afternoon, I will drive you around the grounds here. You will have two Mercedes at your disposal for transporting the Fuehrer. There is also a small airfield and a rail siding here. You will drive either Hitler, Himmler or one of his generals. You will also provide escort security. I will brief you each morning regarding your daily responsibilities. There is a lot of protocol for you to learn, and there can be no missteps."

As the weeks move on, Kurt and the other three Apostles have met and talked with Hitler on multiple occasions. They have taken him to the airfield several times and have accompanied him to Berlin for meetings at the Reich Chancellery. The Fuehrer seems to like them, and they have become his primary security detail. He has even given Kurt permission to pet Blondi.

Kurt is busy with his new assignment and realizes that, at some point in the near future, his job will be to help assassinate the Fuehrer. This thought is constantly with him. The death of his parents also weighs heavy on him. He feels lonely and isolated, and he wonders if his demise is quickly closing in on him. He also thinks constantly about McKenna and their brief time together. She was so unlike any other women he has met. *It was good that I left when I did. I would love to see her again. Maybe after the war is over I could return to Ocean View.*

# McKenna's Letter to Paul
# 1942

McKenna will never forget July 9$^{th}$. She was looking forward to her summer vacation and helping her parents on the farm, hanging out with her friends. Just another laidback summer in Ocean View.

All that changed. Since the incident with Paul, she has really been depressed. She still can't believe he was a German saboteur! A few of her friends from Salisbury have been by to cheer her up, but all she can focus on is her brief time with Paul and the secret feelings she had for him. In the evenings, she wants to be alone. She takes long rides on her horse until the sun sets, or she spends time just sitting on the beach and staring at the waves. She can't get Paul off her mind. How could someone so sweet, so handsome, so caring, betray her?

As the summer winds down, Jeff and Lori are worried about her. One evening when she returns from the beach, Lori is waiting by the door. "McKenna, can we talk? Here, let's sit down." She motions toward the sofa. Lori sits next to her and places her arm on McKenna's shoulder.

"Dad and I can see that you are depressed. You're hiding from us. You're not eating, and you just mope around. You should reconnect with your friends, and we think you should start playing piano again in Baltimore, like you were doing with Brian, Joey and Michael before the semester ended. I know it is all about Paul."

McKenna begins to cry. "Mom, this all seems surreal! He quickly appeared. He was here for a few weeks and then takes a submarine back to Germany! This is a movie scene or a chapter in a novel that I can't comprehend. When he was here, you and I talked about what a nice young man he was. I loved being with him and wanted to spend more time with him. I actually felt that maybe this was someone I could fall in love with. He really swept me off my feet!"

Lori sits closer and gives her a gentle hug. "McKenna, life is full of surprises. You are young and beautiful, and you will fall in love. Sometimes, here at the beach, we feel disconnected from this tragic world war, but it has touched all of us in different ways. Now the war has touched you in a very personal and dramatic way. You've got to forget him. You will be back in class soon, and this will be a busy senior year for you. You will be student teaching and involved in all kinds of activities. Things will get better. I promise!"

"Mom, thank you for the pep talk. I love you. I will get over this, but it will take some time. See you in the morning."

McKenna walks up the stairs to her bedroom, turns on the light, and closes the door. She walks over to her nightstand, opens the top drawer, and reaches for her diary. She pages through the year and finds a blank page. She begins to write a letter to Paul.

*Paul, I know that you will never see me again and will never see this letter. Hopefully by writing this, I will feel better. They say you can never mend a broken heart. Let me start by saying that I think I was falling in love with you. The kiss we shared will never be forgotten. I was hoping our relationship would grow and there would be other kisses, but that will never happen.*

*When I look around the streets of Bethany, I see young men in American military uniforms, including my brother and other close friends of mine. Then I picture you with your pistol, killing them. How horrible to envision the kind, caring person I briefly knew, killing for some crazed monster named Adolf. You have turned my safe little world upside down! Everything you told me was a lie. You betrayed my trust in you.*

*Remember that day when we were sitting on the beach and I told you I was writing a song? I wanted to share with you the opening line: "Once in your life, you will find that one person who captures your heart." I was talking about you! I felt so close to you. Sadly, your life is one of lies and deception. You must be heartless and a man with no feelings. My prayer is that you may, at some time in your life, learn to love.*

*I know that someday I will find peace, love, and happiness and maybe I will forgive you ... someday?*

# Assassination Attempt 1943

On March 10, 1943, Judas (Hintenach) summons the four Apostles to his private office in one of the deep bunkers at the Wolf's Lair. He hands each a piece of paper which outlines a trip the Fuehrer will take on March 21 to Berlin.

Hintenach has a penetrating stare. "Canaris and Himmler have agreed that this is our best opportunity. This paper outlines the tentative plan. Hitler will travel to Berlin to view an exhibition of captured Soviet weaponry at the *Zeughaus* (old arsenal). The Fuehrer will fly into Berlin the morning of the 21st. We will fly in the day before. We will drive three Mercedes to the chancellery building and take him directly to the arsenal. We will have the lead car, the car carrying Hitler along with two members of the SS and the trail car. Kurt and I will be in the trail car. We will bring the cars to the back entrance of the *Zeughaus*. Kurt will be the shooter as Hitler exits his car and walks toward the entrance. When the work is done, I will drive Kurt to Rostock to board a small British plane that will take both of us to England. Canaris has made arrangements to transport the remaining Apostles to Bremen to board a trawler and from there to Lisbon. We will have a more detailed briefing on March 19. That is the day Canaris and Oster will be here to meet with Himmler."

On March 20, Kurt, Hintenach and the other three Apostles fly from the Wolf's Lair to Berlin. They spend the day in seclusion, rehearsing the plan that will unfold. On the morning of the 21st, Kurt is tired and had a sleepless night. He pulls on his uniform and steadies his hand as he places his pistol in his holster. He will join the other Apostles for breakfast. Hintenach knocks on his door.

"This is it. This will be a historical day for you, one that you and the world will always remember. Are you ready? You look sick!"

"I am sick and not really hungry! Let's go meet the others."

The plan calls for all three black Mercedes to be in front of the Reich Chancellery building at two in the afternoon to transport Hitler to the *Zeughaus*, a ride of only 15 minutes. The plans have been slightly altered with two Apostles in the lead car, an SS soldier driving Hitler with one other SS soldier as security, and Kurt driving the trail car along with Hintenach. Kurt wasn't planning on the SS guards escorting Hitler from the car and into the building.

At exactly 2:00, Hitler walks out of the sprawling chancellery building and toward his car. The two SS guards walk one on each side of him. One opens the door, and quickly Hitler is alone in the back seat. One guard drives, and the other sits next to him. The motorcade moves slowly through the streets of Berlin, swastikas flying from the bumpers. Hintenach can see that Kurt is shaking as he grips the steering wheel. Kurt can see the back of the Fuehrer's head through the rear window.

"I was surprised that Hitler wanted the SS to drive him. I was counting on the Apostles to do that. That just raised our risk level!"

"Just settle down. We will be fine. Focus on the plan. It will all be over in a matter of seconds."

The motorcade passes in front of the arsenal, turns the corner, and moves toward the more secure back entrance. Several civilians and armed military are standing there along with Canaris and Himmler. The walk from Hitler's car to the entrance is no more than 50 feet. The Mercedes vehicles stop with engines running. Hitler's security guard exits the car and moves to open the back door. Hitler slowly slides off the seat, stands next to the guard, and straightens his uniform. He stands still, looks around, sniffs the air, and begins to walk alongside his SS guard toward the entrance.

Kurt is watching and unbuckles the strap on his holster. He grips his pistol and quickly exits the car. Hintenach slides over into the driver's seat. Kurt moves in front of his Mercedes, takes his shooter's stance with legs apart, arms outstretched, and fires toward Hitler. Hitler's SS driver sees Kurt pointing his pistol and honks his horn. Just then, the SS security guard next to Hitler quickly turns and shoves Hitler, pushing him to the pavement. The guard falls on top of Hitler, bleeding from a head wound. Kurt fires three more shots toward Hitler and the guard and then runs back toward his car. The other SS security guard is now firing back. Kurt feels a bullet hit his shoulder as he dives into his car and slams the door. Another bullet hits the windshield and rips into the back seat.

Hintenach pulls away, slams first gear, and accelerates into traffic. Kurt is holding his shoulder. Hintenach quickly glances at Kurt.

"I think you killed the SS guard but you missed Hitler. How bad are you hurt?"

Kurt can feel the blood running down his arm and onto the seat of the car. "Don't know. Hurts and a lot of blood." His face is etched in pain.

Raymond will avoid the main roads and drive toward the city of Rostock, 140 miles north of Berlin, on the Baltic Sea. Once in Rostock, they will drive to a small bakery owned by a husband and wife who are in the German Resistance. It sits among a group of shops on a sleepy side street on the fringe of the city. The bakery will provide rest and shelter until nightfall. As Raymond drives the three hours to Rostock, he sees that Kurt is in much pain as he tries to sleep. Much of this part of Germany has been recently bombed by the RAF. There are trucks, cars and people walking with carts full of house goods and clothing, heading south toward Berlin.

The Mercedes navigates through the very empty city. Raymond pulls the car behind Heffner's *Backerei* (Bakery). The Heffner's have been vetted by Canaris. Mrs. Heffner is sitting on a wooden chair on the sidewalk behind the bakery and jumps up when she sees the black Mercedes. She opens the door of the garage, and Raymond slowly moves the car into the tight space.

Kurt is staggering as he makes his way out of the car, a trail of blood following him. He and Hintenach follow her up the back stairs to her apartment, which sits above the bakery. She was a nurse during the Great War and tended to many gunshot wounds. She points Kurt toward a small sofa.

"Here, let's take your shirt off so I can take a look. Do you mind if I ask your name? I'm Nita, and my husband is Wilhelm."

Kurt lays on the sofa and grimaces as she pulls off his shirt. He looks at her with a dazed stare and glassy eyes. "My name is Kurt. My partner is Raymond. Thank you for helping us. How bad is the wound?"

"Let me take a good look and clean you up."

Nita gets a basin of hot water, several small cloths, and alcohol. She cleans the deep gash on his left shoulder and probes the wound with a small wooden knife. From her first aid kit, she finds gauze, cotton balls and tape, as she packs the wound.

She gives Kurt one of Wilhelm's clean shirts. "Let me help you put this on. You are one very lucky young man. Thank God the bullet only grazed you and did not enter. There is a deep gash but nothing fatal! Take this pill and drink this water. Try to get some sleep. When you arrive in England, have a doctor look at it."

Nita makes hot tea and hands a cup to Hintenach. Kurt is fast asleep as she covers him with a blanket. At 6:00, Wilhelm closes the bakery and makes his way up the stairs. He pulls up a chair next to Nita and Raymond. Wilhelm watches Kurt sleep on the sofa. "So, tell me how the operation went? Looks like your man took a bullet. Is our Fuehrer still among us, or should I send flowers?"

"Not as we expected. Kurt was the shooter, and he missed Hitler and hit his SS guard. Maybe next time. Canaris will be very disappointed! Rostock looks empty. Houses boarded up, shops closed, but you are still baking?"

"The Navy still has a few ships here. They have to feed their sailors, so I mainly bake for them. They may pull anchor at any time. I had only two customers all day. We had several bombing raids here over the last month, so everyone wants to get out before they level Rostock just like the attacks on Bremen. I'm thankful the navy buys from me!"

"So, Wilhelm, tell me about the plan for tonight. Is the RAF plane still on schedule?"

"We are ready. I was on the wireless last night with London. At 10:00 tonight, I will take you and your friend in my bakery truck to a farm very close to here that belongs to my daughters and their husbands. It is almost 400,000 square meters (100 acres), and the RAF has landed there before. If the weather is kind to us, you will be on your way. Depending on the plane the RAF sends, you should be eating your breakfast in England!"

At exactly 10:00 p.m., Kurt, Hintenach and Wilhelm make

their way down the steps and into the garage. Wilhelm opens the doors and steps into the desolate street shrouded in darkness. The three make their way around the corner and see the bakery truck sitting by itself in a small parking lot. Wilhelm opens the back door, and Hintenach jumps in and gives Kurt his hand. They sit on the floor in the darkness. Kurt reaches over and touches Hintenach's arm.

"Are you sure that one of my bullets didn't hit the Fuehrer? When the SS guard honked his horn, that's when he turned and saw me with my pistol pointed at him. Bad timing on my part. I know Canaris is livid. Maybe he will cancel our plane ride to London?"

"Don't think about it. You did exactly as was planned and paid the price. It's impossible to control the unexpected, no matter how good your plan is. The good news is we are leaving Germany!"

Wilhelm pulls out into the empty roadway and takes them to the farm. The truck makes its way down a long dirt drive lined with trees and pulls up to a large, stately stone home. It is a clear night with a small moon. Wilhelm's daughters are sitting on the porch, and there is a farm tractor with a wagon full of firewood sitting next to the house. Wilhelm stops the truck as his daughters hurry down the steps to greet him. Wilhelm has a nervous look.

"We've got to move fast. I've got two in the truck."

His daughters, Christine and Joanne, give him a quick hug and kiss. They walk with him to the back of the truck. Christine motions toward the tractor and her husband. "Let's get them in the wagon. Robert will drive the tractor to the landing area. He will light four fires. If the pilot doesn't see the fires, he will not land. Father, you better get back home to Mother! All will be well here. We know the drill. Is the Fuehrer dead?"

Wilhelm shakes his head with a disgusted look as he opens

the back door of the truck. Kurt and Raymond climb down and follow him over to the farm tractor. Joanne hands Raymond a flashlight. The plane should arrive near midnight if all goes according to the plan. If there is a major bombing raid tonight over this part of Germany, the plane will not land.

The tractor bounces along the smoothed-out fields ready for spring planting. Robert tells them that the landing zone is tucked behind a rolling hillside. Kurt and Hintenach jump off the tractor and sit next to a large tree as Robert squares out the landing strip with the four fires burning on its corners. Robert heads back to where Kurt and Raymond are sitting. "I've got four good fires burning, so the pilot shouldn't have any problem locating us. Wilhelm gave them compass coordinates last night when he was in contact with them. The RAF pilots are well trained for these pickups. When we hear the plane, jump in the back of the wagon, and I will take you over to it. The three of us will turn the plane around for takeoff. You jump in, and off you go. The last time we did this, a German patrol fired at the plane as it was trying to land! The pilot aborted, but we were successful a week later. So, you never know what to expect. Keep your fingers crossed."

Kurt stands to stretch his legs and walks over to Robert. "Do you know what type of aircraft they use for these pickups?"

"I think it will be the Westland Lysander. It is perfect for short-field landings on rough terrain but can carry no more than two and the pilot. It's hard to see it when it lands. It's painted all black with no lights. Just before he is touching down, he will turn on his landing lights. There is a fixed ladder over the port side for you to climb, and then you both will squeeze into the rear cockpit. They only do this within a week of a full moon, so your timing is perfect! The pilot has no navigation equipment, only a map and compass. Interesting about the name 'Lysander.'

That is from Greek mythology. Lysander was the name of the Spartan general."

"You did your homework on the aircraft!"

Robert nods his head. "My father was a pilot in the Luftwaffe, and I fell in love with airplanes!"

Just then, the three stand motionless in complete silence. Kurt asks Robert, "Did you hear that?"

"Yes, I think that is your plane. Get in the wagon!"

The plane flies low over the field and lands exactly in the middle of the four signal fires. It lands hard and bumps along the rutted field. The plane stops with the engine running. Kurt and Raymond jump out of the wagon and run over to the plane with Robert trailing them. The three of them quickly push and maneuver the Lysander into position for take-off. They shake hands with Robert and step onto the ladder as the pilot slides back the canopy.

The pilot speaks a little textbook German to them and is surprised when Kurt speaks to him in English. "Yes, we are with the German Resistance and anxious to help the Allied war effort!"

The pilot looks over his shoulder as the plane picks up speed for take-off. "Welcome aboard! Next stop, damp and chilly Newmarket, England."

Raymond, who doesn't speak English, taps Kurt on the shoulder. "What did he say?"

# British Military Intelligence 1943

Dawn is breaking as the plane makes it descent to the small airfield in Newmarket, Suffolk, England. It taxis to the end of the runway, and three RAF jeeps pull up next to the plane. The pilot unlocks their cockpit, and a strong wind greets Raymond and Kurt.

"Gentlemen, welcome to England! Thank God all went according to plan and you can now begin your work with the Allies! Great to have you as passengers!"

They shake the pilot's hand and climb down the ladder. A tall, well decorated Royal Air Force captain greets them along with a German translator.

"Gentlemen, once again welcome! I am Captain Leimbach, and this is my German translator and aide-de-camp, Lieutenant Jon Becker. My papers indicate that you are Lieutenant Kurt Wagner, and you must be Major Raymond Hintenach." Lieutenant Becker translates to Kurt and Hintenach.

"We will show you to your quarters and get you some breakfast, a shower and a change of clothes. You will spend the afternoon with us and our interrogators. I am sure you have a lot to tell us. Your pilot radioed to us that one of you suffered a bullet wound in an assassination attempt on Hitler. Is that correct?"

Kurt raises his hand and replies in English, "Yes, that is correct. I am the one with the bullet wound. The major here is the one who needs the translator."

"We will have our doctor look at you before we start the questioning."

At 3:00 in the afternoon on March 22, 1943, Kurt and Raymond are led to a small office carved into a sprawling metal aircraft hangar next to the runway. It is raining with heavy wind, and the building rattles. Inside the office, they are greeted by Captain Leimbach, Lieutenant Becker, two women in RAF uniforms and one other man in a beautifully tailored London suit. One of the women is working on a large magnetic tape recorder, and the other is busy writing on her steno pad.

"Gentlemen, we will keep you here for only a few hours this afternoon. I know you have had a long day. We wanted to quickly get some important background information about yesterday's assassination attempt while the details are still fresh."

Kurt and Raymond brief them about all the months at the Wolf's Lair and the work of the Apostles, including the leadership of Admiral Canaris in the German Resistance. Leimbach wants to know names, ranks, and locations of the Apostles, but the major questioning comes from the man in the suit, who is handsome with an aristocratic face. He focuses on Admiral Canaris and his involvement with Spain. He also wants to know what the Abwehr knew about the Allies' planning for the D-Day invasion.

Questioning continues for all the following day. Kurt and Raymond are surprised that the man in the suit is not part of today's conversation. After a long afternoon, Leimbach pushes back his chair and stretches as he stands. He moves toward Kurt and Raymond.

"Thank you for your information and your patience. We have decided that it may be more productive to move both of you to London to work with British Military Intelligence MI6. We will give you two days to catch up on your sleep, then we will motorcar you to your new location."

Leimbach hands them a letter-sized manila envelope. "Here is information concerning the London location of your apartment and the location of your office. Also, you will find some spending money for your miscellaneous needs. As you would expect, all of this is top secret and highly classified, including the location of your apartment and your office in London."

Kurt and Raymond share a small room in a brick building behind the aircraft hangar. That evening after eating in the dining hall, Kurt enters their room and finds a British newspaper lying on his bed. On the front page, he sees the bold heading, "Hitler Assassination Attempt Fails." He jumps on his bed, props up his pillow, and is surprised to read all the details that unfolded on March 21. Kurt looks at Raymond. "Let me read this to you! It is the story we told them yesterday. Remarkably accurate!"

A few days later, they arrive in London and settle into a small apartment within walking distance to their office located within an old rundown building located at 54 Broadway. On the first morning of their arrival, they notice a large sign hanging over a double door entrance. It reads, *Kensington Fire Extinguisher Company.* Kurt re-reads his directions. "This has got to be the place."

The door is locked, but they see a telephone hanging next to the entrance. Kurt picks up the receiver, and the phone is answered by a male voice. "May I help you?" According to the instructions, Kurt answers, "Yes, I am here to deliver new fire extinguishers."

"Yes, we are ready for them. Please take them to the rear loading dock and ring the bell."

Kurt and Raymond walk around the block to the rear entrance and ring the bell. The door slowly opens, and a young man in a tie and sport coat motions them in. "May I see your papers?" Kurt and Raymond nod yes and hand the man their identity papers. He looks at their photographs and fingerprints as he examines their documents.

"Welcome to England. Please follow me."

They walk down a dimly lit hall and enter a creaky lift that takes them to the third floor. They follow the young man as he walks into a large, open office area. It is a very busy place with telephones and typewriters and people on the move from office to office. They are led down a maze of hallways. The young man stops and knocks on an office door. As the door slowly opens, Kurt looks surprised as he sees the man in the suit from the previous days of interrogation at the airfield in Newmarket.

"Please come in. Good to see you again. In the way of introductions, my name is Thomas Sinclair, and this is Miss Mary Hiltz. Please take a seat. Mary speaks German, as do I. I know you have had a busy few days. I am sorry we were not introduced at the Newmarket airfield, but that's the way Captain Leimbach wanted it. I am the Deputy Director of MI6, Britain's Secret Intelligence Service, and Miss Hiltz heads our cryptology and translation operations at our location not far from here, known as Bletchley Park. We report directly to General Stewart Menzies, who is the chief of MI6. Seldom do we meet German defectors, especially those that were part of German Intelligence. Mary has also been briefed on your assassination attempt on Hitler. Very courageous! We admire you for your effort and are disappointed that you were not successful. So, now you will help us here as we coordinate the mobilization of Allied forces."

Sinclair speaks in British English, and Mary translates for Raymond. "Based on your background and experience, we know you both will serve our intelligence efforts well. Raymond, we have decided to move you to Bletchley Park to work with Mary and her group. Kurt, you will be assigned to this location. Since every second is important to our war effort, Mary will take Raymond back to your apartment now, so you can gather your things and head on to Bletchley Park. You both will be treated as civilian employees within the Secret Intelligence Service and will be on our payroll. Raymond, you will also be very busy with English language lessons on top of your other assignments."

Mary and Raymond say goodbye to Kurt. Mary tries to move Raymond quickly out of the office. Kurt hurries over to Raymond and warmly shakes his hand.

"Raymond, I know this is not goodbye. I wanted you to know how much your help and protection mean to me. I will never forget our time together or the memories we share. With your help, we are now in a good place."

Raymond says in German, "*Mein Freund für immer* (My forever friend)!"

Ms. Hiltz steps forward and shakes Kurt's hand. "Welcome to our team. I look forward to working with you." She heads out the door with Raymond in tow.

Sinclair closes the office door and offers Kurt a cup of tea. "Kurt, let me explain your position here and the work you will be doing. Also, let me restate that what we do here is highly classified and will be closely monitored for security breaches. As you know, Admiral Canaris is working closely with a variety of resistance groups, especially the French and Italian. They all have offices here and in Bletchley Park. Major General Dwight Eisenhower arrived in London in June of last year (1942) and is in command of Allied forces in Europe. He has a team of intelligence officers working here. As you probably found out in Germany, the Allies are mobilizing forces here in England. Their assemblage will eventually result in the invasion of France sometime next year, perhaps May or June. Since you were part of the German Military Intelligence, your knowledge will greatly assist our strategic planning and logistical efforts, with you concentrating mainly on German troop movements within France. The report I received provided some background information on you. One thing reported is that you have a United States passport and lived in the States for a time when you were a child. Maryland, if I recall. That passport might serve you well as we move forward. So now, let me introduce you to Eisenhower's team here at MI6 that you will be working with."

Sinclair and Kurt walk out of the office and up a flight of stairs, down a long hallway, and into a doorway above which a sign reads, *Fifth Army, Special Services Force*. A young soldier in a US Army uniform comes around the corner.

"Captain Bossen, just the person I wanted to see! Do you have a moment? I want to introduce you to a new member of your team."

Bossen shakes Sinclair's hand and then looks at Kurt.

"Kurt Wagner, this is the US Army officer in charge, Captain Bridger Bossen." Kurt takes a long look at this young captain. Tall, muscular, sandy-haired with penetrating eyes, a ruddy complexion and a strong, forceful military presence.

Bossen firmly shakes Kurt's hand. "So, you are *the* Kurt Wagner, Hitler's bodyguard, the one who carried out the recent assassination attempt on Hitler?"

"That's me. I was a bit off target that day. Looking forward to working with you."

"Captain Bossen, from now on, Kurt is your man. I may need him on a few special assignments, but I will give you ample notice. I know you will keep him busy!"

Captain Bossen has kept Kurt very busy over the last few

months, decrypting and decoding German radio transmissions, analyzing intelligence gathered from low-level Allied fly-overs of German troop movements in northern France, and tracking German supply lines. He has been working closely with the RAF and the US Army Special Services Force. His days have been long. He usually leaves the office very late, eats at the same local pub, and then goes to his apartment. One afternoon in early July (1943), Bossen pokes his head into Kurt's small office.

"Kurt, what are you doing tonight? How about dinner somewhere?"

"Sounds good, Bridger! Would 7:00 work for you?"

Kurt meets Bridger in his office, and they make their way down Broadway to Beak Street. Bridger points ahead to a small pub sitting at the end of a long meandering street. "I like this place, and it's my favorite hangout here in London. Ever been here?"

"No, don't think so. I usually go to the King's Cross, which is close to my apartment."

They enter the Horse and Coach pub and are placed at a small table close to the bar. Kurt notices the tattered furniture and threadbare carpet. It is a lively and busy place with many soldiers milling about. His eyes focus on the piano sitting next to the bar.

"Kurt, I know it's a bit shabby, but they have great food and ale. You will be pleasantly surprised. On Fridays, they have a piano player, and the patrons join in English singalongs." Bridger offers Kurt a few recommendations, and they quickly place their order with the eager waiter.

Their ale arrives, and Kurt takes a long sip. "Not as good as German beer, but it will pass! So, tell me about yourself. How did you land in London with the US Army?"

"Well, it isn't very complicated. I was born in Idaho. Mom's a nurse, and Dad's a teacher. I decided to attend Boise State

University since it was pretty close to home. I joined the ROTC program and graduated in 1940. I also studied German in college but don't speak it very well. Joined the Army just as Pearl Harbor was attacked in 1941. I moved up in rank, and my commanders decided that the war in Europe would be a better fit for me than the war in the Pacific. I really do like military intelligence. I think when we do our work well and are effective, we can save lives and maybe help end this tragic war sooner!"

"You know that London and the Brits are in the thick of it here. I arrived in January of this year (1943) and was greeted with renewed air attacks. They called it the Baby Blitz! I guess they showed you the tunnels under our office building and the shelters. I spent some time there, and thank God we were not hit."

"Did you hear about the Bethnal Green Tube shelter disaster here in London? It killed over 170 people—including a lot of kids all crushed trying to enter the shelter. That happened in March in London's East End. The tragedy was that it was a total false alarm with no airplanes and no bombs, just a stampede. That was, in a way, my first real experience with the horrors of war and man's inhumanity. I also realized that death awaits at any moment."

Kurt sees the intensity in Bridger's eyes. "Like you, Bridger, I have seen the horror on a very personal level. My mother was killed in a bombing raid on Bremen in 1941, and my father was killed in Stalingrad just last year (1942). He was a German soldier and determined that I would follow in his footsteps. My mother never forgave him for pushing me in that direction."

"So sorry, Kurt. Do you have other family?"

"I do have a grandfather who lives in the US, but I have not been in touch with him for many years. He may have passed on, for all I know."

"How did you learn to speak such good English? Did you study it in your German school?"

"Yes, in school. Also, my mother and I spent some time in Maryland with my grandparents when I was young. I did attend one year of elementary school in Baltimore. That is where my grandfather lives."

"Any women in your life?"

"Not really. My work in the German military was intense and didn't leave much time for relationships. I did meet someone I had strong feelings for last summer, but that is a long story!" Kurt quickly changes the subject. "What are you hearing about the invasion? London is really getting crowded, as is most of England. Eisenhower will have to decide soon."

"I am hearing it will be early next year as soon as the weather works in our favor. Italy seems to be more of a priority now. Only a few generals really know, including Churchill and Roosevelt. It will be Eisenhower's call. Oh, if you haven't noticed, there are thousands of single women here in London, so don't be shy!"

It is late, and they have enjoyed their meal and getting to know each other. Kurt places some English pounds on the table. "No, Kurt, this one's on me. You can pay next time. It's been great spending time with you."

Kurt says goodbye to Bridger and makes his way back to his apartment. He thinks about the comment he made at dinner, *I did meet someone I had strong feelings for last summer, but that is a long story!*

It is a stuffy, hot evening as Kurt enters his room and turns on the light. The old fan in his bedroom doesn't work, so he pried open the window. He finds some writing paper and tries to capture his feelings. In his wallet, he finds a small piece of tattered paper. He gently unfolds it and sees the address, *Woodland Avenue, Ocean View, Delaware.*

*July 2, 1943*

*McKenna,*

*I know this letter will surprise you, and I pray that you will take the time to try and understand the feelings it contains. Just about this time last year, we met and spent some time together. You knew me as Paul visiting from Baltimore. I am now in London, England and have been here since March of this year. By now, you know that I was a German saboteur, and I will never be able to apologize enough for my deception. For me, our time together was an unbelievable experience, and you are constantly on my mind. My true story is a long one, and maybe someday I will be able to explain to you my involvement in an assassination attempt to kill Hitler. I have enclosed a copy of an article that appeared in the British newspapers. The article explains most of the details. I was the German soldier who tried to kill Hitler. As the article states, I did not succeed. Fortunately, members of the German Resistance were able to secure for me an escape plan to England. I am now working with the Allied forces here in London, and we will defeat Hitler and destroy the Nazi movement. Please know that there are good Germans and good German soldiers who are working to end the war, remove Hitler, and bring a lasting peace. Please believe that I would never harm you, and I am sorry we met under the cloud of a world war. I will never forget the kiss we shared. I have enclosed my address here in hopes that I may hear from you. Please find it in your heart to forgive me.*

*Kurt Wagner (Paul)*

# Kurt's Letter—McKenna's Future
# 1943

July 15, 1943. Jeff and Lori decide that they want to have a small party to celebrate McKenna's graduation from the Maryland State Teachers College at Salisbury. McKenna graduated in June and still is trying to decide where to teach. She knows she is running out of time. Selbyville Elementary has an opening for a second-grade teaching position. That would mean she would still be living at home. She would prefer to be a music teacher. She knows she must quickly make up her mind. She also has been thinking about applying for a teaching job in Dover or Wilmington or maybe Baltimore. One of her best friends that graduated with her, Belle Waden, will be teaching in Baltimore, and it would be fun if they both lived there and shared an apartment. She thinks she needs a big change in her life, and perhaps a move from boring lower shore Delaware would be an exciting thing to do. *I can't grow anymore here in Ocean View. I need a change of scenery and new friends!*

On Saturday afternoon, the guests begin to arrive. Tables and chairs are sitting on the patio behind the house. Brian, Joey and Michael, the guys that she travels to Baltimore with to play at the Owl Bar in the Belvedere, have set up their instruments.

Brian, Joey and Michael walk over to McKenna. They give her warm hugs. "Congratulations, McKenna! You did it! Where will you be teaching?"

She explains that she is still undecided. Brian tells her that the Belvedere wants them to start playing there again on the weekends beginning in September. "Do you think you will be able to join us? It will be the same deal as last year. Drive up on Friday after you get off school and play a late set beginning around 10:00 p.m. Then again on Saturday evening and back to the shore on Sunday. What do you think?"

"I don't know, Brian. It depends on where I will be. I'm thinking about teaching in Baltimore. If I get a job in Baltimore, I would certainly be able to play there on the weekends. I should know what my plans are within the next few weeks. I'll let you know."

McKenna spots Lee Crosby sitting next to Cameron LaPlante. Lee and Cameron congratulate McKenna. McKenna asks, "So, what have you two been doing? I haven't seen either of you in quite a while. Cameron, you just graduated from the University of Delaware, so congratulations to you. Are you still planning on becoming a veterinarian?"

Cameron moves his chair closer to McKenna. "Yeah, I've been accepted into the veterinary school at Penn State. I really want to attend and have always wanted to be a vet. I'm worried about my pending military service. Since I am in the Army Reserve, I might be called up at any time. Since we entered the war, most of my classmates and friends are in the military. I'm thinking that maybe I should just go full-time Army and then finish my education when the war is over. God knows when that will be! I am still working with Dr. Burton this summer. I really hate to be undecided, so I need to make a decision and move on with my life. Did you hear that Hugh is heading to England? He says that thousands of troops are heading there, and they will be training for an assault on Germany or maybe France. Is Tristan still in the Pacific on the submarine? Sorry, Lee, for being so rude and not letting you tell McKenna about your brother."

Lee rolls her eyes and shakes her head. "McKenna, did you know that I'm working at the Townsend bank where you worked? I like it there, and it is close to home. Have things settled down for you? I still can't believe that you had a German spy living next to you! Can you believe it was a year ago that we had all the excitement? What was his name?"

"He called himself *Paul*. In a way, yes, things are somewhat back to normal. As you can see, the Stickler farm is falling down. The bank has repossessed it, and they tell us it will be auctioned off, but no one knows when. Did you hear that Emma just died of a heart attack two weeks ago? She was in a Virginia prison. Wilmer has been sentenced to life in prison for conspiring with the spy and his participation in the *King James* sinking. So sad for them. They were strange, but their lives were ruined by that Bund organization they belonged to and their love for Hitler! Can you imagine giving up everything because you loved Germany more than the United States?

"Cameron, you asked about Tristan. He is still stationed on the submarine in the Pacific. We just received a letter from him. He is on patrol near Guadalcanal. There is a big battle going on there, and he said that the *USS Chicago* was lost, and many sailors were killed. He is in a danger zone, and we are so worried about him!"

McKenna mingles with the crowd and really enjoys everyone's company. Some of her friends stay way past midnight. The next morning, she is sleepy-eyed as she sits at the table eating a bowl of cereal and drinking coffee. Lori walks into the kitchen holding an envelope.

"McKenna, I just walked down to the mailbox and found this letter addressed to you. It has all kinds of postage on it and looks like it was mailed from London, England. Do you know someone there?"

"No, I can't think of anyone that I know there. Very strange!"

Lori hands the envelope to McKenna, who immediately opens it and pulls out a letter. Lori moves closer to her. As McKenna reads, she begins to cry, and Lori tries to comfort her.

"Mom, this is unbelievable! I am reading a letter from a German spy, who tried to assassinate Hitler and is now living in England, who hopes I will forgive him and wants me to write to him. This has to be a cruel hoax! This can't be true! Why would someone try to hurt my feelings again? Paul is now a Kurt Wagner? This article in the British paper looks real!"

Lori takes the letter and the newspaper clipping from McKenna and begins to read it herself. "Honey, this could be real. A war is going on, and all kinds of crazy things happen that we can't comprehend or understand. I wouldn't dismiss it. It may be true, and it wouldn't surprise me if it was."

Jeff, Lori and McKenna are still trying to understand the letter and to determine if it was really written by Kurt Wagner, who was a German saboteur and freed a POW from the camp in Bear Trap. Jeff has suggested that they contact John Townsend and see if he can provide some advice.

"I'll set up a meeting with Townsend and show him the letter. Since the FBI was involved, they might want to investigate its authenticity. Who knows? But, we really need to get to the bottom of it. I personally don't like German spies sending letters to my daughter!"

Three weeks later, Jeff receives a call from John Townsend, who offers to drop by and give them some information regarding the letter. Townsend arrives early on a Saturday morning and joins them for breakfast.

"Thank you, Lori. This is quite a treat for me, and you are

serving my favorite—blueberry pancakes! Before we eat, let's take care of business, if you don't mind."

Townsend pulls a large envelope out of his briefcase. "I sent a copy of your letter to J. Edgar Hoover, and he forwarded it to his deputy, Clyde Tolson. Clyde and his team did a great job digging into the letter and verifying its authenticity. Here is what he told me, and I will share it with you. In this envelope is his written response, but I can summarize it. The letter is authentic and was sent from a German, Kurt Wagner, 23 years old, who is now in London, England and working for both British Intelligence, they refer to it as MI6, and a US Army intelligence group. He is doing secret work for them, so they wouldn't provide me with details. He did try to kill Hitler on March 21 of this year. He must be a bad shot. He missed Hitler and killed his SS security guard. A German Resistance group working in Germany provided an escape route for him. A small plane picked him up on a landing strip in northern Germany, a place called Rostock. So, he has been in London since then. His father was in the German military and was killed in battle, and his mother was killed in a RAF bombing attack in Bremen, Germany a few years ago. He is the same person who was dropped off by a German sub last year and stayed at the Stickler farm. You know that story all too well. The FBI has informed us that everything he stated in the letter is true. So, there you have it! Since he directed the letter to you, McKenna, the FBI state in their letter that you are free to communicate with him. All his letters are screened before they are mailed, and I am sure he knows that. So now, what you do next is totally up to you. Ok, let's eat!"

Jeff shakes Townsend's hand. "Senator, thank you for getting involved with this. We really didn't know what to do or who to turn to. Oh, by the way, we heard that you bought the Stickler farm. Is that true?"

"Yes, I settle on it next week. As you know, the bank

repossessed it, and there was an auction. I've got to do a lot of work over there and may have to call on you for some assistance. If you know of a good farm manager looking for a challenge, please let me know. I guess you heard about the Sticklers. I liked them and still can't believe how they messed up their lives. Just another tragedy of this horrible war."

On a Monday evening in early August, McKenna is sitting down to dinner with Jeff and Lori. She has a serious look. "Mom, Dad, I think I've made a decision about where I will be teaching in September. I told you that Belle is going to teach in Baltimore. She has been accepted to teach at Gardenville Elementary. We saw it on the Baltimore map. It is not in downtown Baltimore but more toward the county. I received a letter from the Baltimore City Board of Education that said they have accepted my application. They have a music teacher position available at the same school. I have an interview with them next week. So, Belle and I will drive to Baltimore together. After my interview, we will look for an apartment. What do you think?"

Jeff and Lori share a surprised look. Lori stares at McKenna. "Don't make a rash decision. Make sure you are real comfortable with the school and the principal. Also, be sure that you like the neighborhood. Baltimore is a big city, and you and Belle are small—town girls. I don't agree with your decision, but you are a grown woman, so you need to follow your heart. I am going to miss you beyond words! Please be sure you are hired before you commit to an apartment."

Jeff quickly finishes his meal. "McKenna, you are making a very important decision. Think it through very carefully. Baltimore is a long ride from here, and I know you will be homesick. Also, I will worry about you. I really don't want my little girl moving away from her parents. Are you sure this is what you want to do?"

"I will miss both of you, but I have to try this. If I don't like it there or if things don't work out, I can come home. Just keep my room empty!"

Lori touches her hand. "McKenna, we love you, and we will always be here for you. Also, Dad and I were wondering if you ever responded to that letter from Paul—or is it Kurt?"

"No, I never did. He is totally in my past and a distant memory. His life seems very complicated. Is he a hero or a monster? I hope I never hear from him again!"

# D-Day Strategy
# 1944

January 1944. Captain Bridger Bossen just returned from a high-level strategic planning session with a very select group of British and American military brass. Everything discussed was labeled top secret, and now he must inform his team of their new high-priority assignment. He has gathered nine of his team, including Kurt, into a small classroom in the basement of their building at 54 Broadway.

"Good afternoon. I wanted to bring everyone up to date and provide a quick overview of our new assignment. I just left a meeting with Generals Eisenhower and Montgomery. They have targeted May or early June for the invasion of France along the Normandy coast. From what I can gather, this is the first time that a specific timeline and a specific location have been announced."

Bridger walks over to the worn chalkboard and writes: *Operation Fortitude.* The assembled group has a surprised look.

"Ok, I know you are asking yourselves, 'What is Fortitude?' We know that the codename for the invasion of France is Operation Overlord. Fortitude will be a sub-set of Overlord. As you know, for that past few months, we have been working on deception strategies. We have sent false wireless transmissions, planted double agents within the German military, planted false information through diplomatic channels, just to name a few among a long list of other strategies, all in an attempt to confuse the Germans and create chaos in their military operations.

"Now that the Normandy coast is the chosen landing site, this group will launch Operation Fortitude. Our task is to convince the Germans that the bridgehead in France for the Allied landings will be the Pas-de-Calais, not Normandy. We will create a ghost army and fool them with fake equipment like inflatable tanks and vehicles, dummy landing craft and cardboard soldiers. We will create wireless messages that will be intentionally intercepted to convince them that we will not be landing in Normandy. Fake news will be given to the press. If we are successful at this deception and all its moving pieces come together, we will save the lives of thousands of our soldiers because the Germans will deploy their military assets to the wrong landing site. When they do, we will bomb the hell out of them at Calais, while we successfully come ashore along the Normandy beaches. We have only four months to make this work. Expect to work seven days a week and very long days. All leave is cancelled, effective today. I know this team can make it happen! We have *fortitude*!"

One evening, Kurt drags himself to his apartment. He feels so alone and isolated. His new assignment has left little time for friends. Even grabbing a quick drink after work has been difficult. He has been thinking about his grandfather in Baltimore and decides to write him. Kurt thinks about all the great times he enjoyed with him. *My God, Grandfather is almost 75, and I was six years old when I last saw him. That was 18 years ago! I did write and told him that Mother died in the Bremen air attack. Uncle Gerhard and Aunt Elizabeth are both gone. I wonder if he is still alive and living at the same address. I would really love to hear from him. I feel so bad that I have not been in touch with him over the years. Mother would write him faithfully, and I know she always wanted him to visit us or come live with us. Thank God he stayed in the States. He is the only family member I have left.* Kurt sends him a short letter and prays that he is alive and well. *Hopefully he will remember me.*

A month later, Kurt empties out his mail bin at the apartment. He finds a letter postmarked from Baltimore, Maryland. *Oh Lord, it's from Grandfather!*

*My dearest Kurt,*

*Yes, it is me, and please excuse my shaky handwriting! Thank you so much for writing. I have prayed that someday I would hear from you. I am well and still live in the same house you remember when you visited. You know that Uncle Gerhard and Aunt Elizabeth died a few years ago. I still attend Holy Cross Church and help out there as much as I can. Your life appears to have gone in different directions. So, you are no longer in the German military. Thank God you were able to leave Germany. I still am confused concerning how you made your way to London. I am so sorry about the death of your father. Gunter and I were never close, but I did like and respect him. I so miss your mother, and she is constantly on my mind. Let's promise to keep in touch and write each other frequently. I really do want to know what is happening in your life. You are the only family I have, and I love you and miss you so very much!*

*Grandfather*

The last few months have been hectic, and Captain Bossen and his superiors seem pleased with, as Bridger's team calls it, "the Great Hoax." The Allied leadership seems convinced that the Germans think the invasion will take place at Pas-de-Calais and not Normandy. They have monitored considerable troop movement in that direction. The Germans have focused their efforts there. Surveillance reports show that they have built approximately 20 concrete pill boxes per mile of coastline along with mines and other obstacles along the beaches, including concrete observation towers. Pas-de-Calais is only 11 miles from Dover, England as the crow flies across the Channel, so it would make logistical sense to land there.

On May 6, 1944, Bridger attends a meeting regarding the latest updates on the invasion. He is told it looks more like the first week of June and mobilization will work around the dates of June 5 or 6. As he is always told, "It all depends on the weather."

Bridger and Kurt get together for dinner one evening in late May. Most of the major goals and objectives of Operation Fortitude have been accomplished, and Bridger and Kurt just completed an assessment of strategic outcomes. It is now time for them to briefly exhale and to move on to other work.

They are sitting at the bar at the Horse and Coach Pub. Kurt slides Bridger's ale over to him. Bridger raises his glass and taps Kurt's. "A toast to a successful invasion and the end of the war! Kurt, this is hard to imagine, but I was told that, as of May 1, the Allied armies comprise over 3 million soldiers spread over 39 divisions. England is bursting at the seams. Come June 1, our soldiers and their equipment will be placed aboard their landing ships. If all goes according to Eisenhower's plan, we will launch the attack at dawn on either June 5 or 6. I know it will not be easy, and I hope the Germans will be surprised!

"Kurt, I have some news for you. I was told that our group may ship back to the US around the beginning of August, soon after the D-Day invasion. I know that sounds crazy, but I have been told that Roosevelt wants to totally restructure how the United States gathers its intelligence. He wants to model it after the British Secret Intelligence Service—MI6 and MI5. He wants our team back in Washington to begin an initiative to centralize all the various security and intelligence activities under one main governmental division. I can tell you that all your superiors here have been very impressed with the work you have done. We want you on our team back in the States. I think we may even meet with Roosevelt himself concerning the direction he wants to go. I also heard that his point man on this initiative will be his Secretary of the Navy, James Forrestal."

Kurt has an excited and anxious look. "Bridger, you know I love the work that I do, and we have learned a lot from our British counterparts. I can't believe that they would want me working in Washington and not here in England. I really enjoy working with you. Count me in!"

"Kurt, I think we sometimes forget that there is a bigger war going on with the Japs in the Pacific. Our group here has been focused on the invasion and the destruction of Hitler and his Nazi regime. Our generals and the politicos in the States want intelligence-gathering elevated to a much higher and a more broadly focused effort. We can make that happen, and we will be more effective working in Washington than working here in England. A smaller team will stay in England and work on the war effort here, but we will take a more global approach in Washington."

On June 1, Kurt, Bridger and other members of their team make their way south to the Southampton England embarkation area. They set up office in the old South Western Hotel. They are primarily monitoring German radio transmissions and troop movement. The team is told that June 5 is the "go date," but the invasion is abruptly delayed by Eisenhower due to strong winds and rough seas in the Channel. The last-minute decision involves calling back the landing ships that are already underway.

At 4:15 a.m. on June 6, the Supreme Commander of the

Allied forces gives the word to launch the invasion onto the Normandy beaches of France. Over 170,000 Allied troops begin landing along the 50-mile stretch of the Normandy coastline. More than 5,000 ships, thousands of landing craft, and 13,000 aircraft support the D-Day invasion. The day takes its toll with over 9,000 Allied soldiers killed or wounded.

On August 25, 1944, Bridger, Kurt and other members of the Military Intelligence team are transported to the airfield at Newmarket, Suffolk, England. They will fly to Reykjavik, Iceland in a Douglas C-54 Skymaster and then on to the Camp Springs Air Base just outside of Washington D.C., a suburb of Maryland.

Bridger sees Kurt staring out the window as the plane taxis down the runway. "Kurt, I heard this morning, just as we were boarding, that Allied troops, with the help of the French resistance led by General Charles de Gaulle, liberated Paris."

"Wow! That happened much sooner than I thought it would. Patton's Third Army moves fast. I love Paris and spent some time there a few years ago when the Germans first moved in. I was so thankful that it was not bombed and most of the beauty remains. My father was there as well."

"Never been there. I spent most of my time working with the French Resistance, but never landed there. My high school French lessons barely got me by. I would love to visit Paris someday and spend some time checking out France. Maybe the US Army will pay for my vacation there! Someday, you will have to tell me more about your father."

Kurt and Bridger are now part of a very select group of military intelligence officers working for the Department of War. Most of the department has moved to a new location just outside of Washington called the Pentagon, located in Arlington, Virginia. Bridger's team is housed in a stately Victorian row house on Logan Circle only a mile and a half from the capital and the White House.

Bridger and Kurt have decided to share an apartment. They are renting a second-floor apartment on 13$^{th}$ St. N.W. in Washington, very close to where they are working. One evening at dinner, Bridger asks about Kurt's family and his grandfather.

Kurt tells Bridger about the strict discipline of his father and the strained relationship the German military and Nazi party created between his parents. He recounts the devastating news he received from his father about his mother's horrible death in the Bremen bombing and how shocked he was when he was told by Admiral Canaris that his father was killed during the Stalingrad fighting.

"I was shocked when I received a letter from my grandfather before we left England. I took a chance and sent him a letter to the only address I had for him. Mom and I spent a year with him and my grandmother in 1926. That was 18 years ago. He told me he was well and still living at the same address in Baltimore. I remember how he would carve circus animals for me. We went fishing and crabbing together. That was the best year of my life."

"You know we are close to Baltimore. You should take the train over and spend some time with him. You've got some leave time. I think now would be a good time before things heat up here."

# A Visit with Grandfather 1944

Two weeks later, on a Saturday in early October, Kurt takes a cab to Union Station and takes the train north to Baltimore. It is a quick, easy ride, and he arrives in the early afternoon. As he takes the cab to the address he remembers on Cross Street in Federal Hill, he thinks, *I hope my surprise visit won't upset him!*

The cab passes the market where his grandfather worked and pulls up to the curb in front of the row house he remembers as a child. He grabs his duffel bag and lumbers toward the front door. He rings the bell and waits, but there is no answer. He rings the bell again, but still there is no answer. He remembers the alley behind the house. He walks around the block and up the small alley. He opens the gate and walks toward the back door. There is a dog next door barking and snarling at him. *Thank God he's tied up!*

Again, he knocks and knocks, but no answer. As he turns to walk back, a neighbor on the next door back porch sees Kurt and walks over to the fence. The short, bald man with squinty eyes examines Kurt. He looks at his blue denim shirt and khaki pants. *I guess he thinks I'm here to rob the house.*

"Excuse me, young man. Can I help you?"

Kurt walks closer and drops his duffel. "Good afternoon. Why, yes, I'm looking for my grandfather, George Reckman. Have you seen him?"

"You are George's grandson, the one he always talks about? He told me he recently received a letter from you and you were in the Army and stationed in London? Is that true?"

Kurt thinks, *I am being interrogated by this old guy. I guess I do look a bit suspicious?* Kurt quickly explains the latest happenings in his life and that he is living in Washington D.C.

"Well, welcome to Baltimore. I know George will be so happy to see you after all these years. He is at his church, Holy Cross, a few blocks from here. He does odd jobs around the church and rectory. He should be home soon. Would you like to come in and have something to drink?"

"No, thanks. I'll just wait for him on the front porch. Nice meeting you ... and your name, sir?"

"Charles White, but just call me Charlie!"

Kurt walks back to the front porch and sits on the steps. About 20 minutes later, he sees an older man with a cane, slowly limping toward him. *My God, that has got to be grandfather!* Kurt jumps up and quickly walks toward him. "Grandfather, it's me, Kurt!"

George stops, wobbles a bit, and drops his cane. Kurt quickly grabs his arm to steady him. He stares into Kurt's eyes. "Kurt, it is you! I see that little boy look on your face and those beautiful blue eyes—and your hair is still blond. My prayers have been answered!"

He wraps his arms around Kurt and gives him a long, warm hug as he tries to catch his breath. Kurt picks up the cane, and they slowly walk toward the house.

It has been a wonderful visit, but not long enough. George spent long hours reminiscing about the adventures they shared when Kurt and Anna visited with him, the death of Kurt's grandmother and then the deaths of Anna and Gunter. Kurt carefully explained how he became a member of the German Resistance and his admiration for Admiral Canaris. George is having a difficult time understanding that Kurt tried to assassinate Hitler.

Before Kurt leaves, they stop by the market and bring home a dozen steamed blue crabs.

"Grandfather, these are so good and bring back great memories. I remember Mom was afraid of them. How about the time one fell on the floor and chased her? She was so frightened!" George smiles and savors the memory. *If only I could re-live those moments!*

Kurt's visit was a quick one, but now he must return to Washington.

"Kurt, since you are living so close, you must promise me that you will visit more often. We can go fishing, and let's go to a movie. Just promise me."

"Grandfather, I promise. I will visit you often. Now I have your telephone number, so we can really keep in touch. It has been so great to see you!"

# McKenna's New Life
# 1943

In August of 1943, McKenna made the big decision to move to Baltimore along with her friend from college, Belle Waden. They both are now teaching at Gardenville Elementary School in Baltimore. McKenna is teaching music, and Belle is teaching kindergarten. Belle has an old wreck of a car that was her father's, a 1935 Chevrolet sedan. It barely got them to Baltimore from Ocean View, Delaware, but it is now parked behind their apartment which is on White Avenue and only a half mile to school. They can ride the streetcar to work and sometimes walk. On the weekends, they have been exploring downtown Baltimore, the museums, historical sites and department stores. They get back to the beach to visit, mainly during the summer, and Lori and Jeff have visited them on long weekends when school has been closed. Now that her parents have checked out her new surroundings, they feel more comfortable with her decision to move to Baltimore.

Brian has also been in touch with McKenna, and she is playing piano once again with the Shorebirds, the new name of their jazz band. Beginning in October, they are playing every Friday and Saturday at the Owl Bar in the Belvedere Hotel. Belle usually comes along on most nights. Brian finds out from McKenna that Belle sung in her church choir. Belle and McKenna are sitting at the bar, sipping their wine, when Brian walks over.

"Belle, we need a vocalist for our group. McKenna tells me you have a great voice. Would you be interested in joining us? Since the crowds are picking up here, the manager tells me he can afford one more person in our band. What do you think?"

"Brian, that sounds great! I already know most of the songs you have been playing. Do you want me to audition?"

"Not necessary. You can rehearse with McKenna during the week. How about if you start next weekend?"

The Shorebirds are beginning to attract larger crowds, but they have decided to take a summer break. School is out the last week in May. McKenna and Belle decide to travel to the beach and spend the month of June 1944 in Ocean View.

McKenna arrives home on Friday, June 3, and quickly transitions back to farm life. She is feeding the animals, picking produce, weeding the garden, and doing other chores. She remembers how busy the summers are on the farm. She also wants to spend some fun time with her friends. She sees that a new family with two little girls is living in the old Stickler house. She was told that the Army has removed most of the dogs and horses from their farm, which makes farm life a little easier for Jeff and Lori.

With Tristan in the Navy and McKenna in Baltimore, Jeff was looking for some farm help. He found out that Jimmy Crosby was looking for a job. Jimmy played baseball during high school and was on the wrestling team. He is tall, muscular, and loves animals. He seems to like working with Jeff and Lori and keeps them informed about what is happening at the Crosby house. Jimmy tells Jeff, Lori and McKenna that Hugh has been training in England since January of 1944, and he is in command of a fleet of landing craft.

Jeff always rises early. On Tuesday, June 6, 1944, he makes a pot of coffee and turns on the radio. All the stations have the breaking news: "The Allied powers have crossed the English Channel and are landing on the beaches of Normandy, France, beginning the liberation of Western Europe from Nazi control." Jeff is not surprised, and the news media speculated that the invasion was imminent. He wakes Lori and McKenna, and they all gather around the radio.

Jeff sips his coffee. "Another chapter in this horrible world conflict. Remember what Jimmy just told us about Hugh commanding landing craft and training in England? He said that, when Hugh writes, he keeps telling them to stay tuned, that something big is about to happen there and how many troops were gathering in England. Now we know what his training was all about."

On Monday, June 12, the telephone rings, and McKenna answers. Someone is crying as she presses the phone to her ear.

*"McKenna, its Barbara Crosby. I have some horrible news that I must share with you. We just found out that our dear Hugh was killed on D-Day. He was commanding a landing ship full of soldiers. We have been told that it was hit and exploded just a few miles off of the Normandy beach in France. Over 60 soldiers were killed. Needless to say, our family is devastated. We loved our Hugh, and I know he was close to your heart. When will God grant us peace on this earth? All these young boys killed! We will all grieve together! He always told us you were his best friend, and I know he deeply cared for you. Please let your family know."*

McKenna is sobbing as she says goodbye and hangs up the phone. Jeff and Lori are in the barn as McKenna walks toward them with tears streaming down her face.

Lori runs toward her. "McKenna, what is wrong?"

"Mom, Dad, Mrs. Crosby just called. They were just notified that Hugh was killed on D-Day. His ship exploded. What terrible news! I can't imagine the grief and agony his family is going through. I loved him, but we were never *in love.* He was more like a brother to me. Every day, I prayed for him. I would dream about a reunion with him. He always looked so handsome in his uniform. Now I will never see him again. Let's go over to the Crosby house. I want to be with them."

The summer of 1944 is not what McKenna had expected it to be. Hugh would never return to his family and the ocean that he loved. The Crosbys are notified that he is buried in the Normandy American Cemetery in Colleville-sur-Mer, France. There is a memorial service for him at the Bethel Church in Ocean View. For McKenna, the service is, in a way, a release for her deep grief, but once again she feels the bite of depression. She replays in her mind the words she heard at the service spoken by a member of the Coast Guard.

"Today, the words of General George S. Patton ring true: 'It is foolish and wrong to mourn the men who died. Rather, we should thank God that such men lived!'"

She thinks, *Patton was wrong. It is not foolish to mourn for him.* She knows that she and all who knew him will mourn. She will always carry Hugh's memory in her heart.

# Quick Trip to Paris
# 1944

Kurt and Bridger's visit to Paris comes much faster than expected. On September 15, 1944, they again fly to London, and then to the Roissy airfield north of Paris. This is a hurry-up, secret 10-day mission to set up an intelligence network based in Paris with the help of the US Army's 28th Infantry Division. The 28th Infantry just paraded up the Avenue Hoche to the Arc de Triomphe on August 29 to the cheers of the joyous French crowds. Now that the Germans have been removed from Paris, the War Department must quickly establish a strategy so that they stay one step ahead of the Soviets.

Bridger brought over 20,000 dollars in French francs and American currency to pre-pay several well-vetted spies who will now be working for the Allies and spying on the Soviets. Their handlers have been handpicked by General Norman Cota, who is a direct report to General Patton.

The day before they leave to return to Washington, Kurt takes Bridger on a quick tour of a few of the major sites around the city of Paris. Since they are both in their Army uniforms, Bridger calls it his military tour with military privilege. Bridger is able to requisition a jeep, and Kurt is his chauffeur. In 10 hours, Bridger and Kurt see the Notre Dame Cathedral, the Louvre, the Eiffel Tower and the Arc de Triomphe.

They eat dinner at a small restaurant near the Sorbonne University. Bridger does not like the French food and passes most of his meal to Kurt. During dinner, Kurt explains that, when the German army occupied France in 1940, his father was stationed at the *Ecole Militaire*, the military school, which was just a short walk south of the Sorbonne campus.

"Father loved Paris and always promised to bring my mother to visit. Mom never made it. As he gained rank, he never seemed to have time to take her anywhere. Let me put that a different way. He actually never had time for *her*! So sad. I know she would have loved to visit and see its beauty."

Bridger senses the emotion in Kurt's voice. "Ok, pal. We better get back. By the way, you are an outstanding tour guide!"

# Baltimore Reunion 1944

Kurt is back in Washington. One evening in mid-November, he calls his grandfather.

"Grandfather, glad to hear that you are doing well. Just wondering what you are doing for Thanksgiving? I have some leave time, so I could spend a few days with you, and we could have Thanksgiving dinner together."

"Kurt,that would be fantastic! I have no plans, and I would enjoy your company. I'm still a pretty good cook, so I will buy a bird and have a real American feast for you."

"Grandfather, would you mind if I brought a friend of mine to visit and have dinner with us? He is my commanding officer. He is from Idaho, and I know you will like him."

"Would love to meet him. Does he drink beer and speak German? I'll buy a case of your favorite, Natty Boh! I am so glad you called me and can't wait to see you."

On the Tuesday before Thanksgiving 1944, Kurt and Bridger take the train to Baltimore and grab a quick cab ride over to Cross Street. This is Bridger's first trip to Baltimore. They ride by the Washington Monument and the Bromo Seltzer tower. Kurt points out the ships unloading cargo at the harbor. They pass by Holy Cross Church, and the cab stops in front of George's row house. George greets them and immediately hands them two beers.

"Great to meet you, Burger! Kurt told me all about you and your spy work in England."

"Good to meet you as well, Mr. Reckman. Oh, by the way, my name is Bridger, not Burger. Thanks for the beer."

"Sorry about that. My hearing isn't what it used to be, but my memory is pretty good. That beer is a Natty Boh, Baltimore's best. I thought you guys would be thirsty after your train ride. I bet you both are hungry. Let me make some hamburgers and hot dogs. How about some pork and beans to go along with it?"

Kurt and Bridger settle in. On Wednesday evening, George begins to prepare the turkey so he can get it in the oven early Thursday morning. Kurt and Bridger help by cutting celery, onions, and carrots, and they set the table. Kurt finds the dishes and the silverware and sets three place settings. George comes in and repositions the tableware to set a fourth place. Kurt rolls his eyes at Bridger.

"Grandfather, I thought it was only the three of us for dinner tomorrow?"

"I'm sorry Kurt; I should have told you. I invited my next-door neighbor, Charlie. I think you met him the day you surprised me. His wife died about six months ago, and I knew he would be lonely this Thanksgiving."

The next day, the four men are gathered around the old dining room table that Kurt remembers. Some of its scratches were made by him with his toy soldiers. The meal is outstanding, and George is beaming. He makes a pot of coffee and brings to the table his surprise dessert, *Hoska* bread.

"Kurt, you loved this when you were a little boy visiting with your mother. I went to the Czech bakery at the market yesterday and wanted to surprise you."

The conversation is intense, and George wants Kurt and Bridger to tell them about all their adventures.

"I know you can't tell us everything because what you do is top secret, but share what you can. It's got to be so much more exciting than the life Charlie and I have."

Bridger and Kurt do share some of the more exciting aspects of their military life—some serious and some funny. George and Charlie can't believe that Kurt was a saboteur who landed on the Delaware coast and freed a German rocket scientist and returned him to Germany in a submarine. He also can't believe that his grandson, sitting at his Thanksgiving table, was the trigger man who tried to kill Hitler.

"Your stories are like a movie or a radio soap opera. You both are lucky to still be alive."

On Friday night, Bridger and Kurt want to listen to music and enjoy some Baltimore night life.

They see George in the kitchen as they are about to leave.

"Grandfather, we're heading out, and we may be home rather late. Do you think I could have your front door key? Any suggestions where to go for some drinks and music?"

"Well, you are probably asking the wrong guy, but if you are looking for burlesque and ladies of negotiable virtue, then you want to head to Baltimore Street. If you are looking for a more sophisticated place, everyone talks about the old Belvedere Hotel on Chase Street. I hear they have jazz music in the Owl Bar. It's not too far from here, but you should take a cab."

They decide to start off at the Belvedere. As they walk in, they read the sign in the lobby: *Old World elegance still exits at the Belvedere. Our famous guests who have visited include: F. Scott Fitzgerald, President Franklin D. Roosevelt, Will Rogers, Clark Gable, Carole Lombard....*

Bridger stares at Kurt. "This doesn't seem like the kind of place we are looking for!"

"Hey, we're here. Let's have a few beers, and then we can hit Baltimore Street."

They make their way into the bar and discover a large crowd listening to a jazz band performing in a small space next to a large cathedral-type window. They are seated with their back to the band. The bar is long with dark stain, and the walls are exposed brick. Above where they are seated is a large stuffed animal head. Kurt looks at it as he sips his beer.

"Bridger, you're from Idaho. Is that a moose head?"

"I thought you collected animal carvings. Of course that's a moose!"

The jazz band plays a few more numbers before taking a break. As the band makes their way back and begins to set up, Kurt spies a beautiful blond-haired girl sitting at the piano. He vaguely remembers that McKenna said she played the piano at a night club in Baltimore.

"Bridger, you won't believe this! See the girl sitting at the piano? I swear it looks like the girl I was telling you about when I was staying at the farm in Delaware. She lived next door. That has got to be her. I know she played the piano somewhere in Baltimore."

Bridger turns on his stool and takes a long look at McKenna.

"Wow, she is beautiful! Do you think she will recognize you?"

"Well, it was only two years ago. I think she would."

"Go up and say hi to her. See what happens."

Kurt moves to the back of the bar and slowly walks along the wall toward the piano. McKenna is sitting there with her back to him, waiting for the rest of the group to set up. Kurt comes up behind her and slides next to her on the piano bench.

"Excuse me. I know it's been awhile, but could we play something together?"

She glances at him with a startled look. She is shaking. "Oh my God! I can't believe this is happening! Paul, I can't believe it's you! What are you doing here? You told me you were in London!" Tears escape down her cheek as she rests her head on Kurt's shoulder. She takes his hand. "Paul, you never said goodbye to me."

Kurt gives her a gentle kiss. "McKenna, my name is Kurt, and if you let me, I have a very long story to tell you."

THE END

# About the Author

J.R. Miller was born in Baltimore, Maryland, in 1944, two months after the D-Day invasion of France. He attended the University of Baltimore and received a BS degree in Finance. He also holds a Master's degree in Governmental Administration from the Fels School at the University of Pennsylvania. He held executive positions in governmental procurement and was an instructor and consultant for NIGP—The Institute for Public Procurement. He has authored textbooks and taught procurement classes throughout the United States and Canada. Additionally, he was an adjunct professor at Harford Community College in Maryland and the University of Virginia.

J.R. had a home near Ocean View, Delaware and was fascinated by the history of the area, especially during WWII. He was surprised to find the purpose of the fire control towers that sit on the Delaware beaches, the discovery of a prisoner of war camp in Bear Trap, the impact of German submarines just offshore, and the landing of German saboteurs along the Atlantic coast.

World War II had a major impact on the "Quiet Resort," and this story of historical fiction tells a tale of families living in Ocean View and how their lives were transformed by a German boy born in Bremen, Germany. It is a story of love of family, survival and people making difficult choices. It is also captures how the horrors of war are lived at a very personal level.

# Acknowledgement

A very special thank you to my dear family for their love, encouragement and support. This book is the result of a challenge given to me by my grandchildren. Also, thanks to family and friends who reviewed the draft text and provided comments and recommendations!

*Towers on the Beach: WWII Spies and Heroes—From Ocean View, Delaware to Bremen, Germany* is a work of historical fiction. All of the incidents, dialogue and characters with the exception of well-known historical and public figures are products of the author's imagination and are not real. Names of family and friends have been used with permission, but their characters are works of fiction. Events are built around a historical context, but are fictional.

# References/ Acknowledgements— Inspirational Attribution

Citation: Franklin D. Roosevelt: "Radio Address on United Flag Day.," June 14, 1942. Online by Gerhard Peters and John T. Woolley, *The America*

*World War II Magazine-Article by Harvey Ardman regarding the German sub U-202 and its landing in Long Island NY in 1942.*

*War and Remembrance-Herman Wouk*

*All the Light We Cannot See-Anhony Doerr*

*Altar of Resistance-Samuel Marquis*

*Flowers from Berlin-Noel Hynd*

*Portrait of a Spy, The English Spy-Daniel Silva*

*Alan Furst—various novels*

The following web sources were used to help determine historical accuracy.

www.history.com/this-day-in-history/Allies-prepare-for-d-day

www.k9history.com/wwii

www.uscg.mil/history/articles

www.jacksjoint.com/manhattan_beach

www.historynet.com/world-war-ii-german-saboteurs-invade-America-in-1942

www.fbi.gov/about-us/history/famous-cases/nazi-saboteurs

www.americainwwii.com/americans-for-Hitler
www.bbc.co.uk/history/ww2/peopleswarstories

www.fortdupont.org/history
www.mtholyoak.edu/kmmurray/operationoverlord
en.wikipedia.org/uss-jacob-jones
en.wikipedia.org/uscgc_alexander_hamilton

CPSIA information can be obtained
at www.ICGtesting.com
Printed in the USA
BVHW051750181222
654502BV00020B/123

9 781480 858091